T0096018

GREATEST
RUSSIAN
SHORT STORIES

CLASSICS

Published 2023

FiNGERPRINT! **CLASSICS**

An imprint of Prakash Books India Pvt. Ltd.

113/A, Darya Ganj,
New Delhi-110 002
Email: info@prakashbooks.com/sales@prakashbooks.com

facebook www.facebook.com/fingerprintpublishing
twitter www.twitter.com/FingerprintP

Selection and editorial material © Fingerprint! Publishing

ISBN: 978 93 5440 920 2

Processed & printed in India

"*I am a dreamer. I know so little of real life that I just can't help re-living such moments as these in my dreams, for such moments are something I have very rarely experienced. I am going to dream about you the whole night, the whole week, the whole year.*"

"White Nights", Fyodor Dostoevsky

Before the epics of *Iliad* and *Odyssey*, we had the tradition of oral storytelling. This tradition of oral storytelling developed into the genre of short story, as we know it today. Be it folk tales, fairy tales, or fables, we have all grown up with the genre of the short story. And in this repertoire, the Russian short stories occupy a distinctive space.

The nineteenth century gave us some greatest gems of Russian literature. Be it poetry, drama, novels, or short fiction— the recording of human experience by writers was one with such honesty, accuracy, and directness, that the works produced in that century in Russia are still read today with pleasure.

As Thomas Seltzer says, "Everything is subordinated to two main requirements—humanitarian ideals and fidelity to life. This is the secret of the marvellous simplicity of Russian literary art." Russian short story writers are the epitome of intellectual genius, and the stories in this edition are a precise reflection of that. These stories are short and crisp, yet are slices of life that explore the notions of happiness, melancholy, love, and family.

This anthology brings together some such iconic stories written by the most celebrated Russian writers. All these writers were published around the same time, yet their works have a unique charm. Each of them inhabited a unique style of writing which represents human nature in all its colours, and makes us question the injustices of the society.

We have, in this edition, the very famous "The Queen of Spades" by Alexander Pushkin, a story that mixes realism with supernatural elements to portray what greed does to a man. Pushkin stands out amongst all the brilliant writers of Russia.

We also have Anton Chekhov, who is considered by many to be the master of the art of short fiction. "The Lady with the Dog" and "The Bet" are some of his best works. Both of these and some others are part of this edition.

Leo Tolstoy and Fyodor Dostoevsky are regarded as two of the greatest novelists of all time, but their stories are no less compelling. Tolstoy's "How Much Land Does a Man Need", which is a part of this anthology, is "the greatest story that the world of literature knows". Dostoevsky's "White Nights" and "The Heavenly Christmas Tree" are uniquely thought-provoking stories that represent the genius of Dostoevsky.

Ivan Turgenev's short stories were a milestone in Russian realism, and not much needs to be said about Nikolai Gogol. After all, all Russian short stories 'emerged from Gogol's overcoat'. Stories by these two maestros, namely Turgenev's "Death" and Gogol's "Memoirs of a Madman" are also included in this anthology.

This anthology will surely appeal to the reader in you and broaden your knowledge of Russian literature and of life itself.

About this Edition

The iconic short stories from the likes of the greatest Russian writers Alexander Pushkin, Nikolai Gogol, Ivan Turgenev, Fyodor Dostoevsky, Leo Tolstoy, and Anton Chekhov come together in this edition to give you the best experience of the golden age of Russian literature.

Contents

Alexander Pushkin

(1799–1837)

The Queen of Spades

Translated by Mrs Sutherland Edwards

CHAPTER I

There was a card party at the rooms of Narumoff, a lieutenant in the Horse Guards. A long winter night had passed unnoticed, and it was five o'clock in the morning when supper was served. The winners sat down to table with an excellent appetite; the losers let their plates remain empty before them. Little by little, however, with the assistance of the champagne, the conversation became animated, and was shared by all.

"How did you get on this evening, Surin?" said the host to one of his friends.

"Oh, I lost, as usual. I really have no luck. I play *mirandole*. You know that I keep cool. Nothing moves me; I never change my play, and yet I always lose."

"Do you mean to say that all the evening you did not once back the red? Your firmness of character surprises me."

"What do you think of Hermann?" said one of the party, pointing to a young Engineer officer.

"That fellow never made a bet or touched a card in his life, and yet he watches us playing until five in the morning."

"It interests me," said Hermann; "but I am not disposed to risk the necessary in view of the superfluous."

"Hermann is a German, and economical; that is the whole of the secret," cried Tomski. "But what is really astonishing is the Countess Anna Fedotovna!"

"How so?" asked several voices.

"Have you not remarked," said Tomski, "that she never plays?"

"Yes," said Narumoff, "a woman of eighty, who never touches a card; that is indeed something extraordinary!"

"You do not know why?"

"No; is there a reason for it?"

"Just listen. My grandmother, you know, some sixty years ago, went to Paris, and became the rage there. People ran after her in the streets, and called her the 'Muscovite Venus.' Richelieu made love to her, and my grandmother makes out that, by her rigorous demeanour, she almost drove him to suicide. In those days women used to play at faro. One evening at the court she lost, on *parole,* to the Duke of Orleans, a very considerable sum. When she got home, my grandmother removed her beauty spots, took off her hoops, and in this tragic costume went to my grandfather, told him of her misfortune, and asked him for the money she had to pay. My grandfather, now no more, was, so to say, his wife's steward. He feared her like fire; but the sum she named made him leap into the air. He flew into a rage, made a brief calculation, and proved to my grandmother that in six months she had got through half a million rubles. He told her plainly that he had no villages to sell in Paris, his domains being situated in the neighbourhood of Moscow and of Saratoff; and finally refused point blank. You may imagine the fury of my grandmother. She boxed his ears, and passed the night in another room.

"The next day she returned to the charge. For the first time in her life, she condescended to arguments and explanations. In vain did she try to prove to her husband that there were debts and debts, and that she could not treat a prince of the blood like her coachmaker.

"All this eloquence was lost. My grandfather was inflexible. My grandmother did not know where to turn. Happily she was acquainted with a man who was very celebrated at this time. You have heard of the Count of St. Germain, about whom so many marvellous stories were told. You know that he passed for a sort of Wandering Jew, and that he was said to possess an elixir of life and the philosopher's stone.

"Some people laughed at him as a charlatan. Casanova, in his memoirs, says that he was a spy. However that may be, in spite of the mystery of his life, St. Germain was much sought after in good society, and was really an agreeable man. Even to this day my grandmother has preserved a genuine affection for him, and she becomes quite angry when anyone speaks of him with disrespect.

"It occurred to her that he might be able to advance the sum of which she was in need, and she wrote a note begging him to call. The old magician came at once, and found her plunged in the deepest despair. In two or three words she told him everything; related to him her misfortune and the cruelty of her husband, adding that she had no hope except in his friendship and his obliging disposition.

"'Madam,' said St. Germain, after a few moments' reflection, 'I could easily advance you the money you want, but I am sure that you would have no rest until you had repaid me, and I do not want to get you out of one trouble in order to place you in another. There is another way of settling the matter. You must regain the money you have lost.'

"'But, my dear friend,' answered my grandmother, 'I have already told you that I have nothing left.'

"'That does not matter,' answered St. Germain. 'Listen to me, and I will explain.'

"He then communicated to her a secret which any of you would, I am sure, give a good deal to possess."

All the young officers gave their full attention. Tomski stopped to light his Turkish pipe, swallowed a mouthful of smoke, and then went on.

"That very evening my grandmother went to Versailles to play at the Queen's table. The Duke of Orleans held the bank. My grandmother invented a little story by way of excuse for not having paid her debt, and then sat down at the table, and began to stake. She took three cards. She won with the first; doubled her stake on the second, and won again; doubled on the third, and still won."

"Mere luck!" said one of the young officers.

"What a tale!" cried Hermann.

"Were the cards marked?" said a third.

"I don't think so," replied Tom ski, gravely.

"And you mean to say," exclaimed Narumoff, "that you have a grandmother who knows the names of three winning cards, and you have never made her tell them to you?"

"That is the very deuce of it," answered Tomski. "She had three sons, of whom my father was one; all three were determined gamblers, and not one of them was able to extract her secret from her, though it would have been of immense advantage to them, and to me also. Listen to what my uncle told me about it, Count Ivan Ilitch, and he told me on his word of honour.

"Tchaplitzki—the one you remember who died in poverty after devouring millions—lost one day, when he was a young man, to Zoritch about three hundred thousand roubles. He was in despair. My grandmother, who had no mercy for the extravagance of young men, made an exception—I do not know why—in favour of Tchaplitzki. She gave him three cards, telling him to play them one after the other, and exacting from him at the same time his word of honour that he would never afterwards touch a card as long as he lived. Accordingly Tchaplitzki went to Zoritch and asked for his revenge. On the first card he staked fifty thousand rubles. He won, doubled the stake, and won again. Continuing his system he ended by gaining more than he had lost.

"But it is six o'clock! It is really time to go to bed."

Everyone emptied his glass and the party broke up.

CHAPTER II

The old Countess Anna Fedotovna was in her dressing-room, seated before her looking-glass. Three maids were in attendance. One held her pot of rouge, another a box of black pins, a third an enormous lace cap, with flaming ribbons. The Countess had no longer the slightest pretence to beauty, but she preserved all the habits of her youth. She dressed in the style of fifty years before, and gave as much time and attention to her toilet as a fashionable beauty of the last century. Her companion was working at a frame in a corner of the window.

"Good morning, grandmother," said the young officer, as he entered the dressing-room. "Good morning, Mademoiselle Lise. Grandmother, I have come to ask you a favour."

"What is it, Paul?"

"I want to introduce to you one of my friends, and to ask you to give him an invitation to your ball."

"Bring him to the ball and introduce him to me there. Did you go yesterday to the Princess's?"

"Certainly. It was delightful! We danced until five o'clock in the morning. Mademoiselle Eletzki was charming."

"My dear nephew, you are really not difficult to please. As to beauty, you should have seen her grandmother, the Princess Daria Petrovna. But she must be very old the Princess Daria Petrovna!"

"How do you mean old?" cried Tomski thoughtlessly; "she died seven years ago."

The young lady who acted as companion raised her head and made a sign to the officer, who then remembered that it was an understood thing to conceal from the Princess the death of any of her contemporaries. He bit his lips. The Countess, however, was not in any way disturbed on hearing that her old friend was no longer in this world.

"Dead!" she said, "and I never knew it! We were maids of honour in the same year, and when we were presented, the Empress'"—and the old Countess related for the hundredth time an anecdote of her young days. "Paul," she said, as she finished her story, "help me to get up. Lisaveta, where is my snuff-box?"

And, followed by the three maids, she went behind a great screen to finish her toilet. Tomski was now alone with the companion.

"Who is the gentleman you wish to introduce to madame?" asked Lisaveta.

"Narumoff. Do you know him?"

"No. Is he in the army?"

"Yes."

"In the Engineers?"

"No, in the Horse Guards. Why did you think he was in the Engineers?"

The young lady smiled, but made no answer.

"Paul," cried the Countess from behind the screen, "send me a new novel; no matter what. Only see that it is not in the style of the present day."

"What style would you like, grandmother?"

"A novel in which the hero strangles neither his father nor his mother, and in which no one gets drowned. Nothing frightens me so much as the idea of getting drowned."

"But how is it possible to find you such a book? Do you want it in Russian?"

"Are there any novels in Russian? However, send me something or other. You won't forget?"

"I will not forget, grandmother. I am in a great hurry. Goodbye, Lisaveta. What made you fancy Narumoff was in the Engineers?" and Tomski took his departure.

Lisaveta, left alone, took out her embroidery, and sat down close to the window. Immediately afterwards, in the street, at the corner of a neighbouring house, appeared a young officer. The sight of him made the companion blush to her ears. She lowered her head, and almost concealed it in the canvas. At this moment the Counters returned, fully dressed.

"Lisaveta," she said "have the horses put in; we will go out for a drive."

Lisaveta rose from her chair, and began to arrange her embroidery.

"Well, my dear child, are you deaf? Go and tell them to put the horses in at once."

"I am going," replied the young lady, as she went out into the ante-chamber.

A servant now came in, bringing some books from Prince Paul Alexandrovitch.

"Say I am much obliged to him. Lisaveta! Lisaveta! Where has she run off to?"

"I was going to dress."

"We have plenty of time, my dear. Sit down, take the first volume, and read to me."

The companion took the book and read a few lines.

"Louder," said the Countess. "What is the matter with you? Have you a cold? Wait a moment; bring me that stool. A little closer; that will do."

Lisaveta read two pages of the book.

"Throw that stupid book away," said the Countess. "What nonsense! Send it back to Prince Paul, and tell him I am much obliged to him; and the carriage, is it never coming?

"Here it is," replied Lisaveta, going to the window.

"And now you are not dressed. Why do you always keep me waiting? It is intolerable."

Lisaveta ran to her room. She had scarcely been there two minutes when the Countess rang with all her might. Her maids rushed in at one door and her valet at the other.

"You do not seem to hear me when I ring," she cried. "Go and tell Lisaveta that I am waiting for her."

At this moment Lisaveta entered, wearing a new walking dress and a fashionable bonnet.

"At last, miss," cried the Countess. "But what is that you have got on? And why? For whom are you dressing? What sort of weather is it? Quite stormy, I believe."

"No, your Excellency," said the valet; "it is exceedingly fine."

"What do you know about it? Open the ventilator. Just what I told you! A frightful wind, and as icy as can be. Unharness the horses. Lisaveta, my child, we will not go out today. It was scarcely worth while to dress so much."

"What an existence!" said the companion to herself.

Lisaveta Ivanovna was, in fact, a most unhappy creature. "The bread of the stranger is bitter," says Dante, "and his staircase hard to climb." But who can tell the torments of a poor little companion attached to an old lady of quality? The Countess had all the caprices of a woman spoilt by the world. She was avaricious and egotistical, and thought all the more of herself now that she had ceased to play an active part in society. She never missed a ball, and she dressed and painted in the style of a bygone age. She remained in a corner of the room, where she seemed to have been placed expressly to serve as a scarecrow. Everyone on coming in went to her and made her a low bow, but this ceremony once at an end no one spoke a word to her. She received the whole city at her house, observing the strictest etiquette, and never failing to give to everyone his or her proper name. Her innumerable servants, growing pale and fat in the ante-chamber, did absolutely as they liked, so that that the house was pillaged as if its owner were really dead. Lisaveta passed her life in continual torture. If she made tea she was reproached with wasting the sugar. If she read a novel to the Countess she was held responsible for all the absurdities of the author. If she went out with the noble lady for a walk or drive, it was she who was to blame if the weather was bad or the pavement muddy. Her salary, more than modest, was never punctually paid, and she was expected to dress "like everyone else," that is to say, like very few people indeed. When she went into society her position was sad. Everyone knew her; no one paid her any attention. At a ball she sometimes danced, but only when a *vis-à-vis* was wanted. Women would come up to her, take her by the arm, and lead her out of the room if their dress required attending to. She had her portion of self-respect, and felt deeply the misery of her position. She looked with impatience for a liberator to break her chain. But the young men, prudent in the midst of their affected giddiness, took care not to honour her with their attentions, though Lisaveta Ivanovna was a hundred times prettier than the shameless or stupid girls whom they surrounded with their homage. More than once she slunk away from the splendour of the drawing room to shut herself up alone in her little bedroom, furnished with an old screen and a pieced carpet, a chest of drawers, a small looking-glass, and a wooden bedstead. There she shed tears at her ease by the light of a tallow candle in a tin candlestick.

One morning—it was two days after the party at Narumoff's, and a week before the scene we have just sketched—Lisaveta was sitting at her embroidery before the window, when, looking carelessly into the street, she saw an officer, in the uniform of the Engineers, standing motionless with his eyes fixed upon her. She lowered her head, and applied herself to her work more attentively than ever. Five minutes afterwards she locked mechanically into the street, and the officer was still in the same place. Not being in the habit of exchanging glances with young men who passed by her window, she remained with her eyes fixed on her work for nearly two hours, until she was told that lunch was ready. She got up to put her embroidery away, and while doing so, looked into the street, and saw the officer still in the same place. This seemed to her very strange. After lunch she went to the window with a certain emotion, but the officer of Engineers was no longer in the street.

She thought no more of him. But two days afterwards, just as she was getting into the carriage with the Countess, she saw him once more, standing straight before the door. His face was half concealed by a fur collar, but his black eyes sparkled beneath his helmet. Lisaveta was afraid, without knowing why, and she trembled as she took her seat in the carriage.

On returning home, she rushed with a beating heart towards the window. The officer was in his habitual place, with his eyes fixed ardently upon her. She at once withdrew, burning at the same time with curiosity, and moved by a strange feeling which she now experienced for the first time.

No day now passed but the young officer showed himself beneath the window. Before long a dumb acquaintance was established between them. Sitting at her work she felt his presence, and when she raised her head she looked at him for a long time every day. The young man seemed full of gratitude for these innocent favours.

She observed, with the deep and rapid perceptions of youth, that a sudden redness covered the officer's pale cheeks as soon as their eyes met. After about a week she would smile at seeing him for the first time.

When Tomski asked his grandmother's permission to present one of his friends, the heart of the poor young girl beat strongly, and when she heard that it was Narumoff, she bitterly repented having compromised her secret by letting it out to a giddy young man like Paul.

Hermann was the son of a German settled in Russia, from whom he had inherited a small sum of money. Firmly resolved to preserve his independence, he had made it a principle not to touch his private income. He lived on his pay, and did not allow himself the slightest luxury. He was not very communicative; and his reserve rendered it difficult for his comrades to amuse themselves at his expense.

Under an assumed calm he concealed strong passions and a highly-imaginative disposition. But he was always master of himself, and kept himself free from the ordinary faults of young men. Thus, a gambler by temperament, he never touched a card, feeling, as he himself said, that his position did not allow him to "risk the necessary in view of the superfluous." Yet he would pass entire nights before a card-table, watching with feverish anxiety the rapid changes of the game. The anecdote of Count St. Germaines three cards had struck his imagination, and he did nothing but think of it all that night.

"If," he said to himself next day as he was walking along the streets of St. Petersburg, "if she would only tell me her secret—if she would only name the three winning cards! I must get presented to her, that I may pay my court and gain her confidence. Yes! And she is eighty-seven! She may die this week—tomorrow perhaps. But after all, is there a word of truth in the story? No! Economy, Temperance, Work; these are my three winning cards. With them I can double my capital; increase it tenfold. They alone can ensure my independence and prosperity."

Dreaming in this way as he walked along, his attention was attracted by a house built in an antiquated style of architecture. The street was full of carriages, which passed one by one before the old house, now brilliantly illuminated. As the people stepped out of the carriages Hermann saw now the little feet of a young woman, now the military boot of a general.

Then came a clocked stocking; then, again, a diplomatic pump. Fur-lined cloaks and coats passed in procession before a gigantic porter.

Hermann stopped. "Who lives here?" he said to a watchman in his box.

"The Countess Anna Fedotovna." It was Tomski's grandmother.

Hermann started. The story of the three cards came once more upon his imagination. He walked to and fro before the house, thinking of the woman to whom it belonged, of her wealth and her mysterious power. At last he returned to his den. But for some time he could not get to sleep; and when at last sleep came upon him, he saw, dancing before his eyes, cards, a green table, and heaps of rubles and bank-notes. He saw himself doubling stake after stake, always winning, and then filling his pockets with piles of coin, and stuffing his pocket-book with countless bank-notes. When he awoke, he sighed to find that his treasures were but creations of a disordered fancy; and, to drive such thoughts from him, he went out for a walk. But he had not gone far when he found himself once more before the house of the Countess. He seemed to have been attracted there by some irresistible force. He stopped, and looked up at the windows. There he saw a girl's head with beautiful black hair, leaning gracefully over a book or an embroidery-frame. The head was lifted, and he saw a fresh complexion and black eyes.

This moment decided his fate.

CHAPTER III

Lisaveta was just taking off her shawl and her bonnet, when the Countess sent for her. She had had the horses put in again.

While two footmen were helping the old lady into the carriage, Lisaveta saw the young officer at her side. She felt him take her by the hand, lost her head, and found, when the young officer had walked away, that he had left a paper between her fingers. She hastily concealed it in her glove.

During the whole of the drive she neither saw nor heard. When they were in the carriage together the Countess was in the habit of questioning Lisaveta perpetually.

"Who is that man that bowed to us? What is the name of this bridge? What is there written on that signboard?"

Lisaveta now gave the most absurd answers, and was accordingly scolded by the Countess.

"What is the matter with you, my child?" she asked. "What are you thinking about? Or do you really not hear me? I speak distinctly enough, however, and I have not yet lost my head, have I?"

Lisaveta was not listening. When she got back to the house, she ran to her room, locked the door, and took the scrap of paper from her glove. It was not sealed, and it was impossible, therefore, not to read it. The letter contained protestations of love. It was tender, respectful, and translated word for word from a German novel. But Lisaveta did not read German, and she was quite delighted. She was, however, much embarrassed. For the first time in her life she had a secret. Correspond with a young man! The idea of such a thing frightened her. How imprudent she had been! She had reproached herself, but knew not now what to do.

Cease to do her work at the window, and by persistent coldness try and disgust the *young* officer? Send him back his letter? Answer him in a firm, decided manner? What line of conduct was she to pursue? She had no friend, no one to advise her. She at last decided to send an answer. She sat down at her little table, took pen and paper, and began to think. More than once she wrote a sentence and then tore up the paper. What she had written seemed too stiff, or else it was wanting in reserve. At last, after much trouble, she succeeded in composing a few lines which seemed to meet the case.

"I believe," she wrote, "that your intentions are those of an honourable man, and that you would not wish to offend me by any thoughtless conduct. But you must understand that our acquaintance cannot begin in this way. I return your letter, and trust that you will not give me cause to regret my imprudence."

Next day, as soon as Hermann made his appearance, Lisaveta left her embroidery, and went into the drawing room, opened the ventilator, and threw her letter into the street, making sure that the young officer would pick it up.

Hermann, in fact, at once saw it, and picking it up, entered a confectioner's shop in order to read it. Finding nothing discouraging in it, he went home sufficiently pleased with the first step in his love adventure.

Some days afterwards, a young person with lively eyes called to see Miss Lisaveta, on the part of a milliner. Lisaveta wondered what she could want, and suspected, as she received her, some secret intention. She was much surprised, however, when she recognised, on the letter that was now handed to her, the writing of Hermann.

"You make a mistake," she said; "this letter is not for me."

"I beg your pardon," said the milliner, with a slight smile; "be kind enough to read it."

Lisaveta glanced at it. Hermann was asking for an appointment.

"Impossible!" she cried, alarmed both at the boldness of the request, and at the manner in which it was made. "This letter is not for me," she repeated; and she tore it into a hundred pieces.

"If the letter was not for you, why did you tear it up? You should have given it me back, that I might take it to the person it was meant for."

"True," said Lisaveta, quite disconcerted.

"But bring me no more letters, and tell the person who gave you this one that he ought to blush for his conduct."

Hermann, however, was not a man to give up what he had once undertaken. Every day Lisaveta received a fresh letter from him, sent now in one way, now in another. They were no longer translated from the German. Hermann wrote under the influence of a commanding passion, and spoke a language which was his own. Lisaveta could not hold out against such torrents of eloquence. She received the letters, kept them, and at last answered them. Every day her answers were longer and more affectionate, until at last she threw out of the window a letter couched as follows—

"This evening there is a ball at the Embassy. The Countess will be there. We shall remain until two in the morning. You may manage to see me alone. As soon as the Countess leaves home, that is to say towards eleven o'clock, the servants are sure to go out, and there will be no one left but the porter, who will be sure to be asleep in his box. Enter as soon as it strikes eleven, and go upstairs as fast as possible. If you find anyone in the ante-chamber, ask whether the Countess is at home, and you will be told that she is out, and, in that case, you must resign yourself, and go away. In all probability, however, you will meet no one. The Countess's women are together in a distant room. When you are once in the ante-chamber, turn to the left, and walk straight on, until you reach the Countess's bedroom. There, behind a large screen, you will see two doors. The one on the right leads to a dark room. The one on the left leads to a corridor, at the end of which is a little winding staircase, which leads to my parlour."

At, ten o'clock Hermann was already on duty before the Countess's door. It was a frightful night. The winds had been unloosed, and the snow was falling in large flakes; the lamps gave an uncertain light; the streets were deserted; from time to time passed a sledge, drawn by a wretched hack, on the lookout for a fare. Covered by a thick overcoat, Hermann felt neither the wind nor the snow. At last the Countesses carriage drew up. He saw two huge footmen come forward and take beneath the arms a dilapidated spectre, and place it on the cushions well wrapped up in an enormous fur cloak. Immediately afterwards, in a cloak of lighter make, her head crowned with natural flowers, came Lisaveta, who sprang into the carriage like a dart. The door was closed, and the carriage rolled on softly over the snow.

The porter closed the street door, and soon the windows of the first floor became dark. Silence reigned throughout the house. Hermann walked backwards and forwards; then coming to a lamp he looked at his watch. It was twenty minutes to eleven. Leaning against the lamp-post, his eyes fixed on the long hand of his watch, he counted impatiently the minutes which had yet to pass. At eleven o'clock precisely Hermann walked up the steps, pushed open the street door, and went into the vestibule, which was well lighted. As it happened the porter was not there. With a firm and rapid step he rushed up the staircase and reached the ante-chamber. There, before a lamp, a footman was sleeping, stretched out in a dirty greasy dressing-gown. Hermann passed quickly before him and crossed the dining room and the drawing room, where there was no light. But the lamp of the ante-chamber helped him to see. At last he reached the Countess's bedroom. Before a screen covered with old icons (sacred pictures) a golden lamp was burning. Gilt armchairs, sofas of faded colours, furnished with soft cushions, were arranged symmetrically along the walls, which were hung with China silk. He saw two large portraits painted by Madame le Brun. One represented a man of forty, stout and full coloured, dressed in a light green coat, with a decoration on his breast. The second portrait was that of an elegant young woman, with an aquiline nose, powdered hair rolled back on the temples, and with a rose over her ear. Everywhere might be seen shepherds and shepherdesses in Dresden china, with vases of all shapes, clocks by Leroy, work-baskets, fans, and all the thousand playthings for the use of ladies of fashion, discovered in the last century, at the time of Montgolfier's balloons and Mesmer's animal magnetism.

Hermann passed behind the screen, which concealed a little iron bedstead. He saw the two doors; the one on the right leading to the dark room, the one on the left to the corridor. He opened the latter, saw the staircase which led to the poor little companion's parlour, and then, closing this door, went into the dark room.

The time passed slowly. Everything was quiet in the house. The drawing room clock struck midnight, and again there was silence. Hermann was standing up, leaning against the stove, in which there was no fire. He was calm; but his heart beat with quick pulsations, like that of a man determined to brave all dangers he might have to meet, because he knows them to be inevitable. He heard one o'clock strike; then two; and soon afterwards the distant roll of a carriage. He now, in spite of himself, experienced some emotion. The carriage approached rapidly and stopped. There was at once a great noise of servants running about the staircases, and a confusion of voices. Suddenly the rooms were all lit up, and the Countess's three antiquated maids came at once into the bedroom. At last appeared the Countess herself.

The walking mummy sank into a large Voltaire armchair. Hermann looked through the crack in the door; he saw Lisaveta pass close to him, and heard her hurried step as she went up the little winding staircase. For a moment he felt something like remorse; but it soon passed off, and his heart was once more of stone.

The Countess began to undress before a looking-glass. Her headdress of roses was taken off, and her powdered wig separated from her own hair, which was very short and quite white. Pins fell in showers around her. At last she was in her dressing-gown and night cap, and in this costume, more suitable to her age, was less hideous than before.

Like most old people, the Countess was tormented by sleeplessness. She had her armchair rolled towards one of the windows, and told her maids to leave her. The lights were put out, and the room was lighted only by the lamp which burned before the holy images. The Countess, sallow and wrinkled, balanced herself gently from right to left. In her dull eyes could be read an utter absence of thought; and as she moved from side to side, one might have said that she did so not by any action of the will, but through some secret mechanism.

Suddenly this death's-head assumed a new expression; the lips ceased to tremble, and the eyes became alive. A strange man had appeared before the Countess!

It was Hermann.

"Do not be alarmed, madam," said Hermann, in a low voice, but very distinctly. "For the love of Heaven, do not be alarmed. I do not wish to do you the slightest harm; on the contrary, I come to implore a favour of you."

The old woman looked at him in silence, as if she did not understand. Thinking she was deaf, he leaned towards her ear and repeated what he had said; but the Countess still remained silent.

"You can ensure the happiness of my whole life, and without its costing you a farthing. I know that you can name to me three cards—"

The Countess now understood what he required.

"It was a joke," she interrupted. "I swear to you it was only a joke."

"No, madam," replied Hermann in an angry tone. "Remember Tchaplitzki, and how you enabled him to win."

The Countess was agitated. For a moment her features expressed strong emotion; but they soon resumed their former dullness.

"Cannot you name to me," said Hermann, "three winning cards?"

The Countess remained silent. "Why keep this secret for your great-grandchildren," he continued. "They are rich enough without; they do not know the value of money. Of what profit would your three cards be to them? They are debauchees. The man who cannot keep his inheritance will die in want, though he had the science of demons at his command. I am a steady man. I know the value of money. Your three cards will not be lost upon me. Come!"

He stopped tremblingly, awaiting a reply. The Countess did not utter a word. Hermann went upon his knees.

"If your heart has ever known the passion of love; if you can remember its sweet ecstasies; if you Pave ever been touched by the cry of a newborn babe; if any human feeling has ever caused your heart to beat, I entreat you by the love of a husband, a lover, a mother, by all that is sacred in life, not to reject my prayer. Tell me your secret! Reflect! You are old; you Pave not long to live! Remember that the happiness of a man is in your hands; that not only myself, but my children and my grandchildren will bless your memory as a saint."

The old Countess answered not a word.

Hermann rose, and drew a pistol from his pocket.

"Hag!" he exclaimed, "I will make you speak."

At the sight of the pistol the Countess for the second time showed agitation. Her head shook violently she stretched out her hands as if to put the weapon aside. Then suddenly she fell back motionless.

"Come, don't be childish!" said Hermann. "I adjure you for the last time; will you name the three cards?"

The Countess did not answer. Hermann saw that she was dead!

CHAPTER IV

Lisaveta was sitting in her room, still in her ball dress, lost in the deepest meditation. On her return to the house, she had sent away her maid, and had gone upstairs to her room, trembling at the idea of finding Hermann there; desiring, indeed, *not* to find him. One glance showed her that he was not there, and she gave thanks to Providence that he had missed the appointment. She sat down pensively, without thinking of taking off her cloak, and allowed to pass through her memory all the circumstances of the intrigue which had begun such a short time back, and had already advanced so far. Scarcely three weeks had passed since she had first seen the young officer from her window, and already she had written to him, and he had succeeded in inducing her to make an appointment. She knew his name, and that was all. She had received a quantity of letters from him, but he had never spoken to her; she did not know the sound of his voice, and until that evening, strangely enough, she had never heard him spoken of.

But that very evening Tomski, fancying he had noticed that the young Princess Pauline, to whom he had been paying assiduous court, was flirting, contrary to her custom, with, another man, had wished to revenge himself by making a show of indifference. With this noble object he had invited Lisaveta to take part in an interminable mazurka; but he teased her immensely about her partiality for Engineer officers, and pretending all the time to know much more than he really did, hazarded purely in fun a few guesses which were so happy that Lisaveta thought her secret must have been discovered.

"But who tells you all this?" she said with a smile. "A friend of the very officer you know, a most original man."

"And who is this man that is so original?"

"His name is Hermann."

She answered nothing, but her hands and feet seemed to be of ice.

"Hermann is a hero of romance," continued Tomski. "He has the profile of Napoleon, and the soul of Mephistopheles. I believe he has at least three crimes on his conscience . . . But how pale you are!"

"I have a bad headache. But what did this Mr. Hermann tell you? Is not that his name?"

"Hermann is very much displeased with his friend, with the Engineer officer who has made your acquaintance. He says that in his place he would behave very differently. But I am quite sure that Hermann himself has designs upon you. At least, he seems to listen with remarkable interest to all that his friend tells him about you."

"And where has he seen me?"

"Perhaps in church, perhaps in the street; heaven knows where."

At this moment three ladies came forward according to the custom of the mazurka, and asked Tomski to choose between "forgetfulness and regret."*

And the conversation which had so painfully excited the curiosity of Lisaveta came to an end.

The lady who, in virtue of the infidelities permitted by the mazurka, had just been chosen by Tom ski, was the Princess Pauline. During the rapid evolutions which the figure obliged them to make, there was a grand explanation between them, until at last he conducted her to a chair, and returned to his partner.

But Tomski could now think no more, either of Hermann or Lisaveta, and he tried in vain to resume the conversation. But the mazurka was coming to an end, and immediately afterwards the old Countess rose to go.

Tomski's mysterious phrases were nothing more than the usual platitudes of the mazurka, but they had made a deep impression upon the heart of the poor little companion. The portrait sketched by Tomski had struck her as very exact; and with her romantic ideas, she saw in the rather ordinary countenance of her adorer something to fear and admire. She was now sitting down with her cloak off, with bare shoulders; her head, crowned with flowers, falling forward from fatigue, when suddenly the door opened and Hermann entered. She shuddered.

"Where were you?" she said, trembling all over.

---

* The figures and fashions of the mazurka are reproduced in the cotillon of Western Europe.—TRANSLATOR.

"In the Countess's bedroom. I have just left her," replied Hermann. "She is dead."

"Great Heavens! What are you saying?"

"I am afraid," he said, "that I am the cause of her death."

Lisaveta looked at him in consternation, and remembered Tomski's words: "He has at least three crimes on his conscience."

Hermann sat down by the window, and told everything. The young girl listened with terror.

So those letters so full of passion, those burning expressions, this daring obstinate pursuit—all this had been inspired by anything but love! Money alone had inflamed the man's soul. She, who had nothing but a heart to offer, how could she make him happy? Poor child! she had been the blind instrument of a robber, of the murderer of her old benefactress. She wept bitterly in the agony of her repentance. Hermann watched her in silence; but neither the tears of the unhappy girl, nor her beauty, rendered more touching by her grief, could move his heart of iron. He had no remorse in thinking of the Countess's death. One sole thought distressed him—the irreparable loss of the secret which was to have made his fortune.

"You are a monster!" said Lisaveta, after a long silence.

"I did not mean to kill her," replied Hermann coldly. "My pistol was not loaded."

They remained for some time without speaking, without looking at one another. The day was breaking, and Lisaveta put out her candle. She wiped her eyes, drowned in tears, and raised them towards Hermann. He was standing close to the window, his arms crossed, with a frown on his forehead. In this attitude he reminded her involuntarily of the portrait of Napoleon. The resemblance overwhelmed her.

"How am I to get you away?" she said at last. "I thought you might go out by the back stairs. But it would be necessary to go through the Countess's bedroom, and I am too frightened."

"Tell me how to get to the staircase, and I will go alone."

She went to a drawer, took out a key, which she handed to Hermann, and gave him the necessary instructions. Hermann took her icy hand, kissed her on the forehead, and departed.

He went down the staircase, and entered the Countess's bedroom. She was seated quite stiff in her armchair; but her features were in no way contracted. He stopped for a moment, and gazed into her face as if to make sure of the terrible reality. Then he entered the dark room, and, feeling behind the tapestry, found the little door which, opened on to a staircase. As he went down it, strange ideas came into his head. "Going down this staircase," he said to himself, "some sixty years ago, at about this time, may have been seen some man in an embroidered coat with powdered wig, pressing to his breast a cocked hat: some gallant who has long been buried; and now the heart of his aged mistress has ceased to beat."

At the end of the staircase he found another door, which his key opened, and he found himself in the corridor which led to the street.

CHAPTER V

Three days after this fatal night, at nine o'clock in the morning, Hermann entered the convent where the last respects were to be paid to the mortal remains of the old Countess. He felt no remorse, though he could not deny to himself that he was the poor woman's assassin. Having no religion, he was, as usual in such cases, very superstitious; believing that the dead Countess might exercise a malignant influence on his life, he thought to appease her spirit by attending her funeral.

The church was full of people, and it was difficult to get in. The body had been placed on a rich catafalque, beneath a canopy of velvet. The Countess was reposing in an open coffin, her hands joined on her breast, with a dress of white satin, and headdress of lace. Around the catafalque the family was assembled, the servants in black caftans with a knot of ribbons on the shoulder, exhibiting the colours of the Countess's coat of arms. Each of them held a wax candle in his hand. The relations, in deep mourning—children, grandchildren, and great-grandchildren—were all present; but none of them wept.

To have shed tears would have looked like affectation. The Countess was so old that her death could have taken no one by surprise, and she had long been looked upon as already out of the world. The funeral sermon was delivered by a celebrated preacher. In a few simple, touching phrases he painted the final departure of the just, who had passed long years of contrite preparation, for a Christian end. The service concluded in the midst of respectful silence. Then the relations went towards the defunct to take a last farewell After them, in a long procession, all who had been, invited to the ceremony bowed, for the last time, to her who for so many years had been a scarecrow at their entertainments. Finally came the Countess's household; among them was remarked an old governess, of the same age as the deceased, supported by two woman. She had not strength enough to kneel down, but tears flowed from her eyes, as she kissed the hand of her old mistress.

In his turn Hermann advanced towards the coffin. He knelt down for a moment on the flagstones, which were strewed with branches of yew. Then he rose, as pale as death, and walked up the steps of the catafalque. He bowed his head. But suddenly the dead woman seemed to be staring at him; and with a mocking look she opened and shut one eye. Hermann by a sudden movement started and fell backwards. Several persons hurried towards him. At the same moment, close to the church door, Lisaveta fainted.

Throughout the day Hermann suffered from a strange indisposition. In a quiet restaurant, where he took his meals, he, contrary to his habit, drank a great deal of wine, with the object of stupefying himself. But the wine had no effect but to excite his imagination, and give fresh activity to the ideas with which he was preoccupied.

He went home earlier than usual, lay down with his clothes on upon the bed, and fell into a leaden sleep. When he woke up it was night, and the room was lighted up by the rays of the moon. He looked at his watch; it was a quarter to three. He could sleep no more. He sat up on the bed and thought of the old Countess. At this moment someone in the street passed the window, looked into the room, and then went on. Hermann scarcely noticed it; but in another minute he heard the door of the ante-chamber open. He thought, that his orderly, drunk as usual, was returning from some nocturnal excursion; but the step was one to which he was not accustomed. Somebody seemed to be softly walking over the floor in slippers.

The door opened, and a woman, dressed entirely in white, entered the bedroom. Hermann thought it must be his old nurse, and he asked himself what she could want at that time of night.

But the woman in white, crossing the room with a rapid step, was now at the foot of his bed, and Hermann recognised the Countess.

"I come to you against my wish," she said in a firm voice. "I am forced to grant your prayer. Three, seven, ace, will win, if played one after the other; but you must not play more than one card in twenty-four hours, and afterwards, as long as you live, you must never touch a card again. I forgive you my death on condition of your marrying my companion, Lisaveta Ivanovna."

With these words she walked towards the door, and gliding with her slippers over the floor, disappeared. Hermann heard the door of the ante-chamber open, and soon afterwards saw a white figure pass along the street. It stopped for a moment before his window, as if to look at him.

Hermann remained, for some time astounded. Then he got up and went into the next room. His orderly, drunk as usual, was asleep on the floor. He had much difficulty in waking him, and then could not obtain from him the least explanation. The door of the ante-chamber was locked.

Hermann went back to his bedroom, and wrote down all the details of his vision.

CHAPTER VI

Two fixed ideas can no more exist together in the moral world, than in the physical two bodies can occupy the same place at the same time; and "Three, seven, ace" soon drove away Hermann's recollection of the old Countess's last moments. "Three, seven, ace" were now in his head to the exclusion of everything else.

They followed him in his dreams, and appeared to him under strange forms. Threes seemed to be spread before him like magnolias, sevens took the form of Gothic doors, and aces became gigantic spiders.

His thoughts concentrated themselves on one single point. How was he to profit by the secret so dearly purchased? What if he applied for leave to travel? At Paris, he said to himself, he would find some gambling-house where, with his three cards, he could at once make his fortune.

Chance soon came to his assistance. There was at Moscow a society of rich gamblers, presided over by the celebrated Tchekalinski, who had passed all his life playing at cards, and had amassed millions. For while he lost silver only, he gained bank-notes. His magnificent house, his excellent kitchen, his cordial manners, had brought him numerous friends and secured for him general esteem.

When he came to St. Petersburg, the young men of the capital filled his rooms, forsaking balls for his card-parties, and preferring the emotions of gambling to the fascinations of flirting. Hermann was taken to Tchekalinski by Narumoff. They passed through a long suite of rooms, full of the most attentive, obsequious servants. The place was crowded. Generals and high officials were playing at whist; young men were stretched out on the sofas, eating ices and smoking long pipes. In the principal room at the head of a long table, around which were assembled a score of players, the master of the house held a faro bank.

He was a man of about sixty, with a sweet and noble expression of face, and hair white as snow. On his full, florid countenance might be read good humour and benevolence. His eyes shone with a perpetual smile. Narumoff introduced Hermann. Tchekalinski took him by the hand, told him that he was glad to see him, that no one stood on ceremony in his house; and then went on dealing. The deal occupied some time, and stakes were made on more than thirty cards. Tchekalinski waited patiently to allow the winners time to double their stakes, paid what he had lost, listened politely to all observations, and, more politely still, put straight the corners of cards, when in a fit of absence someone had taken the liberty of turning them down. At last when the game was at an end, Tchekalinski collected the cards, shuffled them again, had them cut, and then dealt anew.

"Will you allow me to take a card?" said Hermann, stretching out his arm above a fat man who occupied nearly the whole of one side of the table. Tchekalinski, with a gracious smile, bowed in consent. Naroumoff complimented Hermann, with a laugh, on the cessation of the austerity by which his conduct had hitherto been marked, and wished him all kinds of happiness on the occasion of his first appearance in the character of a gambler.

"There!" said Hermann, after writing some figures on the back of his card.

"How much?" asked the banker, half closing his eyes. "Excuse me, I cannot see."

"Forty-seven thousand rubles," said Hermann.

Everyone's eyes were directed toward the new player.

"He has lost his head," thought Harumoff.

"Allow me to point out to you," said Tchekalinski, with his eternal smile, "that you are playing rather high. We never put down here, as a first stake, more than a hundred and seventy-five rubles."

"Very well," said Hermann; "but do you accept my stake or not?"

Tchekalinski bowed in token of acceptation. "I only wish to point out to you," he said, "that although I am perfectly sure of my friends, I can only play against ready money. I am quite convinced that your word is as good as gold; but to keep up the rules of the game, and to facilitate calculations, I should be obliged to you if you would put the money on your card."

Hermann took a bank-note from his pocket and handed it to Tchekalinski, who, after examining it with a glance, placed it on Hermann's card.

Then he began to deal. He turned up on the right a ten, and on the left a three.

"I win," said Hermann, exhibiting his three.

A murmur of astonishment ran through the assembly. The banker knitted his eyebrows, but speedily his face resumed its everlasting smile.

"Shall I settle at once?" he asked.

"If you will be kind enough to do so," said Hermann.

Tchekalinski took a bundle of bank-notes from his pocket-book, and paid. Hermann pocketed His winnings and left the table.

Narumoff was lost in astonishment. Hermann drank a glass of lemonade and went home.

The next evening he returned to the house. Tchekalinski again held the bank. Hermann went to the table, and this time the players hastened to make room for him. Tchekalinski received him with a most gracious bow. Hermann waited, took a card, and staked on it his forty-seven thousand roubles, together with the like sum which he had gained the evening before.

Tchekalinski began to deal. He turned up on the right a knave, and on the left a seven.

Hermann exhibited a seven.

There was a general exclamation. Tchekalinski was evidently ill at ease, but he counted out the ninety-four thousand roubles to Hermann, who took them in the calmest manner, rose from, the table, and went away.

The next evening, at the accustomed hour, he again appeared. Everyone was expecting him. Generals and high officials had left their whist to watch this extraordinary play. The young officers had quitted their sofas, and even the servants of the house pressed round the table.

When Hermann took his seat, the other players ceased to stake, so impatient were they to see him have it out with the banker, who, still smiling, watched the approach of his antagonist and prepared to meet him. Each of them untied at the same time a pack of cards. Tchekalinski shuffled, and Hermann cut. Then the latter took up a card and covered it with a heap of banknotes. It was like the preliminaries of a duel. A deep silence reigned through the room.

Tchekalinski took up the cards with trembling hands and dealt. On one side he put down a queen and on the other side an ace.

"Ace wins," said Hermann.

"No. Queen loses," said Tchekalinski.

Hermann looked. Instead of ace, he saw a queen of spades before him. He could not trust his eyes! And now as he gazed, in fascination, on the fatal card, he fancied that he saw the queen of spades open and then close her eye, while at the same time she gave a mocking smile. He felt a thrill of nameless horror. The queen of spades resembled the dead Countess!

Hermann is now at the Obukhoff Asylum, room No. 17 a hopeless madman! He answers no questions which we put to him. Only he mumbles to himself without cessation, "Three, seven, ace; three, seven, *queen*!"

The Postmaster

Translated by Mrs Sutherland Edwards

W ho has not cursed the Postmaster; who has not quarrelled with him? Who, in a moment of anger, has not demanded the fatal book to write his ineffectual complaint against extortion, rudeness, and unpunctuality? Who does not consider him a human monster, equal only to our extinct attorney, or, at least, to the brigands of the Murom Woods? Let us, however, be just and place ourselves in his position, and, perhaps, we shall judge him less severely. What is a Postmaster? A real martyr of the 14th class (i.e., of nobility), only protected by his *tchin* (rank) from personal violence; and that not always. I appeal to the conscience of my readers. What is the position of this dictator, as Prince Yiasemsky jokingly calls him? Is it not really that of a galley slave? No rest for him day or night. All the irritation accumulated in the course of a dull journey by the traveller is vented upon the Postmaster. If the weather is intolerable, the road wretched, the driver obstinate, or the horses intractable—the Postmaster is to blame. Entering his humble abode, the traveller looks upon him as his enemy, and the Postmaster is lucky if he gets rid of his uninvited guest soon. But should there happen to be no horses! Heavens! what abuse, what threats are showered upon his head! Through rain and mud he is obliged to seek them, so that during a storm, or in the winter frosts, he is often glad to take refuge in the cold passage in order to snatch a few moments of repose and to escape from the shrieking and pushing of irritated guests.

If a general arrives, the trembling Postmaster supplies him with the two last remaining *troiki* (team of three horses abreast), of which one *troika* ought, perhaps, to have been reserved for the diligence. The general drives on without even a word of thanks. Five minutes later the Postmaster hears—a bell! and the guard throws down his travelling certificate on the table before him! Let us realize all this, and, instead of anger, we shall feel sincere pity for the Postmaster. A few words more. In the course of twenty years I have travelled all over Russia, and know nearly all the mail routes. I have made the acquaintance of several generations of drivers. There are few postmasters whom I do not know personally, and few with whom I have not had dealings. My curious collection of travelling experiences I hope shortly to publish. At present I will only say that, as a class, the Postmaster is presented to the public in a false light. This much-libelled personage is generally a peaceful, obliging, sociable, modest man, and not too fond of money. From his conversation (which the travelling gentry very wrongly despise) much interesting and instructive information may be acquired. As far as I am concerned, I profess that I prefer his talk to that of some *tchinovnik* (official) of the 6th class, travelling for the Government.

It may easily be guessed that I have some friends among the honourable class of postmasters. Indeed, the memory of one of them is very dear to me. Circumstances at one time brought us together, and it is of him that I now intend to tell my dear readers.

In the May of 1816 I chanced to be passing through the Government of——, along a road now no longer existing. I held a small rank, and was travelling with relays of three horses while paying only for two. Consequently the Postmaster stood upon no ceremony with me, but I had often to take from him by force what I considered to be mine by right. Being young and passionate, I was indignant at the meanness and, cowardice of the Postmaster when he handed over the *troika* prepared for me to some official gentleman of higher rank.

It also took me a long time to get over the offence, when a servant, fond of making distinctions, missed me when waiting at the governor's table. Now the one and the other appear to me to be quite in the natural course of things. Indeed, what would become of us, if, instead of the convenient rule that rank gives precedence to rank, the rule were to be reversed, and mind made to give precedence to mind? What disputes would arise! Besides, to whom would the attendants first hand the dishes? But to return to my story.

The day was hot. About three versts from the station it began to spit, and a minute afterwards there was a pouring rain, and I was soon drenched to the skin. Arriving at the station, my first care was to change my clothes, and then I asked for a cup of tea.

"Hi! Dunia!" called out the Postmaster, "Prepare the *samovar* and fetch some cream."

In obedience to this command, a girl of fourteen appeared from behind the partition, and ran out into the passage. I was struck by her beauty.

"Is that your daughter?" I inquired of the Postmaster.

"Yes," he answered, with a look of gratified pride, "and such a good, clever girl, just like her late mother." Then, while he took note of my travelling certificate, I occupied the time in examining the pictures which decorated the walls of his humble abode. They were illustrations of the story of the Prodigal Son. In the firsts a venerable old man in a skull cap and dressing gown, is wishing goodbye to the restless youth who naturally receives his blessing and a bag of money. In another, the dissipated life of the young man is painted in glaring colours; he is sitting at a table surrounded by false friends and shameless women. In the next picture, the ruined youth in his shirt sleeves and a three-cornered hat, is taking care of some swine while sharing their food. His face expresses deep sorrow and contrition. Finally, there was the representation of his return to his father. The kind old man, in the same cap and dressing gown, runs out to meet him; the prodigal son falls on his knees before him; in the distance, the cook is killing the fatted calf, and the eldest son is asking the servants the reason of all this rejoicing. At the foot of each picture I read some appropriate German verses. I remember them all distinctly, as well as some pots of balsams, the bed with the speckled curtains, and many other characteristic surroundings. I can see the stationmaster at this moment; a man about fifty years of age, fresh and strong, in a long green coat, with three medals on faded ribbons.

I had scarcely time to settle with my old driver when Dunia returned with the *samovar*. The little coquette saw at a second glance the impression she had produced upon me. She lowered her large, blue eyes. I spoke to her, and she replied confidently, like a girl accustomed to society. I offered a glass of punch to her father, to Dunia I handed a cup of tea. Then we all three fell into easy conversation, as if we had known each other all our lives.

The horses had been waiting a long while, but I was loth to part from the Postmaster and his daughter. At last I took leave of them, the father wishing me a pleasant journey, while the daughter saw me to the *telega*. In the corridor I stopped and asked permission to kiss her. Dunia consented. I can remember a great many kisses since then, but none which left such a lasting, such a delightful impression.

Several years passed, when circumstances brought me back to the same tract, to the very same places. I recollected the old Postmasters daughter, and rejoiced at the prospect of seeing her again.

"But," I thought, "perhaps the old Postmaster has been changed, and Dunia may be already married." The idea that one or the other might be dead also passed through my mind, and I approached the station of——with sad presentiments. The horses drew up at the small station house. I entered the waiting-room, and instantly recognised the pictures representing the story of the Prodigal Son. The table and the bed stood in their old places, but the flowers on the window sills had disappeared, while all the surroundings showed neglect and decay.

The Postmaster was asleep under his great-coat, but my arrival awoke him and he rose. It was certainly Simeon Virin, but how aged! While he was preparing to make a copy of my travelling certificate, I looked at his grey hairs, and the deep wrinkles in his long, unshaven face, his bent back, and I was amazed to see how three or four years had managed to change a strong, middle-aged man into a frail, old one.

"Do you recognise me?" I asked him, "we are old friends."

"May be," he replied, gloomily, "this is a highway, and many travellers have passed through here."

"Is your Dunia well?" I added. The old man frowned.

"Heaven knows," he answered.

"Apparently, she is married," I said.

The old man pretended not to hear my question, and in a low voice went on reading my travelling certificate. I ceased my inquiries and ordered hot water.

My curiosity was becoming painful, and I hoped that the punch would loosen the tongue of my old friend. I was not mistaken; the old man did not refuse the proffered tumbler. I noticed that the rum dispelled his gloom. At the second glass he became talkative, remembered, or at any rate looked as if he remembered, me, and I heard the story, which at the time interested me and even affected me much.

"So you knew my Dunia?" he began. "But, then, who did not? Oh, Dunia, Dunia! What a beautiful girl you were! You were admired and praised by every traveller. No one had a word to say against her. The ladies gave her presents—one a handkerchief, another a pair of earrings. The gentlemen stopped on purpose, as if to dine or to take supper, but really only to take a longer look at her. However rough a man might be, he became subdued in her presence and spoke graciously to me. Will you believe me, sir? Couriers and special messengers would talk to her for half an hour at the time. She was the support of the house. She kept everything in order, did everything and looked after everything. While I, the old fool that I was, could not see enough of her, or pet her sufficiently. How I loved her! How I indulged my child! Surely her life was a happy one? But, no! fate is not to be avoided."

Then he began to tell me his sorrow in detail. Three years before, one winter evening, while the Postmaster was ruling a new book, his daughter in the next partition was busy making herself a dress, when a *troika* drove up and a traveller, wearing a Circassian hat and a long military overcoat, and muffled in a shawl, entered the room and demanded horses.

The horses were all out. Hearing this, the traveller had raised his voice and his whip, when Dunia, accustomed to such scenes, rushed out from behind the partition and inquired pleasantly whether he would not like something to eat? Her appearance produced the usual effect. The passenger's rage subsided, he agreed to wait for horses, and ordered some supper. He took off his wet hat, unloosed the shawl, and divested himself of his long overcoat.

The traveller was a tall, young hussar with a small black moustache. He settled down comfortably at the Postmaster's and began a lively, conversation with him and his daughter. Supper was served. Meanwhile, the horses returned and the Postmaster ordered them instantly, without being fed, to be harnessed to the traveller's *kibitka*. But returning to the room, he found the young man senseless on the bench where he lay in a faint. Such a headache had attacked him that it was impossible for him to continue his journey. What was to be done? The Postmaster gave up his own bed to him; and it was arranged that if the patient was not better the next morning to send to C——for the doctor.

Next day the hussar was worse. His servant rode to the town to fetch the doctor. Dunia bound up his head with a handkerchief moistened in vinegar, and sat down with her needlework by his bedside. In the presence of the Postmaster the invalid groaned and scarcely said a word.

Nevertheless, he drank two cups of coffee and, still groaning, ordered a good dinner. Dunia never left him. Every time he asked for a drink Dunia handed him the jug of lemonade prepared by herself. After moistening his lips, the patient each time he returned the jug gave her hand a gentle pressure in token of gratitude.

Towards dinner time the doctor arrived. He felt the patient's pulse, spoke to him in German and in Russian, declared that all he required was rest, and said that in a couple of days he would be able to start on his journey. The hussar handed him twenty-five rubles for his visit, and gave him an invitation to dinner, which the doctor accepted. They both ate with a good appetite, and drank a bottle of wine between them. Then, very pleased with one another, they separated.

Another day passed, and the hussar had quite recovered. He became very lively, incessantly joking, first with Dunia, then with the Postmaster, whistling tunes, conversing with the passengers, copying their travelling certificates into the station book, and so ingratiating himself that on the third day the good Postmaster regretted parting with his dear lodger.

It was Sunday, and Dunia was getting ready to attend mass. The hussar's *kibitka* was at the door. He took leave of the Postmaster, after recompensing him handsomely for his board and lodging, wished Dunia goodbye, and proposed to drop her at the church, which was situated at the other end of the village. Dunia hesitated.

"What are you afraid of?" asked her father. "His nobility is not a wolf. He won't eat you. Drive with him as far as the church."

Dunia got into the carriage by the side of the hussar. The servant jumped on the coach box, the coachman gave a whistle, and the horses went off at a gallop.

The poor Postmaster could not understand how he came to allow his Dunia to drive off with the hussar; how he could have been so blind, and what had become of his senses. Before half an hour had passed his heart misgave him. It ached, and he became so uneasy that he could bear the situation no longer, and started for the church himself. Approaching the church, he saw that the people were already dispersing. But Dunia was neither in the churchyard nor at the entrance. He hurried into the church; the priest was just leaving the altar, the clerk was extinguishing the tapers, two old women were still praying in a corner; but Dunia was nowhere to be seen. The poor father could scarcely summon courage to ask the clerk if she had been to mass. The clerk replied that she had not. The Postmaster returned home neither dead nor alive. He had only one hope left; that Dunia in the flightiness of her youth had, perhaps, resolved to drive as far as the next station, where her godmother lived. In patient agitation he awaited the return of the *troika* with which he had allowed her to drive off, but the driver did not come back. At last, towards night, he arrived alone and tipsy, with the fatal news that Dunia had gone on with the hussar.

The old man succumbed to his misfortune, and took to his bed, the same bed where, the day before, the young impostor had lain. Recalling all the circumstances, the Postmaster understood now that the hussar's illness had been shammed. The poor fellow sickened with severe fever, he was removed to C——, and in his place another man was temporarily appointed. The same doctor who had visited the hussar attended him. He assured the Postmaster that the young man had been perfectly well, that he had from the first had suspicions of his evil intentions, but that he had kept silent for fear of his whip.

Whether the German doctor spoke the truth, or was anxious only to prove his great penetration, his assurance brought no consolation to the poor patient. As soon as he was beginning to recover from his illness, the old Postmaster asked his superior postmaster of the town of C——for two months' leave of absence, and without saying a word to anyone, he started off on foot to look for his daughter.

From the station book he discovered that Captain Minsky had left Smolensk for Petersburg. The coachman who drove him said that Dunia had wept all the way, though she seemed to be going of her own free will.

"Perhaps," thought the station master, "I shall bring back my strayed lamb." With this idea he reached St. Petersburg, and stopped with the Ismailovsky regiment, in the quarters of a non-commissioned officer, his old comrade in arms. Beginning his search he soon found out that Captain Minsky was in Petersburg, living at Demuth's Hotel. The Postmaster determined to see him.

Early in the morning he went to Minsky's antechamber, and asked to have his nobility informed that an old soldier wished to see him. The military attendant, in the act of cleaning a boot on a boot-tree, informed him that his master was asleep, and never received anyone before eleven o'clock. The Postmaster left to return at the appointed time. Minsky came out to him in his dressing gown and red skull cap.

"Well, my friend, what do you want?" he inquired.

The old maids heart boiled, tears started to his eyes, and in a trembling voice he could only say, "Your nobility; be divinely merciful!"

Minsky glanced quickly at him, flushed, and seizing him by the hand, led him into his study and locked the door.

"Your nobility!" continued the old man, "what has fallen from the cart is lost; give me back, at any rate, my Dunia. Let her go. Do not ruin her entirely."

"What is done cannot be undone," replied the young man, in extreme confusion. "I am guilty before you, and ready to ask your pardon. But do not imagine that I could neglect Dunia. She shall be happy, I give you my word of honour. Why do you want her? She loves me; she has forsaken her former existence. Neither you nor she can forget what has happened." Then, pushing something up his sleeve, he opened the door, and the Postmaster found himself, he knew not how, in the street.

He stood long motionless, at last catching sight of a roll of papers inside his cuff, he pulled them out and unrolled several crumpled-up fifty ruble notes. His eyes again filled with tears, tears of indignation! He crushed the notes into a ball, threw them on the ground, and, stamping on them with his heel, walked away. After a few steps he stopped, reflected a moment, and turned back.

But the notes were gone. A well-dressed young man, who had observed him, ran towards an *isvoshtchick*, got in hurriedly, and called to the driver to be "off."

The Postmaster did not pursue him. He had resolved to return home to his post-house; but before doing so he wished to see his poor Dunia once more. With this view, a couple of days afterwards he returned to Minsky's lodgings. But the military servant told him roughly that his master received nobody, pushed him out of the antechamber, and slammed the door in his face. The Postmaster stood and stood, and at last went away.

That same day, in the evening, he was walking along the Leteinaia, having been to service at the Church of the All Saints, when a smart *drojki* flew past him, and in it the Postmaster recognised Minsky. The *drojki* stopped in front of a three-storeyed house at the very entrance, and the hussar ran up the steps. A happy thought occurred to the Postmaster. He retraced his steps.

"Whose horses are these?" he inquired of the coachman. "Don't they belong to Minsky?"

"Exactly so," replied the coachman. "Why do you ask?"

"Why! your master told me to deliver a note for him to his Dunia, and I have forgotten where his Dunia lives."

"She lives here on the second floor; but you are too late, my friend, with your note; he is there himself now."

"No matter," answered the Postmaster, who had an undefinable sensation at his heart. "Thanks for your information; I shall be able to manage my business." With these words he ascended the steps.

The door was locked; he rang. There were several seconds of painful delay. Then the key jingled, and the door opened.

"Does Avdotia Simeonovna live here?" he inquired.

"She does," replied the young maid-servant, "What do you want with her?"

The Postmaster did not reply, but walked on.

"You must not, must not," she called after him; "Avdotia Simeonovna has visitors." But the Postmaster, without listening, went on. The first two rooms were dark. In the third there was a light. He approached the open door and stopped. In the room, which was beautifully furnished, sat Minsky in deep thought. Dunia, dressed in all the splendour of the latest fashion, sat on the arm of his easy chair, like a rider on an English side saddle. She was looking tenderly at Minsky, while twisting his black locks round her glittering fingers. Poor Postmaster! His daughter had never before seemed so beautiful to him. In spite of himself, he stood admiring her.

"Who is there?" she asked, without raising her head.

He was silent.

Receiving no reply Dunia looked up, and with a cry she fell on the carpet.

Minsky, in alarm, rushed to pick her up, when suddenly seeing the old Postmaster in the doorway, he left Dunia and approached him, trembling with rage.

"What do you want?" he inquired, clenching his teeth. "Why do you steal after me everywhere, like a burglar? Or do you want to murder me?

Begone!" and with a strong hand he seized the old man by the scruff of the neck and pushed him down the stairs.

The old man went back to his rooms. His friend advised him to take proceedings, but the Postmaster reflected, waved his hand, and decided to give the matter up. Two days afterwards he left Petersburg for his station and resumed his duties.

"This is the third year," he concluded, "that I am living without my Dunia; and I have had no tidings whatever of her. Whether she is alive or not God knows. Many tilings happen. She is not the first, nor the last, whom a wandering blackguard has *enticed* away, kept for a time, and then dropped. There are many such young fools in Petersburg today, in satins and velvets, and tomorrow you see them sweeping the streets in the company of drunkards in rags. When I think sometimes that Dunia, too, may end in the same way, then, in spite of myself, I sin, and wish her in her grave."

Such was the story of my friend, the old Postmaster, the story more than once interrupted by tears, which he wiped away picturesquely with the flap of his coat like the faithful Terentieff in Dmitrieff's beautiful ballad. The tears were partly caused by punch, of which he had consumed five tumblers in the course of his narrative. But whatever their origin, I was deeply affected by them. After parting with him, it was long before I could forget the old Postmaster, and I thought long of poor Dunia.

Lately, again passing through the small place of——, I remembered my friend. I heard that the station over which he ruled had been done away with. To my inquiry, "Is the Postmaster alive?" no one could give a satisfactory answer. Having resolved to pay a visit to the familiar place, I hired horses of my own, and started for the village of N——.

It was autumn. Grey clouds covered the sky; a cold wind blew from the close reaped fields, carrying with it the brown and yellow leaves of the trees which it met. I arrived in the village at sunset, and stopped at the station house. In the passage (where once Dunia had kissed me) a stout woman met me; and to my inquiries, replied that the old Postmaster had died about a year before; that a brewer occupied his house; and that she was the wife of that brewer. I regretted my fruitless journey, and my seven roubles of useless expense.

"Of what did he die?" I asked the brewer's wife.

"Of drink," she answered.

"And where is he buried?"

"Beyond the village, by the side of his late wife."

"Could someone take me to his grave?"

"Certainly! Hi, Vanka! cease playing with the cat and take this gentleman to the cemetery, and show him the Postmaster's grave."

At these words, a ragged boy, with red hair and a squint, ran towards me to lead the way.

"Did you know the poor man?" I asked him, on the road.

"How should I not know him? He taught me to make whistles. When (may he be in heaven!) we met him coming from the tavern, *we* used to run after him calling, 'Daddy! daddy! some nuts,' and he gave us nuts. He idled most of his time away with, us."

"And do the travellers ever speak of him?"

"There are few travellers nowadays, unless the assize judge turns up; and he is too busy to think of the dead. But a lady, passing through last summer, did ask after the old Postmaster, and she went to his grave."

"What was the ladylike?" I inquired curiously.

"A beautiful lady," answered the boy. "She travelled in a coach with six horses, three beautiful little children, a nurse, and a little black dog; and when she heard that the old Postmaster was dead, she wept, and told the children to keep quiet while she went to the cemetery. I offered to show her the way, but the lady said, 'I know the way,' and she gave me a silver *piatak* (twopence) . . . such a kind lady!"

We reached the cemetery. It was a bare place unenclosed, marked with wooden crosses and unshaded by a single tree. Never before had I seen such a melancholy cemetery.

"Here is the grave of the old Postmaster," said the boy to me, as he pointed to a heap of sand into which had been stuck a black cross with a brass *icon* (image).

"Did the lady come here?" I asked.

"She did," replied Vanka. "I saw her from a distance. She lay down here, and remained lying down for a long while. Then she went into the village and saw the priest. She gave him some money and drove off. To me she gave a silver *piatak*. She was a splendid lady!"

And I also gave the boy a silver *piatak,* regretting neither the journey nor the seven roubles that it had cost me.

The Pistol Shot

Translated by Mrs Sutherland Edwards

CHAPTER I

We were stationed at the little village of Z. The life of an officer in the army is well known. Drill and the riding school in the morning; dinner with the colonel or at the Jewish restaurant; and in the evening punch and cards.

At Z. nobody kept open house, and there was no girl that anyone could think of marrying. We used to meet at each other's rooms, where we never saw anything but one another's uniforms. There was only one man among us who did not belong to the regiment. He was about thirty-five, and, of course, we looked upon him as an old fellow. He had the advantage of experience, and his habitual gloom, stern features, and his sharp tongue gave him great influence over his juniors. He was surrounded by a certain mystery. His looks were Russian, but his name was foreign. He had served in the Hussars, and with credit. No one knew what had induced him to retire and settle in this out of the way little village, where he lived in mingled poverty and extravagance. He always went on foot, and wore a shabby black coat. But he was always ready to receive any of our officers; and though his dinners, cooked by a retired soldier, never consisted of more than two or three dishes, champagne flowed at them like water. His income, or how he got it, no one knew, and no one ventured to ask. He had a few books on military subjects and a few novels, which he willingly lent and never asked to have returned. But, on the other hand, he never returned the books he himself borrowed.

His principal recreation was pistol-shooting. The walls of his room were riddled with bullets—a perfect honeycomb. A rich collection of pistols was the only thing luxurious in his modestly furnished villa. His skill as a shot was quite prodigious. If he had undertaken to shoot a pear off someone's cap not a man in our regiment would have hesitated to act as target. Our conversation often turned on duelling; Silvio, so I will call him, never joined in it. When asked if he had ever fought, he answered curtly, "Yes." But he gave no particulars, and it was evident that he disliked such questions. We concluded that the memory of some unhappy victim of his terrible skill preyed heavily upon his conscience. None of us could ever have suspected him of cowardice. There are men whose look alone is enough to repel such a suspicion.

An unexpected incident fairly astonished us. One afternoon about ten officers were dining with Silvio. They drank as usual, that is to say, a great deal. After dinner we asked our host to make a pool. For a long time he refused on the ground that he seldom played. At last he ordered cards to be brought in. With half a hundred gold pieces on the table we sat round him, and the game began. It was Silvio's habit not to speak when playing. He never disputed or explained. If an adversary made a mistake Silvio without a word chalked it down against him. Knowing his way we always let him have it.

But among us on this occasion was an officer who had but lately joined. While playing he absentmindedly scored a point too much. Silvio took the chalk and corrected the score in his own fashion. The officer, supposing him to have made a mistake, began to explain. Silvio went on dealing in silence. The officer, losing patience, took the brush and rubbed out what he thought was wrong. Silvio took the chalk and recorrected it. The officer, heated with wine and play, and irritated by the laughter of the company, thought himself aggrieved, and, in a fit of passion, seized a brass candlestick and threw it at Silvio, who only just managed to avoid the missile. Great was our confusion. Silvio got up, white with rage, and said, with sparkling eyes—

"Sir! have the goodness to withdraw, and you may thank God that this has happened in my own house."

We could have no doubt as to the consequences, and we already looked upon our new comrade as a dead man. He withdrew saying that he was ready to give satisfaction for his offence in any way desired.

The game went on for a few minutes; but feeling that our host was upset we gradually left off playing and dispersed, each to his own quarters. At the riding school next day we were already asking one another whether the young lieutenant was still alive, when he appeared among us. We asked him the same question, and were told that he had not yet heard from Silvio. We were astonished. We went to Silvio's and found him in the courtyard popping bullet after bullet into an ace which he had gummed to the gate. He received us as usual, but made no allusion to what had happened on the previous evening.

Three days passed and the lieutenant was still alive. "Can it be possible," we asked one another in astonishment, "that Silvio will not fight?"

Silvio did not fight. He accepted a flimsy apology, and became reconciled to the man who had insulted him. This lowered him greatly in the opinion of the young men, who, placing bravery above all the other human virtues and regarding it as an excuse for every imaginable vice, were ready to overlook anything sooner than a lack of courage. However, little by little, all was forgotten, and Silvio regained his former influence. I alone could not renew my friendship with him. Being naturally romantic I had surpassed the rest in my attachment to the man whose life was an enigma, and who seemed to me a hero of some mysterious story. He liked me, and with me alone did he drop his sarcastic tone and converse simply and most agreeably on many subjects. But after this unlucky evening the thought that his honour was tarnished, and that it remained so by his own choice, never left me; and this prevented any renewal of our former intimacy. I was ashamed to look at him. Silvio was too sharp and experienced not to notice this and guess the reason. It seemed to vex him, for I observed that once or twice he hinted at an explanation; but I wanted none, and Silvio gave me up. Thenceforth I only met him in the presence of other friends, and our confidential talks were at an end.

The busy occupants of the capital have no idea of the emotions so frequently experienced by residents in the country and in country towns; as, for instance, in awaiting the arrival of the post. On Tuesdays and Fridays the bureau of the regimental staff was crammed with officers. Some were expecting money, others letters or newspapers. The letters were mostly opened on the spot, and the news freely interchanged, the office meanwhile presenting a most lively appearance.

Silvio's letters used to be addressed to our regiment, and he usually called for them himself. On one occasion, a letter having been handed to him, I saw him break the seal and, with a look of great impatience, read the contents. His eyes sparkled. The other officers, each engaged with his own letters, did not notice anything.

"Gentlemen," said Silvio, "circumstances demand my immediate departure. I leave tonight, and I hope you will not refuse to dine with me for the last time. I shall expect you, too," he added, "turning towards me, without fail." With these words he hurriedly left, and we agreed to meet at Silvio's.

I went to Silvio's at the appointed time and found nearly the whole regiment with him. His things were already packed. Nothing remained but the bare shot-marked walls. We sat down to table. The host was in excellent spirits, and his liveliness communicated itself to the rest of the company. Corks popped every moment. Bottles fizzed and tumblers foamed incessantly, and we, with much warmth, wished our departing friend a pleasant journey and every happiness. The evening was far advanced when we rose from table. During the search for hats, Silvio wished everybody goodbye. Then, taking me by the hand, as I was on the point of leaving, he said in a low voice:

"I want to speak to you."

I stopped behind.

The guests had gone and we were left alone.

Sitting down opposite one another we lighted our pipes. Silvio was much agitated, no traces of his former gaiety remained. Deadly pale, with sparkling eyes, and a thick smoke issuing from his mouth, he looked like a demon. Several minutes passed before he broke silence.

"Perhaps we shall never meet again," he said. "Before saying goodbye I want to have a few words with you. You may have remarked that I care little for the opinion of others. But I like you, and should be sorry to leave you under a wrong impression."

He paused, and began refilling his pipe. I looked down and was silent.

"You thought it odd," he continued, "that I did not require satisfaction from that drunken maniac. You will grant, however, that being entitled to the choice of weapons I had his life more or less in my hands. I might attribute my tolerance to generosity, but I will not deceive you; if I could have chastised him without the least risk to myself, without the slightest danger to my own life, then I would on no account have forgiven him."

I looked at Silvio with surprise. Such a confession completely upset me. Silvio continued:

"Precisely so, I had no right to endanger my life. Six years ago I received a slap in the face and my enemy still lives."

My curiosity was greatly excited.

"Did you not fight him?" I inquired. "Circumstances probably separated you?"

"I did fight him," replied Silvio, "and here is a memento of our duel."

He rose and took from a cardboard box a red cap with a gold tassel and gold braid.

"My disposition is well known to you. I have been accustomed to be first in everything. Prom my youth this has been my passion. In my time dissipation was the fashion, and I was the most dissipated man in the army. We used to boast of our drunkenness. I beat at drinking the celebrated Burtsoff, of whom Davidoff has sung in his poems. Duels in our regiment were of daily occurrence. I took part in all of them, either as second or as principal. My comrades adored me, while the commanders of the regiment, who were constantly being changed, looked upon me as an incurable evil.

"I was calmly, or rather boisterously, enjoying my reputation when a certain young man joined our regiment. He was rich, and came of a distinguished family—I will not name him. Never in my life did I meet with so brilliant, so fortunate a fellow!—young, clever, handsome, with the wildest spirits, the most reckless bravery, bearing a celebrated name, possessing funds of which he did not know the amount, but which were inexhaustible. You may imagine the effect he was sure to produce among us. My leadership was shaken. Dazzled by my reputation he began by seeking my friendship. But I received him coldly; at which, without the least sign of regret, he kept aloof from me.

"I took a dislike to him. His success in the regiment and in the society of women brought me to despair. I tried to pick a quarrel with him. To my epigrams he replied with epigrams which always seemed to me more pointed and more piercing than my own, and which were certainly much livelier; for while he joked I was raving.

"Finally, at a ball at the house of a Polish landed proprietor, seeing him receive marked attention from all the ladies, and especially from the lady of the house, who had formerly been on very friendly terms with me, I whispered some low insult in his ear. He flew into a passion and gave me a slap on the cheek. We clutched our swords, the ladies fainted, we were separated, and the same night we drove out to fight.

"It was nearly daybreak. I was standing at the appointed spot with my three seconds. How impatiently I awaited my opponent! The spring sun had risen and it was growing hot. At last I saw him in the distance. He was on foot, accompanied by only one second. We advanced to meet him. He approached, holding in his hand his regimental cap filled full of black cherries.

"The seconds measured twelve paces. It was for me to fire first. But my excitement was so great that I could not depend upon the certainty of my hand, and, in order to give myself time to get calm, I ceded the first shot to my adversary. He would not accept it, and we decided to cast lots.

"The number fell to him; constant favourite of fortune that he was! He aimed and put a bullet through my cap.

"It was now my turn. His life at last was in my hands. I looked at him eagerly, trying to detect if only some faint shadow of uneasiness. But he stood beneath my pistol picking out ripe cherries from his cap and spitting out the stones, some of which fell near me. His indifference enraged me. 'What is the use,' thought I, 'of depriving him of life, when he sets no value upon it.' As this savage thought flitted through my brain I lowered the pistol.

"'You don't seem to be ready for death,' I said, 'you are eating your breakfast, and I don't want to interfere with you.'

"'You don't interfere with me in the least,' he replied. 'Be good enough to fire; or don't fire if you prefer it; the shot remains with you, and I shall be at your service at any moment.'

"I turned to the seconds, informing them that I had no intention of firing that day, and with this the duel ended. I resigned my commission and retired to this little place. Since then not a single day has passed that I have not thought of my revenge; and now the hour has arrived."

Silvio took from his pocket the letter he had received that morning, and handed it to me to read. Someone (it seemed to be his business agent) wrote to him from Moscow, that a certain individual was soon to be married to a young and beautiful girl.

"You guess," said Silvio, "who the certain individual is. I am starting for Moscow. Me shall see whether he will be as indifferent now as he was some time ago, when in presence of death he ate cherries!"

With these words Silvio rose, threw his cap upon the floor, and began pacing up and down the room like a tiger in his cage. I remained silent. Strange contending feelings agitated me.

The servant entered and announced that the horses were ready. Silvio grasped my hand tightly. He got into the *telega*, in which lay two trunks—one containing his pistols, the other some personal effects. We wished goodbye a second time, and the horses galloped off.

CHAPTER II

Many years passed, and family circumstances obliged me to settle in the poor little village of H. Engaged in farming, I sighed in secret for my former merry, careless existence. Most difficult of all I found it to pass in solitude the spring and winter evenings. Until the dinner hour I somehow occupied the time, talking to the *starosta*, driving round to see how the work went on, or visiting the new buildings. But as soon as evening began to draw in, I was at a loss what to do with myself. My books in various bookcases, cupboards, and storerooms I knew by heart. The housekeeper, Kurilovna, related to me all the stories she could remember. The songs of the peasant women made me melancholy. I tried cherry brandy, but that gave me the headache. I must confess, however, that I had some fear of becoming a drunkard from *ennui*, the saddest kind of drunkenness imaginable, of which I had seen many examples in our district.

I had no near neighbours with the exception of two or three melancholy ones, whose conversation consisted mostly of hiccups and sighs. Solitude was preferable to that. Finally I decided to go to bed as early as possible, and to dine as late as possible, thus shortening the evening and lengthening the day; and I found this plan a good one.

Pour versts from my place was a large estate belonging to Count B.; but the steward alone lived there. The Countess had visited her domain once only, just after her marriage, and she then only lived there about a month. However, in the second spring of my retirement, there was a report that the Countess, with her husband, would come to spend the summer on her estate; and they arrived at the beginning of June.

The advent of a rich neighbour is an important event for residents in the country. The landowners and the people of their household talk of it for a couple of months beforehand, and for three years afterwards. As far as I was concerned, I must confess, the expected arrival of a young and beautiful neighbour affected me strongly. I burned with impatience to see her; and the first Sunday after her arrival I started for the village, in order to present myself to the Count and Countess as their near neighbour and humble servant.

The footman showed me into the Count's study, while he went to inform him of my arrival. The spacious room was furnished in a most luxurious manner. Against the walls stood enclosed bookshelves well furnished with books, and surmounted by bronze busts. Over the marble mantelpiece was a large mirror. The floor was covered with green cloth, over which were spread rugs and carpets.

Having got unaccustomed to luxury in my own poor little corner, and not having beheld the wealth of other people for a long while, I was awed; and I awaited the Count with a sort of fear, just as a petitioner from the provinces awaits in an ante-room the arrival of the minister. The doors opened, and a man about thirty-two, and very handsome, entered the apartment. The Count approached me with a frank and friendly look. I tried to be self-possessed, and began to introduce myself, but he forestalled me.

We sat down. His easy and agreeable, conversation soon dissipated my nervous timidity. I was already passing into my usual manner, when suddenly the Countess entered, and I became more confused than ever. She was, indeed, beautiful. The Count presented me. I was anxious to appear at ease, but the more I tried to assume an air of unrestraint, the more awkward I felt myself becoming. They, in order to give me time to recover myself and get accustomed to my new acquaintances, conversed with one another, treating me in good neighbourly fashion without ceremony. Meanwhile, I walked about the room, examining the books and pictures. In pictures I am no *connoisseur*; but one of the Count's attracted my particular notice. It represented a view in Switzerland was not, however, struck by the painting, but by the fact that it was shot through by two bullets, one planted just on the top of the other.

"A good shot," I remarked, turning to the Count.

"Yes," he replied, "a very remarkable shot."

"Do you shoot well?" he added.

"Tolerably," I answered, rejoicing that the conversation had turned at last on a subject which interested me. "At a distance of thirty paces I do not miss a card; I mean, of course, with a pistol that I am accustomed to."

"Really?" said the Countess, with a look of great interest. "And you, my dear, could you hit a card at thirty paces?"

"Some day," replied the Count, "we will try. In my own time I did not shoot badly. But it is four years now since I held a pistol in my hand."

"Oh," I replied, "in that case, I bet, Count, that you will not hit a card even at twenty paces. The pistol demands daily practice. I know that from experience. In our regiment I was reckoned one of the bests shots. Once I happened not to take a pistol in hand for a whole month; I had sent my own to the gunsmith's. Well, what do you think, Count? The first time I began again to shoot I four times running missed a bottle at twenty paces. The captain of our company, who was a wit, happened to be present, and he said to me: 'Your hand, my friend, refuses to raise itself against the bottle!' No, Count, you must not neglect to practise, or you will soon lose all skill. The best shot I ever knew used to shoot every day, and at least three times every day, before dinner. This was as much his habit as the preliminary glass of vodka."

The Count and Countess seemed pleased that I had begun to talk.

"And what sort of a shot was he?" asked the Count.

"This sort, Count. If he saw a fly settle on the wall—you smile, Countess, but I assure you it is a fact. When he saw the fly, he would call out, 'Kuska, my pistol!' Kuska brought him the loaded pistol. A crack, and the fly was crushed into the wall!"

"That is astonishing!" said the Count. "And what was his name?"

"Silvio was his name."

"Silvio!" exclaimed the Count, starting from his seat. "*You* knew Silvio?"

"How could I fail to know him? We were comrades; he was received at our mess like a brother officer. It is now about five years since I last had tidings of him. Then you, Count, also knew him?"

"I knew him very well. Did he never tell you of one very extraordinary incident in his life?"

"Do you mean the slap in the face, Count, that he received from a blackguard at a ball?"

"He did not tell you the name of this blackguard?"

"No, Count, he did not. Forgive me," I added, guessing the truth, "forgive me—I did not—could it really have been you?"

"It was myself," replied the Count, greatly agitated. "And the shots in the picture are a memento of our last meeting."

"Oh, my dear," said the Countess, "for God's sake do not relate it! It frightens me to think of it."

"No," replied the Count; "I must tell him all. He knows how I insulted his friend. He shall also know how Silvio revenged himself."

The Count pushed a chair towards me, and with the liveliest interest I listened to the following story—

"Five years ago," began the Count, "I got married. The honeymoon I spent here, in this village. To this house I am indebted for the happiest moments of my life, and for one of its saddest remembrances.

"One afternoon we went out riding together. My wife's horse became restive. She was frightened, got off the horse, handed the reins over to me; and walked home. I rode on before her. In the yard I saw a travelling carriage, and I was told that in my study sat a man who would not give his name, but simply said that he wanted to see me on business. I entered the study, and saw in the darkness a man, dusty and unshaven. He stood there, by the fireplace. I approached him, trying to recollect his face.

"'You don't remember me, Count?' he said, in a tremulous voice.

"'Silvio!' I cried, and I confess I felt that my hair was standing on end.

"'Exactly so,' he added. 'You owe me a shot; I have come to claim it. Are you ready?'

"A pistol protruded from his side pocket.

"I measured twelve paces, and stood there in that corner, begging him to fire quickly, before my wife came in.

"He hesitated, and asked for a light. Candles were brought in. I locked the doors, gave orders that no one should enter, and again called upon him to fire. He took out his pistol and aimed.

"I counted the seconds . . . I thought of her . . . A terrible moment passed! Then Silvio lowered his hand.

"'I only regret,' he said, that the pistol is not loaded with cherry-stones. My bullet is heavy; and it always seems to me that an affair of this kind is net a duel, but a murder. I am not accustomed to aim at unarmed men. Let us begin again from the beginning. Let us cast lots as to who shall fire first.'

"My head went round. I think I objected. Finally, however, we loaded another pistol and rolled up two pieces of paper. These he placed inside his cap; the one through which, at our first meeting, I had put the bullet. I again drew the lucky number.

"'Count, you have the devil's luck,' he said, with a smile which I shall never forget.

"I don't know what I was about, or how it happened that he succeeded in inducing me. But I fired and hit that picture."

The Count pointed with his finger to the picture with the shot-marks His face had become red with agitation. The Countess was whiter than her own handkerchief; and I could not restrain an exclamation.

"I fired," continued the Count, "and, thank Heaven, missed. Then Silvio—at this moment he was really terrible—then Silvio raised his pistol to take aim at me.

"Suddenly the door flew open, Masha rushed into the room. She threw herself upon my neck with a loud shriek. Her presence restored to me-all my courage.

"'My dear,' I said to her, 'don't you see that we are only joking? How frightened you look! Go and drink a glass of water and then come back; I will introduce you to an old friend and comrade.'

Masha was still in doubt.

"'Tell me; is my husband speaking the truth?' she asked, turning to the terrible Silvio. 'Is it true that you are only joking?'

"'He is always joking. Countess,' Silvio replied. 'He once in a joke gave me a slap in the face; in joke he put a bullet through this cap while I was wearing it; and in joke, too, he missed me when he fired just now. And now I have a fancy for a joke.'

"With these words he raised his pistol as if to shoot me down before her eyes."

Masha threw herself at his feet.

'Rise, Masha! For shame!' I cried, in my passion. 'And you, sir, cease to amuse yourself at the expense of an unhappy woman. Will you fire or not?'

"'I will not,' replied Silvio. 'I am satisfied. I have witnessed your agitation—your terror. I forced you to fire at me. That is enough; you will remember me. I leave you to your conscience.'

"He was now about to go; but he stopped at the door, looked round at the picture which my shot had passed through, fired at it almost without taking aim, and disappeared.

"My wife had sunk down fainting. The servants had not ventured to stop Silvio, whom they looked upon with terror. He passed out to the steps, called his coachman, and before I could collect myself drove off."

The Count was silent. I had now heard the end of the story of which the beginning had long before surprised me. The hero of it I never saw again. I heard, however, that Silvio, during the rising of Alexander Ipsilanti, commanded a detach of insurgents and was killed in action.

Nikolai Gogol

(1809–1852)

Memoirs of a Madman

Translated by Claud Field

*O*ctober 3rd.—A strange occurrence has taken place today. I got up fairly late, and when Mawra brought me my clean boots, I asked her how late it was. When I heard it had long struck ten, I dressed as quickly as possible.

To tell the truth, I would rather not have gone to the office at all today, for I know beforehand that our department-chief will look as sour as vinegar. For some time past he has been in the habit of saying to me, "Look here, my friend; there is something wrong with your head. You often rush about as though you were possessed. Then you make such confused abstracts of the documents that the devil himself cannot make them out; you write the title without any capital letters, and add neither the date nor the docket-number." The long-legged scoundrel! He is certainly envious of me, because I sit in the director's work-room, and mend His Excellency's pens. In a word, I should not have gone to the office if I had not hoped to meet the accountant, and perhaps squeeze a little advance out of this skinflint.

A terrible man, this accountant! As for his advancing one's salary once in a way—you might sooner expect the skies to fall. You may beg and beseech him, and be on the very verge of ruin—this grey devil won't budge an inch. At the same time, his own cook at home, as all the world knows, boxes his ears.

I really don't see what good one gets by serving in our department. There are no plums there. In the fiscal and judicial offices it is quite different. There some ungainly fellow sits in a corner and writes and writes; he has such a shabby coat and such an ugly mug that one would like to spit on both of them. But you should see what a splendid country-house he has rented. He would not condescend to accept a gilt porcelain cup as a present. "You can give that to your family doctor," he would say. Nothing less than a pair of chestnut horses, a fine carriage, or a beaver-fur coat worth three hundred roubles would be good enough for him. And yet he seems so mild and quiet, and asks so amiably, "Please lend me your penknife; I wish to mend my pen." Nevertheless, he knows how to scarify a petitioner till he has hardly a whole stitch left on his body.

In our office it must be admitted everything is done in a proper and gentlemanly way; there is more cleanness and elegance than one will ever find in Government offices. The tables are mahogany, and everyone is addressed as "sir." And truly, were it not for this official propriety, I should long ago have sent in my resignation.

I put on my old cloak, and took my umbrella, as a light rain was falling. No one was to be seen on the streets except some women, who had flung their skirts over their heads. Here and there one saw a cabman or a shopman with his umbrella up. Of the higher classes one only saw an official here and there. One I saw at the street-crossing, and thought to myself, "Ah! my friend, you are not going to the office, but after that young lady who walks in front of you. You are just like the officers who run after every petticoat they see."

As I was thus following the train of my thoughts, I saw a carriage stop before a shop just as I was passing it. I recognised it at once; it was our director's carriage. "He has nothing to do in the shop," I said to myself; "it must be his daughter."

I pressed myself close against the wall. A lackey opened the carriage door, and, as I had expected, she fluttered like a bird out of it. How proudly she looked right and left; how she drew her eyebrows together, and shot lightnings from her eyes—good heavens! I am lost, hopelessly lost!

But why must she come out in such abominable weather? And yet they say women are so mad on their finery!

She did not recognise me. I had wrapped myself as closely as possible in my cloak. It was dirty and old-fashioned, and I would not have liked to have been seen by her wearing it. Now they wear cloaks with long collars, but mine has only a short double collar, and the cloth is of inferior quality.

Her little dog could not get into the shop, and remained outside. I know this dog; its name is "Meggy."

Before I had been standing there a minute, I heard a voice call, "Good day, Meggy!"

Who the deuce was that? I looked round and saw two ladies hurrying by under an umbrella—one old, the other fairly young. They had already passed me when I heard the same voice say again, "For shame, Meggy!"

What was that? I saw Meggy sniffing at a dog which ran behind the ladies. The deuce! I thought to myself, "I am not drunk? That happens pretty seldom."

"No, Fidel, you are wrong," I heard Meggy say quite distinctly. "I was—bow—wow!—I was—bow! wow! wow!—very ill."

What an extraordinary dog! I was, to tell the truth, quite amazed to hear it talk human language. But when I considered the matter well, I ceased to be astonished. In fact, such things have already happened in the world. It is said that in England a fish put its head out of water and said a word or two in such an extraordinary language that learned men have been puzzling over them for three years, and have not succeeded in interpreting them yet. I also read in the paper of two cows who entered a shop and asked for a pound of tea.

Meanwhile what Meggy went on to say seemed to me still more remarkable. She added, "I wrote to you lately, Fidel; perhaps Polkan did not bring you the letter."

Now I am willing to forfeit a whole month's salary if I ever heard of dogs writing before. This has certainly astonished me. For some little time past I hear and see things which no other man has heard and seen.

"I will," I thought, "follow that dog in order to get to the bottom of the matter. Accordingly, I opened my umbrella and went after the two ladies. They went down Bean Street, turned through Citizen Street and Carpenter Street, and finally halted on the Cuckoo Bridge before a large house. I know this house; it is Sverkoff's. What a monster he is! What sort of people live there! How many cooks, how many bagmen! There are brother officials of mine also there packed on each other like herrings. And I have a friend there, a fine player on the cornet."

The ladies mounted to the fifth story. "Very good," thought I; "I will make a note of the number, in order to follow up the matter at the first opportunity."

***

October 4th.—Today is Wednesday, and I was as usual in the office. I came early on purpose, sat down, and mended all the pens.

Our director must be a very clever man. The whole room is full of bookcases. I read the titles of some of the books; they were very learned, beyond the comprehension of people of my class, and all in French and German. I look at his face; see! how much dignity there is in his eyes. I never hear a single superfluous word from his mouth, except that when he hands over the documents, he asks "What sort of weather is it?"

No, he is not a man of our class; he is a real statesman. I have already noticed that I am a special favourite of his. If now his daughter also—ah! what folly—let me say no more about it!

I have read the *Northern Bee*. What foolish people the French are! By heavens! I should like to tackle them all, and give them a thrashing. I have also read a fine description of a ball given by a landowner of Kursk. The landowners of Kursk write a fine style.

Then I noticed that it was already half-past twelve, and the director had not yet left his bedroom. But about half-past one something happened which no pen can describe.

The door opened. I thought it was the director; I jumped up with my documents from the seat, and—then—she—herself—came into the room. Ye saints! how beautifully she was dressed. Her garments were whiter than a swan's plumage—oh how splendid! A sun, indeed, a real sun!

She greeted me and asked, "Has not my father come yet?"

Ah! what a voice. A canary bird! A real canary bird!

"Your Excellency," I wanted to exclaim, "don't have me executed, but if it must be done, then kill me rather with your own angelic hand." But, God knows why, I could not bring it out, so I only said, "No, he has not come yet."

She glanced at me, looked at the books, and let her handkerchief fall. Instantly I started up, but slipped on the infernal polished floor, and nearly broke my nose. Still I succeeded in picking up the handkerchief.

Ye heavenly choirs, what a handkerchief! So tender and soft, of the finest cambric. It had the scent of a general's rank!

She thanked me, and smiled so amiably that her sugar lips nearly melted. Then she left the room.

After I had sat there about an hour, a flunkey came in and said, "You can go home, Mr Ivanovitch; the director has already gone out!"

I cannot stand these lackeys! They hang about the vestibules, and scarcely vouchsafe to greet one with a nod. Yes, sometimes it is even worse; once one of these rascals offered me his snuff-box without even getting up from his chair. "Don't you know then, you country-bumpkin, that I am an official and of aristocratic birth?"

This time, however, I took my hat and overcoat quietly; these people naturally never think of helping one on with it. I went home, lay a good while on the bed, and wrote some verses in my note:

> "'Tis an hour since I saw thee,
>   And it seems a whole long year;
>   If I loathe my own existence,
>   How can I live on, my dear?"

I think they are by Pushkin.

In the evening I wrapped myself in my cloak, hastened to the director's house, and waited there a long time to see if she would come out and get into the carriage. I only wanted to see her once, but she did not come.

***

November 6th.—Our chief clerk has gone mad. When I came to the office today he called me to his room and began as follows: "Look here, my friend, what wild ideas have got into your head?"

"How! What? None at all," I answered.

"Consider well. You are already past forty; it is quite time to be reasonable. What do you imagine? Do you think I don't know all your tricks? Are you trying to pay court to the director's daughter? Look at yourself and realise what you are! A nonentity, nothing else. I would not give a kopeck for you. Look well in the glass. How can you have such thoughts with such a caricature of a face?"

May the devil take him! Because his own face has a certain resemblance to a medicine-bottle, because he has a curly bush of hair on his head, and sometimes combs it upwards, and sometimes plasters it down in all kinds of queer ways, he thinks that he can do everything. I know well, I know why he is angry with me. He is envious; perhaps he has noticed the tokens of favour which have been graciously shown me. But why should I bother about him? A councillor! What sort of important animal is that? He wears a gold chain with his watch, buys himself boots at thirty roubles a pair; may the deuce take him! Am I a tailor's son or some other obscure cabbage? I am a nobleman! I can also work my way up. I am just forty-two—an age when a man's real career generally begins. Wait a bit, my friend! I too may get to a superior's rank; or perhaps, if God is gracious, even to a higher one. I shall make a name which will far outstrip yours. You think there are no able men except yourself? I only need to order a fashionable coat and wear a tie like yours, and you would be quite eclipsed.

But I have no money—that is the worst part of it!

***

November 8th.—I was at the theatre. "The Russian House-Fool" was performed. I laughed heartily. There was also a kind of musical comedy which contained amusing hits at barristers. The language was very broad; I wonder the censor passed it. In the comedy lines occur which accuse the merchants of cheating; their sons are said to lead immoral lives, and to behave very disrespectfully towards the nobility.

The critics also are criticised; they are said only to be able to find fault, so that authors have to beg the public for protection.

Our modern dramatists certainly write amusing things. I am very fond of the theatre. If I have only a kopeck in my pocket, I always go there. Most of my fellow-officials are uneducated boors, and never enter a theatre unless one throws free tickets at their head.

One actress sang divinely. I thought also of—but silence!

***

November 9th.—About eight o'clock I went to the office. The chief clerk pretended not to notice my arrival. I for my part also behaved as though he were not in existence. I read through and collated documents. About four o'clock I left. I passed by the director's house, but no one was to be seen. After dinner I lay for a good while on the bed.

***

November 11th.—Today I sat in the director's room, mended twenty-three pens for him, and for Her—for Her Excellence, his daughter, four more.

The director likes to see many pens lying on his table. What a head he must have! He continually wraps himself in silence, but I don't think the smallest trifle escapes his eye. I should like to know what he is generally thinking of, what is really going on in this brain; I should like to get acquainted with the whole manner of life of these gentlemen, and get a closer view of their cunning courtiers' arts, and all the activities of these circles. I have often thought of asking His Excellence about them; but— the deuce knows why!—every time my tongue failed me and I could get nothing out but my meteorological report.

I wish I could get a look into the spare-room whose door I so often see open. And a second small room behind the spare-room excites my curiosity. How splendidly it is fitted up; what a quantity of mirrors and choice china it contains! I should also like to cast a glance into those regions where Her Excellency, the daughter, wields the sceptre. I should like to see how all the scent-bottles and boxes are arranged in her boudoir, and the flowers which exhale so delicious a scent that one is half afraid to breathe. And her clothes lying about which are too ethereal to be called clothes—but silence!

Today there came to me what seemed a heavenly inspiration. I remembered the conversation between the two dogs which I had overheard on the Nevski Prospect. "Very good," I thought; "now I see my way clear. I must get hold of the correspondence which these two silly dogs have carried on with each other. In it I shall probably find many things explained."

I had already once called Meggy to me and said to her, "Listen, Meggy! Now we are alone together; if you like, I will also shut the door so that no one can see us. Tell me now all that you know about your mistress. I swear to you that I will tell no one."

But the cunning dog drew in its tail, ruffled up its hair, and went quite quietly out of the door, as though it had heard nothing.

I had long been of the opinion that dogs are much cleverer than men. I also believed that they could talk, and that only a certain obstinacy kept them from doing so. They are especially watchful animals, and nothing escapes their observation. Now, cost what it may, I will go tomorrow to Sverkoff's house in order to ask after Fidel, and if I have luck, to get hold of all the letters which Meggy has written to her.

***

November 12th.—Today about two o'clock in the afternoon I started in order, by some means or other, to see Fidel and question her.

I cannot stand this smell of Sauerkraut which assails one's olfactory nerves from all the shops in Citizen Street. There also exhales such an odour from under each house door, that one must hold one's nose and pass by quickly. There ascends also so much smoke and soot from the artisans' shops that it is almost impossible to get through it.

When I had climbed up to the sixth story, and had rung the bell, a rather pretty girl with a freckled face came out. I recognised her as the companion of the old lady. She blushed a little and asked "What do you want?"

"I want to have a little conversation with your dog."

She was a simple-minded girl, as I saw at once. The dog came running and barking loudly. I wanted to take hold of it, but the abominable beast nearly caught hold of my nose with its teeth. But in a corner of the room I saw its sleeping-basket. Ah! that was what I wanted. I went to it, rummaged in the straw, and to my great satisfaction drew out a little packet of small pieces of paper. When the hideous little dog saw this, it first bit me in the calf of the leg, and then, as soon as it had become aware of my theft, it began to whimper and to fawn on me; but I said, "No, you little beast; goodbye!" and hastened away.

I believe the girl thought me mad; at any rate she was thoroughly alarmed.

When I reached my room I wished to get to work at once, and read through the letters by daylight, since I do not see well by candle-light; but the wretched Mawra had got the idea of sweeping the floor. These blockheads of Finnish women are always clean where there is no need to be.

I then went for a little walk and began to think over what had happened. Now at last I could get to the bottom of all facts, ideas and motives! These letters would explain everything. Dogs are clever fellows; they know all about politics, and I will certainly find in the letters all I want, especially the character of the director and all his relationships. And through these letters I will get information about her who—but silence!

Towards evening I came home and lay for a good while on the bed.

***

November 13th.—Now let us see! The letter is fairly legible but the handwriting is somewhat doggish.

***

"DEAR FIDEL!—I cannot get accustomed to your ordinary name, as if they could not have found a better one for you! Fidel! How tasteless! How ordinary! But this is not the time to discuss it. I am very glad that we thought of corresponding with each other."

(The letter is quite correctly written. The punctuation and spelling are perfectly right. Even our head clerk does not write so simply and clearly, though he declares he has been at the University. Let us go on.)

"I think that it is one of the most refined joys of this world to interchange thoughts, feelings, and impressions."

(H'm! This idea comes from some book which has been translated from German. I can't remember the title.)

"I speak from experience, although I have not gone farther into the world than just before our front door. Does not my life pass happily and comfortably? My mistress, whom her father calls Sophie, is quite in love with me."

(Ah! Ah!—but better be silent!)

"Her father also often strokes me. I drink tea and coffee with cream. Yes, my dear, I must confess to you that I find no satisfaction in those large, gnawed-at bones which Polkan devours in the kitchen. Only the bones of wild fowl are good, and that only when the marrow has not been sucked out of them. They taste very nice with a little sauce, but there should be no green stuff in it. But I know nothing worse than the habit of giving dogs balls of bread kneaded up. Someone sits at table, kneads a bread-ball with dirty fingers, calls you and sticks it in your mouth. Good manners forbid your refusing it, and you eat it—with disgust it is true, but you eat it."

(The deuce! What is this? What rubbish! As if she could find nothing more suitable to write about! I will see if there is anything more reasonable on the second page.)

"I am quite willing to inform you of everything that goes on here. I have already mentioned the most important person in the house, whom Sophie calls 'Papa.' He is a very strange man."

(Ah! Here we are at last! Yes, I knew it; they have a politician's penetrating eye for all things. Let us see what she says about "Papa.")

". . . a strange man. Generally he is silent; he only speaks seldom, but about a week ago he kept on repeating to himself, 'Shall I get it or not?' In one hand he took a sheet of paper; the other he stretched out as though to receive something, and repeated, 'Shall I get it or not?' Once he turned to me with the question, 'What do you think, Meggy?' I did not understand in the least what he meant, sniffed at his boots, and went away. A week later he came home with his face beaming. That morning he was visited by several officers in uniform who congratulated him. At the dinner-table he was in a better humour than I have ever seen him before."

(Ah! he is ambitious then! I must make a note of that.)

"Pardon, my dear, I hasten to conclude, etc., etc. Tomorrow I will finish the letter."

***

"Now, good morning; here I am again at your service. Today my mistress Sophie . . ."

(Ah! we will see what she says about Sophie. Let us go on!)

". . . was in an unusually excited state. She went to a ball, and I was glad that I could write to you in her absence. She likes going to balls, although she gets dreadfully irritated while dressing. I cannot understand, my dear, what is the pleasure in going to a ball. She comes home from the ball at six o'clock in the early morning, and to judge by her pale and emaciated face, she has had nothing to eat. I could, frankly speaking, not endure such an existence. If I could not get partridge with sauce, or the wing of a roast chicken, I don't know what I should do. Porridge with sauce is also tolerable, but I can get up no enthusiasm for carrots, turnips, and artichokes."

***

The style is very unequal! One sees at once that it has not been written by a man. The beginning is quite intelligent, but at the end the canine nature breaks out. I will read another letter; it is rather long and there is no date.

***

"Ah, my dear, how delightful is the arrival of spring! My heart beats as though it expected something. There is a perpetual ringing in my ears, so that I often stand with my foot raised, for several minutes at a time, and listen towards the door. In confidence I will tell you that I have many admirers. I often sit on the window-sill and let them pass in review. Ah! if you knew what miscreations there are among them; one, a clumsy house-dog, with stupidity written on his face, walks the street with an important air and imagines that he is an extremely important person, and that the eyes of all the world are fastened on him. I don't pay him the least attention, and pretend not to see him at all.

"And what a hideous bulldog has taken up his post opposite my window! If he stood on his hind-legs, as the monster probably cannot, he would be taller by a head than my mistress's papa, who himself has a stately figure. This lout seems, moreover, to be very impudent. I growl at him, but he does not seem to mind that at all. If he at least would only wrinkle his forehead! Instead of that, he stretches out his tongue, droops his big ears, and stares in at the window—this rustic boor! But do you think, my dear, that my heart remains proof against all temptations? Alas no! If you had only seen that gentlemanly dog who crept through the fence of the neighbouring house. 'Treasure' is his name. Ah, my dear, what a delightful snout he has!"

(To the deuce with the stuff! What rubbish it is! How can one blacken paper with such absurdities. Give me a man. I want to see a man! I need some food to nourish and refresh my mind, and get this silliness instead. I will turn the page to see if there is anything better on the other side.)

"Sophie sat at the table and sewed something. I looked out of the window and amused myself by watching the passers-by. Suddenly a flunkey entered and announced a visitor—'Mr Teploff.'

"'Show him in!' said Sophie, and began to embrace me. 'Ah! Meggy, Meggy, do you know who that is? He is dark, and belongs to the Royal Household; and what eyes he has! Dark and brilliant as fire.'

"Sophie hastened into her room. A minute later a young gentleman with black whiskers entered. He went to the mirror, smoothed his hair, and looked round the room. I turned away and sat down in my place.

"Sophie entered and returned his bow in a friendly manner.

"I pretended to observe nothing, and continued to look out of the window. But I leant my head a little on one side to hear what they were talking about. Ah, my dear! what silly things they discussed—how a lady executed the wrong figure in dancing; how a certain Boboff, with his expansive shirt-frill, had looked like a stork and nearly fallen down; how a certain Lidina imagined she had blue eyes when they were really green, etc.

"I do not know, my dear, what special charm she finds in her Mr Teploff, and why she is so delighted with him."

(It seems to me myself that there is something wrong here. It is impossible that this Teploff should bewitch her. We will see further.)

"If this gentleman of the Household pleases her, then she must also be pleased, according to my view, with that official who sits in her papa's writing-room. Ah, my dear, if you know what a figure he is! A regular tortoise!"

(What official does she mean?)

"He has an extraordinary name. He always sits there and mends the pens. His hair looks like a truss of hay. Her papa always employs him instead of a servant."

(I believe this abominable little beast is referring to me. But what has my hair got to do with hay?)

"Sophie can never keep from laughing when she sees him."

***

You lie, cursed dog! What a scandalous tongue! As if I did not know that it is envy which prompts you, and that here there is treachery at work—yes, the treachery of the chief clerk. This man hates me implacably; he has plotted against me, he is always seeking to injure me. I'll look through one more letter; perhaps it will make the matter clearer.

***

"Fidel, my dear, pardon me that I have not written for so long. I was floating in a dream of delight. In truth, some author remarks, 'Love is a second life.' Besides, great changes are going on in the house. The young chamberlain is always here. Sophie is wildly in love with him. Her papa is quite contented. I heard from Gregor, who sweeps the floor, and is in the habit of talking to himself, that the marriage will soon be celebrated. Her papa will at any rate get his daughter married to a general, a colonel, or a chamberlain."

***

Deuce take it! I can read no more. It is all about chamberlains and generals. I should like myself to be a general—not in order to sue for her hand and all that—no, not at all; I should like to be a general merely in order to see people wriggling, squirming, and hatching plots before me.

And then I should like to tell them that they are both of them not worth spitting on. But it is vexatious! I tear the foolish dog's letters up in a thousand pieces.

***

December 3rd.—It is not possible that the marriage should take place; it is only idle gossip. What does it signify if he is a chamberlain! That is only a dignity, not a substantial thing which one can see or handle. His chamberlain's office will not procure him a third eye in his forehead. Neither is his nose made of gold; it is just like mine or anyone else's nose. He does not eat and cough, but smells and sneezes with it. I should like to get to the bottom of the mystery—whence do all these distinctions come? Why am I only a titular councillor?

Perhaps I am really a count or a general, and only appear to be a titular councillor. Perhaps I don't even know who and what I am. How many cases there are in history of a simple gentleman, or even a burgher or peasant,

75

suddenly turning out to be a great lord or baron? Well, suppose that I appear suddenly in a general's uniform, on the right shoulder an epaulette, on the left an epaulette, and a blue sash across my breast, what sort of a tune would my beloved sing then? What would her papa, our director, say? Oh, he is ambitious! He is a freemason, certainly a freemason; however much he may conceal it, I have found it out. When he gives anyone his hand, he only reaches out two fingers. Well, could not I this minute be nominated a general or a superintendent? I should like to know why I am a titular councillor—why just that, and nothing more?

***

December 5th.—Today I have been reading papers the whole morning. Very strange things are happening in Spain. I have not understood them all. It is said that the throne is vacant, the representatives of the people are in difficulties about finding an occupant, and riots are taking place.

All this appears to me very strange. How can the throne be vacant? It is said that it will be occupied by a woman. A woman cannot sit on a throne. That is impossible. Only a king can sit on a throne. They say that there is no king there, but that is not possible. There cannot be a kingdom without a king. There must be a king, but he is hidden away somewhere. Perhaps he is actually on the spot, and only some domestic complications, or fears of the neighbouring Powers, France and other countries, compel him to remain in concealment; there might also be other reasons.

***

December 8th.—I was nearly going to the office, but various considerations kept me from doing so. I keep on thinking about these Spanish affairs. How is it possible that a woman should reign? It would not be allowed, especially by England. In the rest of Europe the political situation is also critical; the Emperor of Austria——

These events, to tell the truth, have so shaken and shattered me, that I could really do nothing all day. Mawra told me that I was very absent-minded at table. In fact, in my absent-mindedness I threw two plates on the ground so that they broke in pieces.

After dinner I felt weak, and did not feel up to making abstracts of reports. I lay most of the time on my bed, and thought of the Spanish affairs.

***

The year 2000: April 43rd.—Today is a day of splendid triumph. Spain has a king; he has been found, and I am he. I discovered it today; all of a sudden it came upon me like a flash of lightning.

I do not understand how I could imagine that I am a titular councillor. How could such a foolish idea enter my head? It was fortunate that it occurred to no one to shut me up in an asylum. Now it is all clear, and as plain as a pikestaff. Formerly—I don't know why—everything seemed veiled in a kind of mist. That is, I believe, because people think that the human brain is in the head. Nothing of the sort; it is carried by the wind from the Caspian Sea.

For the first time I told Mawra who I am. When she learned that the king of Spain stood before her, she struck her hands together over her head, and nearly died of alarm. The stupid thing had never seen the king of Spain before!

I comforted her, however, at once by assuring her that I was not angry with her for having hitherto cleaned my boots badly. Women are stupid things; one cannot interest them in lofty subjects. She was frightened because she thought all kings of Spain were like Philip II. But I explained to her that there was a great difference between me and him. I did not go to the office. Why the deuce should I? No, my dear friends, you won't get me there again! I am not going to worry myself with your infernal documents any more.

***

Marchember 86. Between day and night.—Today the office-messenger came and summoned me, as I had not been there for three weeks. I went just for the fun of the thing. The chief clerk thought I would bow humbly before him, and make excuses; but I looked at him quite indifferently, neither angrily nor mildly, and sat down quietly at my place as though I noticed no one. I looked at all this rabble of scribblers, and thought, "If you only knew who is sitting among you! Good heavens! what a to-do you would make. Even the chief clerk would bow himself to the earth before me as he does now before the director."

A pile of reports was laid before me, of which to make abstracts, but I did not touch them with one finger.

After a little time there was a commotion in the office, and there a report went round that the director was coming. Many of the clerks vied with each other to attract his notice; but I did not stir. As he came through our room, each one hastily buttoned up his coat; but I had no idea of doing anything of the sort. What is the director to me? Should I stand up before him? Never. What sort of a director is he? He is a bottle-stopper, and no director. A quite ordinary, simple bottle-stopper—nothing more. I felt quite amused as they gave me a document to sign.

They thought I would simply put down my name—"So-and-so, Clerk." Why not? But at the top of the sheet, where the director generally writes his name, I inscribed "Ferdinand VIII." in bold characters. You should have seen what a reverential silence ensued. But I made a gesture with my hand, and said, "Gentlemen, no ceremony please!" Then I went out, and took my way straight to the director's house.

He was not at home. The flunkey wanted not to let me in, but I talked to him in such a way that he soon dropped his arms.

I went straight to Sophie's dressing-room. She sat before the mirror. When she saw me, she sprang up and took a step backwards; but I did not tell her that I was the king of Spain.

But I told her that a happiness awaited her, beyond her power to imagine; and that in spite of all our enemies' devices we should be united. That was all which I wished to say to her, and I went out. Oh, what cunning creatures these women are! Now I have found out what woman really is. Hitherto no one knew whom a woman really loves; I am the first to discover it—she loves the devil. Yes, joking apart, learned men write nonsense when they pronounce that she is this and that; she loves the devil—that is all. You see a woman looking through her lorgnette from a box in the front row. One thinks she is watching that stout gentleman who wears an order. Not a bit of it! She is watching the devil who stands behind his back. He has hidden himself there, and beckons to her with his finger. And she marries him—actually—she marries him!

That is all ambition, and the reason is that there is under the tongue a little blister in which there is a little worm of the size of a pin's head. And this is constructed by a barber in Bean Street; I don't remember his name at the moment, but so much is certain that, in conjunction with a midwife, he wants to spread Mohammedanism all over the world, and that in consequence of this a large number of people in France have already adopted the faith of Islam.

***

No date. The day had no date.—I went for a walk incognito on the Nevski Prospect. I avoided every appearance of being the king of Spain. I felt it below my dignity to let myself be recognised by the whole world, since I must first present myself at court. And I was also restrained by the fact that I have at present no Spanish national costume. If I could only get a cloak! I tried to have a consultation with a tailor, but these people are real asses! Moreover, they neglect their business, dabble in speculation, and have become loafers. I will have a cloak made out of my new official uniform which I have only worn twice. But to prevent this botcher of a tailor spoiling it, I will make it myself with closed doors, so that no one sees me. Since the cut must be altogether altered, I have used the scissors myself.

***

I don't remember the date. The devil knows what month it was. The cloak is quite ready. Mawra exclaimed aloud when I put it on. I will, however, not present myself at court yet; the Spanish deputation has not yet arrived. It would not be befitting if I appeared without them. My appearance would be less imposing. From hour to hour I expect them.

***

The 1st.—The extraordinary long delay of the deputies in coming astonishes me. What can possibly keep them? Perhaps France has a hand in the matter; it is certainly hostilely inclined. I went to the post office to inquire whether the Spanish deputation had come. The postmaster is an extraordinary blockhead who knows nothing. "No," he said to me, "there is no Spanish deputation here; but if you want to send them a letter, we will forward it at the fixed rate." The deuce! What do I want with a letter? Letters are nonsense. Letters are written by apothecaries . . .

***

Madrid, February 30th.—So I am in Spain after all! It has happened so quickly that I could hardly take it in. The Spanish deputies came early this morning, and I got with them into the carriage. This unexpected promptness seemed to me strange. We drove so quickly that in half an hour we were at the Spanish frontier. Over all Europe now there are cast-iron roads, and the steamers go very fast. A wonderful country, this Spain!

As we entered the first room, I saw numerous persons with shorn heads. I guessed at once that they must be either grandees or soldiers, at least to judge by their shorn heads.

The Chancellor of the State, who led me by the hand, seemed to me to behave in a very strange way; he pushed me into a little room and said, "Stay here, and if you call yourself 'King Ferdinand' again, I will drive the wish to do so out of you."

I knew, however, that that was only a test, and I reasserted my conviction; on which the Chancellor gave me two such severe blows with a stick on the back, that I could have cried out with the pain. But I restrained myself, remembering that this was a usual ceremony of old-time chivalry when one was inducted into a high position, and in Spain the laws of chivalry prevail up to the present day. When I was alone, I determined to study State affairs; I discovered that Spain and China are one and the same country, and it is only through ignorance that people regard them as separate kingdoms. I advise everyone urgently to write down the word "Spain" on a sheet of paper; he will see that it is quite the same as China.

But I feel much annoyed by an event which is about to take place tomorrow; at seven o'clock the earth is going to sit on the moon. This is foretold by the famous English chemist, Wellington. To tell the truth, I often felt uneasy when I thought of the excessive brittleness and fragility of the moon. The moon is generally repaired in Hamburg, and very imperfectly. It is done by a lame cooper, an obvious blockhead who has no idea how to do it. He took waxed thread and olive-oil—hence that pungent smell over all the earth which compels people to hold their noses. And this makes the moon so fragile that no men can live on it, but only noses. Therefore we cannot see our noses, because they are on the moon.

When I now pictured to myself how the earth, that massive body, would crush our noses to dust, if it sat on the moon, I became so uneasy, that I immediately put on my shoes and stockings and hastened into the council-hall to give the police orders to prevent the earth sitting on the moon.

The grandees with the shorn heads, whom I met in great numbers in the hall, were very intelligent people, and when I exclaimed, "Gentlemen! let us save the moon, for the earth is going to sit on it," they all set to work to fulfil my imperial wish, and many of them clambered up the wall in order to take the moon down. At that moment the Imperial Chancellor came in. As soon as he appeared, they all scattered, but I alone, as king, remained. To my astonishment, however, the Chancellor beat me with the stick and drove me to my room. So powerful are ancient customs in Spain!

***

January in the same year, following after February.—I can never understand what kind of a country this Spain really is. The popular customs and rules of court etiquette are quite extraordinary. I do not understand them at all, at all. Today my head was shorn, although I exclaimed as loudly as I could, that I did not want to be a monk. What happened afterwards, when they began to let cold water trickle on my head, I do not know. I have never experienced such hellish torments. I nearly went mad, and they had difficulty in holding me. The significance of this strange custom is entirely hidden from me. It is a very foolish and unreasonable one.

Nor can I understand the stupidity of the kings who have not done away with it before now. Judging by all the circumstances, it seems to me as though I had fallen into the hands of the Inquisition, and as though the man whom I took to be the Chancellor was the Grand Inquisitor. But yet I cannot understand how the king could fall into the hands of the Inquisition. The affair may have been arranged by France—especially Polignac—he is a hound, that Polignac! He has sworn to compass my death, and now he is hunting me down. But I know, my friend, that you are only a tool of the English. They are clever fellows, and have a finger in every pie. All the world knows that France sneezes when England takes a pinch of snuff.

***

The 25th.—Today the Grand Inquisitor came into my room; when I heard his steps in the distance, I hid myself under a chair. When he did not see me, he began to call. At first he called "Poprishchin!" I made no answer. Then he called "Axanti Ivanovitch! Titular Councillor! Nobleman!" I still kept silence. "Ferdinand the Eighth, King of Spain!" I was on the point of putting out my head, but I thought, "No, brother, you shall not deceive me! You shall not pour water on my head again!"

But he had already seen me and drove me from under the chair with his stick. The cursed stick really hurts one. But the following discovery compensated me for all the pain, i.e. that every cock has his Spain under his feathers. The Grand Inquisitor went angrily away, and threatened me with some punishment or other. I felt only contempt for his powerless spite, for I know that he only works like a machine, like a tool of the English.

***

34 March. February, 349.—No, I have no longer power to endure. O God! what are they going to do with me? They pour cold water on my head. They take no notice of me, and seem neither to see nor hear. Why do they torture me? What do they want from one so wretched as myself? What can I give them? I possess nothing. I cannot bear all their tortures; my head aches as though everything were turning round in a circle. Save me! Carry me away! Give me three steeds swift as the wind! Mount your seat, coachman, ring bells, gallop horses, and carry me straight out of this world. Farther, ever farther, till nothing more is to be seen!

Ah! the heaven bends over me already; a star glimmers in the distance; the forest with its dark trees in the moonlight rushes past; a bluish mist floats under my feet; music sounds in the cloud; on the one side is the sea, on the other, Italy; beyond I also see Russian peasants' houses. Is not my parents' house there in the distance? Does not my mother sit by the window? O mother, mother, save your unhappy son! Let a tear fall on his aching head! See how they torture him! Press the poor orphan to your bosom! He has no rest in this world; they hunt him from place to place.

Mother, mother, have pity on your sick child! And do you know that the Bey of Algiers has a wart under his nose?

Ivan Turgenev

(1818–1883)

Death

Translated by Constance Garnett

I have a neighbour, a young landowner and a young sportsman. One fine July morning I rode over to him with a proposition that we should go out grouse-shooting together. He agreed. "Only let's go," he said, "to my underwoods at Zusha; I can seize the opportunity to have a look at Tchapligino; you know my oakwood; they're felling timber there." "By all means." He ordered his horse to be saddled, put on a green coat with bronze buttons, stamped with a boar's head, a game-bag embroidered in crewels, and a silver flask, slung a new-fangled French gun over his shoulder, turned himself about with some satisfaction before the looking-glass, and called his dog, Hope, a gift from his cousin, an old maid with an excellent heart, but no hair on her head. We started. My neighbour took with him the village constable, Arhip, a stout, squat peasant with a square face and jaws of antediluvian proportions, and an overseer he had recently hired from the Baltic provinces, a youth of nineteen, thin, flaxen-haired, and short-sighted, with sloping shoulders and a long neck, Herr Gottlieb von der Kock. My neighbour had himself only recently come into the property. It had come to him by inheritance from an aunt, the widow of a councillor of state, Madame Kardon-Kataev, an excessively stout woman, who did nothing but lie in her bed, sighing and groaning. We reached the underwoods. "You wait for me here at the clearing," said Ardalion Mihalitch (my neighbour) addressing his companions. The German bowed, got off his horse, pulled a book out of his pocket—a novel of Johanna Schopenhauer's, I fancy—and sat down under a bush; Arhip remained in the sun without stirring a muscle for an hour. We beat about among the bushes, but did not come on a single covey. Ardalion Mihalitch announced his intention of going on to the wood. I myself had no faith, somehow, in our luck that day; I, too, sauntered after him. We got back to the clearing. The German noted the page, got up, put the book in his pocket, and with some difficulty mounted his bob-tailed, broken-winded mare, who neighed and kicked at the slightest touch; Arhip shook himself, gave a tug at both reins at once, swung his legs, and at last succeeded in starting his torpid and dejected nag. We set off.

I had been familiar with Ardalion Mihalitch's wood from my childhood. I had often strolled in Tchapligino with my French tutor, Monsieur Désiré Fleury, the kindest of men (who had, however, almost ruined my constitution for life by dosing me with Leroux's mixture every evening). The whole wood consisted of some two or three hundred immense oaks and ash-trees. Their stately, powerful trunks were magnificently black against the transparent golden green of the nut bushes and mountain-ashes; higher up, their wide knotted branches stood out in graceful lines against the clear blue sky, unfolding into a tent overhead; hawks, honey-buzzards and kestrels flew whizzing under the motionless tree-tops; variegated wood-peckers tapped loudly on the stout bark; the blackbird's bell-like trill was heard suddenly in the thick foliage, following on the ever-changing note of the gold-hammer; in the bushes below was the chirp and twitter of hedge-warblers, siskins, and peewits; finches ran swiftly along the paths; a hare would steal along the edge of the wood, halting cautiously as he ran; a squirrel would hop sporting from tree to tree, then suddenly sit still, with its tail over its head. In the grass among the high ant-hills under the delicate shade of the lovely, feathery, deep-indented bracken, were violets and lilies of the valley, and funguses, russet, yellow, brown, red and crimson; in the patches of grass among the spreading bushes red strawberries were to be found . . . And oh, the shade in the wood! In the most stifling heat, at mid-day, it was like night in the wood: such peace, such fragrance, such freshness . . . I had spent happy times in Tchapligino, and so, I must own, it was with melancholy feelings I entered the wood I knew so well. The ruinous, snowless winter of 1840 had not spared my old friends, the oaks and the ashes; withered, naked, covered here and there with sickly foliage, they struggled mournfully up above the young growth which "took their place, but could never replace them." [Footnote: In 1840 there were severe frosts, and no snow fell up to the very end of December; all the wintercorn was frozen, and many splendid oak-forests were destroyed by that merciless winter. It will be hard to replace them; the productive force of the land is apparently diminishing; in the "interdicted" wastelands (visited by processions with holy images, and so not to be touched), instead of the noble trees of former days, birches and aspens grow of themselves; and, indeed, they have no idea among us of planting woods at all.—*Author's Note*.]

Some trees, still covered with leaves below, fling their lifeless, ruined branches upwards, as it were, in reproach and despair; in others, stout, dead, dry branches are thrust out of the midst of foliage still thick, though with none of the luxuriant abundance of old; others have fallen altogether, and lie rotting like corpses on the ground. And—who could have dreamed of this in former days?—there was no shade—no shade to be found anywhere in Tchapligino! "Ah," I thought, looking at the dying trees: "isn't it shameful and bitter for you?" . . . Koltsov's lines recurred to me:

> "What has become
> Of the mighty voices,
> The haughty strength,
> The royal pomp?
> Where now is the
> Wealth of green? . . . "

"How is it, Ardalion Mihalitch," I began, "that they didn't fell these trees the very next year? You see they won't give for them now a tenth of what they would have done before."

He merely shrugged his shoulders.

"You should have asked my aunt that; the timber merchants came, offered money down, pressed the matter, in fact."

"*Mein Gott! mein Gott!*" Von der Kock cried at every step. "Vat a bity, vat a bity!"

"What's a bity!" observed my neighbour with a smile.

"That is; how bitiful, I meant to say."

What particularly aroused his regrets were the oaks lying on the ground—and, indeed, many a miller would have given a good sum for them. But the constable Arhip preserved an unruffled composure, and did not indulge in any lamentations; on the contrary, he seemed even to jump over them and crack his whip on them with a certain satisfaction.

We were getting near the place where they were cutting down the trees, when suddenly a shout and hurried talk was heard, following on the crash of a falling tree, and a few instants after a young peasant, pale and dishevelled, dashed out of the thicket towards us.

"What is it? where are you running?" Ardalion Mihalitch asked him.

He stopped at once.

"Ah, Ardalion Mihalitch, sir, an accident!"

"What is it?"

"Maksim, sir, crushed by a tree."

"How did it happen? . . . Maksim the foreman?"

"The foreman, sir. We'd started cutting an ash-tree, and he was standing looking on . . . He stood there a bit, and then off he went to the well for some water—wanted a drink, seemingly—when suddenly the ash-tree began creaking and coming straight towards him. We shout to him: 'Run, run, run!' . . . He should have rushed to one side, but he up and ran straight before him . . . He was scared, to be sure. The ash-tree covered him with its top branches. But why it fell so soon, the Lord only knows! . . . Perhaps it was rotten at the core."

"And so it crushed Maksim?"

"Yes, sir."

"To death?"

"No, sir, he's still alive—but as good as dead; his arms and legs are crushed. I was running for Seliverstitch, for the doctor."

Ardalion Mihalitch told the constable to gallop to the village for Seliverstitch, while he himself pushed on at a quick trot to the clearing . . . I followed him.

We found poor Maksim on the ground. The peasants were standing about him. We got off our horses. He hardly moaned at all; from time to time he opened his eyes wide, looked round, as it were, in astonishment, and bit his lips, fast turning blue . . . The lower part of his face was twitching; his hair was matted on his brow; his breast heaved irregularly: he was dying. The light shade of a young lime-tree glided softly over his face.

We bent down to him. He recognised Ardalion Mihalitch.

"Please sir," he said to him, hardly articulately, "send . . . for the priest . . . tell . . . the Lord . . . has punished me . . . arms, legs, all smashed . . . today's . . . Sunday . . . and I . . . I . . . see . . . didn't let the lads off . . . work."

He ceased, out of breath.

"And my money . . . for my wife . . . after deducting . . . Onesim here knows . . . whom I . . . what I owe."

"We've sent for the doctor, Maksim," said my neighbour; "perhaps you may not die yet."

He tried to open his eyes, and with an effort raised the lids.

"No, I'm dying. Here . . . here it is coming . . . here it . . . Forgive me, lads, if in any way . . ."

"God will forgive you, Maksim Andreitch," said the peasants thickly with one voice, and they took off their caps; "do you forgive us!"

He suddenly shook his head despairingly, his breast heaved with a painful effort, and he fell back again.

"We can't let him lie here and die, though," cried Ardalion Mihalitch; "lads, give us the mat from the cart, and carry him to the hospital."

Two men ran to the cart.

"I bought a horse . . . yesterday," faltered the dying man, "off Efim . . . Sitchovsky . . . paid earnest money . . . so the horse is mine . . . Give it . . . to my wife . . ."

They began to move him on to the mat . . . He trembled all over, like a wounded bird, and stiffened . . .

"He is dead," muttered the peasants.

We mounted our horses in silence and rode away.

The death of poor Maksim set me musing. How wonderfully indeed the Russian peasant dies! The temper in which he meets his end cannot be called indifference or stolidity; he dies as though he were performing a solemn rite, coolly and simply.

A few years ago a peasant belonging to another neighbour of mine in the country got burnt in the drying shed, where the corn is put. (He would have remained there, but a passing pedlar pulled him out half-dead; he plunged into a tub of water, and with a run broke down the door of the burning outhouse.) I went to his hut to see him. It was dark, smoky, stifling, in the hut. I asked, "Where is the sick man?" "There, sir, on the stove," the sorrowing peasant woman answered me in a sing-song voice.

I went up; the peasant was lying covered with a sheepskin, breathing heavily. "Well, how do you feel?" The injured man stirred on the stove; all over burns, within sight of death as he was, tried to rise. "Lie still, lie still, lie still . . . Well, how are you?" "In a bad way, surely," said he. "Are you in pain?" No answer. "Is there anything you want?"—No answer. "Shouldn't I send you some tea, or anything." "There's no need." I moved away from him and sat down on the bench. I sat there a quarter of an hour; I sat there half an hour—the silence of the tomb in the hut. In the corner behind the table under the holy pictures crouched a little girl of twelve years old, eating a piece of bread. Her mother threatened her every now and then. In the outer room there was coming and going, noise and talk: the brother's wife was chopping cabbage. "Hey, Aksinya," said the injured man at last. "What?" "Some kvas." Aksinya gave him some kvas. Silence again. I asked in a whisper, "Have they given him the sacrament?" "Yes." So, then, everything was in order: he was waiting for death, that was all. I could not bear it, and went away . . .

Again, I recall how I went one day to the hospital in the village of Krasnogorye to see the surgeon Kapiton, a friend of mine, and an enthusiastic sportsman.

This hospital consisted of what had once been the lodge of the manor-house; the lady of the manor had founded it herself; in other words, she ordered a blue board to be nailed up above the door with an inscription in white letters: "Krasnogorye Hospital," and had herself handed to Kapiton a red album to record the names of the patients in. On the first page of this album one of the toadying parasites of this Lady Bountiful had inscribed the following lines:

"Dans ces beaux lieux, où règne l'allégresse
Ce temple fut ouvert par la Beauté;
De vos seigneurs admirez la tendresse
Bons habitants de Krasnogorié!"

while another gentleman had written below:

"Et moi aussi j'aime la nature!
JEAN KOBYLIATNIKOFF."

The surgeon bought six beds at his own expense, and had set to work in a thankful spirit to heal God's people. Besides him, the staff consisted of two persons; an engraver, Pavel, liable to attacks of insanity, and a one-armed peasant woman, Melikitrisa, who performed the duties of cook. Both of them mixed the medicines and dried and infused herbs; they, too, controlled the patients when they were delirious. The insane engraver was sullen in appearance and sparing of words; at night he would sing a song about "lovely Venus," and would besiege everyone he met with a request for permission to marry a girl called Malanya, who had long been dead. The one-armed peasant woman used to beat him and set him to look after the turkeys. Well, one day I was at Kapiton's. We had begun talking over our last day's shooting, when suddenly a cart drove into the yard, drawn by an exceptionally stout horse, such as are only found belonging to millers. In the cart sat a thick-set peasant, in a new greatcoat, with a beard streaked with grey. "Hullo, Vassily Dmitritch," Kapiton shouted from the window; "please come in . . . The miller of Liobovshin," he whispered to me. The peasant climbed groaning out of the cart, came into the surgeon's room, and after looking for the holy pictures, crossed himself, bowing to them. "Well, Vassily Dmitritch, any news? . . . But you must be ill; you don't look well." "Yes, Kapiton Timofeitch, there's something not right." "What's wrong with you?" "Well, it was like this, Kapiton Timofeitch. Not long ago I bought some mill-stones in the town, so I took them home, and as I went to lift them out of the cart, I strained myself, or something; I'd a sort of rick in the loins, as though something had been torn away, and ever since I've been out of sorts. Today I feel worse than ever." "Hm," commented Kapiton, and he took a pinch of snuff; "that's a rupture, no doubt. But is it long since this happened?" "It's ten days now." "Ten days?" (The surgeon drew a long inward breath and shook his head.) "Let me examine you." "Well, Vassily Dmitritch," he pronounced at last, "I am sorry for you, heartily sorry, but things aren't right with you at all; you're seriously ill; stay here with me; I will do everything I can, for my part, though I can't answer for anything." "So bad as that?" muttered the astounded peasant. "Yes, Vassily Dmitritch, it is bad; if you'd come to me a day or two sooner, it would have been nothing much; I could have cured you in a trice; but now inflammation has set in; before we know where we are, there'll be mortification." "But it can't be, Kapiton Timofeitch." "I tell you it is so." "But how comes it?" (The surgeon shrugged his shoulders.) "And I must

die for a trifle like that?" "I don't say that . . . only you must stop here."
The peasant pondered and pondered, his eyes fixed on the floor, then he
glanced up at us, scratched his head, and picked up his cap. "Where are you
off to, Vassily Dmitritch?" "Where? why, home to be sure, if it's so bad.
I must put things to rights, if it's like that." "But you'll do yourself harm,
Vassily Dmitritch; you will, really; I'm surprised how you managed to get
here; you must stop." "No, brother, Kapiton Timofeitch, if I must die, I'll
die at home; why die here? I've got a home, and the Lord knows how it
will end." "No one can tell yet, Vassily Dmitritch, how it will end . . . Of
course, there is danger, considerable danger; there's no disputing that . . .
but for that reason you ought to stay here." (The peasant shook his head.)
"No, Kapiton Timofeitch, I won't stay . . . but perhaps you will prescribe
me a medicine." "Medicine alone will be no good." "I won't stay, I tell you."
"Well, as you like . . . Mind you don't blame me for it afterwards."

The surgeon tore a page out of the album, and, writing out a prescription,
gave him some advice as to what he could do besides. The peasant took the
sheet of paper, gave Kapiton half-a-rouble, went out of the room, and took
his seat in the cart. "Well, goodbye, Kapiton Timofeitch, don't remember
evil against me, and remember my orphans, if anything . . ." "Oh, do stay,
Vassily!" The peasant simply shook his head, struck the horse with the
reins, and drove out of the yard. The road was muddy and full of holes;
the miller drove cautiously, without hurry, guiding his horse skilfully, and
nodding to the acquaintances he met. Three days later he was dead.

The Russians, in general, meet death in a marvellous way. Many of
the dead come back now to my memory. I recall you, my old friend, who
left the university with no degree, Avenir Sorokoumov, noblest, best of
men! I see once again your sickly, consumptive face, your lank brown
tresses, your gentle smile, your ecstatic glance, your long limbs; I can hear
your weak, caressing voice. You lived at a Great Russian landowner's,
called Gur Krupyanikov, taught his children, Fofa and Zyozya, Russian
grammar, geography, and history, patiently bore all the ponderous jokes
of the said Gur, the coarse familiarities of the steward, the vulgar pranks
of the spiteful urchins; with a bitter smile, but without repining, you
complied with the caprices of their bored and exacting mother; but to
make up for it all, what bliss, what peace was yours in the evening, after
supper, when, free at last of all duties, you sat at the window pensively
smoking a pipe, or greedily turned the pages of a greasy and mutilated

number of some solid magazine, brought you from the town by the land-surveyor—just such another poor, homeless devil as yourself! How delighted you were then with any sort of poem or novel; how readily the tears started into your eyes; with what pleasure you laughed; what genuine love for others, what generous sympathy for everything good and noble, filled your pure youthful soul! One must tell the truth: you were not distinguished by excessive sharpness of wit; Nature had endowed you with neither memory nor industry; at the university you were regarded as one of the least promising students; at lectures you slumbered, at examinations you preserved a solemn silence; but who was beaming with delight and breathless with excitement at a friend's success, a friend's triumphs? . . . Avenir! . . . Who had a blind faith in the lofty destiny of his friends? who extolled them with pride? who championed them with angry vehemence? who was innocent of envy as of vanity? who was ready for the most disinterested self-sacrifice? who eagerly gave way to men who were not worthy to untie his latchet? . . . That was you, all you, our good Avenir! I remember how broken-heartedly you parted from your comrades, when you were going away to be a tutor in the country; you were haunted by presentiment of evil . . . And, indeed, your lot was a sad one in the country; you had no one there to listen to with veneration, no one to admire, no one to love . . . The neighbours—rude sons of the steppes, and polished gentlemen alike—treated you as a tutor: some, with rudeness and neglect, others carelessly. Besides, you were not pre-possessing in person; you were shy, given to blushing, getting hot and stammering . . . Even your health was no better for the country air: you wasted like a candle, poor fellow! It is true your room looked out into the garden; wild cherries, apple-trees, and limes strewed their delicate blossoms on your table, your ink-stand, your books; on the wall hung a blue silk watch-pocket, a parting present from a kind-hearted, sentimental German governess with flaxen curls and little blue eyes; and sometimes an old friend from Moscow would come out to you and throw you into ecstasies with new poetry, often even with his own. But, oh, the loneliness, the insufferable slavery of a tutor's lot! the impossibility of escape, the endless autumns and winters, the ever-advancing disease! . . . Poor, poor Avenir!

I paid Sorokoumov a visit not long before his death. He was then hardly able to walk. The landowner, Gur Krupyanikov, had not turned him out of the house, but had given up paying him a salary, and had taken another tutor for Zyozya . . . Fofa had been sent to a school of cadets. Avenir was sitting near the window in an old easy-chair. It was exquisite weather. The clear autumn sky was a bright blue above the dark-brown line of bare limes; here and there a few last leaves of lurid gold rustled and whispered about them. The earth had been covered with frost, now melting into dewdrops in the sun, whose ruddy rays fell aslant across the pale grass; there was a faint crisp resonance in the air; the voices of the labourers in the garden reached us clearly and distinctly. Avenir wore an old Bokhara dressing-gown; a green neckerchief threw a deathly hue over his terribly sunken face. He was greatly delighted to see me, held out his hand, began talking and coughing at once. I made him be quiet, and sat down by him . . . On Avenir's knee lay a manuscript book of Koltsov's poems, carefully copied out; he patted it with a smile. "That's a poet," he stammered, with an effort repressing his cough; and he fell to declaiming in a voice scarcely audible:

> "Can the eagle's wings
>   Be chained and fettered?
> Can the pathways of heaven
>   Be closed against him?"

I stopped him: the doctor had forbidden him to talk. I knew what would please him. Sorokoumov never, as they say, "kept up" with the science of the day; but he was always anxious to know what results the leading intellects had reached. Sometimes he would get an old friend into a corner and begin questioning him; he would listen and wonder, take every word on trust, and even repeat it all after him. He took a special interest in German philosophy. I began discoursing to him about Hegel (this all happened long ago, as you may gather). Avenir nodded his head approvingly, raised his eyebrows, smiled, and whispered: "I see! I see! ah, that's splendid! splendid!" . . . The childish curiosity of this poor, dying, homeless outcast, moved me, I confess, to tears. It must be noted that Avenir, unlike the general run of consumptives, did not deceive himself in regard to his disease . . . But what of that?—he did not sigh, nor grieve; he did not even once refer to his position . . .

Rallying his strength, he began talking of Moscow, of old friends, of Pushkin, of the drama, of Russian literature; he recalled our little suppers, the heated debates of our circle; with regret he uttered the names of two or three friends who were dead . . .

"Do you remember Dasha?" he went on. "Ah, there was a heart of pure gold! What a heart! and how she loved me! . . . What has become of her now? Wasted and fallen away, poor dear, I daresay!"

I had not the courage to disillusion the sick man; and, indeed, why should he know that his Dasha was now broader than she was long, and that she was living under the protection of some merchants, the brothers Kondatchkov, that she used powder and paint, and was for ever swearing and scolding?

"But can't we," I thought, looking at his wasted face, "get him away from here? Perhaps there may still be a chance of curing him." But Avenir cut short my suggestion.

"No, brother, thanks," he said; "it makes no difference where one dies. I shan't live till the winter, you see . . . Why give trouble for nothing? I'm used to this house. It's true the people . . ."

"They're unkind, eh?" I put in.

"No, not unkind! but wooden-headed creatures. However, I can't complain of them. There are neighbours: there's a Mr. Kasatkin's daughter, a cultivated, kind, charming girl . . . not proud . . ."

Sorokoumov began coughing again.

"I shouldn't mind anything," he went on, after taking breath, "if they'd only let me smoke my pipe . . . But I'll have my pipe, if I die for it!" he added, with a sly wink. "Thank God, I have had life enough! I have known so many fine people."

"But you should, at least, write to your relations," I interrupted.

"Why write to them? They can't be any help; when I die they'll hear of it. But, why talk about it . . . I'd rather you'd tell me what you saw abroad."

I began to tell him my experiences. He seemed positively to gloat over my story. Towards evening I left, and ten days later I received the following letter from Mr. Krupyanikov:

I have the honour to inform you, my dear sir, that your friend, the student, living in my house, Mr. Avenir Sorokoumov, died at two o'clock in the afternoon, three days ago, and was buried today, at my expense, in the parish church. He asked me to forward you the books and manuscripts enclosed herewith. He was found to have twenty-two roubles and a half, which, with the rest of his belongings, pass into the possession of his relatives. Your friend died fully conscious, and, I may say, with so little sensibility that he showed no signs of regret even when the whole family of us took a last farewell of him. My wife, Kleopatra Aleksandrovna, sends you her regards. The death of your friend has, of course, affected her nerves; as regards myself, I am, thank God, in good health, and have the honour to remain, your humble servant,

G. KRUPYANIKOV

Many more examples recur to me, but one cannot relate everything. I will confine myself to one.

I was present at an old lady's death-bed; the priest had begun reading the prayers for the dying over her, but, suddenly noticing that the patient seemed to be actually dying, he made haste to give her the cross to kiss. The lady turned away with an air of displeasure. "You're in too great a hurry, father," she said, in a voice almost inarticulate; "in too great a hurry." . . . She kissed the cross, put her hand under the pillow and expired. Under the pillow was a silver rouble; she had meant to pay the priest for the service at her own death . . .

Yes, the Russians die in a wonderful way.

Fyodor Dostoevsky

(1821–1881)

The Heavenly
Christmas Tree

Translated by Constance Garnett

I am a novelist, and I suppose I have made up this story. I write "I
suppose," though I know for a fact that I have made it up, but yet I
keep fancying that it must have happened somewhere at some time,
that it must have happened on Christmas Eve in some great town in a time
of terrible frost.

I have a vision of a boy, a little boy, six years old or even younger. This
boy woke up that morning in a cold damp cellar. He was dressed in a sort
of little dressing-gown and was shivering with cold. There was a cloud of
white steam from his breath, and sitting on a box in the corner, he blew
the steam out of his mouth and amused himself in his dullness watching
it float away. But he was terribly hungry. Several times that morning he
went up to the plank bed where his sick mother was lying on a mattress as
thin as a pancake, with some sort of bundle under her head for a pillow.
How had she come here? She must have come with her boy from some
other town and suddenly fallen ill. The landlady who let the "corners"
had been taken two days before to the police station, the lodgers were
out and about as the holiday was so near, and the only one left had been
lying for the last twenty-four hours dead drunk, not having waited for
Christmas. In another corner of the room a wretched old woman of eighty,
who had once been a children's nurse but was now left to die friendless,
was moaning and groaning with rheumatism, scolding and grumbling at

the boy so that he was afraid to go near her corner. He had got a drink of water in the outer room, but could not find a crust anywhere, and had been on the point of waking his mother a dozen times. He felt frightened at last in the darkness: it had long been dusk, but no light was kindled. Touching his mother's face, he was surprised that she did not move at all, and that she was as cold as the wall. "It is very cold here," he thought. He stood a little, unconsciously letting his hands rest on the dead woman's shoulders, then he breathed on his fingers to warm them, and then quietly fumbling for his cap on the bed, he went out of the cellar. He would have gone earlier, but was afraid of the big dog which had been howling all day at the neighbour's door at the top of the stairs. But the dog was not there now, and he went out into the street.

Mercy on us, what a town! He had never seen anything like it before. In the town from which he had come, it was always such black darkness at night. There was one lamp for the whole street, the little, low-pitched, wooden houses were closed up with shutters, there was no one to be seen in the street after dusk, all the people shut themselves up in their houses, and there was nothing but the howling of packs of dogs, hundreds and thousands of them barking and howling all night. But there it was so warm and he was given food, while here—oh, dear, if he only had something to eat! And what a noise and rattle here, what light and what people, horses and carriages, and what a frost! The frozen steam hung in clouds over the horses, over their warmly breathing mouths; their hoofs clanged against the stones through the powdery snow, and everyone pushed so, and—oh, dear, how he longed for some morsel to eat, and how wretched he suddenly felt. A policeman walked by and turned away to avoid seeing the boy.

Here was another street—oh, what a wide one, here he would be run over for certain; how everyone was shouting, racing and driving along, and the light, the light! And what was this? A huge glass window, and through the window a tree reaching up to the ceiling; it was a fir tree, and on it were ever so many lights, gold papers and apples and little dolls and horses; and there were children clean and dressed in their best running about the room, laughing and playing and eating and drinking something. And then a little girl began dancing with one of the boys, what a pretty little girl! And he could hear the music through the window. The boy looked and wondered and laughed, though his toes were aching with the cold and his fingers were red and stiff so that it hurt him to move them. And all at once the boy remembered how his toes and fingers hurt him, and began crying, and ran on; and again through another window-pane he saw another Christmas tree, and on a table cakes of all sorts—almond cakes, red cakes and yellow cakes, and three grand young ladies were sitting there, and they gave the cakes to any one who went up to them, and the door kept opening, lots of gentlemen and ladies went in from the street. The boy crept up, suddenly opened the door and went in. Oh, how they shouted at him and waved him back! One lady went up to him hurriedly and slipped a kopeck into his hand, and with her own hands opened the door into the street for him! How frightened he was. And the kopeck rolled away and clinked upon the steps; he could not bend his red fingers to hold it tight. The boy ran away and went on, where he did not know. He was ready to cry again but he was afraid, and ran on and on and blew his fingers. And he was miserable because he felt suddenly so lonely and terrified, and all at once, mercy on us! What was this again? People were standing in a crowd admiring. Behind a glass window there were three little dolls, dressed in red and green dresses, and exactly, exactly as though they were alive. One was a little old man sitting and playing a big violin, the two others were standing close by and playing little violins and nodding in time, and looking at one another, and their lips moved, they were speaking, actually speaking, only one couldn't hear through the glass. And at first the boy thought they were alive, and when he grasped that they were dolls he laughed. He had never seen such dolls before, and had no idea there were such dolls! And he wanted to cry, but he felt amused, amused by the dolls. All at once he fancied that someone caught at his smock behind: a wicked big boy was standing beside him and suddenly hit him on the head, snatched off his cap and tripped him up. The boy fell down on the ground, at once there was a shout, he was numb with fright, he jumped up and ran away. He ran, and not knowing where he was going, ran in at the gate of someone's courtyard, and sat down behind a stack of wood: "They won't find me here, besides it's dark!"

He sat huddled up and was breathless from fright, and all at once, quite suddenly, he felt so happy: his hands and feet suddenly left off aching and grew so warm, as warm as though he were on a stove; then he shivered all over, then he gave a start, why, he must have been asleep. How nice to have a sleep here! "I'll sit here a little and go and look at the dolls again," said the boy, and smiled thinking of them. "Just as though they were alive! . . ." And suddenly he heard his mother singing over him. "Mammy, I am asleep; how nice it is to sleep here!"

"Come to my Christmas tree, little one," a soft voice suddenly whispered over his head.

He thought that this was still his mother, but no, it was not she. Who it was calling him, he could not see, but someone bent over and embraced him in the darkness; and he stretched out his hands to him, and . . . and all at once—oh, what a bright light! Oh, what a Christmas tree! And yet it was not a fir tree, he had never seen a tree like that! Where was he now? Everything was bright and shining, and all round him were dolls; but no, they were not dolls, they were little boys and girls, only so bright and shining. They all came flying round him, they all kissed him, took him and carried him along with them, and he was flying himself, and he saw that his mother was looking at him and laughing joyfully. "Mammy, Mammy; oh, how nice it is here, Mammy!" And again he kissed the children and wanted to tell them at once of those dolls in the shop window. "Who are you, boys? Who are you, girls?" he asked, laughing and admiring them.

"This is Christ's Christmas tree," they answered. "Christ always has a Christmas tree on this day, for the little children who have no tree of their own . . ." And he found out that all these little boys and girls were children just like himself; that some had been frozen in the baskets in which they had as babies been laid on the doorsteps of well-to-do Petersburg people, others had been boarded out with Finnish women by the Foundling and had been suffocated, others had died at their starved mother's breasts (in the Samara famine), others had died in the third-class railway carriages from the foul air; and yet they were all here, they were all like angels about Christ, and He was in the midst of them and held out His hands to them and blessed them and their sinful mothers . . . And the mothers of these children stood on one side weeping; each one knew her boy or girl, and the children flew up to them and kissed them and wiped away their tears with their little hands, and begged them not to weep because they were so happy.

And down below in the morning the porter found the little dead body of the frozen child on the woodstack; they sought out his mother too . . . She had died before him. They met before the Lord God in heaven.

Why have I made up such a story, so out of keeping with an ordinary diary, and a writer's above all? And I promised two stories dealing with real events! But that is just it, I keep fancying that all this may have happened really—that is, what took place in the cellar and on the woodstack; but as for Christ's Christmas tree, I cannot tell you whether that could have happened or not.

White Nights

Translated by Constance Garnett

A SENTIMENTAL STORY FROM
THE DIARY OF A DREAMER

FIRST NIGHT

It was a wonderful night, such a night as is only possible when we are young, dear reader. The sky was so starry, so bright that, looking at it, one could not help asking oneself whether ill-humoured and capricious people could live under such a sky. That is a youthful question too, dear reader, very youthful, but may the Lord put it more frequently into your heart! . . . Speaking of capricious and ill-humoured people, I cannot help recalling my moral condition all that day. From early morning I had been oppressed by a strange despondency. It suddenly seemed to me that I was lonely, that everyone was forsaking me and going away from me. Of course, any one is entitled to ask who "everyone" was. For though I had been living almost eight years in Petersburg I had hardly an acquaintance. But what did I want with acquaintances? I was acquainted with all Petersburg as it was; that was why I felt as though they were all deserting me when all Petersburg packed up and went to its summer villa. I felt afraid of being left alone, and for three whole days I wandered about the town in profound dejection, not knowing what to do with myself. Whether I walked in the Nevsky, went to the Gardens or sauntered on the embankment, there was not one face of those I had been accustomed to meet at the same time and place all the year. They, of course, do not know me, but I know them. I know them intimately, I have almost made a study of their faces, and am delighted when they are gay, and downcast when they are under a cloud. I have almost struck up a friendship with one old man whom I meet every blessed day, at the same hour in Fontanka. Such a grave, pensive countenance; he is always whispering to himself and brandishing his left arm, while in his right hand he holds a long gnarled stick with a gold knob. He even notices me and takes a warm interest in me. If I happen not to be at a certain time in the same spot in Fontanka, I am certain he feels disappointed. That is how it is that we almost bow to each other, especially when we are both in good humour. The other day, when we had not seen each other for two days and met on the third, we were actually touching our hats, but, realizing in time, dropped our hands and passed each other with a look of interest.

I know the houses too. As I walk along they seem to run forward in the streets to look out at me from every window, and almost to say: "Good morning! How do you do? I am quite well, thank God, and I am to have a new storey in May," or, "How are you? I am being redecorated tomorrow;" or, "I was almost burnt down and had such a fright," and so on. I have my favourites among them, some are dear friends; one of them intends to be treated by the architect this summer. I shall go every day on purpose to see that the operation is not a failure. God forbid! But I shall never forget an incident with a very pretty little house of a light pink colour. It was such a charming little brick house, it looked so hospitably at me, and so proudly at its ungainly neighbours, that my heart rejoiced whenever I happened to pass it. Suddenly last week I walked along the street, and when I looked at my friend I heard a plaintive, "They are painting me yellow!" The villains! The barbarians! They had spared nothing, neither columns, nor cornices, and my poor little friend was as yellow as a canary. It almost made me bilious. And to this day I have not had the courage to visit my poor disfigured friend, painted the colour of the Celestial Empire.

So now you understand, reader, in what sense I am acquainted with all Petersburg.

I have mentioned already that I had felt worried for three whole days before I guessed the cause of my uneasiness. And I felt ill at ease in the street—this one had gone and that one had gone, and what had become of the other?—and at home I did not feel like myself either. For two evenings I was puzzling my brains to think what was amiss in my corner; why I felt so uncomfortable in it. And in perplexity I scanned my grimy green walls, my ceiling covered with a spider's web, the growth of which Matrona has so successfully encouraged. I looked over all my furniture, examined every chair, wondering whether the trouble lay there (for if one chair is not standing in the same position as it stood the day before, I am not myself). I looked at the window, but it was all in vain . . . I was not a bit the better for it! I even bethought me to send for Matrona, and was giving her some fatherly admonitions in regard to the spider's web and sluttishness in general; but she simply stared at me in amazement and went away without saying a word, so that the spider's web is comfortably hanging in its place to this day. I only at last this morning realized what was wrong. Aie! Why, they are giving me the slip and making off to their summer villas! Forgive the triviality of the expression, but I am in no mood for fine language . . . for everything that had been in Petersburg had gone or was going away for the holidays; for every respectable gentleman of dignified appearance who took a cab was at once transformed, in my eyes, into a respectable head of a household who after his daily duties were over, was making his way to the bosom of his family, to the summer villa; for all the passers-by had now quite a peculiar air which seemed to say to everyone they met: "We are only here for the moment, gentlemen, and in another two hours we shall be going off to the summer villa." If a window opened after delicate fingers, white as snow, had tapped upon the pane, and the head of a pretty girl was thrust out, calling to a street-seller with pots of flowers—at once on the spot I fancied that those flowers were being bought not simply in order to enjoy the flowers and the spring in stuffy town lodgings, but because they would all be very soon moving into the country and could take the flowers with them. What is more, I made such progress in my new peculiar sort of investigation that I could distinguish correctly from the mere air of each in what summer villa he was living. The inhabitants of Kamenny and Aptekarsky Islands or of the Peterhof Road were marked by the studied elegance of their manner, their fashionable summer suits, and the fine carriages in which they drove to town. Visitors to Pargolovo and places further away impressed one at first sight by their reasonable and dignified air; the tripper to Krestovsky Island could be recognized by his look of irrepressible gaiety. If I chanced to meet a long procession of waggoners walking lazily with the reins in their hands beside waggons loaded with regular mountains of furniture, tables, chairs, ottomans and sofas and domestic utensils of all sorts, frequently with a decrepit cook sitting on the top of it all, guarding her master's property as though it were the apple of her eye; or if I saw boats heavily loaded with household goods crawling along the Neva or Fontanka to the Black River or the Islands—the waggons and the boats were multiplied tenfold, a hundredfold, in my eyes. I fancied that everything was astir and moving, everything was going in regular caravans to the summer villas. It seemed as though Petersburg threatened to become a wilderness, so that at last I felt ashamed, mortified and sad that I had nowhere to go for the holidays and no reason to go away. I was ready to go away with every waggon, to drive off with every gentleman of respectable appearance who took a cab; but no one—absolutely no one—invited me; it seemed they had forgotten me, as though really I were a stranger to them!

I took long walks, succeeding, as I usually did, in quite forgetting where I was, when I suddenly found myself at the city gates. Instantly I felt light-hearted, and I passed the barrier and walked between cultivated fields and meadows, unconscious of fatigue, and feeling only all over as though a burden were falling off my soul. All the passers-by gave me such friendly looks that they seemed almost greeting me, they all seemed so pleased at something. They were all smoking cigars, everyone of them. And I felt pleased as I never had before. It was as though I had suddenly found myself in Italy—so strong was the effect of nature upon a half-sick townsman like me, almost stifling between city walls.

There is something inexpressibly touching in nature round Petersburg, when at the approach of spring she puts forth all her might, all the powers bestowed on her by Heaven, when she breaks into leaf, decks herself out and spangles herself with flowers . . . Somehow I cannot help being reminded of a frail, consumptive girl, at whom one sometimes looks with compassion, sometimes with sympathetic love, whom sometimes one simply does not notice; though suddenly in one instant she becomes, as though by chance, inexplicably lovely and exquisite, and, impressed and intoxicated, one cannot help asking oneself what power made those sad, pensive eyes flash with such fire? What summoned the blood to those pale, wan cheeks? What bathed with passion those soft features? What set that bosom heaving? What so suddenly called strength, life and beauty into the poor girl's face, making it gleam with such a smile, kindle with such bright, sparkling laughter? You look round, you seek for someone, you conjecture . . . But the moment passes, and next day you meet, maybe, the same pensive and preoccupied look as before, the same pale face, the same meek and timid movements, and even signs of remorse, traces of a mortal anguish and regret for the fleeting distraction . . . And you grieve that the momentary beauty has faded so soon never to return, that it flashed upon you so treacherously, so vainly, grieve because you had not even time to love her . . .

And yet my night was better than my day! This was how it happened.

I came back to the town very late, and it had struck ten as I was going towards my lodgings. My way lay along the canal embankment, where at that hour you never meet a soul. It is true that I live in a very remote part of the town. I walked along singing, for when I am happy I am always humming to myself like every happy man who has no friend or acquaintance with whom to share his joy. Suddenly I had a most unexpected adventure.

Leaning on the canal railing stood a woman with her elbows on the rail, she was apparently looking with great attention at the muddy water of the canal. She was wearing a very charming yellow hat and a jaunty little black mantle. "She's a girl, and I am sure she is dark," I thought. She did not seem to hear my footsteps, and did not even stir when I passed by with bated breath and loudly throbbing heart.

"Strange," I thought; "she must be deeply absorbed in something," and all at once I stopped as though petrified. I heard a muffled sob. Yes! I was not mistaken, the girl was crying, and a minute later I heard sob after sob. Good Heavens! My heart sank. And timid as I was with women, yet this was such a moment! . . . I turned, took a step towards her, and should certainly have pronounced the word "Madam!" if I had not known that that exclamation has been uttered a thousand times in every Russian society novel. It was only that reflection stopped me. But while I was seeking for a word, the girl came to herself, looked round, started, cast down her eyes and slipped by me along the embankment. I at once followed her; but she, divining this, left the embankment, crossed the road and walked along the pavement. I dared not cross the street after her. My heart was fluttering like a captured bird. All at once a chance came to my aid.

Along the same side of the pavement there suddenly came into sight, not far from the girl, a gentleman in evening dress, of dignified years, though by no means of dignified carriage; he was staggering and cautiously leaning against the wall. The girl flew straight as an arrow, with the timid haste one sees in all girls who do not want any one to volunteer to accompany them home at night, and no doubt the staggering gentleman would not have pursued her, if my good luck had not prompted him.

Suddenly, without a word to any one, the gentleman set off and flew full speed in pursuit of my unknown lady. She was racing like the wind, but the staggering gentleman was overtaking—overtook her. The girl uttered a shriek, and . . . I bless my luck for the excellent knotted stick, which happened on that occasion to be in my right hand. In a flash I was on the other side of the street; in a flash the obtrusive gentleman had taken in the position, had grasped the irresistible argument, fallen back without a word, and only when we were very far away protested against my action in rather vigorous language. But his words hardly reached us.

"Give me your arm," I said to the girl. "And he won't dare to annoy us further."

She took my arm without a word, still trembling with excitement and terror. Oh, obtrusive gentleman! How I blessed you at that moment! I stole a glance at her, she was very charming and dark—I had guessed right.

On her black eyelashes there still glistened a tear—from her recent terror or her former grief—I don't know. But there was already a gleam of a smile on her lips. She too stole a glance at me, faintly blushed and looked down.

"There, you see; why did you drive me away? If I had been here, nothing would have happened . . ."

"But I did not know you; I thought that you too . . ."

"Why, do you know me now?"

"A little! Here, for instance, why are you trembling?"

"Oh, you are right at the first guess!" I answered, delighted that my girl had intelligence; that is never out of place in company with beauty. "Yes, from the first glance you have guessed the sort of man you have to do with. Precisely; I am shy with women, I am agitated, I don't deny it, as much so as you were a minute ago when that gentleman alarmed you. I am in some alarm now. It's like a dream, and I never guessed even in my sleep that I should ever talk with any woman."

"What? Really? . . ."

"Yes; if my arm trembles, it is because it has never been held by a pretty little hand like yours. I am a complete stranger to women; that is, I have never been used to them. You see, I am alone . . . I don't even know how to talk to them. Here, I don't know now whether I have not said something silly to you! Tell me frankly; I assure you beforehand that I am not quick to take offence? . . ."

"No, nothing, nothing, quite the contrary. And if you insist on my speaking frankly, I will tell you that women like such timidity; and if you want to know more, I like it too, and I won't drive you away till I get home."

"You will make me," I said, breathless with delight, "lose my timidity, and then farewell to all my chances . . ."

"Chances! What chances—of what? That's not so nice."

"I beg your pardon, I am sorry, it was a slip of the tongue; but how can you expect one at such a moment to have no desire . . ."

"To be liked, eh?"

"Well, yes; but do, for goodness' sake, be kind. Think what I am! Here, I am twenty-six and I have never seen any one. How can I speak well, tactfully, and to the point? It will seem better to you when I have told you everything openly . . . I don't know how to be silent when my heart is speaking. Well, never mind . . . Believe me, not one woman, never, never! No acquaintance of any sort! And I do nothing but dream every day that at last I shall meet someone. Oh, if only you knew how often I have been in love in that way . . ."

"How? With whom? . . ."

"Why, with no one, with an ideal, with the one I dream of in my sleep. I make up regular romances in my dreams. Ah, you don't know me! It's true, of course, I have met two or three women, but what sort of women were they? They were all landladies, that . . . But I shall make you laugh if I tell you that I have several times thought of speaking, just simply speaking, to some aristocratic lady in the street, when she is alone, I need hardly say; speaking to her, of course, timidly, respectfully, passionately; telling her that I am perishing in solitude, begging her not to send me away; saying that I have no chance of making the acquaintance of any woman; impressing upon her that it is a positive duty for a woman not to repulse so timid a prayer from such a luckless man as me. That, in fact, all I ask is, that she should say two or three sisterly words with sympathy, should not repulse me at first sight; should take me on trust and listen to what I say; should laugh at me if she likes, encourage me, say two words to me, only two words, even though we never meet again afterwards! . . . But you are laughing; however, that is why I am telling you . . ."

"Don't be vexed; I am only laughing at your being your own enemy, and if you had tried you would have succeeded, perhaps, even though it had been in the street; the simpler the better . . . No kind-hearted woman, unless she were stupid or, still more, vexed about something at the moment, could bring herself to send you away without those two words which you ask for so timidly . . . But what am I saying? Of course she would take you for a madman. I was judging by myself; I know a good deal about other people's lives."

"Oh, thank you," I cried; "you don't know what you have done for me now!"

"I am glad! I am glad! But tell me how did you find out that I was the sort of woman with whom . . . well, whom you think worthy . . . of attention and friendship . . . in fact, not a landlady as you say? What made you decide to come up to me?"

"What made me? . . . But you were alone; that gentleman was too insolent; it's night. You must admit that it was a duty . . ."

"No, no; I mean before, on the other side—you know you meant to come up to me."

"On the other side? Really I don't know how to answer; I am afraid to . . . Do you know I have been happy today? I walked along singing; I went out into the country; I have never had such happy moments. You . . . perhaps it was my fancy . . . Forgive me for referring to it; I fancied you were crying, and I . . . could not bear to hear it . . . it made my heart ache . . . Oh, my goodness! Surely I might be troubled about you? Surely there was no harm in feeling brotherly compassion for you . . . I beg your pardon, I said compassion . . . Well, in short, surely you would not be offended at my involuntary impulse to go up to you? . . ."

"Stop, that's enough, don't talk of it," said the girl, looking down, and pressing my hand. "It's my fault for having spoken of it; but I am glad I was not mistaken in you . . . But here I am home; I must go down this turning, it's two steps from here . . . Goodbye, thank you! . . ."

"Surely . . . surely you don't mean . . . that we shall never see each other again? . . . Surely this is not to be the end?"

"You see," said the girl, laughing, "at first you only wanted two words, and now . . . However, I won't say anything . . . perhaps we shall meet . . ."

"I shall come here tomorrow," I said. "Oh, forgive me, I am already making demands . . ."

"Yes, you are not very patient . . . you are almost insisting."

"Listen, listen!" I interrupted her. "Forgive me if I tell you something else . . . I tell you what, I can't help coming here tomorrow, I am a dreamer; I have so little real life that I look upon such moments as this now, as so rare, that I cannot help going over such moments again in my dreams. I shall be dreaming of you all night, a whole week, a whole year. I shall certainly come here tomorrow, just here to this place, just at the same hour, and I shall be happy remembering today. This place is dear to me already. I have already two or three such places in Petersburg. I once shed tears over memories . . . like you . . . Who knows, perhaps you were weeping ten minutes ago over some memory . . . But, forgive me, I have forgotten myself again; perhaps you have once been particularly happy here . . ."

"Very good," said the girl, "perhaps I will come here tomorrow, too, at ten o'clock. I see that I can't forbid you . . . The fact is, I have to be here; don't imagine that I am making an appointment with you; I tell you beforehand that I have to be here on my own account. But . . . well, I tell you straight out, I don't mind if you do come. To begin with, something unpleasant might happen as it did today, but never mind that . . . In short, I should simply like to see you . . . to say two words to you. Only, mind, you must not think the worse of me now! Don't think I make appointments so lightly . . . I shouldn't make it except that . . . But let that be my secret! Only a compact beforehand . . ."

"A compact! Speak, tell me, tell me all beforehand; I agree to anything, I am ready for anything," I cried delighted. "I answer for myself, I will be obedient, respectful . . . you know me . . ."

"It's just because I do know you that I ask you to come tomorrow," said the girl, laughing. "I know you perfectly. But mind you will come on the condition, in the first place (only be good, do what I ask—you see, I speak frankly), you won't fall in love with me . . . That's impossible, I assure you. I am ready for friendship; here's my hand . . . But you mustn't fall in love with me, I beg you!"

"I swear," I cried, gripping her hand . . .

"Hush, don't swear, I know you are ready to flare up like gunpowder. Don't think ill of me for saying so. If only you knew . . . I, too, have no one to whom I can say a word, whose advice I can ask. Of course, one does not look for an adviser in the street; but you are an exception. I know you as though we had been friends for twenty years . . . You won't deceive me, will you? . . ."

"You will see . . . the only thing is, I don't know how I am going to survive the next twenty-four hours."

"Sleep soundly. Goodnight, and remember that I have trusted you already. But you exclaimed so nicely just now, 'Surely one can't be held responsible for every feeling, even for brotherly sympathy!' Do you know, that was so nicely said, that the idea struck me at once, that I might confide in you?"

"For God's sake do; but about what? What is it?"

"Wait till tomorrow. Meanwhile, let that be a secret. So much the better for you; it will give it a faint flavour of romance. Perhaps I will tell you tomorrow, and perhaps not . . . I will talk to you a little more beforehand; we will get to know each other better . . ."

"Oh yes, I will tell you all about myself tomorrow! But what has happened? It is as though a miracle had befallen me . . . My God, where am I? Come, tell me aren't you glad that you were not angry and did not drive me away at the first moment, as any other woman would have done? In two minutes you have made me happy for ever. Yes, happy; who knows, perhaps, you have reconciled me with myself, solved my doubts! . . . Perhaps such moments come upon me . . . But there I will tell you all about it tomorrow, you shall know everything, everything . . ."

"Very well, I consent; you shall begin . . ."

"Agreed."

"Goodbye till tomorrow!"

"Till tomorrow!"

And we parted. I walked about all night; I could not make up my mind to go home. I was so happy . . . Tomorrow!

SECOND NIGHT

"Well, so you have survived!" she said, pressing both my hands.

"I've been here for the last two hours; you don't know what a state I have been in all day."

"I know, I know. But to business. Do you know why I have come? Not to talk nonsense, as I did yesterday. I tell you what, we must behave more sensibly in future. I thought a great deal about it last night."

"In what way—in what must we be more sensible? I am ready for my part; but, really, nothing more sensible has happened to me in my life than this, now."

"Really? In the first place, I beg you not to squeeze my hands so; secondly, I must tell you that I spent a long time thinking about you and feeling doubtful today."

"And how did it end?"

"How did it end? The upshot of it is that we must begin all over again, because the conclusion I reached today was that I don't know you at all; that I behaved like a baby last night, like a little girl; and, of course, the fact of it is, that it's my soft heart that is to blame—that is, I sang my own praises, as one always does in the end when one analyses one's conduct. And therefore to correct my mistake, I've made up my mind to find out all about you minutely. But as I have no one from whom I can find out anything, you must tell me everything fully yourself. Well, what sort of man are you? Come, make haste—begin—tell me your whole history."

"My history!" I cried in alarm. "My history! But who has told you I have a history? I have no history . . ."

"Then how have you lived, if you have no history?" she interrupted, laughing.

"Absolutely without any history! I have lived, as they say, keeping myself to myself, that is, utterly alone—alone, entirely alone. Do you know what it means to be alone?"

"But how alone? Do you mean you never saw any one?"

"Oh no, I see people, of course; but still I am alone."

"Why, do you never talk to any one?"

"Strictly speaking, with no one."

"Who are you then? Explain yourself! Stay, I guess: most likely, like me you have a grandmother. She is blind and will never let me go anywhere, so that I have almost forgotten how to talk; and when I played some pranks two years ago, and she saw there was no holding me in, she called me up and pinned my dress to hers, and ever since we sit like that for days together; she knits a stocking, though she's blind, and I sit beside her, sew or read aloud to her—it's such a queer habit, here for two years I've been pinned to her . . ."

Fyodor Dostoevsky

"Good Heavens! what misery! But no, I haven't a grandmother like that."

"Well, if you haven't why do you sit at home? . . ."

"Listen, do you want to know the sort of man I am?"

"Yes, yes!"

"In the strict sense of the word?"

"In the very strictest sense of the word."

"Very well, I am a type!"

"Type, type! What sort of type?" cried the girl, laughing, as though she had not had a chance of laughing for a whole year. "Yes, it's very amusing talking to you. Look, here's a seat, let us sit down. No one is passing here, no one will hear us, and—begin your history. For it's no good your telling me, I know you have a history; only you are concealing it. To begin with, what is a type?"

"A type? A type is an original, it's an absurd person!" I said, infected by her childish laughter. "It's a character. Listen; do you know what is meant by a dreamer?"

"A dreamer! Indeed I should think I do know. I am a dreamer myself. Sometimes, as I sit by grandmother, all sorts of things come into my head. Why, when one begins dreaming one lets one's fancy run away with one—why, I marry a Chinese Prince! . . . Though sometimes it is a good thing to dream! But, goodness knows! Especially when one has something to think of apart from dreams," added the girl, this time rather seriously.

"Excellent! If you have been married to a Chinese Emperor, you will quite understand me. Come, listen . . . But one minute, I don't know your name yet."

"At last! You have been in no hurry to think of it!"

"Oh, my goodness! It never entered my head, I felt quite happy as it was . . ."

"My name is Nastenka."

"Nastenka! And nothing else?"

"Nothing else! Why, is not that enough for you, you insatiable person?"

"Not enough? On the contrary, it's a great deal, a very great deal, Nastenka; you kind girl, if you are Nastenka for me from the first."

"Quite so! Well?"

"Well, listen, Nastenka, now for this absurd history."

I sat down beside her, assumed a pedantically serious attitude, and began as though reading from a manuscript—

"There are, Nastenka, though you may not know it, strange nooks in Petersburg. It seems as though the same sun as shines for all Petersburg people does not peep into those spots, but some other different new one, bespoken expressly for those nooks, and it throws a different light on everything. In these corners, dear Nastenka, quite a different life is lived, quite unlike the life that is surging round us, but such as perhaps exists in some unknown realm, not among us in our serious, over-serious, time. Well, that life is a mixture of something purely fantastic, fervently ideal, with something (alas! Nastenka) dingily prosaic and ordinary, not to say incredibly vulgar."

"Foo! Good Heavens! What a preface! What do I hear?"

"Listen, Nastenka. (It seems to me I shall never be tired of calling you Nastenka.) Let me tell you that in these corners live strange people— dreamers. The dreamer—if you want an exact definition—is not a human being, but a creature of an intermediate sort. For the most part he settles in some inaccessible corner, as though hiding from the light of day; once he slips into his corner, he grows to it like a snail, or, anyway, he is in that respect very much like that remarkable creature, which is an animal and a house both at once, and is called a tortoise. Why do you suppose he is so fond of his four walls, which are invariably painted green, grimy, dismal and reeking unpardonably of tobacco smoke? Why is it that when this absurd gentleman is visited by one of his few acquaintances (and he ends by getting rid of all his friends), why does this absurd person meet him with such embarrassment, changing countenance and overcome with confusion, as though he had only just committed some crime within his four walls; as though he had been forging counterfeit notes, or as though he were writing verses to be sent to a journal with an anonymous letter, in which he states that the real poet is dead, and that his friend thinks it his sacred duty to publish his things? Why, tell me, Nastenka, why is it conversation is not easy between the two friends? Why is there no laughter? Why does no lively word fly from the tongue of the perplexed newcomer, who at other times may be very fond of laughter, lively words, conversation about the fair sex, and other cheerful subjects? And why does this friend, probably a new friend and on his first visit—for there will hardly be a second, and the friend will never come again—why is the friend himself so confused, so tongue-tied, in spite of his wit (if he has any), as he looks at the downcast face of his host, who in his turn becomes utterly helpless and at his wits' end after gigantic but fruitless efforts to smooth things over and enliven the conversation, to show his knowledge of polite society, to talk, too, of the fair sex, and by such humble endeavour, to please the poor man, who like a fish out of water has mistakenly come to visit him? Why does the gentleman, all at once remembering some very necessary business which never existed, suddenly seize his hat and hurriedly make off, snatching away his hand from the warm grip of his host, who was trying his utmost to show his regret and retrieve the lost position? Why does the friend chuckle as he goes out of the door, and swear never to come and see this queer creature again, though the queer creature is really a very good fellow, and at the same time he cannot refuse his imagination the little diversion of comparing the queer fellow's countenance during their conversation with the expression of an unhappy kitten treacherously captured, roughly handled, frightened and subjected to all sorts of indignities by children, till, utterly crestfallen, it hides away from them under a chair in the dark, and there must needs at its leisure bristle up, spit, and wash its insulted face with both paws, and long afterwards look angrily at life and nature, and even at the bits saved from the master's dinner for it by the sympathetic housekeeper?"

"Listen," interrupted Nastenka, who had listened to me all the time in amazement, opening her eyes and her little mouth. "Listen; I don't know in the least why it happened and why you ask me such absurd questions; all I know is, that this adventure must have happened word for word to you."

"Doubtless," I answered, with the gravest face.

"Well, since there is no doubt about it, go on," said Nastenka, "because I want very much to know how it will end."

"You want to know, Nastenka, what our hero, that is I—for the hero of the whole business was my humble self—did in his corner? You want to know why I lost my head and was upset for the whole day by the unexpected visit of a friend? You want to know why I was so startled, why I blushed when the door of my room was opened, why I was not able to entertain my visitor, and why I was crushed under the weight of my own hospitality?"

"Why, yes, yes," answered Nastenka, "that's the point. Listen. You describe it all splendidly, but couldn't you perhaps describe it a little less splendidly? You talk as though you were reading it out of a book."

"Nastenka," I answered in a stern and dignified voice, hardly able to keep from laughing, "dear Nastenka, I know I describe splendidly, but, excuse me, I don't know how else to do it. At this moment, dear Nastenka, at this moment I am like the spirit of King Solomon when, after lying a thousand years under seven seals in his urn, those seven seals were at last taken off. At this moment, Nastenka, when we have met at last after such a long separation—for I have known you for ages, Nastenka, because I have been looking for someone for ages, and that is a sign that it was you I was looking for, and it was ordained that we should meet now—at this moment a thousand valves have opened in my head, and I must let myself flow in a river of words, or I shall choke. And so I beg you not to interrupt me, Nastenka, but listen humbly and obediently, or I will be silent."

"No, no, no! Not at all. Go on! I won't say a word!"

"I will continue. There is, my friend Nastenka, one hour in my day which I like extremely. That is the hour when almost all business, work and duties are over, and everyone is hurrying home to dinner, to lie down, to rest, and on the way all are cogitating on other more cheerful subjects relating to their evenings, their nights, and all the rest of their free time. At that hour our hero—for allow me, Nastenka, to tell my story in the third person, for one feels awfully ashamed to tell it in the first person—and so at that hour our hero, who had his work too, was pacing along after the others. But a strange feeling of pleasure set his pale, rather crumpled-looking face working. He looked not with indifference on the evening glow which was slowly fading on the cold Petersburg sky. When I say he looked, I am lying: he did not look at it, but saw it as it were without realizing, as though tired or preoccupied with some other more interesting subject, so that he could scarcely spare a glance for anything about him. He was pleased because till next day he was released from business irksome to him, and happy as a schoolboy let out from the classroom to his games and mischief. Take a look at him, Nastenka; you will see at once that joyful emotion has already had an effect on his weak nerves and morbidly excited fancy. You see he is thinking of something . . . Of dinner, do you imagine? Of the evening? What is he looking at like that? Is it at that gentleman of dignified appearance who is bowing so picturesquely to the lady who rolls by in a carriage drawn by prancing horses? No, Nastenka; what are all those trivialities to him now! He is rich now with his *own individual* life; he has suddenly become rich, and it is not for nothing that the fading sunset sheds its farewell gleams so gaily before him, and calls forth a swarm of impressions from his warmed heart. Now he hardly notices the road, on which the tiniest details at other times would strike him. Now 'the Goddess of Fancy' (if you have read Zhukovsky, dear Nastenka) has already with fantastic hand spun her golden warp and begun weaving upon it patterns of marvellous magic life—and who knows, maybe, her fantastic hand has borne him to the seventh crystal heaven far from the excellent granite pavement on which he was walking his way? Try stopping him now, ask him suddenly where he is standing now, through what streets he is going— he will, probably remember nothing, neither where he is going nor where he is standing now, and flushing with vexation he will certainly tell some lie to save appearances. That is why he starts, almost cries out, and looks round with horror when a respectable old lady stops him politely in the middle of the pavement and asks her way. Frowning with vexation he strides on, scarcely noticing that more than one passer-by smiles and turns round to look after him, and that a little girl, moving out of his way in alarm, laughs aloud, gazing open-eyed at his broad meditative smile and gesticulations. But fancy catches up in its playful flight the old woman, the curious passers-by, and the laughing child, and the peasants spending their nights in their barges on Fontanka (our hero, let us suppose, is walking along the canal-side at that moment), and capriciously weaves everyone and everything into the canvas like a fly in a spider's web. And it is only after the queer fellow has returned to his comfortable den with fresh stores for his mind to work on, has sat down and finished his dinner, that he comes to himself, when Matrona who waits upon him—always thoughtful and depressed—clears the table and gives him his pipe; he comes to himself then and recalls with surprise that he has dined, though he has absolutely no notion how it has happened. It has grown dark in the room; his soul is sad and empty; the whole kingdom of fancies drops to pieces about him, drops to pieces without a trace, without a sound, floats away like a dream, and he cannot himself remember what he was dreaming. But a vague sensation faintly stirs his heart and sets it aching, some new desire temptingly tickles and excites his fancy, and imperceptibly evokes a swarm of fresh phantoms. Stillness reigns in the little room; imagination is fostered by solitude and idleness; it is faintly smouldering, faintly simmering, like the water with which old Matrona is making her coffee as she moves quietly about in the kitchen close by. Now it breaks out spasmodically; and the book, picked up aimlessly and at random, drops from my dreamer's hand before he has reached the third page. His imagination is again stirred and at work, and again a new world, a new fascinating life opens vistas before him. A fresh dream—fresh happiness! A fresh rush of delicate, voluptuous poison! What is real life to him! To his corrupted eyes we live, you and I, Nastenka, so torpidly, slowly, insipidly; in his eyes we are all so dissatisfied with our fate, so exhausted by our life! And, truly, see how at first sight everything is cold, morose, as though ill-humoured among us . . . Poor things! thinks our dreamer. And it is no wonder that he thinks it! Look at these magic phantasms, which so enchantingly, so whimsically, so carelessly and freely group before him in such a magic, animated picture, in which the most prominent figure in the foreground is of course himself, our dreamer, in his precious person. See what varied adventures, what an endless swarm of ecstatic dreams. You ask, perhaps, what he is dreaming of. Why ask that?—why, of everything . . . of the lot of the poet, first unrecognized, then crowned with laurels; of friendship with Hoffmann, St. Bartholomew's Night, of Diana Vernon, of playing the hero at the taking of Kazan by Ivan Vassilyevitch, of Clara Mowbray, of Effie Deans, of the council of the prelates and Huss before them, of the rising of the dead in 'Robert the Devil' (do you remember the music, it smells of the churchyard!), of Minna and Brenda, of the battle of Berezina, of the reading of a poem at Countess V. D.'s, of Danton, of Cleopatra *ei suoi amanti*, of a little house in Kolomna, of a little home of one's own and beside one a dear creature who listens to one on a winter's evening, opening her little mouth and eyes as you are listening to me now, my angel . . . No, Nastenka, what is there, what is there for him, voluptuous sluggard, in this life, for which you and I have such a longing? He thinks that this is a poor pitiful life, not foreseeing that for him too, maybe, sometime the mournful hour may strike, when for one day of that pitiful life he would give all his years of phantasy, and would give them not only for joy and for happiness, but without caring to make distinctions in that hour of sadness, remorse and unchecked grief. But so far that threatening has not arrived—he desires nothing, because he is superior to all desire, because he has everything, because he is satiated, because he is the artist of his own life, and creates it for himself every hour to suit his latest whim. And you know this fantastic world of fairyland is so easily, so naturally created! As though it were not a delusion! Indeed, he is ready to believe at some moments that all this life is not suggested by feeling, is not mirage, not a delusion of the imagination, but that it is concrete, real, substantial! Why is it, Nastenka, why is it at such moments one holds one's breath? Why, by what sorcery, through what incomprehensible caprice, is the pulse quickened, does a tear start from the dreamer's eye, while his pale moist cheeks glow, while his whole being is suffused with an inexpressible sense of consolation? Why is it that whole sleepless nights pass like a flash in inexhaustible gladness and happiness, and when the dawn gleams rosy at the window and daybreak floods the gloomy room with uncertain, fantastic light, as in Petersburg, our dreamer, worn out and exhausted, flings himself on his bed and drops asleep with thrills of delight in his morbidly overwrought spirit, and with a weary sweet ache in his heart? Yes, Nastenka, one deceives oneself and unconsciously believes that real true passion is stirring one's soul; one unconsciously believes that there is something living, tangible in one's immaterial dreams! And is it delusion? Here love, for instance, is bound up with all its fathomless joy, all its torturing agonies in his bosom . . . Only look at him, and you will be convinced! Would you believe, looking at him, dear Nastenka, that he has never known her whom he loves in his ecstatic dreams? Can it be that he has only seen her in seductive visions, and that this passion has been nothing but a dream? Surely they must have spent years hand in hand together—alone the two of them, casting off all the world and each uniting his or her life with the other's? Surely when the hour of parting came she must have lain sobbing and grieving on his bosom, heedless of the tempest raging under the sullen sky, heedless of the wind which snatches and bears away the tears from her black eyelashes? Can all of that have been a dream—and that garden, dejected, forsaken, run wild, with its little moss-grown paths, solitary, gloomy, where they used to walk so happily together, where they hoped, grieved, loved, loved each other so long, "so long and so fondly?" And that queer ancestral house where she spent so many years lonely and sad with her morose old husband, always silent and splenetic, who frightened them, while timid as children they hid their love from each other? What torments they suffered, what agonies of terror, how innocent, how pure was their love, and how (I need hardly say, Nastenka) malicious people were! And, good Heavens! surely he met her afterwards, far from their native shores, under alien skies, in the hot south in the divinely eternal city, in the dazzling splendour of the ball to the crash of music, in a *palazzo* (it must be in a *palazzo*), drowned in a sea of lights, on the balcony, wreathed in myrtle and roses, where, recognizing him, she hurriedly removes her mask and whispering, 'I am free,' flings herself trembling into his arms, and with a cry of rapture, clinging to one another, in one instant they forget their sorrow and their parting and all their agonies, and the gloomy house and the old man and the dismal garden in that distant land, and the seat on which with a last passionate kiss she tore herself away from his arms numb with anguish and despair . . . Oh, Nastenka, you must admit that one would start, betray confusion, and blush like a schoolboy who has just stuffed in his pocket an apple stolen from a neighbour's garden, when your uninvited visitor, some stalwart, lanky fellow, a festive soul fond of a joke, opens your door and shouts out as though nothing were happening: 'My dear boy, I have this minute come from Pavlovsk.' My goodness! the old count is dead, unutterable happiness is close at hand—and people arrive from Pavlovsk!"

Finishing my pathetic appeal, I paused pathetically. I remembered that I had an intense desire to force myself to laugh, for I was already feeling that a malignant demon was stirring within me, that there was a lump in my throat, that my chin was beginning to twitch, and that my eyes were growing more and more moist.

I expected Nastenka, who listened to me opening her clever eyes, would break into her childish, irrepressible laugh; and I was already regretting that I had gone so far, that I had unnecessarily described what had long been simmering in my heart, about which I could speak as though from a written account of it, because I had long ago passed judgment on myself and now could not resist reading it, making my confession, without expecting to be understood; but to my surprise she was silent, waiting a little, then she faintly pressed my hand and with timid sympathy asked—

"Surely you haven't lived like that all your life?"

"All my life, Nastenka," I answered; "all my life, and it seems to me I shall go on so to the end."

"No, that won't do," she said uneasily, "that must not be; and so, maybe, I shall spend all my life beside grandmother. Do you know, it is not at all good to live like that?"

"I know, Nastenka, I know!" I cried, unable to restrain my feelings longer. "And I realize now, more than ever, that I have lost all my best years! And now I know it and feel it more painfully from recognizing that

God has sent me you, my good angel, to tell me that and show it. Now that I sit beside you and talk to you it is strange for me to think of the future, for in the future—there is loneliness again, again this musty, useless life; and what shall I have to dream of when I have been so happy in reality beside you! Oh, may you be blessed, dear girl, for not having repulsed me at first, for enabling me to say that for two evenings, at least, I have lived."

"Oh, no, no!" cried Nastenka and tears glistened in her eyes. "No, it mustn't be so any more; we must not part like that! what are two evenings?"

"Oh, Nastenka, Nastenka! Do you know how far you have reconciled me to myself? Do you know now that I shall not think so ill of myself, as I have at some moments? Do you know that, maybe, I shall leave off grieving over the crime and sin of my life? for such a life is a crime and a sin. And do not imagine that I have been exaggerating anything—for goodness' sake don't think that, Nastenka: for at times such misery comes over me, such misery . . . Because it begins to seem to me at such times that I am incapable of beginning a life in real life, because it has seemed to me that I have lost all touch, all instinct for the actual, the real; because at last I have cursed myself; because after my fantastic nights I have moments of returning sobriety, which are awful! Meanwhile, you hear the whirl and roar of the crowd in the vortex of life around you; you hear, you see, men living in reality; you see that life for them is not forbidden, that their life does not float away like a dream, like a vision; that their life is being eternally renewed, eternally youthful, and not one hour of it is the same as another; while fancy is so spiritless, monotonous to vulgarity and easily scared, the slave of shadows, of the idea, the slave of the first cloud that shrouds the sun, and overcasts with depression the true Petersburg heart so devoted to the sun—and what is fancy in depression! One feels that this *inexhaustible* fancy is weary at last and worn out with continual exercise, because one is growing into manhood, outgrowing one's old ideals: they are being shattered into fragments, into dust; if there is no other life one must build one up from the fragments. And meanwhile the soul longs and craves for something else! And in vain the dreamer rakes over his old dreams, as though seeking a spark among the embers, to fan them into flame, to warm his chilled heart by the rekindled fire, and to rouse up in it again all that was so sweet, that touched his heart, that set his blood boiling, drew tears from his eyes, and so luxuriously deceived him! Do you know, Nastenka, the point I have reached? Do you know that I am forced now to celebrate the anniversary of my own sensations, the anniversary of that which was once so sweet, which never existed in reality—for this anniversary is kept in memory of those same foolish, shadowy dreams—and to do this because those foolish dreams are no more, because I have nothing to earn them with; you know even dreams do not come for nothing! Do you know that I love now to recall and visit at certain dates the places where I was once happy in my own way? I love to build up my present in harmony with the irrevocable past, and I often wander like a shadow, aimless, sad and dejected, about the streets and crooked lanes of Petersburg. What memories they are! To remember, for instance, that here just a year ago, just at this time, at this hour, on this pavement, I wandered just as lonely, just as dejected as today. And one remembers that then one's dreams were sad, and though the past was no better one feels as though it had somehow been better, and that life was more peaceful, that one was free from the black thoughts that haunt one now; that one was free from the gnawing of conscience—the gloomy, sullen gnawing which now gives me no rest by day or by night. And one asks oneself where are one's dreams. And one shakes one's head and says how rapidly the years fly by! And again one asks oneself what has one done with one's years. Where have you buried your best days? Have you lived or not? Look, one says to oneself, look how cold the world is growing. Some more years will pass, and after them will come gloomy solitude; then will come old age trembling on its crutch, and after it misery and desolation. Your fantastic world will grow pale, your dreams will fade and die and will fall like the yellow leaves from the trees . . . Oh, Nastenka! you know it will be sad to be left alone, utterly alone, and to have not even anything to regret—nothing, absolutely nothing . . . for all that you have lost, all that, all was nothing, stupid, simple nullity, there has been nothing but dreams!"

"Come, don't work on my feelings any more," said Nastenka, wiping away a tear which was trickling down her cheek. "Now it's over! Now we shall be two together. Now, whatever happens to me, we will never part. Listen; I am a simple girl, I have not had much education, though grandmother did get a teacher for me, but truly I understand you, for all that you have described I have been through myself, when grandmother pinned me to her dress. Of course, I should not have described it so well as you have; I am not educated," she added timidly, for she was still feeling a sort of respect for my pathetic eloquence and lofty style; "but I am very glad that you have been quite open with me. Now I know you thoroughly, all of you. And do you know what? I want to tell you my history too, all without concealment, and after that you must give me advice. You are a very clever man; will you promise to give me advice?"

"Ah, Nastenka," I cried, "though I have never given advice, still less sensible advice, yet I see now that if we always go on like this that it will be very sensible, and that each of us will give the other a great deal of sensible advice! Well, my pretty Nastenka, what sort of advice do you want? Tell me frankly; at this moment I am so gay and happy, so bold and sensible, that it won't be difficult for me to find words."

"No, no!" Nastenka interrupted, laughing. "I don't only want sensible advice, I want warm brotherly advice, as though you had been fond of me all your life!"

"Agreed, Nastenka, agreed!" I cried delighted; "and if I had been fond of you for twenty years, I couldn't have been fonder of you than I am now."

"Your hand," said Nastenka.

"Here it is," said I, giving her my hand.

"And so let us begin my history!"

NASTENKA'S HISTORY

"Half my story you know already—that is, you know that I have an old grandmother . . ."

"If the other half is as brief as that . . ." I interrupted, laughing.

"Be quiet and listen. First of all you must agree not to interrupt me, or else, perhaps I shall get in a muddle! Come, listen quietly.

"I have an old grandmother. I came into her hands when I was quite a little girl, for my father and mother are dead. It must be supposed that grandmother was once richer, for now she recalls better days. She taught me French, and then got a teacher for me. When I was fifteen (and now I am seventeen) we gave up having lessons. It was at that time that I got into mischief; what I did I won't tell you; it's enough to say that it wasn't very important. But grandmother called me to her one morning and said that as she was blind she could not look after me; she took a pin and pinned my dress to hers, and said that we should sit like that for the rest of our lives if, of course, I did not become a better girl. In fact, at first it was impossible to get away from her: I had to work, to read and to study all beside grandmother. I tried to deceive her once, and persuaded Fekla to sit in my place. Fekla is our charwoman, she is deaf. Fekla sat there instead of me; grandmother was asleep in her armchair at the time, and I went off to see a friend close by. Well, it ended in trouble. Grandmother woke up while I was out, and asked some questions; she thought I was still sitting quietly in my place. Fekla saw that grandmother was asking her something, but could not tell what it was; she wondered what to do, undid the pin and ran away . . ."

At this point Nastenka stopped and began laughing. I laughed with her. She left off at once.

"I tell you what, don't you laugh at grandmother. I laugh because it's funny . . . What can I do, since grandmother is like that; but yet I am fond of her in a way. Oh, well, I did catch it that time. I had to sit down in my place at once, and after that I was not allowed to stir.

"Oh, I forgot to tell you that our house belongs to us, that is to grandmother; it is a little wooden house with three windows as old as grandmother herself, with a little upper storey; well, there moved into our upper storey a new lodger."

"Then you had an old lodger," I observed casually.

"Yes, of course," answered Nastenka, "and one who knew how to hold his tongue better than you do. In fact, he hardly ever used his tongue at all. He was a dumb, blind, lame, dried-up little old man, so that at last he could not go on living, he died; so then we had to find a new lodger, for we could not live without a lodger—the rent, together with grandmother's pension, is almost all we have. But the new lodger, as luck would have it, was a young man, a stranger not of these parts. As he did not haggle over the rent, grandmother accepted him, and only afterwards she asked me: 'Tell me, Nastenka, what is our lodger like—is he young or old?' I did not want to lie, so I told grandmother that he wasn't exactly young and that he wasn't old."

"'And is he pleasant looking?' asked grandmother.

"Again I did not want to tell a lie: 'Yes, he is pleasant looking, grandmother,' I said. And grandmother said: 'Oh, what a nuisance, what a nuisance! I tell you this, grandchild, that you may not be looking after him. What times these are! Why a paltry lodger like this, and he must be pleasant looking too; it was very different in the old days!'"

"Grandmother was always regretting the old days—she was younger in old days, and the sun was warmer in old days, and cream did not turn so sour in old days—it was always the old days! I would sit still and hold my tongue and think to myself: why did grandmother suggest it to me? Why did she ask whether the lodger was young and good-looking? But that was all, I just thought it, began counting my stitches again, went on knitting my stocking, and forgot all about it.

"Well, one morning the lodger came in to see us; he asked about a promise to paper his rooms. One thing led to another. Grandmother was talkative, and she said: 'Go, Nastenka, into my bedroom and bring me my reckoner.' I jumped up at once; I blushed all over, I don't know why, and forgot I was sitting pinned to grandmother; instead of quietly undoing the pin, so that the lodger should not see—I jumped so that grandmother's chair moved. When I saw that the lodger knew all about me now, I blushed, stood still as though I had been shot, and suddenly began to cry—I felt so ashamed and miserable at that minute, that I didn't know where to look! Grandmother called out, 'What are you waiting for?' and I went on worse than ever. When the lodger saw, saw that I was ashamed on his account, he bowed and went away at once!

"After that I felt ready to die at the least sound in the passage. 'It's the lodger,' I kept thinking; I stealthily undid the pin in case. But it always turned out not to be, he never came. A fortnight passed; the lodger sent word through Fyokla that he had a great number of French books, and that they were all good books that I might read, so would not grandmother like me to read them that I might not be dull? Grandmother agreed with gratitude, but kept asking if they were moral books, for if the books were immoral it would be out of the question, one would learn evil from them."

"'And what should I learn, grandmother? What is there written in them?'

"'Ah,' she said, 'what's described in them, is how young men seduce virtuous girls; how, on the excuse that they want to marry them, they carry them off from their parents' houses; how afterwards they leave these unhappy girls to their fate, and they perish in the most pitiful way. I read a great many books,' said grandmother, 'and it is all so well described that one sits up all night and reads them on the sly. So mind you don't read them, Nastenka,' said she. 'What books has he sent?'

"'They are all Walter Scott's novels, grandmother.'

"'Walter Scott's novels! But stay, isn't there some trick about it? Look, hasn't he stuck a love-letter among them?'

"'No, grandmother,' I said, 'there isn't a love-letter.'

"'But look under the binding; they sometimes stuff it under the bindings, the rascals!'

"'No, grandmother, there is nothing under the binding.'

"'Well, that's all right.'

"So we began reading Walter Scott, and in a month or so we had read almost half. Then he sent us more and more. He sent us Pushkin, too; so that at last I could not get on without a book and left off dreaming of how fine it would be to marry a Chinese Prince.

"That's how things were when I chanced one day to meet our lodger on the stairs. Grandmother had sent me to fetch something. He stopped, I blushed and he blushed; he laughed, though, said good morning to me, asked after grandmother, and said, 'Well, have you read the books?' I answered that I had. 'Which did you like best?' he asked. I said, 'Ivanhoe, and Pushkin best of all,' and so our talk ended for that time.

"A week later I met him again on the stairs. That time grandmother had not sent me, I wanted to get something for myself. It was past two, and the lodger used to come home at that time. 'Good afternoon,' said he. I said good afternoon, too.

"'Aren't you dull,' he said, 'sitting all day with your grandmother?'

"When he asked that, I blushed, I don't know why; I felt ashamed, and again I felt offended—I suppose because other people had begun to ask me about that. I wanted to go away without answering, but I hadn't the strength.

"'Listen,' he said, 'you are a good girl. Excuse my speaking to you like that, but I assure you that I wish for your welfare quite as much as your grandmother. Have you no friends that you could go and visit?'

"I told him I hadn't any, that I had had no friend but Mashenka, and she had gone away to Pskov.

"'Listen,' he said, 'would you like to go to the theatre with me?'

"'To the theatre. What about grandmother?'

"'But you must go without your grandmother's knowing it,' he said.

"'No,' I said, 'I don't want to deceive grandmother. Goodbye.'

"'Well, goodbye,' he answered, and said nothing more.

"Only after dinner he came to see us; sat a long time talking to grandmother; asked her whether she ever went out anywhere, whether she had acquaintances, and suddenly said: 'I have taken a box at the opera for this evening; they are giving *The Barber of Seville*. My friends meant to go, but afterwards refused, so the ticket is left on my hands.' '*The Barber of Seville*,' cried grandmother; 'why, the same they used to act in old days?'

"'Yes, it's the same barber,' he said, and glanced at me. I saw what it meant and turned crimson, and my heart began throbbing with suspense.

"'To be sure, I know it,' said grandmother; 'why, I took the part of Rosina myself in old days, at a private performance!'

"'So wouldn't you like to go today?' said the lodger. 'Or my ticket will be wasted.'

"'By all means let us go,' said grandmother; why shouldn't we? And my Nastenka here has never been to the theatre.'

"My goodness, what joy! We got ready at once, put on our best clothes, and set off. Though grandmother was blind, still she wanted to hear the music; besides, she is a kind old soul, what she cared most for was to amuse me, we should never have gone of ourselves.

"What my impressions of *The Barber of Seville* were I won't tell you; but all that evening our lodger looked at me so nicely, talked so nicely, that I saw at once that he had meant to test me in the morning when he proposed that I should go with him alone. Well, it was joy! I went to bed so proud, so gay, my heart beat so that I was a little feverish, and all night I was raving about *The Barber of Seville*.

"I expected that he would come and see us more and more often after that, but it wasn't so at all. He almost entirely gave up coming. He would just come in about once a month, and then only to invite us to the theatre. We went twice again. Only I wasn't at all pleased with that; I saw that he was simply sorry for me because I was so hardly treated by grandmother, and that was all. As time went on, I grew more and more restless, I couldn't sit still, I couldn't read, I couldn't work; sometimes I laughed and did something to annoy grandmother, at another time I would cry. At last I grew thin and was very nearly ill. The opera season was over, and our lodger had quite given up coming to see us; whenever we met—always on the same staircase, of course—he would bow so silently, so gravely, as though he did not want to speak, and go down to the front door, while I went on standing in the middle of the stairs, as red as a cherry, for all the blood rushed to my head at the sight of him.

"Now the end is near. Just a year ago, in May, the lodger came to us and said to grandmother that he had finished his business here, and that he must go back to Moscow for a year. When I heard that, I sank into a chair half dead; grandmother did not notice anything; and having informed us that he should be leaving us, he bowed and went away.

"What was I to do? I thought and thought and fretted and fretted, and at last I made up my mind. Next day he was to go away, and I made up my mind to end it all that evening when grandmother went to bed. And so it happened. I made up all my clothes in a parcel—all the linen I needed—and with the parcel in my hand, more dead than alive, went upstairs to our lodger. I believe I must have stayed an hour on the staircase. When I opened his door he cried out as he looked at me. He thought I was a ghost, and rushed to give me some water, for I could hardly stand up. My heart beat so violently that my head ached, and I did not know what I was doing. When I recovered I began by laying my parcel on his bed, sat down beside it, hid my face in my hands and went into floods of tears. I think he understood it all at once, and looked at me so sadly that my heart was torn.

"'Listen,' he began, 'listen, Nastenka, I can't do anything; I am a poor man, for I have nothing, not even a decent berth. How could we live, if I were to marry you?'

"We talked a long time; but at last I got quite frantic, I said I could not go on living with grandmother, that I should run away from her, that I did not want to be pinned to her, and that I would go to Moscow if he liked, because I could not live without him. Shame and pride and love were all clamouring in me at once, and I fell on the bed almost in convulsions, I was so afraid of a refusal.

"He sat for some minutes in silence, then got up, came up to me and took me by the hand.

"'Listen, my dear good Nastenka, listen; I swear to you that if I am ever in a position to marry, you shall make my happiness. I assure you that now you are the only one who could make me happy. Listen, I am going to Moscow and shall be there just a year; I hope to establish my position. When I come back, if you still love me, I swear that we will be happy. Now it is impossible, I am not able, I have not the right to promise anything. Well, I repeat, if it is not within a year it will certainly be some time; that is, of course, if you do not prefer any one else, for I cannot and dare not bind you by any sort of promise.'

"That was what he said to me, and next day he went away. We agreed together not to say a word to grandmother: that was his wish. Well, my history is nearly finished now. Just a year has past. He has arrived; he has been here three days, and, and—

"And what?" I cried, impatient to hear the end.

"And up to now has not shown himself!" answered Nastenka, as though screwing up all her courage. "There's no sign or sound of him."

Here she stopped, paused for a minute, bent her head, and covering her face with her hands broke into such sobs that it sent a pang to my heart to hear them. I had not in the least expected such a *dénouement*.

"Nastenka," I began timidly in an ingratiating voice, "Nastenka! For goodness' sake don't cry! How do you know? Perhaps he is not here yet . . ."

"He is, he is," Nastenka repeated. "He is here, and I know it. We *made an agreement* at the time, that evening, before he went away: when we said all that I have told you, and had come to an understanding, then we came out here for a walk on this embankment. It was ten o'clock; we sat on this seat. I was not crying then; it was sweet to me to hear what he said . . . And he said that he would come to us directly he arrived, and if I did not refuse him, then we would tell grandmother about it all. Now he is here, I know it, and yet he does not come!"

And again she burst into tears.

"Good God, can I do nothing to help you in your sorrow?" I cried jumping up from the seat in utter despair. "Tell me, Nastenka, wouldn't it be possible for me to go to him?"

"Would that be possible?" she asked suddenly, raising her head.

"No, of course not," I said pulling myself up; "but I tell you what, write a letter."

"No, that's impossible, I can't do that," she answered with decision, bending her head and not looking at me.

"How impossible—why is it impossible?" I went on, clinging to my idea. "But, Nastenka, it depends what sort of letter; there are letters and letters and . . . Ah, Nastenka, I am right; trust to me, trust to me, I will not give you bad advice. It can all be arranged! You took the first step—why not now?"

"I can't. I can't! It would seem as though I were forcing myself on him . . ."

"Ah, my good little Nastenka," I said, hardly able to conceal a smile; "no, no, you have a right to, in fact, because he made you a promise.

Besides, I can see from everything that he is a man of delicate feeling; that he behaved very well," I went on, more and more carried away by the logic of my own arguments and convictions. "How did he behave? He bound himself by a promise: he said that if he married at all he would marry no one but you; he gave you full liberty to refuse him at once . . . Under such circumstances you may take the first step; you have the right; you are in the privileged position—if, for instance, you wanted to free him from his promise . . ."

"Listen; how would you write?"

"Write what?"

"This letter."

"I tell you how I would write: 'Dear Sir . . .'"

"Must I really begin like that, 'Dear Sir'?"

"You certainly must! Though, after all, I don't know, I imagine . . ."

"Well, well, what next?"

"'Dear Sir,—I must apologize for—' But, no, there's no need to apologize; the fact itself justifies everything. Write simply":

I am writing to you. Forgive me my impatience; but I have been happy for a whole year in hope; am I to blame for being unable to endure a day of doubt now? Now that you have come, perhaps you have changed your mind. If so, this letter is to tell you that I do not repine, nor blame you. I do not blame you because I have no power over your heart, such is my fate!

You are an honourable man. You will not smile or be vexed at these impatient lines. Remember they are written by a poor girl; that she is alone; that she has no one to direct her, no one to advise her, and that she herself could never control her heart. But forgive me that a doubt has stolen—if only for one instant—into my heart. You are not capable of insulting, even in thought, her who so loved and so loves you.

"Yes, yes; that's exactly what I was thinking!" cried Nastenka, and her eyes beamed with delight. "Oh, you have solved my difficulties: God has sent you to me! Thank you, thank you!"

"What for? What for? For God's sending me?" I answered, looking delighted at her joyful little face. "Why, yes; for that too."

"Ah, Nastenka! Why, one thanks some people for being alive at the same time with one; I thank you for having met me, for my being able to remember you all my life!"

"Well, enough, enough! But now I tell you what, listen: we made an agreement then that as soon as he arrived he would let me know, by leaving a letter with some good simple people of my acquaintance who know nothing about it; or, if it were impossible to write a letter to me, for a letter does not always tell everything, he would be here at ten o'clock on the day he arrived, where we had arranged to meet. I know he has arrived already; but now it's the third day, and there's no sign of him and no letter. It's impossible for me to get away from grandmother in the morning. Give my letter tomorrow to those kind people I spoke to you about: they will send it on to him, and if there is an answer you bring it tomorrow at ten o'clock."

"But the letter, the letter! You see, you must write the letter first! So perhaps it must all be the day after tomorrow."

"The letter . . ." said Nastenka, a little confused, "the letter . . . but . . ."

But she did not finish. At first she turned her little face away from me, flushed like a rose, and suddenly I felt in my hand a letter which had evidently been written long before, all ready and sealed up. A familiar sweet and charming reminiscence floated through my mind.

"R, o—Ro; s, i—si; n, a—na," I began.

"Rosina!" we both hummed together; I almost embracing her with delight, while she blushed as only she could blush, and laughed through the tears which gleamed like pearls on her black eyelashes.

"Come, enough, enough! Goodbye now," she said speaking rapidly. "Here is the letter, here is the address to which you are to take it. Goodbye, till we meet again! Till tomorrow!"

She pressed both my hands warmly, nodded her head, and flew like an arrow down her side street. I stood still for a long time following her with my eyes.

"Till tomorrow! till tomorrow!" was ringing in my ears as she vanished from my sight.

THIRD NIGHT

Today was a gloomy, rainy day without a glimmer of sunlight, like the old age before me. I am oppressed by such strange thoughts, such gloomy

sensations; questions still so obscure to me are crowding into my brain—
and I seem to have neither power nor will to settle them. It's not for me to
settle all this!

Today we shall not meet. Yesterday, when we said goodbye, the clouds
began gathering over the sky and a mist rose. I said that tomorrow it would
be a bad day; she made no answer, she did not want to speak against her
wishes; for her that day was bright and clear, not one cloud should obscure
her happiness.

"If it rains we shall not see each other," she said, "I shall not come."

I thought that she would not notice today's rain, and yet she has not
come.

Yesterday was our third interview, our third white night . . .

But how fine joy and happiness makes any one! How brimming
over with love the heart is! One seems longing to pour out one's whole
heart; one wants everything to be gay, everything to be laughing. And
how infectious that joy is! There was such a softness in her words, such
a kindly feeling in her heart towards me yesterday . . . How solicitous
and friendly she was; how tenderly she tried to give me courage! Oh, the
coquetry of happiness! While I . . . I took it all for the genuine thing, I
thought that she . . .

But, my God, how could I have thought it? How could I have been so
blind, when everything had been taken by another already, when nothing
was mine; when, in fact, her very tenderness to me, her anxiety, her
love . . . yes, love for me, was nothing else but joy at the thought of seeing
another man so soon, desire to include me, too, in her happiness? . . .
When he did not come, when we waited in vain, she frowned, she grew
timid and discouraged. Her movements, her words, were no longer so
light, so playful, so gay; and, strange to say, she redoubled her attentiveness
to me, as though instinctively desiring to lavish on me what she desired
for herself so anxiously, if her wishes were not accomplished. My Nastenka
was so downcast, so dismayed, that I think she realized at last that I loved
her, and was sorry for my poor love. So when we are unhappy we feel the
unhappiness of others more; feeling is not destroyed but concentrated . . .

I went to meet her with a full heart, and was all impatience. I had
no presentiment that I should feel as I do now, that it would not all end
happily. She was beaming with pleasure; she was expecting an answer. The
answer was himself. He was to come, to run at her call. She arrived a whole

hour before I did. At first she giggled at everything, laughed at every word I said. I began talking, but relapsed into silence.

"Do you know why I am so glad," she said, "so glad to look at you?—why I like you so much today?"

"Well?" I asked, and my heart began throbbing.

"I like you because you have not fallen in love with me. You know that some men in your place would have been pestering and worrying me, would have been sighing and miserable, while you are so nice!"

Then she wrung my hand so hard that I almost cried out. She laughed.

"Goodness, what a friend you are!" she began gravely a minute later. "God sent you to me. What would have happened to me if you had not been with me now? How disinterested you are! How truly you care for me! When I am married we will be great friends, more than brother and sister; I shall care almost as I do for him . . ."

I felt horribly sad at that moment, yet something like laughter was stirring in my soul.

"You are very much upset," I said; "you are frightened; you think he won't come."

"Oh dear!" she answered; "if I were less happy, I believe I should cry at your lack of faith, at your reproaches. However, you have made me think and have given me a lot to think about; but I shall think later, and now I will own that you are right. Yes, I am somehow not myself; I am all suspense, and feel everything as it were too lightly. But hush! that's enough about feelings . . ."

At that moment we heard footsteps, and in the darkness we saw a figure coming towards us. We both started; she almost cried out; I dropped her hand and made a movement as though to walk away. But we were mistaken, it was not he.

"What are you afraid of? Why did you let go of my hand?" she said, giving it to me again. "Come, what is it? We will meet him together; I want him to see how fond we are of each other."

"How fond we are of each other!" I cried. ("Oh, Nastenka, Nastenka," I thought, "how much you have told me in that saying! Such fondness at *certain* moments makes the heart cold and the soul heavy. Your hand is cold, mine burns like fire. How blind you are, Nastenka! . . . Oh, how unbearable a happy person is sometimes! But I could not be angry with you!")

At last my heart was too full.

"Listen, Nastenka!" I cried. "Do you know how it has been with me all day."

"Why, how, how? Tell me quickly! Why have you said nothing all this time?"

"To begin with, Nastenka, when I had carried out all your commissions, given the letter, gone to see your good friends, then . . . then I went home and went to bed."

"Is that all?" she interrupted, laughing.

"Yes, almost all," I answered restraining myself, for foolish tears were already starting into my eyes. "I woke an hour before our appointment, and yet, as it were, I had not been asleep. I don't know what happened to me. I came to tell you all about it, feeling as though time were standing still, feeling as though one sensation, one feeling must remain with me from that time for ever; feeling as though one minute must go on for all eternity, and as though all life had come to a standstill for me . . . When I woke up it seemed as though some musical motive long familiar, heard somewhere in the past, forgotten and voluptuously sweet, had come back to me now. It seemed to me that it had been clamouring at my heart all my life, and only now . . ."

"Oh my goodness, my goodness," Nastenka interrupted, "what does all that mean? I don't understand a word."

"Ah, Nastenka, I wanted somehow to convey to you that strange impression . . ." I began in a plaintive voice, in which there still lay hid a hope, though a very faint one.

"Leave off. Hush!" she said, and in one instant the sly puss had guessed.

Suddenly she became extraordinarily talkative, gay, mischievous; she took my arm, laughed, wanted me to laugh too, and every confused word I uttered evoked from her prolonged ringing laughter . . . I began to feel angry, she had suddenly begun flirting.

"Do you know," she began, "I feel a little vexed that you are not in love with me? There's no understanding human nature! But all the same, Mr. Unapproachable, you cannot blame me for being so simple; I tell you everything, everything, whatever foolish thought comes into my head."

"Listen! That's eleven, I believe," I said as the slow chime of a bell rang out from a distant tower. She suddenly stopped, left off laughing and began to count.

"Yes, it's eleven," she said at last in a timid, uncertain voice.

I regretted at once that I had frightened her, making her count the strokes, and I cursed myself for my spiteful impulse; I felt sorry for her, and did not know how to atone for what I had done.

I began comforting her, seeking for reasons for his not coming, advancing various arguments, proofs. No one could have been easier to deceive than she was at that moment; and, indeed, any one at such a moment listens gladly to any consolation, whatever it may be, and is overjoyed if a shadow of excuse can be found.

"And indeed it's an absurd thing," I began, warming to my task and admiring the extraordinary clearness of my argument, "why, he could not have come; you have muddled and confused me, Nastenka, so that I too, have lost count of the time . . . Only think: he can scarcely have received the letter; suppose he is not able to come, suppose he is going to answer the letter, could not come before tomorrow. I will go for it as soon as it's light tomorrow and let you know at once. Consider, there are thousands of possibilities; perhaps he was not at home when the letter came, and may not have read it even now! Anything may happen, you know."

"Yes, yes!" said Nastenka. "I did not think of that. Of course anything may happen?" she went on in a tone that offered no opposition, though some other far-away thought could be heard like a vexatious discord in it. "I tell you what you must do," she said, "you go as early as possible tomorrow morning, and if you get anything let me know at once. You know where I live, don't you?"

And she began repeating her address to me.

Then she suddenly became so tender, so solicitous with me. She seemed to listen attentively to what I told her; but when I asked her some question she was silent, was confused, and turned her head away. I looked into her eyes—yes, she was crying.

"How can you? How can you? Oh, what a baby you are! what childishness! . . . Come, come!"

She tried to smile, to calm herself, but her chin was quivering and her bosom was still heaving.

"I was thinking about you," she said after a minute's silence. "You are so kind that I should be a stone if I did not feel it. Do you know what has occurred to me now? I was comparing you two. Why isn't he you? Why isn't he like you? He is not as good as you, though I love him more than you."

I made no answer. She seemed to expect me to say something.

"Of course, it may be that I don't understand him fully yet. You know I was always as it were afraid of him; he was always so grave, as it were so proud. Of course I know it's only that he seems like that, I know there is more tenderness in his heart than in mine . . . I remember how he looked at me when I went in to him—do you remember?—with my bundle; but yet I respect him too much, and doesn't that show that we are not equals?"

"No, Nastenka, no," I answered, "it shows that you love him more than anything in the world, and far more than yourself."

"Yes, supposing that is so," answered Nastenka naïvely. "But do you know what strikes me now? Only I am not talking about him now, but speaking generally; all this came into my mind some time ago. Tell me, how is it that we can't all be like brothers together? Why is it that even the best of men always seem to hide something from other people and to keep something back? Why not say straight out what is in one's heart, when one knows that one is not speaking idly? As it is everyone seems harsher than he really is, as though all were afraid of doing injustice to their feelings, by being too quick to express them."

"Oh, Nastenka, what you say is true; but there are many reasons for that," I broke in suppressing my own feelings at that moment more than ever.

"No, no!" she answered with deep feeling. "Here you, for instance, are not like other people! I really don't know how to tell you what I feel; but it seems to me that you, for instance . . . at the present moment . . . it seems to me that you are sacrificing something for me," she added timidly, with a fleeting glance at me. "Forgive me for saying so, I am a simple girl you know. I have seen very little of life, and I really sometimes don't know how to say things," she added in a voice that quivered with some hidden feeling, while she tried to smile; "but I only wanted to tell you that I am grateful, that I feel it all too . . . Oh, may God give you happiness for it! What you told me about your dreamer is quite untrue now—that is, I mean, it's not true of you. You are recovering, you are quite a different man from what you described. If you ever fall in love with someone, God give you happiness with her! I won't wish anything for her, for she will be happy with you. I know, I am a woman myself, so you must believe me when I tell you so."

She ceased speaking, and pressed my hand warmly. I too could not speak without emotion. Some minutes passed.

"Yes, it's clear he won't come tonight," she said at last raising her head. "It's late."

"He will come tomorrow," I said in the most firm and convincing tone.

"Yes," she added with no sign of her former depression. "I see for myself now that he could not come till tomorrow. Well, goodbye, till tomorrow. If it rains perhaps I shall not come. But the day after tomorrow, I shall come. I shall come for certain, whatever happens; be sure to be here, I want to see you, I will tell you everything."

And then when we parted she gave me her hand and said, looking at me candidly: "We shall always be together, shan't we?"

Oh, Nastenka, Nastenka! If only you knew how lonely I am now!

As soon as it struck nine o'clock I could not stay indoors, but put on my things, and went out in spite of the weather. I was there, sitting on our seat. I went to her street, but I felt ashamed, and turned back without looking at their windows, when I was two steps from her door. I went home more depressed than I had ever been before. What a damp, dreary day! If it had been fine I should have walked about all night . . .

But tomorrow, tomorrow! Tomorrow she will tell me everything. The letter has not come today, however. But that was to be expected. They are together by now . . .

FOURTH NIGHT

My God, how it has all ended! What it has all ended in! I arrived at nine o'clock. She was already there. I noticed her a good way off; she was standing as she had been that first time, with her elbows on the railing, and she did not hear me coming up to her.

"Nastenka!" I called to her, suppressing my agitation with an effort.

She turned to me quickly.

"Well?" she said. "Well? Make haste!"

I looked at her in perplexity.

"Well, where is the letter? Have you brought the letter?" she repeated clutching at the railing.

"No, there is no letter," I said at last. "Hasn't he been to you yet?" She turned fearfully pale and looked at me for a long time without moving. I had shattered her last hope.

"Well, God be with him," she said at last in a breaking voice; "God be with him if he leaves me like that."

She dropped her eyes, then tried to look at me and could not. For several minutes she was struggling with her emotion. All at once she turned away, leaning her elbows against the railing and burst into tears.

"Oh don't, don't!" I began; but looking at her I had not the heart to go on, and what was I to say to her?

"Don't try and comfort me," she said; "don't talk about him; don't tell me that he will come, that he has not cast me off so cruelly and so inhumanly as he has. What for—what for? Can there have been something in my letter, that unlucky letter?"

At that point sobs stifled her voice; my heart was torn as I looked at her.

"Oh, how inhumanly cruel it is!" she began again. "And not a line, not a line! He might at least have written that he does not want me, that he rejects me—but not a line for three days! How easy it is for him to wound, to insult a poor, defenceless girl, whose only fault is that she loves him! Oh, what I've suffered during these three days! Oh, dear! When I think that I was the first to go to him, that I humbled myself before him, cried, that I begged of him a little love! . . . and after that! Listen," she said, turning to me, and her black eyes flashed, "it isn't so! It can't be so; it isn't natural. Either you are mistaken or I; perhaps he has not received the letter? Perhaps he still knows nothing about it? How could any one—judge for yourself, tell me, for goodness' sake explain it to me, I can't understand it—how could any one behave with such barbarous coarseness as he has behaved to me? Not one word! Why, the lowest creature on earth is treated more compassionately. Perhaps he has heard something, perhaps someone has told him something about me," she cried, turning to me inquiringly: "What do you think?"

"Listen, Nastenka, I shall go to him tomorrow in your name."

"Yes?"

"I will question him about everything; I will tell him everything."

"Yes, yes?"

"You write a letter. Don't say no, Nastenka, don't say no! I will make him respect your action, he shall hear all about it, and if—"

"No, my friend, no," she interrupted. "Enough! Not another word, not another line from me—enough! I don't know him; I don't love him any more. I will . . . forget him."

Fyodor Dostoevsky

She could not go on.

"Calm yourself, calm yourself! Sit here, Nastenka," I said, making her sit down on the seat.

"I am calm. Don't trouble. It's nothing! It's only tears, they will soon dry. Why, do you imagine I shall do away with myself, that I shall throw myself into the river?"

My heart was full: I tried to speak, but I could not.

"Listen," she said taking my hand. "Tell me: you wouldn't have behaved like this, would you? You would not have abandoned a girl who had come to you of herself, you would not have thrown into her face a shameless taunt at her weak foolish heart? You would have taken care of her? You would have realized that she was alone, that she did not know how to look after herself, that she could not guard herself from loving you, that it was not her fault, not her fault—that she had done nothing . . . Oh dear, oh dear!"

"Nastenka!" I cried at last, unable to control my emotion. "Nastenka, you torture me! You wound my heart, you are killing me, Nastenka! I cannot be silent! I must speak at last, give utterance to what is surging in my heart!"

As I said this I got up from the seat. She took my hand and looked at me in surprise.

"What is the matter with you?" she said at last.

"Listen," I said resolutely. "Listen to me, Nastenka! What I am going to say to you now is all nonsense, all impossible, all stupid! I know that this can never be, but I cannot be silent. For the sake of what you are suffering now, I beg you beforehand to forgive me!"

"What is it? What is it?" she said drying her tears and looking at me intently, while a strange curiosity gleamed in her astonished eyes. "What is the matter?"

"It's impossible, but I love you, Nastenka! There it is! Now everything is told," I said with a wave of my hand. "Now you will see whether you can go on talking to me as you did just now, whether you can listen to what I am going to say to you." . . .

"Well, what then?" Nastenka interrupted me. "What of it? I knew you loved me long ago, only I always thought that you simply liked me very much . . . Oh dear, oh dear!"

"At first it was simply liking, Nastenka, but now, now! I am just in the same position as you were when you went to him with your bundle.

In a worse position than you, Nastenka, because he cared for no one else as you do."

"What are you saying to me! I don't understand you in the least. But tell me, what's this for; I don't mean what for, but why are you . . . so suddenly . . . Oh dear, I am talking nonsense! But you . . ."

And Nastenka broke off in confusion. Her cheeks flamed; she dropped her eyes.

"What's to be done, Nastenka, what am I to do? I am to blame. I have abused your . . . But no, no, I am not to blame, Nastenka; I feel that, I know that, because my heart tells me I am right, for I cannot hurt you in any way, I cannot wound you! I was your friend, but I am still your friend, I have betrayed no trust. Here my tears are falling, Nastenka. Let them flow, let them flow—they don't hurt anybody. They will dry, Nastenka."

"Sit down, sit down," she said, making me sit down on the seat. "Oh, my God!"

"No, Nastenka, I won't sit down; I cannot stay here any longer, you cannot see me again; I will tell you everything and go away. I only want to say that you would never have found out that I loved you. I should have kept my secret. I would not have worried you at such a moment with my egoism. No! But I could not resist it now; you spoke of it yourself, it is your fault, your fault and not mine. You cannot drive me away from you . . ."

"No, no, I don't drive you away, no!" said Nastenka, concealing her confusion as best she could, poor child.

"You don't drive me away? No! But I meant to run from you myself. I will go away, but first I will tell you all, for when you were crying here I could not sit unmoved, when you wept, when you were in torture at being—at being—I will speak of it, Nastenka—at being forsaken, at your love being repulsed, I felt that in my heart there was so much love for you, Nastenka, so much love! And it seemed so bitter that I could not help you with my love, that my heart was breaking and I . . . I could not be silent, I had to speak, Nastenka, I had to speak!"

"Yes, yes! tell me, talk to me," said Nastenka with an indescribable gesture. "Perhaps you think it strange that I talk to you like this, but . . . speak! I will tell you afterwards! I will tell you everything."

"You are sorry for me, Nastenka, you are simply sorry for me, my dear little friend! What's done can't be mended. What is said cannot be taken back. Isn't that so? Well, now you know. That's the starting-point.

Very well. Now it's all right, only listen. When you were sitting crying I thought to myself (oh, let me tell you what I was thinking!), I thought, that (of course it cannot be, Nastenka), I thought that you . . . I thought that you somehow . . . quite apart from me, had ceased to love him. Then—I thought that yesterday and the day before yesterday, Nastenka—then I would—I certainly would—have succeeded in making you love me; you know, you said yourself, Nastenka, that you almost loved me. Well, what next? Well, that's nearly all I wanted to tell you; all that is left to say is how it would be if you loved me, only that, nothing more! Listen, my friend— for any way you are my friend—I am, of course, a poor, humble man, of no great consequence; but that's not the point (I don't seem to be able to say what I mean, Nastenka, I am so confused), only I would love you, I would love you so, that even if you still loved him, even if you went on loving the man I don't know, you would never feel that my love was a burden to you. You would only feel every minute that at your side was beating a grateful, grateful heart, a warm heart ready for your sake . . . Oh Nastenka, Nastenka! What have you done to me?"

"Don't cry; I don't want you to cry," said Nastenka getting up quickly from the seat. "Come along, get up, come with me, don't cry, don't cry," she said, drying her tears with her handkerchief; "let us go now; maybe I will tell you something . . . If he has forsaken me now, if he has forgotten me, though I still love him (I do not want to deceive you) . . . but listen, answer me. If I were to love you, for instance, that is, if I only . . . Oh my friend, my friend! To think, to think how I wounded you, when I laughed at your love, when I praised you for not falling in love with me. Oh dear! How was it I did not foresee this, how was it I did not foresee this, how could I have been so stupid? But . . . Well, I have made up my mind, I will tell you."

"Look here, Nastenka, do you know what? I'll go away, that's what I'll do. I am simply tormenting you. Here you are remorseful for having laughed at me, and I won't have you . . . in addition to your sorrow . . . Of course it is my fault, Nastenka, but goodbye!"

"Stay, listen to me: can you wait?"

"What for? How?"

"I love him; but I shall get over it, I must get over it, I cannot fail to get over it; I am getting over it, I feel that . . . Who knows? Perhaps it will all end today, for I hate him, for he has been laughing at me, while you have been weeping here with me, for you have not repulsed me as he has, for you love me while he has never loved me, for in fact, I love you myself . . . Yes, I love you! I love you as you love me; I have told you so before, you heard it yourself—I love you because you are better than he is, because you are nobler than he is, because, because he—"

The poor girl's emotion was so violent that she could not say more; she laid her head upon my shoulder, then upon my bosom, and wept bitterly. I comforted her, I persuaded her, but she could not stop crying; she kept pressing my hand, and saying between her sobs: "Wait, wait, it will be over in a minute! I want to tell you . . . you mustn't think that these tears—it's nothing, it's weakness, wait till it's over." . . . At last she left off crying, dried her eyes and we walked on again. I wanted to speak, but she still begged me to wait. We were silent . . . At last she plucked up courage and began to speak.

"It's like this," she began in a weak and quivering voice, in which, however, there was a note that pierced my heart with a sweet pang; "don't think that I am so light and inconstant, don't think that I can forget and change so quickly. I have loved him for a whole year, and I swear by God that I have never, never, even in thought, been unfaithful to him . . . He has despised me, he has been laughing at me—God forgive him! But he has insulted me and wounded my heart. I . . . I do not love him, for I can only love what is magnanimous, what understands me, what is generous; for I am like that myself and he is not worthy of me—well, that's enough of him. He has done better than if he had deceived my expectations later, and shown me later what he was . . . Well, it's over! But who knows, my dear friend," she went on pressing my hand, "who knows, perhaps my whole love was a mistaken feeling, a delusion—perhaps it began in mischief, in nonsense, because I was kept so strictly by grandmother? Perhaps I ought to love another man, not him, a different man, who would have pity on me and . . . and . . . But don't let us say any more about that," Nastenka broke off, breathless with emotion, "I only wanted to tell you . . . I wanted to tell you that if, although I love him (no, did love him), if, in spite of this you still say . . . If you feel that your love is so great that it may at last drive from my heart my old feeling—if you will have pity on me—if you do not want to leave me alone to my fate, without hope, without consolation—if you are ready to love me always as you do now—I swear to you that gratitude . . . that my love will be at last worthy of your love . . . Will you take my hand?"

"Nastenka!" I cried breathless with sobs. "Nastenka, oh Nastenka!"

"Enough, enough! Well, now it's quite enough," she said, hardly able to control herself. "Well, now all has been said, hasn't it! Hasn't it! You are happy—I am happy too. Not another word about it, wait; spare me . . . talk of something else, for God's sake."

"Yes, Nastenka, yes! Enough about that, now I am happy. I—Yes, Nastenka, yes, let us talk of other things, let us make haste and talk. Yes! I am ready."

And we did not know what to say: we laughed, we wept, we said thousands of things meaningless and incoherent; at one moment we walked along the pavement, then suddenly turned back and crossed the road; then we stopped and went back again to the embankment; we were like children.

"I am living alone now, Nastenka," I began, "but tomorrow! Of course you know, Nastenka, I am poor, I have only got twelve hundred roubles, but that doesn't matter."

"Of course not, and granny has her pension, so she will be no burden. We must take granny."

"Of course we must take granny. But there's Matrona."

"Yes, and we've got Fyokla too!"

"Matrona is a good woman, but she has one fault: she has no imagination, Nastenka, absolutely none; but that doesn't matter."

"That's all right—they can live together; only you must move to us tomorrow."

"To you? How so? All right, I am ready."

"Yes, hire a room from us. We have a top floor, it's empty. We had an old lady lodging there, but she has gone away; and I know granny would like to have a young man. I said to her, 'Why a young man?' And she said, 'Oh, because I am old; only don't you fancy, Nastenka, that I want him as a husband for you.' So I guessed it was with that idea."

"Oh, Nastenka!"

And we both laughed.

"Come, that's enough, that's enough. But where do you live? I've forgotten."

"Over that way, near X bridge, Barannikov's Buildings."

"It's that big house?"

"Yes, that big house."

"Oh, I know, a nice house; only you know you had better give it up and come to us as soon as possible."

"Tomorrow, Nastenka, tomorrow; I owe a little for my rent there but that doesn't matter. I shall soon get my salary."

"And do you know I will perhaps give lessons; I will learn something myself and then give lessons."

"Capital! And I shall soon get a bonus."

"So by tomorrow you will be my lodger."

"And we will go to *The Barber of Seville*, for they are soon going to give it again."

"Yes, we'll go," said Nastenka, "but better see something else and not *The Barber of Seville*."

"Very well, something else. Of course that will be better, I did not think—"

As we talked like this we walked along in a sort of delirium, a sort of intoxication, as though we did not know what was happening to us. At one moment we stopped and talked for a long time at the same place; then we went on again, and goodness knows where we went; and again tears and again laughter. All of a sudden Nastenka would want to go home, and I would not dare to detain her but would want to see her to the house; we set off, and in a quarter of an hour found ourselves at the embankment by our seat. Then she would sigh, and tears would come into her eyes again; I would turn chill with dismay . . . But she would press my hand and force me to walk, to talk, to chatter as before.

"It's time I was home at last; I think it must be very late," Nastenka said at last. "We must give over being childish."

"Yes, Nastenka, only I shan't sleep tonight; I am not going home."

"I don't think I shall sleep either; only see me home."

"I should think so!"

"Only this time we really must get to the house."

"We must, we must."

"Honour bright? For you know one must go home some time!"

"Honour bright," I answered laughing.

"Well, come along!"

"Come along! Look at the sky, Nastenka. Look! Tomorrow it will be a lovely day; what a blue sky, what a moon! Look; that yellow cloud is covering it now, look, look! No, it has passed by. Look, look!"

But Nastenka did not look at the cloud; she stood mute as though turned to stone; a minute later she huddled timidly close up to me. Her hand trembled in my hand; I looked at her. She pressed still more closely to me.

At that moment a young man passed by us. He suddenly stopped, looked at us intently, and then again took a few steps on. My heart began throbbing.

"Who is it, Nastenka?" I said in an undertone.

"It's he," she answered in a whisper, huddling up to me, still more closely, still more tremulously . . . I could hardly stand on my feet.

"Nastenka, Nastenka! It's you!" I heard a voice behind us and at the same moment the young man took several steps towards us.

My God, how she cried out! How she started! How she tore herself out of my arms and rushed to meet him! I stood and looked at them, utterly crushed. But she had hardly given him her hand, had hardly flung herself into his arms, when she turned to me again, was beside me again in a flash, and before I knew where I was she threw both arms round my neck and gave me a warm, tender kiss. Then, without saying a word to me, she rushed back to him again, took his hand, and drew him after her.

I stood a long time looking after them. At last the two vanished from my sight.

MORNING

My night ended with the morning. It was a wet day. The rain was falling and beating disconsolately upon my window pane; it was dark in the room and grey outside. My head ached and I was giddy; fever was stealing over my limbs.

"There's a letter for you, sir; the postman brought it," Matrona said stooping over me.

"A letter? From whom?" I cried jumping up from my chair.

"I don't know, sir, better look—maybe it is written there whom it is from."

I broke the seal. It was from her!

***

"Oh, forgive me, forgive me! I beg you on my knees to forgive me! I deceived you and myself. It was a dream, a mirage . . . My heart aches for you today; forgive me, forgive me!

"Don't blame me, for I have not changed to you in the least. I told you that I would love you, I love you now, I more than love you. Oh, my God! If only I could love you both at once! Oh, if only you were he!"

["Oh, if only he were you," echoed in my mind. I remembered your words, Nastenka!]

"God knows what I would do for you now! I know that you are sad and dreary. I have wounded you, but you know when one loves a wrong is soon forgotten. And you love me.

"Thank you, yes, thank you for that love! For it will live in my memory like a sweet dream which lingers long after awakening; for I shall remember for ever that instant when you opened your heart to me like a brother and so generously accepted the gift of my shattered heart to care for it, nurse it, and heal it . . . If you forgive me, the memory of you will be exalted by a feeling of everlasting gratitude which will never be effaced from my soul . . . I will treasure that memory: I will be true to it, I will not betray it, I will not betray my heart: it is too constant. It returned so quickly yesterday to him to whom it has always belonged.

"We shall meet, you will come to us, you will not leave us, you will be for ever a friend, a brother to me. And when you see me you will give me your hand . . . yes? You will give it to me, you have forgiven me, haven't you? You love me *as before*?

"Oh, love me, do not forsake me, because I love you so at this moment, because I am worthy of your love, because I will deserve it . . . my dear! Next week I am to be married to him. He has come back in love, he has never forgotten me. You will not be angry at my writing about him. But I want to come and see you with him; you will like him, won't you?

Forgive me, remember and love your

NASTENKA."

***

I read that letter over and over again for a long time; tears gushed to my eyes. At last it fell from my hands and I hid my face.

"Dearie! I say, dearie—" Matrona began.

"What is it, Matrona?"

"I have taken all the cobwebs off the ceiling; you can have a wedding or give a party."

I looked at Matrona. She was still a hearty, *youngish* old woman, but I don't know why all at once I suddenly pictured her with lustreless eyes, a wrinkled face, bent, decrepit . . . I don't know why I suddenly pictured my room grown old like Matrona. The walls and the floors looked discoloured, everything seemed dingy; the spiders' webs were thicker than ever. I don't know why, but when I looked out of the window it seemed to me that the house opposite had grown old and dingy too, that the stucco on the columns was peeling off and crumbling, that the cornices were cracked and blackened, and that the walls, of a vivid deep yellow, were patchy.

Either the sunbeams suddenly peeping out from the clouds for a moment were hidden again behind a veil of rain, and everything had grown dingy again before my eyes; or perhaps the whole vista of my future flashed before me so sad and forbidding, and I saw myself just as I was now, fifteen years hence, older, in the same room, just as solitary, with the same Matrona grown no cleverer for those fifteen years.

But to imagine that I should bear you a grudge, Nastenka! That I should cast a dark cloud over your serene, untroubled happiness; that by my bitter reproaches I should cause distress to your heart, should poison it with secret remorse and should force it to throb with anguish at the moment of bliss; that I should crush a single one of those tender blossoms which you have twined in your dark tresses when you go with him to the altar . . . Oh never, never! May your sky be clear, may your sweet smile be bright and untroubled, and may you be blessed for that moment of blissful happiness which you gave to another, lonely and grateful heart!

My God, a whole moment of happiness! Is that too little for the whole of a man's life?

Leo Tolstoy

(1828–1910)

Where Love Is, There God Is Also

Translated by Nathan Haskell Dole

In the city lived the shoemaker, Martuin Avdyeitch. He lived in a basement, in a little room with one window. The window looked out on the street. Through the window he used to watch the people passing by; although only their feet could be seen, yet by the boots, Martuin Avdyeitch recognized the people. Martuin Avdyeitch had lived long in one place, and had many acquaintances. Few pairs of boots in his district had not been in his hands once and again. Some he would half-sole, some he would patch, some he would stitch around, and occasionally he would also put on new uppers. And through the window he often recognized his work.

Avdyeitch had plenty to do, because he was a faithful workman, used good material, did not make exorbitant charges, and kept his word. If it was possible for him to finish an order by a certain time, he would accept it; otherwise, he would not deceive you,—he would tell you so beforehand. And all knew Avdyeitch, and he was never out of work.

Avdyeitch had always been a good man; but as he grew old, he began to think more about his soul, and get nearer to God. Martuin's wife had died when he was still living with his master. His wife left him a boy three years old. None of their other children had lived. All the eldest had died in childhood. Martuin at first intended to send his little son to his sister in the village, but afterward he felt sorry for him; he thought to himself—

"It will be hard for my Kapitoshka to live in a strange family. I shall keep him with me."

And Avdyeitch left his master, and went into lodgings with his little son. But God gave Avdyeitch no luck with his children. As Kapitoshka grew older, he began to help his father, and would have been a delight to him, but a sickness fell on him, he went to bed, suffered a week, and died. Martuin buried his son, and fell into despair. So deep was this despair that he began to complain of God. Martuin fell into such a melancholy state, that more than once he prayed to God for death, and reproached God because He had not taken him who was an old man, instead of his beloved only son. Avdyeitch also ceased to go to church.

And once a little old man from the same district came from Troïtsa to see Avdyeitch; for seven years he had been wandering about. Avdyeitch talked with him, and began to complain about his sorrows.

"I have no desire to live any longer," he said, "I only wish I was dead. That is all I pray God for. I am a man without anything to hope for now."

And the little old man said to him—

"You don't talk right, Martuin, we must not judge God's doings. The world moves, not by our skill, but by God's will. God decreed for your son to die,—for you—to live. So it is for the best. And you are in despair, because you wish to live for your own happiness."

"But what shall one live for?" asked Martuin.

And the little old man said—

"We must live for God, Martuin. He gives you life, and for His sake you must live. When you begin to live for Him, you will not grieve over anything, and all will seem easy to you."

Martuin kept silent for a moment, and then said, "But how can one live for God?"

And the little old man said—

"Christ has taught us how to live for God. You know how to read? Buy a Testament, and read it; there you will learn how to live for God. Everything is explained there."

And these words kindled a fire in Avdyeitch's heart. And he went that very same day, bought a New Testament in large print, and began to read.

At first Avdyeitch intended to read only on holidays; but as he began to read, it so cheered his soul that he used to read every day. At times he would become so absorbed in reading, that all the kerosene in the lamp would burn out, and still he could not tear himself away. And so Avdyeitch used to read every evening.

And the more he read, the clearer he understood what God wanted of him, and how one should live for God; and his heart kept growing easier and easier. Formerly, when he lay down to sleep, he used to sigh and groan, and always thought of his Kapitoshka; and now his only exclamation was—

"Glory to Thee! glory to Thee, Lord! Thy will be done."

And from that time Avdyeitch's whole life was changed. In other days he, too, used to drop into a public-house as a holiday amusement, to drink a cup of tea; and he was not averse to a little brandy, either. He would take a drink with some acquaintance, and leave the saloon, not intoxicated, exactly, yet in a happy frame of mind, and inclined to talk nonsense, and shout, and use abusive language at a person. Now he left off that sort of thing. His life became quiet and joyful. In the morning he would sit down to work, finish his allotted task, then take the little lamp from the hook, put it on the table, get his book from the shelf, open it, and sit down to read. And the more he read, the more he understood, and the brighter and happier it grew in his heart.

Once it happened that Martuin read till late into the night. He was reading the Gospel of Luke. He was reading over the sixth chapter; and he was reading the verses—

"And unto him that smiteth thee on the one cheek offer also the other; and him that taketh away thy cloak forbid not to take thy coat also. Give to every man that asketh of thee; and of him that taketh away thy goods ask them not again. And as ye would that men should do to you, do ye also to them likewise."

He read farther also those verses, where God speaks:

"And why call ye me, Lord, Lord, and do not the things which I say? Whosoever cometh to me, and heareth my sayings, and doeth them, I will shew you to whom he is like: he is like a man which built an house, and digged deep, and laid the foundation on a rock: and when the flood arose, the stream beat vehemently upon that house, and could not shake it; for it was founded upon a rock. But he that heareth, and doeth not, is like a man that without a foundation built an house upon the earth; against which the stream did beat vehemently, and immediately it fell; and the ruin of that house was great."

Avdyeitch read these words, and joy filled his soul. He took off his spectacles, put them down on the book, leaned his elbows on the table, and became lost in thought. And he began to measure his life by these words. And he thought to himself—

"Is my house built on the rock, or on the sand? 'Tis well if on the rock. It is so easy when you are alone by yourself; it seems as if you had done everything as God commands; but when you forget yourself, you sin again. Yet I shall still struggle on. It is very good. Help me, Lord!"

Thus ran his thoughts; he wanted to go to bed, but he felt loath to tear himself away from the book. And he began to read farther in the seventh chapter. He read about the centurion, he read about the widow's son, he read about the answer given to John's disciples, and finally he came to that place where the rich Pharisee desired the Lord to sit at meat with him; and he read how the woman that was a sinner anointed His feet, and washed them with her tears, and how He forgave her. He reached the forty-fourth verse, and began to read—

"And he turned to the woman, and said unto Simon, Seest thou this woman? I entered into thine house, thou gavest me no water for my feet: but she hath washed my feet with tears, and wiped them with the hairs of her head. Thou gavest me no kiss: but this woman since the time I came in hath not ceased to kiss my feet. My head with oil thou didst not anoint: but this woman hath anointed my feet with ointment."

He finished reading these verses, and thought to himself—

"Thou gavest me no water for my feet, thou gavest me no kiss. My head with oil thou didst not anoint."

And again Avdyeitch took off his spectacles, put them down on the book, and again he became lost in thought.

"It seems that Pharisee must have been such a man as I am. I, too, apparently have thought only of myself,—how I might have my tea, be warm and comfortable, but never to think about my guest. He thought about himself, but there was not the least care taken of the guest. And who was his guest? The Lord Himself. If He had come to me, should I have done the same way?"

Avdyeitch rested his head upon both his arms, and did not notice that he fell asleep.

"Martuin!" suddenly seemed to sound in his ears.

Martuin started from his sleep—

"Who is here?"

He turned around, glanced toward the door—no one.

Again he fell into a doze. Suddenly, he plainly heard—

"Martuin! Ah, Martuin! look tomorrow on the street. I am coming."

Martuin awoke, rose from the chair, began to rub his eyes. He himself could not tell whether he heard those words in his dream, or in reality. He turned down his lamp, and went to bed.

At daybreak next morning, Avdyeitch rose, made his prayer to God, lighted the stove, put on the shchi and the kasha, put the water in the samovar, put on his apron, and sat down by the window to work.

And while he was working, he kept thinking about all that had happened the day before. It seemed to him at one moment that it was a dream, and now he had really heard a voice.

"Well," he said to himself, "such things have been."

Martuin was sitting by the window, and looking out more than he was working. When anyone passed by in boots which he did not know, he would bend down, look out of the window, in order to see, not only the feet, but also the face.

The dvornik passed by in new felt boots, the water-carrier passed by; then there came up to the window an old soldier of Nicholas's time, in an old pair of laced felt boots, with a shovel in his hands. Avdyeitch recognized him by his felt boots. The old man's name was Stepanuitch; and a neighbouring merchant, out of charity, gave him a home with him. He was required to assist the dvornik. Stepanuitch began to shovel away the snow from in front of Avdyeitch's window. Avdyeitch glanced at him, and took up his work again.

"Pshaw! I must be getting crazy in my old age," said Avdyeitch, and laughed at himself. "Stepanuitch is clearing away the snow, and I imagine that Christ is coming to see me. I was entirely out of my mind, old dotard that I am!"

Avdyeitch sewed about a dozen stitches, and then felt impelled to look through the window again. He looked out again through the window, and saw that Stepanuitch had leaned his shovel against the wall, and was warming himself, and resting. He was an old, broken-down man; evidently he had not strength enough even to shovel the snow. Avdyeitch said to himself—

"I will give him some tea; by the way, the samovar has only just gone out." Avdyeitch laid down his awl, rose from his seat, put the samovar on the table, poured out the tea, and tapped with his finger at the glass. Stepanuitch turned around, and came to the window. Avdyeitch beckoned to him, and went to open the door.

"Come in, warm yourself a little," he said. "You must be cold."

"May Christ reward you for this! my bones ache," said Stepanuitch.

Stepanuitch came in, and shook off the snow, tried to wipe his feet, so as not to soil the floor, but staggered.

"Don't trouble to wipe your feet. I will clean it up myself; we are used to such things. Come in and sit down," said Avdyeitch. "Here, drink a cup of tea."

And Avdyeitch lifted two glasses, and handed one to his guest; while he himself poured his tea into a saucer, and began to blow it.

Stepanuitch finished drinking his glass of tea, turned the glass upside down, put the half-eaten lump of sugar on it, and began to express his thanks. But it was evident he wanted some more.

"Have some more," said Avdyeitch, filling both his own glass and his guest's. Avdyeitch drank his tea, but from time to time glanced out into the street.

"Are you expecting anyone?" asked his guest.

"Am I expecting anyone? I am ashamed even to tell whom I expect. I am, and I am not, expecting someone; but one word has kindled a fire in my heart. Whether it is a dream, or something else, I do not know. Don't you see, brother, I was reading yesterday the Gospel about Christ the Batyushka; how He suffered, how He walked on the earth. I suppose you have heard about it?"

"Indeed I have," replied Stepanuitch; "but we are people in darkness, we can't read."

"Well, now, I was reading about that very thing,—how He walked on the earth; I read, you know, how He came to the Pharisee, and the Pharisee did not treat Him hospitably. Well, and so, my brother, I was reading yesterday, about this very thing, and was thinking to myself how he did not receive Christ, the Batyushka, with honour. Suppose, for example, He should come to me, or anyone else, I said to myself, I should not even know how to receive Him. And he gave Him no reception at all. Well! while I was thus thinking, I fell asleep, brother, and I heard someone call me by name. I got up; the voice, just as if someone whispered, said, 'Be on the watch; I shall come tomorrow.' And this happened twice. Well! would you believe it, it got into my head? I scolded myself—and yet I am expecting Him, the Batyushka."

Stepanuitch shook his head, and said nothing; he finished drinking his glass of tea, and put it on the side; but Avdyeitch picked up the glass again, and filled it once more.

"Drink some more for your good health. You see, I have an idea that, when the Batyushka went about on this earth, He disdained no one, and had more to do with the simple people. He always went to see the simple people. He picked out His disciples more from among folk like such sinners as we are, from the working class. Said He, whoever exalts himself, shall be humbled, and he who is humbled shall become exalted. Said He, you call me Lord, and, said He, I wash your feet. Whoever wishes, said He, to be the first, the same shall be a servant to all. Because, said He, blessed are the poor, the humble, the kind, the generous."

And Stepanuitch forgot about his tea; he was an old man, and easily moved to tears. He was listening, and the tears rolled down his face.

"Come, now, have some more tea," said Avdyeitch; but Stepanuitch made the sign of the cross, thanked him, turned down his glass, and arose.

"Thanks to you," he says, "Martuin Avdyeitch, for treating me kindly, and satisfying me, soul and body."

"You are welcome; come in again; always glad to see a friend," said Avdyeitch.

Stepanuitch departed; and Martuin poured out the rest of the tea, drank it up, put away the dishes, and sat down again by the window to work, to stitch on a patch. He kept stitching away, and at the same time looking through the window. He was expecting Christ, and was all the while thinking of Him and His deeds, and his head was filled with the different speeches of Christ.

Two soldiers passed by: one wore boots furnished by the crown, and the other one, boots that he had made; then the master of the next house passed by in shining galoshes; then a baker with a basket passed by. All passed by; and now there came also by the window a woman in woolen stockings and rustic bashmaks on her feet. She passed by the window, and stood still near the window-case.

Avdyeitch looked up at her from the window, and saw it was a stranger, a woman poorly clad, and with a child; she was standing by the wall with her back to the wind, trying to wrap up the child, and she had nothing to wrap it up in. The woman was dressed in shabby summer clothes; and from behind the frame, Avdyeitch could hear the child crying, and the woman trying to pacify it; but she was not able to pacify it.

Avdyeitch got up, went to the door, ascended the steps, and cried—

"My good woman. Hey! my good woman!"

The woman heard him and turned around.

"Why are you standing in the cold with the child? Come into my room, where it is warm; you can manage it better. Here, this way!"

The woman was astonished. She saw an old, old man in an apron, with spectacles on his nose, calling her to him. She followed him. They descended the steps and entered the room; the old man led the woman to his bed.

"There," says he, "sit down, my good woman, nearer to the stove; you can get warm, and nurse the little one."

"I have no milk for him. I myself have not eaten anything since morning," said the woman; but, nevertheless, she took the baby to her breast.

Avdyeitch shook his head, went to the table, brought out the bread and a dish, opened the oven door, poured into the dish some cabbage soup, took out the pot with the gruel, but it was not cooked as yet; so he filled the dish with shchi only, and put it on the table. He got the bread, took the towel down from the hook, and spread it upon the table.

"Sit down," he says, "and eat, my good woman; and I will mind the little one. You see, I once had children of my own; I know how to handle them."

The woman crossed herself, sat down at the table, and began to eat; while Avdyeitch took a seat on the bed near the infant. Avdyeitch kept smacking and smacking to it with his lips; but it was a poor kind of smacking, for he had no teeth. The little one kept on crying. And it occured to Avdyeitch to threaten the little one with his finger; he waved, waved his finger right before the child's mouth, and hastily withdrew it. He did not put it to its mouth, because his finger was black, and soiled with wax. And the little one looked at his finger, and became quiet; then it began to smile, and Avdyeitch also was glad. While the woman was eating, she told who she was, and whither she was going.

Said she—

"I am a soldier's wife. It is now seven months since they sent my husband away off, and no tidings. I lived out as cook; the baby was born; no one cared to keep me with a child. This is the third month that I have been struggling along without a place. I ate up all I had. I wanted to engage as a wet-nurse—no one would take me—I am too thin, they say. I have just been to the merchant's wife, where lives a young woman I know, and so they promised to take us in. I thought that was the end of it. But she told me to come next week. And she lives a long way off. I got tired out; and it tired him, too, my heart's darling. Fortunately, our landlady takes pity on us for the sake of Christ, and gives us a room, else I don't know how I should manage to get along."

Avdyeitch sighed, and said:

"Haven't you any warm clothes?"

"Now is the time, friend, to wear warm clothes; but yesterday I pawned my last shawl for a twenty-kopek piece."

The woman came to the bed, and took the child; and Avdyeitch rose, went to the partition, rummaged round, and succeeded in finding an old coat.

"Na!" says he; "It is a poor thing, yet you may turn it to some use."

The woman looked at the coat and looked at the old man; she took the coat, and burst into tears; and Avdyeitch turned away his head; crawling under the bed, he pushed out a little trunk, rummaged in it, and sat down again opposite the woman.

And the woman said—

"May Christ bless you, little grandfather! He must have sent me to your window. My little baby would have frozen to death. When I started out it was warm, but now it has grown cold. And He, the Batyushka, led you to look through the window and take pity on me, an unfortunate."

Avdyeitch smiled, and said—

"Indeed, He did that! I have been looking through the window, my good woman, for some wise reason."

And Martuin told the soldier's wife his dream, and how he heard the voice,—how the Lord promised to come and see him that day.

"All things are possible," said the woman. She rose, put on the coat, wrapped up her little child in it; and, as she started to take leave, she thanked Avdyeitch again.

"Take this, for Christ's sake," said Avdyeitch, giving her a twenty-kopek piece; "redeem your shawl."

She made the sign of the cross, and Avdyeitch made the sign of the cross and went with her to the door.

The woman went away. Avdyeitch ate some shchi, washed the dishes, and sat down again to work. While he was working he still remembered the window; when the window grew darker he immediately looked out to see who was passing by. Acquaintances passed by and strangers passed by, and there was nothing out of the ordinary.

But here Avdyeitch saw that an old apple woman had stopped in front of his window. She carried a basket with apples. Only a few were left, as she had evidently sold them nearly all out; and over her shoulder she had a bag full of chips. She must have gathered them up in some new building, and was on her way home. One could see that the bag was heavy on her shoulder; she tried to shift it to the other shoulder. So she lowered the bag on the sidewalk, stood the basket with the apples on a little post, and began to shake down the splinters in the bag. And while she was shaking her bag, a little boy in a torn cap came along, picked up an apple from the basket, and was about to make his escape; but the old woman noticed it, turned around, and caught the youngster by his sleeve. The little boy began to struggle, tried to tear himself away; but the old woman grasped him with both hands, knocked off his cap, and caught him by the hair.

The little boy was screaming, the old woman was scolding. Avdyeitch lost no time in putting away his awl; he threw it upon the floor, sprang to the door,—he even stumbled on the stairs, and dropped his spectacles,—and rushed out into the street.

The old woman was pulling the youngster by his hair, and was scolding and threatening to take him to the policeman; the youngster was defending himself, and denying the charge.

"I did not take it," he said; "What are you licking me for? Let me go!"

Avdyeitch tried to separate them. He took the boy by his arm, and said—

"Let him go, babushka; forgive him, for Christ's sake."

"I will forgive him so that he won't forget it till the new broom grows. I am going to take the little villain to the police."

Avdyeitch began to entreat the old woman—

"Let him go, babushka," he said, "he will never do it again. Let him go, for Christ's sake."

The old woman let him loose; the boy started to run, but Avdyeitch kept him back.

"Ask the babushka's forgiveness," he said, "and don't you ever do it again; I saw you take the apple."

The boy burst into tears, and began to ask forgiveness.

"There now! that's right; and here's an apple for you."

And Avdyeitch took an apple from the basket, and gave it to the boy. "I will pay you for it, babushka," he said to the old woman.

"You ruin them that way, the good-for-nothings," said the old woman. "He ought to be treated so that he would remember it for a whole week."

"Eh, babushka, babushka," said Avdyeitch, "that is right according to our judgment, but not according to God's. If he is to be whipped for an apple, then what ought to be done to us for our sins?"

The old woman was silent.

And Avdyeitch told her the parable of the master who forgave a debtor all that he owed him, and how the debtor went and began to choke one who owed him.

The old woman listened, and the boy stood listening.

"God has commanded us to forgive," said Avdyeitch, "else we, too, may not be forgiven. All should be forgiven, and the thoughtless especially."

The old woman shook her head, and sighed.

"That's so," said she; "but the trouble is that they are very much spoiled."

"Then we who are older must teach them," said Avdyeitch.

"That's just what I say," remarked the old woman. "I myself have had seven of them,—only one daughter is left."

And the old woman began to relate where and how she lived with her daughter, and how many grandchildren she had. "Here," she says, "my strength is only so-so, and yet I have to work. I pity the youngsters—my grandchildren—but what nice children they are! No one gives me such a welcome as they do. Aksintka won't go to anyone but me. 'Babushka, dear babushka, lovliest.'"

And the old woman grew quite sentimental.

"Of course, it is a childish trick. God be with him," said she, pointing to the boy.

The woman was just about to lift the bag up on her shoulder, when the boy ran up, and said—

"Let me carry it, babushka; it is on my way."

The old woman nodded her head, and put the bag on the boy's back.

And side by side they passed along the street.

And the old woman even forgot to ask Avdyeitch to pay for the apple. Avdyeitch stood motionless, and kept gazing after them; and he heard them talking all the time as they walked away. After Avdyeitch saw them disappear, he returned to his room; he found his eye-glasses on the stairs,— they were not broken; he picked up his awl, and sat down to work again.

After working a little while, it grew darker, so that he could not see to sew; he saw the lamplighter passing by to light the street-lamps.

"It must be time to make a light," he said to himself; so he got his little lamp ready, hung it up, and he took himself again to his work. He had one boot already finished; he turned it around, looked at it: "Well done." He put away his tools, swept off the cuttings, cleared off the bristles and ends, took the lamp, set it on the table, and took down the Gospels from the shelf. He intended to open the book at the very place where he had yesterday put a piece of leather as a mark, but it happened to open at another place; and the moment Avdyeitch opened the Testament, he recollected his last night's dream. And as soon as he remembered it, it seemed as if he heard someone stepping about behind him. Avdyeitch looked around, and saw—there, in the dark corner, it seemed as if people were standing; he was at a loss to know who they were. And a voice whispered in his ear—

"Martuin—ah, Martuin! did you not recognize me?"

"Who?" exclaimed Avdyeitch.

"Me," repeated the voice. "It was I;" and Stepanuitch stepped forth from the dark corner; he smiled, and like a little cloud faded away, and soon vanished.

"And it was I," said the voice.

From the dark corner stepped forth the woman with her child; the woman smiled, the child laughed, and they also vanished,

"And it was I," continued the voice; both the old woman and the boy with the apple stepped forward; both smiled and vanished.

Avdyeitch's soul rejoiced; he crossed himself, put on his spectacles, and began to read the Evangelists where it happened to open. On the upper part of the page he read—

"*For I was an hungered, and ye gave me meat; I was thirsty, and ye gave me drink; I was a stranger, and ye took me in.*"

And on the lower part of the page he read this—

"*Inasmuch as ye have done it unto one of the least of these my brethren, ye have done it unto me.*"—St. Matthew, Chap. xxv.

And Avdyeitch understood that his dream had not deceived him; that the Saviour really called on him that day, and that he really received Him.

How Much Land Does a Man Need?

Translated by Louise and Aylmer Maude

I

An elder sister came to visit her younger sister in the country. The elder was married to a tradesman in town, the younger to a peasant in the village. As the sisters sat over their tea talking, the elder began to boast of the advantages of town life: saying how comfortably they lived there, how well they dressed, what fine clothes her children wore, what good things they ate and drank, and how she went to the theatre, promenades, and entertainments.

The younger sister was piqued, and in turn disparaged the life of a tradesman, and stood up for that of a peasant.

"I would not change my way of life for yours," said she. "We may live roughly, but at least we are free from anxiety. You live in better style than we do, but though you often earn more than you need, you are very likely to lose all you have. You know the proverb, 'Loss and gain are brothers twain.' It often happens that people who are wealthy one day are begging their bread the next. Our way is safer. Though a peasant's life is not a fat one, it is a long one. We shall never grow rich, but we shall always have enough to eat."

The elder sister said sneeringly:

"Enough? Yes, if you like to share with the pigs and the calves! What do you know of elegance or manners! However much your good man may slave, you will die as you are living—on a dung heap—and your children the same."

"Well, what of that?" replied the younger. "Of course our work is rough and coarse. But, on the other hand, it is sure; and we need not bow to any one. But you, in your towns, are surrounded by temptations; today all may be right, but tomorrow the Evil One may tempt your husband with cards, wine, or women, and all will go to ruin. Don't such things happen often enough?"

Pahom, the master of the house, was lying on the top of the oven, and he listened to the women's chatter.

"It is perfectly true," thought he. "Busy as we are from childhood tilling Mother Earth, we peasants have no time to let any nonsense settle in our heads. Our only trouble is that we haven't land enough. If I had plenty of land, I shouldn't fear the Devil himself!"

The women finished their tea, chatted a while about dress, and then cleared away the tea-things and lay down to sleep.

But the Devil had been sitting behind the oven, and had heard all that was said. He was pleased that the peasant's wife had led her husband into boasting, and that he had said that if he had plenty of land he would not fear the Devil himself.

"All right," thought the Devil. "We will have a tussle. I'll give you land enough; and by means of that land I will get you into my power."

II

Close to the village there lived a lady, a small landowner, who had an estate of about three hundred acres. She had always lived on good terms with the peasants, until she engaged as her steward an old soldier, who took to burdening the people with fines. However careful Pahom tried to be, it happened again and again that now a horse of his got among the lady's oats, now a cow strayed into her garden, now his calves found their way into her meadows—and he always had to pay a fine.

Pahom paid, but grumbled, and, going home in a temper, was rough with his family. All through that summer Pahom had much trouble because of this steward; and he was even glad when winter came and the cattle had to be stabled. Though he grudged the fodder when they could no longer graze on the pasture-land, at least he was free from anxiety about them.

In the winter the news got about that the lady was going to sell her land, and that the keeper of the inn on the high road was bargaining for it. When the peasants heard this they were very much alarmed.

"Well," thought they, "if the innkeeper gets the land he will worry us with fines worse than the lady's steward. We all depend on that estate."

So the peasants went on behalf of their Commune, and asked the lady not to sell the land to the innkeeper; offering her a better price for it themselves. The lady agreed to let them have it. Then the peasants tried to arrange for the Commune to buy the whole estate, so that it might be held by all in common. They met twice to discuss it, but could not settle the matter; the Evil One sowed discord among them, and they could not agree. So they decided to buy the land individually, each according to his means; and the lady agreed to this plan as she had to the other.

Presently Pahom heard that a neighbour of his was buying fifty acres, and that the lady had consented to accept one half in cash and to wait a year for the other half. Pahom felt envious.

"Look at that," thought he, "the land is all being sold, and I shall get none of it." So he spoke to his wife.

"Other people are buying," said he, "and we must also buy twenty acres or so. Life is becoming impossible. That steward is simply crushing us with his fines."

So they put their heads together and considered how they could manage to buy it. They had one hundred roubles laid by. They sold a colt, and one half of their bees; hired out one of their sons as a labourer, and took his wages in advance; borrowed the rest from a brother-in-law, and so scraped together half the purchase money.

Having done this, Pahom chose out a farm of forty acres, some of it wooded, and went to the lady to bargain for it. They came to an agreement, and he shook hands with her upon it, and paid her a deposit in advance. Then they went to town and signed the deeds; he paying half the price down, and undertaking to pay the remainder within two years.

So now Pahom had land of his own. He borrowed seed, and sowed it on the land he had bought. The harvest was a good one, and within a year he had managed to pay off his debts both to the lady and to his brother-in-law. So he became a landowner, ploughing and sowing his own land, making hay on his own land, cutting his own trees, and feeding his cattle on his own pasture. When he went out to plough his fields, or to look at his growing corn, or at his grass meadows, his heart would fill with joy. The grass that grew and the flowers that bloomed there, seemed to him unlike any that grew elsewhere. Formerly, when he had passed by that land, it had appeared the same as any other land, but now it seemed quite different.

III

So Pahom was well contented, and everything would have been right if the neighbouring peasants would only not have trespassed on his corn-fields and meadows. He appealed to them most civilly, but they still went on: now the Communal herdsmen would let the village cows stray into his meadows; then horses from the night pasture would get among his corn. Pahom turned them out again and again, and forgave their owners, and for a long time he forbore from prosecuting any one. But at last he lost patience and complained to the District Court. He knew it was the peasants' want of land, and no evil intent on their part, that caused the trouble; but he thought:

"I cannot go on overlooking it, or they will destroy all I have. They must be taught a lesson."

So he had them up, gave them one lesson, and then another, and two or three of the peasants were fined. After a time Pahom's neighbours began to bear him a grudge for this, and would now and then let their cattle on his land on purpose. One peasant even got into Pahom's wood at night and cut down five young lime trees for their bark. Pahom passing through the wood one day noticed something white. He came nearer, and saw the stripped trunks lying on the ground, and close by stood the stumps, where the tree had been. Pahom was furious.

"If he had only cut one here and there it would have been bad enough," thought Pahom, "but the rascal has actually cut down a whole clump. If I could only find out who did this, I would pay him out."

He racked his brains as to who it could be. Finally he decided: "It must be Simon—no one else could have done it." So he went to Simon's homestead to have a look around, but he found nothing, and only had an angry scene. However he now felt more certain than ever that Simon had done it, and he lodged a complaint. Simon was summoned. The case was tried, and re-tried, and at the end of it all Simon was acquitted, there being no evidence against him. Pahom felt still more aggrieved, and let his anger loose upon the Elder and the Judges.

"You let thieves grease your palms," said he. "If you were honest folk yourselves, you would not let a thief go free."

So Pahom quarrelled with the Judges and with his neighbours. Threats to burn his building began to be uttered. So though Pahom had more land, his place in the Commune was much worse than before.

About this time a rumour got about that many people were moving to new parts.

"There's no need for me to leave my land," thought Pahom. "But some of the others might leave our village, and then there would be more room for us. I would take over their land myself, and make my estate a bit bigger. I could then live more at ease. As it is, I am still too cramped to be comfortable."

One day Pahom was sitting at home, when a peasant passing through the village, happened to call in. He was allowed to stay the night, and supper was given him. Pahom had a talk with this peasant and asked him where he came from. The stranger answered that he came from beyond the Volga, where he had been working. One word led to another, and the man went on to say that many people were settling in those parts. He told how some people from his village had settled there. They had joined the Commune, and had had twenty-five acres per man granted them. The land was so good, he said, that the rye sown on it grew as high as a horse, and so thick that five cuts of a sickle made a sheaf. One peasant, he said, had brought nothing with him but his bare hands, and now he had six horses and two cows of his own.

Pahom's heart kindled with desire. He thought:

"Why should I suffer in this narrow hole, if one can live so well elsewhere? I will sell my land and my homestead here, and with the money I will start afresh over there and get everything new. In this crowded place one is always having trouble. But I must first go and find out all about it myself."

Towards summer he got ready and started. He went down the Volga on a steamer to Samara, then walked another three hundred miles on foot, and at last reached the place. It was just as the stranger had said. The peasants had plenty of land: every man had twenty-five acres of Communal land given him for his use, and any one who had money could buy, besides, at fifty-cents an acre as much good freehold land as he wanted.

Having found out all he wished to know, Pahom returned home as autumn came on, and began selling off his belongings. He sold his land at a profit, sold his homestead and all his cattle, and withdrew from membership of the Commune. He only waited till the spring, and then started with his family for the new settlement.

IV

As soon as Pahom and his family arrived at their new abode, he applied for admission into the Commune of a large village. He stood treat to the Elders, and obtained the necessary documents. Five shares of Communal land were given him for his own and his sons' use: that is to say—125 acres (not altogether, but in different fields) besides the use of the Communal pasture. Pahom put up the buildings he needed, and bought cattle. Of the Communal land alone he had three times as much as at his former home, and the land was good corn-land. He was ten times better off than he had been. He had plenty of arable land and pasturage, and could keep as many head of cattle as he liked.

At first, in the bustle of building and settling down, Pahom was pleased with it all, but when he got used to it he began to think that even here he had not enough land. The first year, he sowed wheat on his share of the Communal land, and had a good crop. He wanted to go on sowing wheat, but had not enough Communal land for the purpose, and what he had already used was not available; for in those parts wheat is only sown on virgin soil or on fallow land. It is sown for one or two years, and then the land lies fallow till it is again overgrown with prairie grass. There were many who wanted such land, and there was not enough for all; so that people quarrelled about it. Those who were better off, wanted it for growing wheat, and those who were poor, wanted it to let to dealers, so that they might raise money to pay their taxes. Pahom wanted to sow more wheat; so he rented land from a dealer for a year. He sowed much wheat and had a fine crop, but the land was too far from the village—the wheat had to be carted more than ten miles. After a time Pahom noticed that some peasant-dealers were living on separate farms, and were growing wealthy; and he thought:

"If I were to buy some freehold land, and have a homestead on it, it would be a different thing, altogether. Then it would all be nice and compact."

The question of buying freehold land recurred to him again and again.

He went on in the same way for three years; renting land and sowing wheat. The seasons turned out well and the crops were good, so that he began to lay money by. He might have gone on living contentedly, but he grew tired of having to rent other people's land every year, and having to scramble for it. Wherever there was good land to be had, the peasants would rush for it and it was taken up at once, so that unless you were sharp about it you got none. It happened in the third year that he and a dealer together rented a piece of pasture land from some peasants; and they had already ploughed it up, when there was some dispute, and the peasants went to law about it, and things fell out so that the labour was all lost. "If it were my own land," thought Pahom, "I should be independent, and there would not be all this unpleasantness."

So Pahom began looking out for land which he could buy; and he came across a peasant who had bought thirteen hundred acres, but having got into difficulties was willing to sell again cheap. Pahom bargained and haggled with him, and at last they settled the price at 1,500 roubles, part in cash and part to be paid later. They had all but clinched the matter, when a passing dealer happened to stop at Pahom's one day to get a feed for his horse. He drank tea with Pahom, and they had a talk. The dealer said that he was just returning from the land of the Bashkirs, far away, where he had bought thirteen thousand acres of land all for 1,000 roubles. Pahom questioned him further, and the tradesman said:

"All one need do is to make friends with the chiefs. I gave away about one hundred roubles' worth of dressing-gowns and carpets, besides a case of tea, and I gave wine to those who would drink it; and I got the land for less than two cents an acre. And he showed Pahom the title-deeds, saying:

"The land lies near a river, and the whole prairie is virgin soil."

Pahom plied him with questions, and the tradesman said:

"There is more land there than you could cover if you walked a year, and it all belongs to the Bashkirs. They are as simple as sheep, and land can be got almost for nothing."

"There now," thought Pahom, "with my one thousand roubles, why should I get only thirteen hundred acres, and saddle myself with a debt besides. If I take it out there, I can get more than ten times as much for the money."

V

Pahom inquired how to get to the place, and as soon as the tradesman had left him, he prepared to go there himself. He left his wife to look after the homestead, and started on his journey taking his man with him. They stopped at a town on their way, and bought a case of tea, some wine, and other presents, as the tradesman had advised. On and on they went until they had gone more than three hundred miles, and on the seventh day they came to a place where the Bashkirs had pitched their tents. It was all just as the tradesman had said. The people lived on the steppes, by a river, in felt-covered tents. They neither tilled the ground, nor ate bread. Their cattle and horses grazed in herds on the steppe. The colts were tethered behind the tents, and the mares were driven to them twice a day. The mares were milked, and from the milk kumiss was made. It was the women who prepared kumiss, and they also made cheese. As far as the men were concerned, drinking kumiss and tea, eating mutton, and playing on their pipes, was all they cared about. They were all stout and merry, and all the summer long they never thought of doing any work. They were quite ignorant, and knew no Russian, but were good-natured enough.

As soon as they saw Pahom, they came out of their tents and gathered round their visitor. An interpreter was found, and Pahom told them he had come about some land. The Bashkirs seemed very glad; they took Pahom and led him into one of the best tents, where they made him sit on some down cushions placed on a carpet, while they sat round him. They gave him tea and kumiss, and had a sheep killed, and gave him mutton to eat. Pahom took presents out of his cart and distributed them among the Bashkirs, and divided amongst them the tea. The Bashkirs were delighted. They talked a great deal among themselves, and then told the interpreter to translate.

"They wish to tell you," said the interpreter, "that they like you, and that it is our custom to do all we can to please a guest and to repay him for his gifts. You have given us presents, now tell us which of the things we possess please you best, that we may present them to you."

"What pleases me best here," answered Pahom, "is your land. Our land is crowded, and the soil is exhausted; but you have plenty of land and it is good land. I never saw the like of it."

The interpreter translated. The Bashkirs talked among themselves for a while. Pahom could not understand what they were saying, but saw that they were much amused, and that they shouted and laughed. Then they were silent and looked at Pahom while the interpreter said:

"They wish me to tell you that in return for your presents they will gladly give you as much land as you want. You have only to point it out with your hand and it is yours."

The Bashkirs talked again for a while and began to dispute. Pahom asked what they were disputing about, and the interpreter told him that some of them thought they ought to ask their Chief about the land and not act in his absence, while others thought there was no need to wait for his return.

VI

While the Bashkirs were disputing, a man in a large fox-fur cap appeared on the scene. They all became silent and rose to their feet. The interpreter said, "This is our Chief himself."

Pahom immediately fetched the best dressing-gown and five pounds of tea, and offered these to the Chief. The Chief accepted them, and seated himself in the place of honour. The Bashkirs at once began telling him something. The Chief listened for a while, then made a sign with his head for them to be silent, and addressing himself to Pahom, said in Russian:

"Well, let it be so. Choose whatever piece of land you like; we have plenty of it."

"How can I take as much as I like?" thought Pahom. "I must get a deed to make it secure, or else they may say, 'It is yours,' and afterwards may take it away again."

"Thank you for your kind words," he said aloud. "You have much land, and I only want a little. But I should like to be sure which bit is mine. Could it not be measured and made over to me? Life and death are in God's hands. You good people give it to me, but your children might wish to take it away again."

"You are quite right," said the Chief. "We will make it over to you."

"I heard that a dealer had been here," continued Pahom, "and that you gave him a little land, too, and signed title-deeds to that effect. I should like to have it done in the same way."

The Chief understood.

"Yes," replied he, "that can be done quite easily. We have a scribe, and we will go to town with you and have the deed properly sealed."

"And what will be the price?" asked Pahom.

"Our price is always the same: one thousand roubles a day."

Pahom did not understand.

"A day? What measure is that? How many acres would that be?"

"We do not know how to reckon it out," said the Chief. "We sell it by the day. As much as you can go round on your feet in a day is yours, and the price is one thousand roubles a day."

Pahom was surprised.

"But in a day you can get round a large tract of land," he said.

The Chief laughed.

"It will all be yours!" said he. "But there is one condition: If you don't return on the same day to the spot whence you started, your money is lost."

"But how am I to mark the way that I have gone?"

"Why, we shall go to any spot you like, and stay there. You must start from that spot and make your round, taking a spade with you. Wherever you think necessary, make a mark. At every turning, dig a hole and pile up the turf; then afterwards we will go round with a plough from hole to hole. You may make as large a circuit as you please, but before the sun sets you must return to the place you started from. All the land you cover will be yours."

Pahom was delighted. It was decided to start early next morning. They talked a while, and after drinking some more kumiss and eating some more mutton, they had tea again, and then the night came on. They gave Pahom a feather-bed to sleep on, and the Bashkirs dispersed for the night, promising to assemble the next morning at daybreak and ride out before sunrise to the appointed spot.

VII

Pahom lay on the feather-bed, but could not sleep. He kept thinking about the land.

"What a large tract I will mark off!" thought he. "I can easily go thirty-five miles in a day. The days are long now, and within a circuit of thirty-five miles what a lot of land there will be! I will sell the poorer land, or let it to peasants, but I'll pick out the best and farm it. I will buy two ox-teams, and hire two more labourers. About a hundred and fifty acres shall be plough-land, and I will pasture cattle on the rest."

Pahom lay awake all night, and dozed off only just before dawn. Hardly were his eyes closed when he had a dream. He thought he was lying in that same tent, and heard somebody chuckling outside. He wondered who it could be, and rose and went out, and he saw the Bashkir Chief sitting in front of the tent holding his side and rolling about with laughter. Going nearer to the Chief, Pahom asked: "What are you laughing at?" But he saw that it was no longer the Chief, but the dealer who had recently stopped at his house and had told him about the land. Just as Pahom was going to ask, "Have you been here long?" he saw that it was not the dealer, but the peasant who had come up from the Volga, long ago, to Pahom's old home. Then he saw that it was not the peasant either, but the Devil himself with hoofs and horns, sitting there and chuckling, and before him lay a man barefoot, prostrate on the ground, with only trousers and a shirt on. And Pahom dreamt that he looked more attentively to see what sort of a man it was lying there, and he saw that the man was dead, and that it was himself! He awoke horror-struck.

"What things one does dream," thought he.

Looking round he saw through the open door that the dawn was breaking.

"It's time to wake them up," thought he. "We ought to be starting."

He got up, roused his man (who was sleeping in his cart), bade him harness; and went to call the Bashkirs.

"It's time to go to the steppe to measure the land," he said.

The Bashkirs rose and assembled, and the Chief came, too. Then they began drinking kumiss again, and offered Pahom some tea, but he would not wait.

"If we are to go, let us go. It is high time," said he.

VIII

The Bashkirs got ready and they all started: some mounted on horses, and some in carts. Pahom drove in his own small cart with his servant, and took a spade with him. When they reached the steppe, the morning red was beginning to kindle. They ascended a hillock (called by the Bashkirs a shikhan) and dismounting from their carts and their horses, gathered in one spot. The Chief came up to Pahom and stretched out his arm towards the plain:

"See," said he, "all this, as far as your eye can reach, is ours. You may have any part of it you like."

Pahom's eyes glistened: it was all virgin soil, as flat as the palm of your hand, as black as the seed of a poppy, and in the hollows different kinds of grasses grew breast high.

The Chief took off his fox-fur cap, placed it on the ground and said:

"This will be the mark. Start from here, and return here again. All the land you go round shall be yours."

Pahom took out his money and put it on the cap. Then he took off his outer coat, remaining in his sleeveless under coat. He unfastened his girdle and tied it tight below his stomach, put a little bag of bread into the breast of his coat, and tying a flask of water to his girdle, he drew up the tops of his boots, took the spade from his man, and stood ready to start. He considered for some moments which way he had better go—it was tempting everywhere.

"No matter," he concluded, "I will go towards the rising sun."

He turned his face to the east, stretched himself, and waited for the sun to appear above the rim.

"I must lose no time," he thought, "and it is easier walking while it is still cool."

The sun's rays had hardly flashed above the horizon, before Pahom, carrying the spade over his shoulder, went down into the steppe.

Pahom started walking neither slowly nor quickly. After having gone a thousand yards he stopped, dug a hole and placed pieces of turf one on another to make it more visible. Then he went on; and now that he had walked off his stiffness he quickened his pace. After a while he dug another hole.

Pahom looked back. The hillock could be distinctly seen in the sunlight, with the people on it, and the glittering tires of the cartwheels. At a rough guess Pahom concluded that he had walked three miles. It was growing warmer; he took off his under-coat, flung it across his shoulder, and went on again. It had grown quite warm now; he looked at the sun, it was time to think of breakfast.

"The first shift is done, but there are four in a day, and it is too soon yet to turn. But I will just take off my boots," said he to himself.

He sat down, took off his boots, stuck them into his girdle, and went on. It was easy walking now.

"I will go on for another three miles," thought he, "and then turn to the left. The spot is so fine, that it would be a pity to lose it. The further one goes, the better the land seems."

He went straight on a for a while, and when he looked round, the hillock was scarcely visible and the people on it looked like black ants, and he could just see something glistening there in the sun.

"Ah," thought Pahom, "I have gone far enough in this direction, it is time to turn. Besides I am in a regular sweat, and very thirsty."

He stopped, dug a large hole, and heaped up pieces of turf. Next he untied his flask, had a drink, and then turned sharply to the left. He went on and on; the grass was high, and it was very hot.

Pahom began to grow tired: he looked at the sun and saw that it was noon.

"Well," he thought, "I must have a rest."

He sat down, and ate some bread and drank some water; but he did not lie down, thinking that if he did he might fall asleep. After sitting a little while, he went on again. At first he walked easily: the food had strengthened him; but it had become terribly hot, and he felt sleepy; still he went on, thinking: "An hour to suffer, a lifetime to live."

He went a long way in this direction also, and was about to turn to the left again, when he perceived a damp hollow: "It would be a pity to leave that out," he thought. "Flax would do well there." So he went on past the hollow, and dug a hole on the other side of it before he turned the corner. Pahom looked towards the hillock. The heat made the air hazy: it seemed to be quivering, and through the haze the people on the hillock could scarcely be seen.

"Ah!" thought Pahom, "I have made the sides too long; I must make this one shorter." And he went along the third side, stepping faster. He looked at the sun: it was nearly half way to the horizon, and he had not yet done two miles of the third side of the square. He was still ten miles from the goal.

"No," he thought, "though it will make my land lopsided, I must hurry back in a straight line now. I might go too far, and as it is I have a great deal of land."

So Pahom hurriedly dug a hole, and turned straight towards the hillock.

IX

Pahom went straight towards the hillock, but he now walked with difficulty. He was done up with the heat, his bare feet were cut and bruised, and his legs began to fail. He longed to rest, but it was impossible if he meant to get back before sunset. The sun waits for no man, and it was sinking lower and lower.

"Oh dear," he thought, "if only I have not blundered trying for too much! What if I am too late?"

He looked towards the hillock and at the sun. He was still far from his goal, and the sun was already near the rim. Pahom walked on and on; it was very hard walking, but he went quicker and quicker. He pressed on, but was still far from the place. He began running, threw away his coat, his boots, his flask, and his cap, and kept only the spade which he used as a support.

"What shall I do," he thought again, "I have grasped too much, and ruined the whole affair. I can't get there before the sun sets."

And this fear made him still more breathless. Pahom went on running, his soaking shirt and trousers stuck to him, and his mouth was parched. His breast was working like a blacksmith's bellows, his heart was beating like a hammer, and his legs were giving way as if they did not belong to him. Pahom was seized with terror lest he should die of the strain.

Though afraid of death, he could not stop. "After having run all that way they will call me a fool if I stop now," thought he. And he ran on and on, and drew near and heard the Bashkirs yelling and shouting to him, and their cries inflamed his heart still more. He gathered his last strength and ran on.

The sun was close to the rim, and cloaked in mist looked large, and red as blood. Now, yes now, it was about to set! The sun was quite low, but he was also quite near his aim. Pahom could already see the people on the hillock waving their arms to hurry him up. He could see the fox-fur cap on the ground, and the money on it, and the Chief sitting on the ground holding his sides. And Pahom remembered his dream.

"There is plenty of land," thought he, "but will God let me live on it? I have lost my life, I have lost my life! I shall never reach that spot!"

Pahom looked at the sun, which had reached the earth: one side of it had already disappeared. With all his remaining strength he rushed on, bending his body forward so that his legs could hardly follow fast enough to keep him from falling. Just as he reached the hillock it suddenly grew dark. He looked up—the sun had already set. He gave a cry: "All my labour has been in vain," thought he, and was about to stop, but he heard the Bashkirs still shouting, and remembered that though to him, from below, the sun seemed to have set, they on the hillock could still see it. He took a long breath and ran up the hillock. It was still light there. He reached the top and saw the cap. Before it sat the Chief laughing and holding his sides. Again Pahom remembered his dream, and he uttered a cry: his legs gave way beneath him, he fell forward and reached the cap with his hands.

"Ah, what a fine fellow!" exclaimed the Chief. "He has gained much land!"

Pahom's servant came running up and tried to raise him, but he saw that blood was flowing from his mouth. Pahom was dead!

The Bashkirs clicked their tongues to show their pity.

His servant picked up the spade and dug a grave long enough for Pahom to lie in, and buried him in it. Six feet from his head to his heels was all he needed.

Ivan the Fool

Translated by Louise and Aylmer Maude

I

Once upon a time, in a certain province of a certain country, there lived a rich peasant, who had three sons: Simon the Soldier, Tarás the Stout, and Iván the Fool, besides an unmarried daughter, Martha, who was deaf and dumb. Simon the Soldier went to the wars to serve the king; Tarás the Stout went to a merchant's in town to trade, and Iván the Fool stayed at home with the lass, to till the ground till his back bent.

Simon the Soldier obtained high rank and an estate, and married a nobleman's daughter. His pay was large and his estate was large, but yet he could not make ends meet. What the husband earned his lady wife squandered, and they never had money enough.

So Simon the Soldier went to his estate to collect the income, but his steward said, "Where is any income to come from? We have neither cattle, nor tools, nor horse, nor plough, nor harrow. We must first get all these, and then the money will come."

Then Simon the Soldier went to his father and said: "You, father, are rich, but have given me nothing. Divide what you have, and give me a third part, that I may improve my estate."

But the old man said: "You brought nothing into my house; why should I give you a third part? It would be unfair to Iván and to the girl."

But Simon answered, "He is a fool; and she is an old maid, and deaf and dumb besides; what's the good of property to them?"

The old man said, "We will see what Iván says about it."

And Iván said, "Let him take what he wants."

So Simon the Soldier took his share of his father's goods and removed them to his estate, and went off again to serve the king.

Tarás the Stout also gathered much money, and married into a merchant's family, but still he wanted more. So he, also, came to his father and said, "Give me my portion."

But the old man did not wish to give Tarás a share either, and said, "You brought nothing here. Iván has earned all we have in the house, and why should we wrong him and the girl?"

But Tarás said, "What does he need? He is a fool! He cannot marry, no one would have him; and the dumb lass does not need anything either. Look here, Iván!" said he, "Give me half the corn; I don't want the tools, and of the livestock I will take only the grey stallion, which is of no use to you for the plough."

Iván laughed and said, "Take what you want. I will work to earn some more."

So they gave a share to Tarás also; and he carted the corn away to town, and took the grey stallion. And Iván was left with one old mare, to lead his peasant life as before, and to support his father and mother.

II

Now the old Devil was vexed that the brothers had not quarrelled over the division, but had parted peacefully; and he summoned three imps.

"Look here," said he, "there are three brothers: Simon the Soldier, Tarás the Stout, and Iván the Fool. They should have quarrelled, but are living peaceably and meet on friendly terms. The fool Iván has spoilt the whole business for me. Now you three go and tackle those three brothers, and worry them till they scratch each other's eyes out! Do you think you can do it?"

"Yes, we'll do it," said they.

"How will you set about it?"

"Why," said they, "first we'll ruin them. And when they haven't a crust to eat we'll tie them up together, and then they'll fight each other, sure enough!"

"That's capital; I see you understand your business. Go, and don't come back till you've set them by the ears, or I'll skin you alive!"

The imps went off into a swamp, and began to consider how they should set to work. They disputed and disputed, each wanting the lightest job; but at last they decided to cast lots which of the brothers each imp should tackle. If one imp finished his task before the others, he was to come and help them. So the imps cast lots, and appointed a time to meet again in the swamp to learn who had succeeded and who needed help.

The appointed time came round, and the imps met again in the swamp as agreed. And each began to tell how matters stood. The first, who had undertaken Simon the Soldier, began: "My business is going on well. Tomorrow Simon will return to his father's house."

His comrades asked, "How did you manage it?"

"First," says he, "I made Simon so bold that he offered to conquer the whole world for his king; and the king made him his general and sent him to fight the King of India. They met for battle, but the night before, I damped all the powder in Simon's camp, and made more straw soldiers for the Indian King than you could count. And when Simon's soldiers saw the straw soldiers surrounding them, they grew frightened. Simon ordered them to fire; but their cannons and guns would not go off. Then Simon's soldiers were quite frightened, and ran like sheep, and the Indian King slaughtered them. Simon was disgraced. He has been deprived of his estate, and tomorrow they intend to execute him. There is only one day's work left for me to do; I have just to let him out of prison that he may escape home. Tomorrow I shall be ready to help whichever of you needs me."

Then the second imp, who had Tarás in hand, began to tell how he had fared. "I don't want any help," said he, "my job is going all right. Tarás can't hold out for more than a week. First I caused him to grow greedy and fat. His covetousness became so great that whatever he saw he wanted to buy. He has spent all his money in buying immense lots of goods, and still continues to buy. Already he has begun to use borrowed money. His debts hang like a weight round his neck, and he is so involved that he can never get clear. In a week his bills come due, and before then I will spoil all his stock. He will be unable to pay and will have to go home to his father."

Then they asked the third imp (Iván's), "And how are you getting on?"

"Well," said he, "my affair goes badly. First I spat into his drink to make his stomach ache, and then I went into his field and hammered the ground hard as a stone that he should not be able to till it. I thought he wouldn't plough it, but like the fool that he is, he came with his plough and began to make a furrow. He groaned with the pain in his stomach, but went on ploughing. I broke his plough for him, but he went home, got out another, and again started ploughing. I crept under the earth and caught hold of the ploughshares, but there was no holding them; he leant heavily upon the plough, and the ploughshare was sharp and cut my hands. He has all but finished ploughing the field, only one little strip is left. Come, brothers, and help me; for if we don't get the better of him, all our labour is lost. If the fool holds out and keeps on working the land, his brothers will never know want, for he will feed them both."

Simon the Soldier's imp promised to come next day to help, and so they parted.

<h2 style="text-align:center">III</h2>

Iván had ploughed up the whole fallow, all but one little strip. He came to finish it. Though his stomach ached, the ploughing must be done. He freed the harness ropes, turned the plough, and began to work. He drove one furrow, but coming back the plough began to drag as if it had caught in a root. It was the imp, who had twisted his legs round the ploughshare and was holding it back.

"What a strange thing!" thought Iván. "There were no roots here at all, and yet here's a root."

Iván pushed his hand deep into the furrow, groped about, and, feeling something soft, seized hold of it and pulled it out. It was black like a root, but it wriggled. Why, it was a live imp!

"What a nasty thing!" said Iván, and he lifted his hand to dash it against the plough, but the imp squealed out:

"Don't hurt me, and I'll do anything you tell me to."

"What can you do?"

"Anything you tell me to."

Iván scratched his head.

"My stomach aches," said he; "can you cure that?"

"Certainly I can."

"Well then, do so."

The imp went down into the furrow, searched about, scratched with his claws, and pulled out a bunch of three little roots, which he handed to Iván.

"Here," says he, "whoever swallows one of these will be cured of any illness."

Iván took the roots, separated them, and swallowed one. The pain in his stomach was cured at once. The imp again begged to be let off; "I will jump right into the earth, and never come back," said he.

"All right," said Iván; "begone, and God be with you!"

And as soon as Iván mentioned God, the imp plunged into the earth like a stone thrown into the water. Only a hole was left.

Iván put the other two pieces of root into his cap and went on with his ploughing. He ploughed the strip to the end, turned his plough over, and went home. He unharnessed the horse, entered the hut, and there he saw his elder brother, Simon the Soldier and his wife, sitting at supper. Simon's estate had been confiscated, he himself had barely managed to escape from prison, and he had come back to live in his father's house.

Simon saw Iván, and said: "I have come to live with you. Feed me and my wife till I get another appointment."

"All right," said Iván, "you can stay with us."

But when Iván was about to sit down on the bench, the lady disliked the smell, and said to her husband: "I cannot sup with a dirty peasant."

So Simon the Soldier said, "My lady says you don't smell nice. You'd better go and eat outside."

"All right," said Iván; "any way I must spend the night outside, for I have to pasture the mare."

So he took some bread, and his coat, and went with the mare into the fields.

IV

Having finished his work that night, Simon's imp came, as agreed, to find Iván's imp and help him to subdue the fool. He came to the field and searched and searched; but instead of his comrade he found only a hole.

"Clearly," thought he, "some evil has befallen my comrade. I must take his place. The field is ploughed up, so the fool must be tackled in the meadow."

So the imp went to the meadows and flooded Iván's hayfield with water, which left the grass all covered with mud.

Iván returned from the pasture at dawn, sharpened his scythe, and went to mow the hayfield. He began to mow, but had only swung the scythe once or twice when the edge turned so that it would not cut at all, but needed resharpening. Iván struggled on for awhile, and then said: "It's no good. I must go home and bring a tool to straighten the scythe, and I'll get a chunk of bread at the same time. If I have to spend a week here, I won't leave till the mowing's done."

The imp heard this and thought to himself, "This fool is a tough 'un; I can't get round him this way. I must try some other dodge."

Iván returned, sharpened his scythe, and began to mow. The imp crept into the grass and began to catch the scythe by the heel, sending the point into the earth. Iván found the work very hard, but he mowed the whole meadow, except one little bit which was in the swamp. The imp crept into the swamp and, thought he to himself, "Though I cut my paws I will not let him mow."

Iván reached the swamp. The grass didn't seem thick, but yet it resisted the scythe. Iván grew angry and began to swing the scythe with all his might. The imp had to give in; he could not keep up with the scythe, and, seeing it was a bad business, he scrambled into a bush. Iván swung the scythe, caught the bush, and cut off half the imp's tail. Then he finished mowing the grass, told his sister to rake it up, and went himself to mow the rye. He went with the scythe, but the dock-tailed imp was there first, and entangled the rye so that the scythe was of no use. But Iván went home and got his sickle, and began to reap with that and he reaped the whole of the rye.

"Now it's time," said he, "to start on the oats."

The dock-tailed imp heard this, and thought, "I couldn't get the better of him on the rye, but I shall on the oats. Only wait till the morning."

In the morning the imp hurried to the oat field, but the oats were already mowed down! Iván had mowed them by night, in order that less grain should shake out. The imp grew angry.

"He has cut me all over and tired me out—the fool. It is worse than war. The accursed fool never sleeps; one can't keep up with him. I will get into his stacks now and rot them."

So the imp entered the rye, and crept among the sheaves, and they began to rot. He heated them, grew warm himself, and fell asleep.

Iván harnessed the mare, and went with the lass to cart the rye. He came to the heaps, and began to pitch the rye into the cart. He tossed two sheaves and again thrust his fork—right into the imp's back. He lifts the fork and sees on the prongs a live imp; dock-tailed, struggling, wriggling, and trying to jump.

"What, you nasty thing, are you here again?"

"I'm another," said the imp. "The first was my brother. I've been with your brother Simon."

"Well," said Iván, "whoever you are, you've met the same fate!"

He was about to dash him against the cart, but the imp cried out: "Let me off, and I will not only let you alone, but I'll do anything you tell me to do."

"What can you do?"

"I can make soldiers out of anything you like."

"But what use are they?"

"You can turn them to any use; they can do anything you please."

"Can they sing?"

"Yes, if you want them to."

"All right; you may make me some."

And the imp said, "Here, take a sheaf of rye, then bump it upright on the ground, and simply say:

"O sheaf! my slave
This order gave:
Where a straw has been
Let a soldier be seen!"

Iván took the sheaf, struck it on the ground, and said what the imp had told him to. The sheaf fell asunder, and all the straws changed into soldiers, with a trumpeter and a drummer playing in front, so that there was a whole regiment.

Iván laughed.

"How clever!" said he. "This is fine! How pleased the girls will be!"

"Now let me go," said the imp.

"No," said Iván, "I must make my soldiers of thrashed straw, otherwise good grain will be wasted. Teach me how to change them back again into the sheaf. I want to thrash it."

And the imp said, "Repeat:

"Let each be a straw
Who was soldier before,
For my true slave
This order gave!"

Iván said this, and the sheaf reappeared.

Again the imp began to beg, 'Now let me go!'

"All right." And Iván pressed him against the side of the cart, held him down with his hand, and pulled him off the fork.

"God be with you," said he.

And as soon as he mentioned God, the imp plunged into the earth like a stone into water. Only a hole was left.

Iván returned home, and there was his other brother, Tarás with his wife, sitting at supper.

Tarás the Stout had failed to pay his debts, had run away from his creditors, and had come home to his father's house. When he saw Iván, "Look here," said he, "till I can start in business again, I want you to keep me and my wife."

"All right," said Iván, "you can live here, if you like."

Iván took off his coat and sat down to table, but the merchant's wife said: "I cannot sit at table with this clown, he smells of perspiration."

Then Tarás the Stout said, "Iván, you smell too strong. Go and eat outside."

"All right," said Iván, taking some bread and going into the yard. "It is time, anyhow, for me to go and pasture the mare."

V

Tarás's imp, being also free that night, came, as agreed, to help his comrades subdue Iván the Fool. He came to the cornfield, looked and looked for his comrades—no one was there. He only found a hole. He went to the meadow, and there he found an imp's tail in the swamp, and another hole in the rye stubble.

"Evidently, some ill-luck has befallen my comrades," thought he. "I must take their place and tackle the fool."

So the imp went to look for Iván, who had already stacked the corn and was cutting trees in the wood. The two brothers had begun to feel crowded, living together, and had told Iván to cut down trees to build new houses for them.

The imp ran to the wood, climbed among the branches, and began to hinder Iván from felling the trees. Iván undercut one tree so that it should fall clear, but in falling it turned askew and caught among some branches. Iván cut a pole with which to lever it aside, and with difficulty contrived to bring it to the ground. He set to work to fell another tree—again the same thing occurred; and with all his efforts he could hardly get the tree clear. He began on a third tree, and again the same thing happened.

Iván had hoped to cut down half a hundred small trees, but had not felled even half a score, and now the night was come and he was tired out. The steam from him spread like a mist through the wood, but still he stuck to his work. He undercut another tree, but his back began to ache so that he could not stand. He drove his axe into the tree and sat down to rest.

The imp, noticing that Iván had stopped work, grew cheerful.

"At last," thought he, "he is tired out! He will give it up. Now I can take a rest myself."

He seated himself astride a branch and chuckled. But soon Iván got up, pulled the axe out, swung it, and smote the tree from the opposite side with such force that the tree gave way at once and came crashing down. The imp had not expected this, and had no time to get his feet clear, and the tree in breaking, gripped his paw. Iván began to lop off the branches, when he noticed a live imp hanging in the tree! Iván was surprised.

"What, you nasty thing," says he, "so you are here again!"

"I am another one," says the imp. "I have been with your brother Tarás."

"Whoever you are, you have met your fate," said Iván, and swinging his axe he was about to strike him with the haft, but the imp begged for mercy: "Don't strike me," said he, "and I will do anything you tell me to."

"What can you do?"

"I can make money for you, as much as you want."

"All right, make some." So the imp showed him how to do it.

"Take," said he, "some leaves from this oak and rub them in your hands, and gold will fall out on the ground."

Iván took some leaves and rubbed them, and gold ran down from his hands.

"This stuff will do fine," said he, "for the fellows to play with on their holidays."

"Now let me go," said the imp.

"All right," said Iván, and taking a lever he set the imp free. "Now begone! And God be with you," says he.

And as soon as he mentioned God, the imp plunged into the earth, like a stone into water. Only a hole was left.

VI

So the brothers built houses, and began to live apart; and Iván finished the harvest work, brewed beer, and invited his brothers to spend the next holiday with him. His brothers would not come.

"We don't care about peasant feasts," said they.

So Iván entertained the peasants and their wives, and drank until he was rather tipsy. Then he went into the street to a ring of dancers; and going up to them he told the women to sing a song in his honour; "for," said he, "I will give you something you never saw in your lives before!"

The women laughed and sang his praises, and when they had finished they said, "Now let us have your gift."

"I will bring it directly," said he.

He took a seed-basket and ran into the woods. The women laughed. "He is a fool!" said they, and they began to talk of something else.

But soon Iván came running back, carrying the basket full of something heavy.

"Shall I give it you?"

"Yes! give it to us."

Iván took a handful of gold and threw it to the women. You should have seen them throw themselves upon it to pick it up! And the men around scrambled for it, and snatched it from one another. One old woman was nearly crushed to death. Iván laughed.

"Oh, you fools!" says he. "Why did you crush the old grandmother? Be quiet, and I will give you some more," and he threw them some more. The people all crowded round, and Iván threw them all the gold he had. They asked for more, but Iván said, "I have no more just now. Another time I'll give you some more. Now let us dance, and you can sing me your songs."

The women began to sing.

"Your songs are no good," says he.

"Where will you find better ones?" say they.

"I'll soon show you," says he.

He went to the barn, took a sheaf, thrashed it, stood it up, and bumped it on the ground.

"Now," said he:

> "O sheaf! my slave
> This order gave:
> Where a straw has been
> Let a soldier be seen!"

And the sheaf fell asunder and became so many soldiers. The drums and trumpets began to play. Iván ordered the soldiers to play and sing. He led them out into the street, and the people were amazed. The soldiers played and sang, and then Iván (forbidding any one to follow him) led them back to the thrashing ground, changed them into a sheaf again, and threw it in its place.

He then went home and lay down in the stables to sleep.

VII

Simon the Soldier heard of all these things next morning, and went to his brother.

"Tell me," says he, "where you got those soldiers from, and where you have taken them to?"

"What does it matter to you?" said Iván.

"What does it matter? Why, with soldiers one can do anything. One can win a kingdom."

Iván wondered.

"Really!" said he; "Why didn't you say so before? I'll make you as many as you like. It's well the lass and I have thrashed so much straw."

Iván took his brother to the barn and said:

"Look here; if I make you some soldiers, you must take them away at once, for if we have to feed them, they will eat up the whole village in a day."

Simon the Soldier promised to lead the soldiers away; and Iván began to make them. He bumped a sheaf on the thrashing floor—a company appeared. He bumped another sheaf, and there was a second company. He made so many that they covered the field.

"Will that do?" he asked.

Simon was overjoyed, and said: "That will do! Thank you, Iván!"

"All right," said Iván. "If you want more, come back, and I'll make them. There is plenty of straw this season."

Simon the Soldier at once took command of his army, collected and organized it, and went off to make war.

Hardly had Simon the Soldier gone, when Tarás the Stout came along. He, too, had heard of yesterday's affair, and he said to his brother:

"Show me where you get gold money! If I only had some to start with, I could make it bring me in money from all over the world."

Iván was astonished.

"Really!" said he. "You should have told me sooner. I will make you as much as you like."

His brother was delighted.

"Give me three baskets-full to begin with."

"All right," said Iván. "Come into the forest; or better still, let us harness the mare, for you won't be able to carry it all."

They drove to the forest, and Iván began to rub the oak leaves. He made a great heap of gold.

"Will that do?"

Tarás was overjoyed.

"It will do for the present," said he. "Thank you, Iván!"

"All right," says Iván, "if you want more, come back for it. There are plenty of leaves left."

Tarás the Stout gathered up a whole cartload of money, and went off to trade.

So the two brothers went away: Simon to fight, and Tarás to buy and sell. And Simon the Soldier conquered a kingdom for himself; and Tarás the Stout made much money in trade.

When the two brothers met, each told the other: Simon how he got the soldiers, and Tarás how he got the money. And Simon the Soldier said to his brother, "I have conquered a kingdom and live in grand style, but I have not money enough to keep my soldiers."

And Tarás the Stout said, "And I have made much money, but the trouble is, I have no one to guard it."

Then said Simon the Soldier, "Let us go to our brother. I will tell him to make more soldiers, and will give them to you to guard your money, and you can tell him to make money for me to feed my men."

And they drove away to Iván; and Simon said, "Dear brother, I have not enough soldiers; make me another couple of ricks or so."

Iván shook his head.

"No!" says he, "I will not make any more soldiers."

"But you promised you would."

"I know I promised, but I won't make any more."

"But why not, fool?"

"Because your soldiers killed a man. I was ploughing the other day near the road, and I saw a woman taking a coffin along in a cart, and crying. I asked her who was dead. She said, 'Simon's soldiers have killed my husband in the war.' I thought the soldiers would only play tunes, but they have killed a man. I won't give you any more."

And he stuck to it, and would not make any more soldiers.

Tarás the Stout, too, began to beg Iván to make him more gold money. But Iván shook his head.

"No, I won't make any more," said he.

"Didn't you promise?"

"I did, but I'll make no more," said he.

"Why not, fool?"

"Because your gold coins took away the cow from Michael's daughter."

"How?"

"Simply took it away! Michael's daughter had a cow. Her children used to drink the milk. But the other day her children came to me to ask for milk. I said, 'Where's your cow?' They answered, 'The steward of Tarás the Stout came and gave mother three bits of gold, and she gave him the cow, so we have nothing to drink.' I thought you were only going to play with the gold pieces, but you have taken the children's cow away. I will not give you any more."

And Iván stuck to it and would not give him any more. So the brothers went away. And as they went they discussed how they could meet their difficulties. And Simon said:

"Look here, I tell you what to do. You give me money to feed my soldiers, and I will give you half my kingdom with soldiers enough to guard your money." Tarás agreed. So the brothers divided what they possessed, and both became kings, and both were rich.

VIII

Iván lived at home, supporting his father and mother and working in the fields with his dumb sister. Now it happened that Iván's yard-dog fell sick, grew mangy, and was near dying. Iván, pitying it, got some bread from his sister, put it in his cap, carried it out, and threw it to the dog. But the cap was torn, and together with the bread one of the little roots fell to the ground. The old dog ate it up with the bread, and as soon as she had swallowed it she jumped up and began to play, bark, and wag her tail—in short became quite well again.

The father and mother saw it and were amazed.

"How did you cure the dog?" asked they.

Iván answered: "I had two little roots to cure any pain, and she swallowed one."

Now about that time it happened that the King's daughter fell ill, and the King proclaimed in every town and village, that he would reward any one who could heal her, and if any unmarried man could heal the King's daughter he should have her for his wife. This was proclaimed in Iván's village as well as everywhere else.

His father and mother called Iván, and said to him: "Have you heard what the King has proclaimed? You said you had a root that would cure any sickness. Go and heal the King's daughter, and you will be made happy for life."

"All right," said he.

And Iván prepared to go, and they dressed him in his best. But as he went out of the door he met a beggar woman with a crippled hand.

"I have heard," said she, "that you can heal people. I pray you cure my arm, for I cannot even put on my boots myself."

"All right," said Iván, and giving the little root to the beggar woman he told her to swallow it. She swallowed it, and was cured. She was at once able to move her arm freely.

His father and mother came out to accompany Iván to the King, but when they heard that he had given away the root, and that he had nothing left to cure the King's daughter with, they began to scold him.

"You pity a beggar woman, but are not sorry for the King's daughter!" said they. But Iván felt sorry for the King's daughter also. So he harnessed the horse, put straw in the cart to sit on, and sat down to drive away.

"Where are you going, fool?"

"To cure the King's daughter."

"But you've nothing left to cure her with?"

"Never mind," said he, and drove off.

He drove to the King's palace, and as soon as he stepped on the threshold the King's daughter got well.

The King was delighted, and had Iván brought to him, and had him dressed in fine robes.

"Be my son-in-law," said he.

"All right," said Iván.

And Iván married the Princess. Her father died soon after, and Iván became King. So all three brothers were now kings.

IX

The three brothers lived and reigned. The eldest brother, Simon the Soldier, prospered. With his straw soldiers he levied real soldiers. He ordered throughout his whole kingdom a levy of one soldier from every ten houses, and each soldier had to be tall, and clean in body and in face. He gathered many such soldiers and trained them; and when any one opposed him, he sent these soldiers at once, and got his own way, so that everyone began to fear him, and his life was a comfortable one. Whatever he cast his eyes on and wished for, was his. He sent soldiers, and they brought him all he desired.

Tarás the Stout also lived comfortably. He did not waste the money he got from Iván, but increased it largely. He introduced law and order into his kingdom. He kept his money in coffers, and taxed the people. He instituted a poll-tax, tolls for walking and driving, and a tax on shoes and stockings and dress trimmings. And whatever he wished for he got. For the sake of money, people brought him everything, and they offered to work for him—for everyone wanted money.

Iván the Fool, also, did not live badly. As soon as he had buried his father-in-law, he took off all his royal robes and gave them to his wife to put away in a chest; and he again donned his hempen shirt, his breeches and peasant shoes, and started again to work.

"It's dull for me," said he. "I'm getting fat and have lost my appetite and my sleep." So he brought his father and mother and his dumb sister to live with him, and worked as before.

People said, "But you are a king!"

"Yes," said he, "but even a king must eat."

One of his ministers came to him and said, "We have no money to pay salaries."

"All right," says he, "then don't pay them."

"Then no one will serve."

"All right; let them not serve. They will have more time to work; let them cart manure. There is plenty of scavenging to be done."

And people came to Iván to be tried. One said, "He stole my money." And Iván said, "All right, that shows that he wanted it."

And they all got to know that Iván was a fool. And his wife said to him, "People say that you are a fool."

"All right," said Iván.

His wife thought and thought about it, but she also was a fool.

"Shall I go against my husband? Where the needle goes the thread follows," said she.

So she took off her royal dress, put it away in a chest, and went to the dumb girl to learn to work. And she learned to work and began to help her husband.

And all the wise men left Iván's kingdom; only the fools remained.

Nobody had money. They lived and worked. They fed themselves; and they fed others.

X

The old Devil waited and waited for news from the imps of their having ruined the three brothers. But no news came. So he went himself to inquire about it. He searched and searched, but instead of finding the three imps he found only the three holes.

"Evidently they have failed," thought he. "I shall have to tackle it myself."

So he went to look for the brothers, but they were no longer in their old places. He found them in three different kingdoms. All three were living and reigning. This annoyed the old Devil very much.

"Well," said he, "I must try my own hand at the job."

First he went to King Simon. He did not go to him in his own shape, but disguised himself as a general, and drove to Simon's palace.

"I hear, King Simon," said he, "that you are a great warrior, and as I know that business well, I desire to serve you."

King Simon questioned him, and seeing that he was a wise man, took him into his service.

The new commander began to teach King Simon how to form a strong army.

"First," said he, "we must levy more soldiers, for there are in your kingdom many people unemployed. We must recruit all the young men without exception. Then you will have five times as many soldiers as formerly. Secondly, we must get new rifles and cannons. I will introduce rifles that will fire a hundred balls at once; they will fly out like peas. And I will get cannons that will consume with fire either man, or horse, or wall. They will burn up everything!"

Simon the King listened to the new commander, ordered all young men without exception to be enrolled as soldiers, and had new factories built in which he manufactured large quantities of improved rifles and cannons. Then he made haste to declare war against a neighbouring king. As soon as he met the other army, King Simon ordered his soldiers to rain balls against it and shoot fire from the cannons, and at one blow he burned and crippled half the enemy's army. The neighbouring king was so thoroughly frightened that he gave way and surrendered his kingdom. King Simon was delighted.

"Now," said he, "I will conquer the King of India."

But the Indian King had heard about King Simon, and had adopted all his inventions, and added more of his own. The Indian King enlisted not only all the young men, but all the single women also, and got together a greater army even than King Simon's. And he copied all King Simon's rifles and cannons, and invented a way of flying through the air to throw explosive bombs from above.

King Simon set out to fight the Indian King, expecting to beat him as he had beaten the other king; but the scythe that had cut so well had lost its edge. The King of India did not let Simon's army come within gunshot, but sent his women through the air to hurl down explosive bombs on to Simon's army. The women began to rain down bombs on to the army like borax upon cockroaches. The army ran away, and Simon the King was left alone. So the Indian King took Simon's kingdom, and Simon the Soldier fled as best he might.

Having finished with this brother, the old Devil went to King Tarás. Changing himself into a merchant, he settled in Tarás's kingdom, started a house of business, and began spending money. He paid high prices for everything, and everybody hurried to the new merchant's to get money. And so much money spread among the people that they began to pay all their taxes promptly, and paid up all their arrears, and King Tarás rejoiced.

"Thanks to the new merchant," thought he, "I shall have more money than ever; and my life will be yet more comfortable."

And Tarás the King began to form fresh plans, and began to build a new palace. He gave notice that people should bring him wood and stone, and come to work, and he fixed high prices for everything. King Tarás thought people would come in crowds to work as before, but to his surprise all the wood and stone was taken to the merchant's, and all the workmen went there too. King Tarás increased his price, but the merchant bid yet more. King Tarás had much money, but the merchant had still more, and outbid the King at every point.

The King's palace was at a standstill; the building did not get on.

King Tarás planned a garden, and when autumn came he called for the people to come and plant the garden, but nobody came. All the people were engaged digging a pond for the merchant. Winter came, and King Tarás wanted to buy sable furs for a new overcoat. He sent to buy them, but the messengers returned and said, "There are no sables left. The merchant has all the furs. He gave the best price, and made carpets of the skins."

King Tarás wanted to buy some stallions. He sent to buy them, but the messengers returned saying, "The merchant has all the good stallions; they are carrying water to fill his pond."

All the King's affairs came to a standstill. Nobody would work for him, for everyone was busy working for the merchant; and they only brought King Tarás the merchant's money to pay their taxes.

And the King collected so much money that he had nowhere to store it, and his life became wretched. He ceased to form plans, and would have been glad enough simply to live, but he was hardly able even to do that. He ran short of everything. One after another his cooks, coachmen, and servants left him to go to the merchant. Soon he lacked even food. When he sent to the market to buy anything, there was nothing to be got—the merchant had bought up everything, and people only brought the King money to pay their taxes.

Tarás the King got angry and banished the merchant from the country. But the merchant settled just across the frontier, and went on as before. For the sake of the merchant's money, people took everything to him instead of to the King.

Things went badly with King Tarás. For days together he had nothing to eat, and a rumour even got about that the merchant was boasting that he would buy up the King himself! King Tarás got frightened, and did not know what to do.

At this time Simon the Soldier came to him, saying, "Help me, for the King of India has conquered me."

But King Tarás himself was over head and ears in difficulties. "I myself," said he, "have had nothing to eat for two days."

XI

Having done with the two brothers, the old Devil went to Iván. He changed himself into a General, and coming to Iván began to persuade him that he ought to have an army.

"It does not become a king," said he, "to be without an army. Only give me the order, and I will collect soldiers from among your people, and form one."

Iván listened to him. "All right," said Iván, "form an army, and teach them to sing songs well. I like to hear them do that."

So the old Devil went through Iván's kingdom to enlist men. He told them to go and be entered as soldiers, and each should have a quart of spirits and a fine red cap.

The people laughed.

"We have plenty of spirits," said they. "We make it ourselves; and as for caps, the women make all kinds of them, even striped ones with tassels."

So nobody would enlist.

The old Devil came to Iván and said: "Your fools won't enlist of their own free will. We shall have to make them."

"All right," said Iván, "you can try."

So the old Devil gave notice that all the people were to enlist, and that Iván would put to death any one who refused.

The people came to the General and said, "You say that if we do not

199

go as soldiers the King will put us to death, but you don't say what will happen if we do enlist. We have heard say that soldiers get killed!"

"Yes, that happens sometimes."

When the people heard this they became obstinate.

"We won't go," said they. "Better meet death at home. Either way we must die."

"Fools! You are fools!" said the old Devil. "A soldier may be killed or he may not, but if you don't go, King Iván will have you killed for certain."

The people were puzzled, and went to Iván the Fool to consult him.

"A General has come," said they, "who says we must all become soldiers. 'If you go as soldiers,' says he, 'you may be killed or you may not, but if you don't go, King Iván will certainly kill you.' Is this true?"

Iván laughed and said, "How can I, alone, put all you to death? If I were not a fool I would explain it to you, but as it is, I don't understand it myself."

"Then," said they, "we will not serve."

"All right," says he, "don't."

So the people went to the General and refused to enlist. And the old Devil saw that this game was up, and he went off and ingratiated himself with the King of Tarakán.

"Let us make war," says he, "and conquer King Iván's country. It is true there is no money, but there is plenty of corn and cattle and everything else."

So the King of Tarakán prepared to make war. He mustered a great army, provided rifles and cannons, marched to the frontier, and entered Iván's kingdom.

And people came to Iván and said, "The King of Tarakán is coming to make war on us."

"All right," said Iván, "let him come."

Having crossed the frontier, the King of Tarakán sent scouts to look for Iván's army. They looked and looked, but there was no army! They waited and waited for one to appear somewhere, but there were no signs of an army, and nobody to fight with. The King of Tarakán then sent to seize the villages. The soldiers came to a village, and the people, both men and women, rushed out in astonishment to stare at the soldiers. The soldiers began to take their corn and cattle; the people let them have it, and did not resist. The soldiers went on to another village; the same thing happened again. The soldiers went on for one day, and for two days, and everywhere the same thing happened. The people let them have everything, and no one resisted, but only invited the soldiers to live with them.

"Poor fellows," said they, "if you have a hard life in your own land, why don't you come and stay with us altogether?"

The soldiers marched and marched: still no army, only people living and feeding themselves and others, and not resisting, but inviting the soldiers to stay and live with them. The soldiers found it dull work, and they came to the King of Tarakán and said, "We cannot fight here, lead us elsewhere. War is all right, but what is this? It is like cutting pea-soup! We will not make war here any more."

The King of Tarakán grew angry, and ordered his soldiers to overrun the whole kingdom, to destroy the villages, to burn the grain and the houses, and to slaughter the cattle. "And if you do not obey my orders," said he, "I will execute you all."

The soldiers were frightened, and began to act according to the King's orders. They began to burn houses and corn, and to kill cattle. But the fools still offered no resistance, and only wept. The old men wept, and the old women wept, and the young people wept.

"Why do you harm us?" they said. "Why do you waste good things? If you need them, why do you not take them for yourselves?"

At last the soldiers could stand it no longer. They refused to go any further, and the army disbanded and fled.

XII

The old Devil had to give it up. He could not get the better of Iván with soldiers. So he changed himself into a fine gentleman, and settled down in Iván's kingdom. He meant to overcome him by means of money, as he had overcome Tarás the Stout.

"I wish," says he, "to do you a good turn, to teach you sense and reason. I will build a house among you and organize a trade."

"All right," said Iván, "come and live among us if you like."

Next morning the fine gentleman went out into the public square with a big sack of gold and a sheet of paper, and said, "You all live like swine. I wish to teach you how to live properly. Build me a house according to this plan. You shall work, I will tell you how, and I will pay you with gold coins." And he showed them the gold.

The fools were astonished; there was no money in use among them; they bartered their goods, and paid one another with labour. They looked at the gold coins with surprise.

"What nice little things they are!" said they.

And they began to exchange their goods and labour for the gentleman's gold pieces. And the old Devil began, as in Tarás's kingdom, to be free with his gold, and the people began to exchange everything for gold and to do all sorts of work for it.

The old Devil was delighted, and thought he to himself, "Things are going right this time. Now I shall ruin the Fool as I did Tarás, and I shall buy him up body and soul."

But as soon as the fools had provided themselves with gold pieces they gave them to the women for necklaces. The lasses plaited them into their tresses, and at last the children in the street began to play with the little pieces. Everybody had plenty of them, and they stopped taking them. But the fine gentleman's mansion was not yet half-built, and the grain and cattle for the year were not yet provided. So he gave notice that he wished people to come and work for him, and that he wanted cattle and grain; for each thing, and for each service, he was ready to give many more pieces of gold.

But nobody came to work and nothing was brought. Only sometimes a boy or a little girl would run up to exchange an egg for a gold coin, but nobody else came, and he had nothing to eat. And being hungry, the fine gentleman went through the village to try and buy something for dinner. He tried at one house, and offered a gold piece for a fowl, but the housewife wouldn't take it.

"I have a lot already," said she.

He tried at a widow's house to buy a herring, and offered a gold piece.

"I don't want it, my good sir," said she. "I have no children to play with it, and I myself already have three coins as curiosities."

He tried at a peasant's house to get bread, but neither would the peasant take money.

"I don't need it," said he, "but if you are begging 'for Christ's sake,' wait a bit and I'll tell the housewife to cut you a piece of bread."

At that the Devil spat, and ran away. To hear Christ's name mentioned, let alone receiving anything for Christ's sake, hurt him more than sticking a knife into him.

And so he got no bread. Everyone had gold, and no matter where the old Devil went, nobody would give anything for money, but everyone said, "Either bring something else, or come and work, or receive what you want in charity for Christ's sake."

But the old Devil had nothing but money; for work he had no liking, and as for taking anything "for Christ's sake" he could not do that. The old Devil grew very angry.

"What more do you want, when I give you money?" said he. "You can buy everything with gold, and hire any kind of labourer." But the fools did not heed him.

"No, we do not want money," said they. "We have no payments to make, and no taxes, so what should we do with it?"

The old Devil lay down to sleep—supperless.

The affair was told to Iván the Fool. People came and asked him, "What are we to do? A fine gentleman has turned up, who likes to eat and drink and dress well, but he does not like to work, does not beg in 'Christ's name,' but only offers gold pieces to everyone. At first people gave him all he wanted, until they had plenty of gold pieces, but now no one gives him anything. What's to be done with him? He will die of hunger before long."

Iván listened.

"All right," says he, "we must feed him. Let him live by turn at each house as a shepherd does."

There was no help for it. The old Devil had to begin making the round.

In due course the turn came for him to go to Iván's house. The old Devil came in to dinner, and the dumb girl was getting it ready.

She had often been deceived by lazy folk who came early to dinner— without having done their share of work—and ate up all the porridge, so it had occurred to her to find out the sluggards by their hands. Those who had horny hands, she put at the table, but the others got only the scraps that were left over.

The old Devil sat down at the table, but the dumb girl seized him by the hands and looked at them—there were no hard places there: the hands were clean and smooth, with long nails. The dumb girl gave a grunt and pulled the Devil away from the table. And Iván's wife said to him, "Don't be offended, fine gentleman. My sister-in-law does not allow any one to come to table who hasn't horny hands. But wait awhile, after the folk have eaten you shall have what is left."

The old Devil was offended that in the King's house they wished him to feed like a pig. He said to Iván, "It is a foolish law you have in your kingdom that everyone must work with his hands. It's your stupidity that invented it. Do people work only with their hands? What do you think wise men work with?"

And Iván said, "How are we fools to know? We do most of our work with our hands and our backs."

"That is because you are fools! But I will teach you how to work with the head. Then you will know that it is more profitable to work with the head than with the hands."

Iván was surprised.

"If that is so," said he, "then there is some sense in calling us fools!"

And the old Devil went on. "Only it is not easy to work with one's head. You give me nothing to eat, because I have no hard places on my hands, but you do not know that it is a hundred times more difficult to work with the head. Sometimes one's head quite splits."

Iván became thoughtful.

"Why, then, friend, do you torture yourself so? Is it pleasant when the head splits? Would it not be better to do easier work with your hands and your back?"

But the Devil said, "I do it all out of pity for you fools. If I didn't torture myself you would remain fools for ever. But, having worked with my head, I can now teach you."

Iván was surprised.

"Do teach us!" said he, "so that when our hands get cramped we may use our heads for a change."

And the Devil promised to teach the people. So Iván gave notice throughout the kingdom that a fine gentleman had come who would teach everybody how to work with their heads; that with the head more could be done than with the hands; and that the people ought all to come and learn.

Now there was in Iván's kingdom a high tower, with many steps leading up to a lantern on the top. And Iván took the gentleman up there that everyone might see him.

So the gentleman took his place on the top of the tower and began to speak, and the people came together to see him. They thought the gentleman would really show them how to work with the head without using the hands. But the old Devil only taught them in many words how they might live without working. The people could make nothing of it. They looked and considered, and at last went off to attend to their affairs.

The old Devil stood on the tower a whole day, and after that a second day, talking all the time. But standing there so long he grew hungry, and the fools never thought of taking food to him up in the tower. They thought that if he could work with his head better than with his hands, he could at any rate easily provide himself with bread.

The old Devil stood on the top of the tower yet another day, talking away. People came near, looked on for awhile, and then went away.

And Iván asked, "Well, has the gentleman begun to work with his head yet?"

"Not yet," said the people; "he's still spouting away."

The old Devil stood on the tower one day more, but he began to grow weak, so that he staggered and hit his head against one of the pillars of the lantern. One of the people noticed it and told Iván's wife, and she ran to her husband, who was in the field.

"Come and look," said she. "They say the gentleman is beginning to work with his head."

Iván was surprised.

"Really?" says he, and he turned his horse round, and went to the tower. And by the time he reached the tower the old Devil was quite exhausted with hunger, and was staggering and knocking his head against the pillars. And just as Iván arrived at the tower, the Devil stumbled, fell, and came bump, bump, bump, straight down the stairs to the bottom, counting each step with a knock of his head!

"Well!" says Iván, "the fine gentleman told the truth when he said that 'sometimes one's head quite splits.' This is worse than blisters; after such work there will be swellings on the head."

The old Devil tumbled out at the foot of the stairs, and struck his head against the ground. Iván was about to go up to him to see how much work he had done—when suddenly the earth opened and the old Devil fell through. Only a hole was left.

Iván scratched his head.

"What a nasty thing," says he. "It's one of those devils again! What a whopper! He must be the father of them all."

Iván is still living, and people crowd to his kingdom. His own brothers have come to live with him, and he feeds them, too. To everyone who comes and says, "Give me food!" Iván says, "All right. You can stay with us; we have plenty of everything."

Only there is one special custom in his kingdom; whoever has horny hands comes to table, but whoever has not, must eat what the others leave.

1885

Anton Chekhov

(1860–1904)

The Lady with the Dog

Translated by Constance Garnett

I

It was said that a new person had appeared on the sea-front: a lady with a little dog. Dmitri Dmitritch Gurov, who had by then been a fortnight at Yalta, and so was fairly at home there, had begun to take an interest in new arrivals. Sitting in Verney's pavilion, he saw, walking on the sea-front, a fair-haired young lady of medium height, wearing a *béret*; a white Pomeranian dog was running behind her.

And afterwards he met her in the public gardens and in the square several times a day. She was walking alone, always wearing the same *béret*, and always with the same white dog; no one knew who she was, and everyone called her simply "the lady with the dog."

"If she is here alone without a husband or friends, it wouldn't be amiss to make her acquaintance," Gurov reflected.

He was under forty, but he had a daughter already twelve years old, and two sons at school. He had been married young, when he was a student in his second year, and by now his wife seemed half as old again as he. She was a tall, erect woman with dark eyebrows, staid and dignified, and, as she said of herself, intellectual. She read a great deal, used phonetic spelling, called her husband, not Dmitri, but Dimitri, and he secretly considered her unintelligent, narrow, inelegant, was afraid of her, and did not like to be at home. He had begun being unfaithful to her long ago—had been unfaithful to her often, and, probably on that account, almost always spoke ill of women, and when they were talked about in his presence, used to call them "the lower race."

It seemed to him that he had been so schooled by bitter experience that he might call them what he liked, and yet he could not get on for two days together without "the lower race." In the society of men he was bored and not himself, with them he was cold and uncommunicative; but when he was in the company of women he felt free, and knew what to say to them and how to behave; and he was at ease with them even when he was silent. In his appearance, in his character, in his whole nature, there was something attractive and elusive which allured women and disposed them in his favour; he knew that, and some force seemed to draw him, too, to them.

Experience often repeated, truly bitter experience, had taught him long ago that with decent people, especially Moscow people—always slow to move and irresolute—every intimacy, which at first so agreeably diversifies life and appears a light and charming adventure, inevitably grows into a regular problem of extreme intricacy, and in the long run the situation becomes unbearable. But at every fresh meeting with an interesting woman this experience seemed to slip out of his memory, and he was eager for life, and everything seemed simple and amusing.

One evening he was dining in the gardens, and the lady in the *béret* came up slowly to take the next table. Her expression, her gait, her dress, and the way she did her hair told him that she was a lady, that she was married, that she was in Yalta for the first time and alone, and that she was dull there . . . The stories told of the immorality in such places as Yalta are to a great extent untrue; he despised them, and knew that such stories were for the most part made up by persons who would themselves have been glad to sin if they had been able; but when the lady sat down at the next table three paces from him, he remembered these tales of easy conquests, of trips to the mountains, and the tempting thought of a swift, fleeting love affair, a romance with an unknown woman, whose name he did not know, suddenly took possession of him.

He beckoned coaxingly to the Pomeranian, and when the dog came up to him he shook his finger at it. The Pomeranian growled: Gurov shook his finger at it again.

The lady looked at him and at once dropped her eyes.

"He doesn't bite," she said, and blushed.

"May I give him a bone?" he asked; and when she nodded he asked courteously, "Have you been long in Yalta?"

"Five days."

"And I have already dragged out a fortnight here."

There was a brief silence.

"Time goes fast, and yet it is so dull here!" she said, not looking at him.

"That's only the fashion to say it is dull here. A provincial will live in Belyov or Zhidra and not be dull, and when he comes here it's 'Oh, the dulness! Oh, the dust!' One would think he came from Grenada."

She laughed. Then both continued eating in silence, like strangers, but after dinner they walked side by side; and there sprang up between them the light jesting conversation of people who are free and satisfied, to whom it does not matter where they go or what they talk about. They walked and talked of the strange light on the sea: the water was of a soft warm lilac hue, and there was a golden streak from the moon upon it. They talked of how sultry it was after a hot day. Gurov told her that he came from Moscow, that he had taken his degree in Arts, but had a post in a bank; that he had trained as an opera-singer, but had given it up, that he owned two houses in Moscow . . . And from her he learnt that she had grown up in Petersburg, but had lived in S——since her marriage two years before, that she was staying another month in Yalta, and that her husband, who needed a holiday too, might perhaps come and fetch her. She was not sure whether her husband had a post in a Crown Department or under the Provincial Council—and was amused by her own ignorance. And Gurov learnt, too, that she was called Anna Sergeyevna.

Afterwards he thought about her in his room at the hotel—thought she would certainly meet him next day; it would be sure to happen. As he got into bed he thought how lately she had been a girl at school, doing lessons like his own daughter; he recalled the diffidence, the angularity, that was still manifest in her laugh and her manner of talking with a stranger. This must have been the first time in her life she had been alone in surroundings in which she was followed, looked at, and spoken to merely from a secret motive which she could hardly fail to guess. He recalled her slender, delicate neck, her lovely grey eyes.

"There's something pathetic about her, anyway," he thought, and fell asleep.

II

A week had passed since they had made acquaintance. It was a holiday. It was sultry indoors, while in the street the wind whirled the dust round and round, and blew people's hats off. It was a thirsty day, and Gurov often went into the pavilion, and pressed Anna Sergeyevna to have syrup and water or an ice. One did not know what to do with oneself.

In the evening when the wind had dropped a little, they went out on the groyne to see the steamer come in. There were a great many people walking about the harbour; they had gathered to welcome someone, bringing bouquets. And two peculiarities of a well-dressed Yalta crowd were very conspicuous: the elderly ladies were dressed like young ones, and there were great numbers of generals.

Owing to the roughness of the sea, the steamer arrived late, after the sun had set, and it was a long time turning about before it reached the groyne. Anna Sergeyevna looked through her lorgnette at the steamer and the passengers as though looking for acquaintances, and when she turned to Gurov her eyes were shining. She talked a great deal and asked disconnected questions, forgetting next moment what she had asked; then she dropped her lorgnette in the crush.

The festive crowd began to disperse; it was too dark to see people's faces. The wind had completely dropped, but Gurov and Anna Sergeyevna still stood as though waiting to see someone else come from the steamer. Anna Sergeyevna was silent now, and sniffed the flowers without looking at Gurov.

"The weather is better this evening," he said. "Where shall we go now? Shall we drive somewhere?"

She made no answer.

Then he looked at her intently, and all at once put his arm round her and kissed her on the lips, and breathed in the moisture and the fragrance of the flowers; and he immediately looked round him, anxiously wondering whether any one had seen them.

"Let us go to your hotel," he said softly. And both walked quickly.

The room was close and smelt of the scent she had bought at the Japanese shop. Gurov looked at her and thought: "What different people one meets in the world!" From the past he preserved memories of careless, good-natured women, who loved cheerfully and were grateful to him for the happiness he gave them, however brief it might be; and of women like his wife who loved without any genuine feeling, with superfluous phrases, affectedly, hysterically, with an expression that suggested that it was not love nor passion, but something more significant; and of two or three others, very beautiful, cold women, on whose faces he had caught a glimpse of a rapacious expression—an obstinate desire to snatch from life more than it could give, and these were capricious, unreflecting, domineering, unintelligent women not in their first youth, and when Gurov grew cold to them their beauty excited his hatred, and the lace on their linen seemed to him like scales.

But in this case there was still the diffidence, the angularity of inexperienced youth, an awkward feeling; and there was a sense of consternation as though someone had suddenly knocked at the door. The attitude of Anna Sergeyevna—"the lady with the dog"—to what had happened was somehow peculiar, very grave, as though it were her fall— so it seemed, and it was strange and inappropriate. Her face dropped and faded, and on both sides of it her long hair hung down mournfully; she mused in a dejected attitude like "the woman who was a sinner" in an old-fashioned picture.

"It's wrong," she said. "You will be the first to despise me now."

There was a watermelon on the table. Gurov cut himself a slice and began eating it without haste. There followed at least half an hour of silence.

Anna Sergeyevna was touching; there was about her the purity of a good, simple woman who had seen little of life. The solitary candle burning on the table threw a faint light on her face, yet it was clear that she was very unhappy.

"How could I despise you?" asked Gurov. "You don't know what you are saying."

"God forgive me," she said, and her eyes filled with tears. "It's awful."

"You seem to feel you need to be forgiven."

"Forgiven? No. I am a bad, low woman; I despise myself and don't attempt to justify myself. It's not my husband but myself I have deceived. And not only just now; I have been deceiving myself for a long time. My husband may be a good, honest man, but he is a flunkey! I don't know what he does there, what his work is, but I know he is a flunkey! I was twenty when I was married to him. I have been tormented by curiosity; I wanted something better. 'There must be a different sort of life,' I said to myself. I wanted to live! To live, to live! . . . I was fired by curiosity . . . you don't understand it, but, I swear to God, I could not control myself; something happened to me: I could not be restrained. I told my husband I was ill, and came here . . . And here I have been walking about as though I were dazed, like a mad creature; . . . and now I have become a vulgar, contemptible woman whom any one may despise."

Gurov felt bored already, listening to her. He was irritated by the naïve tone, by this remorse, so unexpected and inopportune; but for the tears in her eyes, he might have thought she was jesting or playing a part.

"I don't understand," he said softly. "What is it you want?"

She hid her face on his breast and pressed close to him.

"Believe me, believe me, I beseech you . . ." she said. "I love a pure, honest life, and sin is loathsome to me. I don't know what I am doing. Simple people say: 'The Evil One has beguiled me.' And I may say of myself now that the Evil One has beguiled me."

"Hush, hush! . . ." he muttered.

He looked at her fixed, scared eyes, kissed her, talked softly and affectionately, and by degrees she was comforted, and her gaiety returned; they both began laughing.

Afterwards when they went out there was not a soul on the sea-front. The town with its cypresses had quite a deathlike air, but the sea still broke noisily on the shore; a single barge was rocking on the waves, and a lantern was blinking sleepily on it.

They found a cab and drove to Oreanda.

"I found out your surname in the hall just now: it was written on the board—Von Diderits," said Gurov. "Is your husband a German?"

"No; I believe his grandfather was a German, but he is an Orthodox Russian himself."

At Oreanda they sat on a seat not far from the church, looked down at the sea, and were silent. Yalta was hardly visible through the morning mist; white clouds stood motionless on the mountain-tops. The leaves did not stir on the trees, grasshoppers chirruped, and the monotonous hollow sound of the sea rising up from below, spoke of the peace, of the eternal sleep awaiting us. So it must have sounded when there was no Yalta, no Oreanda here; so it sounds now, and it will sound as indifferently and monotonously when we are all no more. And in this constancy, in this complete indifference to the life and death of each of us, there lies hid, perhaps, a pledge of our eternal salvation, of the unceasing movement of life upon earth, of unceasing progress towards perfection. Sitting beside a young woman who in the dawn seemed so lovely, soothed and spellbound in these magical surroundings—the sea, mountains, clouds, the open sky—Gurov thought how in reality everything is beautiful in this world when one reflects: everything except what we think or do ourselves when we forget our human dignity and the higher aims of our existence.

A man walked up to them—probably a keeper—looked at them and walked away. And this detail seemed mysterious and beautiful, too. They saw a steamer come from Theodosia, with its lights out in the glow of dawn.

"There is dew on the grass," said Anna Sergeyevna, after a silence.

"Yes. It's time to go home."

They went back to the town.

Then they met every day at twelve o'clock on the sea-front, lunched and dined together, went for walks, admired the sea. She complained that she slept badly, that her heart throbbed violently; asked the same questions, troubled now by jealousy and now by the fear that he did not respect her sufficiently. And often in the square or gardens, when there was no one near them, he suddenly drew her to him and kissed her passionately. Complete idleness, these kisses in broad daylight while he looked round in dread of someone's seeing them, the heat, the smell of the sea, and the continual passing to and fro before him of idle, well-dressed, well-fed people, made a new man of him; he told Anna Sergeyevna how beautiful she was, how fascinating. He was impatiently passionate, he would not move a step away from her, while she was often pensive and continually urged him to confess that he did not respect her, did not love her in the least, and thought of her as nothing but a common woman. Rather late almost every evening they drove somewhere out of town, to Oreanda or to the waterfall; and the expedition was always a success, the scenery invariably impressed them as grand and beautiful.

They were expecting her husband to come, but a letter came from him, saying that there was something wrong with his eyes, and he entreated his wife to come home as quickly as possible. Anna Sergeyevna made haste to go.

"It's a good thing I am going away," she said to Gurov. "It's the finger of destiny!"

She went by coach and he went with her. They were driving the whole day. When she had got into a compartment of the express, and when the second bell had rung, she said:

"Let me look at you once more . . . look at you once again. That's right."

She did not shed tears, but was so sad that she seemed ill, and her face was quivering.

"I shall remember you . . . think of you," she said. "God be with you; be happy. Don't remember evil against me. We are parting forever—it must be so, for we ought never to have met. Well, God be with you."

The train moved off rapidly, its lights soon vanished from sight, and a minute later there was no sound of it, as though everything had conspired together to end as quickly as possible that sweet delirium, that madness. Left alone on the platform, and gazing into the dark distance, Gurov listened to the chirrup of the grasshoppers and the hum of the telegraph wires, feeling as though he had only just waked up. And he thought, musing, that there had been another episode or adventure in his life, and it, too, was at an end, and nothing was left of it but a memory . . . He was moved, sad, and conscious of a slight remorse. This young woman whom he would never meet again had not been happy with him; he was genuinely warm and affectionate with her, but yet in his manner, his tone, and his caresses there had been a shade of light irony, the coarse condescension of a happy man who was, besides, almost twice her age. All the time she had called him kind, exceptional, lofty; obviously he had seemed to her different from what he really was, so he had unintentionally deceived her . . .

Here at the station was already a scent of autumn; it was a cold evening.

"It's time for me to go north," thought Gurov as he left the platform. "High time!"

III

At home in Moscow everything was in its winter routine; the stoves were heated, and in the morning it was still dark when the children were having breakfast and getting ready for school, and the nurse would light the lamp for a short time. The frosts had begun already. When the first snow has fallen, on the first day of sledge-driving it is pleasant to see the white earth, the white roofs, to draw soft, delicious breath, and the season brings back the days of one's youth. The old limes and birches, white with hoar-frost, have a good-natured expression; they are nearer to one's heart than cypresses and palms, and near them one doesn't want to be thinking of the sea and the mountains.

Gurov was Moscow born; he arrived in Moscow on a fine frosty day, and when he put on his fur coat and warm gloves, and walked along Petrovka, and when on Saturday evening he heard the ringing of the bells, his recent trip and the places he had seen lost all charm for him. Little by little he became absorbed in Moscow life, greedily read three newspapers a day, and declared he did not read the Moscow papers on principle! He already felt a longing to go to restaurants, clubs, dinner-parties, anniversary celebrations, and he felt flattered at entertaining distinguished lawyers and artists, and at playing cards with a professor at the doctors' club. He could already eat a whole plateful of salt fish and cabbage.

In another month, he fancied, the image of Anna Sergeyevna would be shrouded in a mist in his memory, and only from time to time would visit him in his dreams with a touching smile as others did. But more than a month passed, real winter had come, and everything was still clear in his memory as though he had parted with Anna Sergeyevna only the day before. And his memories glowed more and more vividly. When in the evening stillness he heard from his study the voices of his children, preparing their lessons, or when he listened to a song or the organ at the restaurant, or the storm howled in the chimney, suddenly everything would rise up in his memory: what had happened on the groyne, and the early morning with the mist on the mountains, and the steamer coming from Theodosia, and the kisses. He would pace a long time about his room, remembering it all and smiling; then his memories passed into dreams, and in his fancy the past was mingled with what was to come. Anna Sergeyevna did not visit him in dreams, but followed him about everywhere like a shadow and haunted him. When he shut his eyes he saw her as though she were living before him, and she seemed to him lovelier, younger, tenderer than she was; and he imagined himself finer than he had been in Yalta. In the evenings she peeped out at him from the bookcase, from the fireplace, from the corner—he heard her breathing, the caressing rustle of her dress. In the street he watched the women, looking for someone like her.

He was tormented by an intense desire to confide his memories to someone. But in his home it was impossible to talk of his love, and he had no one outside; he could not talk to his tenants nor to any one at the bank. And what had he to talk of? Had he been in love, then? Had there been anything beautiful, poetical, or edifying or simply interesting in his relations with Anna Sergeyevna? And there was nothing for him but to talk vaguely of love, of woman, and no one guessed what it meant; only his wife twitched her black eyebrows, and said:

"The part of a lady-killer does not suit you at all, Dimitri."

One evening, coming out of the doctors' club with an official with whom he had been playing cards, he could not resist saying:

"If only you knew what a fascinating woman I made the acquaintance of in Yalta!"

The official got into his sledge and was driving away, but turned suddenly and shouted:

"Dmitri Dmitritch!"

"What?"

"You were right this evening: the sturgeon was a bit too strong!"

These words, so ordinary, for some reason moved Gurov to indignation, and struck him as degrading and unclean. What savage manners, what people! What senseless nights, what uninteresting, uneventful days! The rage for card-playing, the gluttony, the drunkenness, the continual talk always about the same thing. Useless pursuits and conversations always about the same things absorb the better part of one's time, the better part of one's strength, and in the end there is left a life grovelling and curtailed, worthless and trivial, and there is no escaping or getting away from it—just as though one were in a madhouse or a prison.

Gurov did not sleep all night, and was filled with indignation. And he had a headache all next day. And the next night he slept badly; he sat up in bed, thinking, or paced up and down his room. He was sick of his children, sick of the bank; he had no desire to go anywhere or to talk of anything.

In the holidays in December he prepared for a journey, and told his wife he was going to Petersburg to do something in the interests of a young friend—and he set off for S——. What for? He did not very well know himself. He wanted to see Anna Sergeyevna and to talk with her—to arrange a meeting, if possible.

He reached S——in the morning, and took the best room at the hotel, in which the floor was covered with grey army cloth, and on the table was an inkstand, grey with dust and adorned with a figure on horseback, with its hat in its hand and its head broken off. The hotel porter gave him the necessary information; Von Diderits lived in a house of his own in Old Gontcharny Street—it was not far from the hotel: he was rich and lived in good style, and had his own horses; everyone in the town knew him. The porter pronounced the name "Dridirits."

Gurov went without haste to Old Gontcharny Street and found the house. Just opposite the house stretched a long grey fence adorned with nails.

"One would run away from a fence like that," thought Gurov, looking from the fence to the windows of the house and back again.

He considered: today was a holiday, and the husband would probably be at home. And in any case it would be tactless to go into the house and upset her. If he were to send her a note it might fall into her husband's hands, and then it might ruin everything. The best thing was to trust to chance. And he kept walking up and down the street by the fence, waiting for the chance. He saw a beggar go in at the gate and dogs fly at him; then an hour later he heard a piano, and the sounds were faint and indistinct. Probably it was Anna Sergeyevna playing. The front door suddenly opened, and an old woman came out, followed by the familiar white Pomeranian. Gurov was on the point of calling to the dog, but his heart began beating violently, and in his excitement he could not remember the dog's name.

He walked up and down, and loathed the grey fence more and more, and by now he thought irritably that Anna Sergeyevna had forgotten him, and was perhaps already amusing herself with someone else, and that that was very natural in a young woman who had nothing to look at from morning till night but that confounded fence. He went back to his hotel room and sat for a long while on the sofa, not knowing what to do, then he had dinner and a long nap.

"How stupid and worrying it is!" he thought when he woke and looked at the dark windows: it was already evening. "Here I've had a good sleep for some reason. What shall I do in the night?"

He sat on the bed, which was covered by a cheap grey blanket, such as one sees in hospitals, and he taunted himself in his vexation:

"So much for the lady with the dog . . . so much for the adventure . . . You're in a nice fix . . ."

That morning at the station a poster in large letters had caught his eye. "The Geisha" was to be performed for the first time. He thought of this and went to the theatre.

"It's quite possible she may go to the first performance," he thought.

The theatre was full. As in all provincial theatres, there was a fog above the chandelier, the gallery was noisy and restless; in the front row the local dandies were standing up before the beginning of the performance, with their hands behind them; in the Governor's box the Governor's daughter, wearing a boa, was sitting in the front seat, while the Governor himself lurked modestly behind the curtain with only his hands visible; the orchestra was a long time tuning up; the stage curtain swayed. All the time the audience were coming in and taking their seats Gurov looked at them eagerly.

Anna Sergeyevna, too, came in. She sat down in the third row, and when Gurov looked at her his heart contracted, and he understood clearly that for him there was in the whole world no creature so near, so precious, and so important to him; she, this little woman, in no way remarkable, lost in a provincial crowd, with a vulgar lorgnette in her hand, filled his whole life now, was his sorrow and his joy, the one happiness that he now desired for himself, and to the sounds of the inferior orchestra, of the wretched provincial violins, he thought how lovely she was. He thought and dreamed.

A young man with small side-whiskers, tall and stooping, came in with Anna Sergeyevna and sat down beside her; he bent his head at every step and seemed to be continually bowing. Most likely this was the husband whom at Yalta, in a rush of bitter feeling, she had called a flunkey. And there really was in his long figure, his side-whiskers, and the small bald patch on his head, something of the flunkey's obsequiousness; his smile was sugary, and in his buttonhole there was some badge of distinction like the number on a waiter.

During the first interval the husband went away to smoke; she remained alone in her stall. Gurov, who was sitting in the stalls, too, went up to her and said in a trembling voice, with a forced smile:

"Good evening."

She glanced at him and turned pale, then glanced again with horror, unable to believe her eyes, and tightly gripped the fan and the lorgnette in her hands, evidently struggling with herself not to faint. Both were silent. She was sitting, he was standing, frightened by her confusion and not venturing to sit down beside her. The violins and the flute began tuning up. He felt suddenly frightened; it seemed as though all the people in the boxes were looking at them. She got up and went quickly to the door; he followed her, and both walked senselessly along passages, and up and down stairs, and figures in legal, scholastic, and civil service uniforms, all wearing badges, flitted before their eyes. They caught glimpses of ladies, of fur coats hanging on pegs; the draughts blew on them, bringing a smell of stale tobacco. And Gurov, whose heart was beating violently, thought:

"Oh, heavens! Why are these people here and this orchestra! . . ."

And at that instant he recalled how when he had seen Anna Sergeyevna off at the station he had thought that everything was over and they would never meet again. But how far they were still from the end!

On the narrow, gloomy staircase over which was written "To the Amphitheatre," she stopped.

"How you have frightened me!" she said, breathing hard, still pale and overwhelmed. "Oh, how you have frightened me! I am half dead. Why have you come? Why?"

"But do understand, Anna, do understand . . ." he said hastily in a low voice. "I entreat you to understand . . ."

She looked at him with dread, with entreaty, with love; she looked at him intently, to keep his features more distinctly in her memory.

"I am so unhappy," she went on, not heeding him. "I have thought of nothing but you all the time; I live only in the thought of you. And I wanted to forget, to forget you; but why, oh, why, have you come?"

On the landing above them two schoolboys were smoking and looking down, but that was nothing to Gurov; he drew Anna Sergeyevna to him, and began kissing her face, her cheeks, and her hands.

"What are you doing, what are you doing!" she cried in horror, pushing him away. "We are mad. Go away today; go away at once . . . I beseech you by all that is sacred, I implore you . . . There are people coming this way!"

Someone was coming up the stairs.

"You must go away," Anna Sergeyevna went on in a whisper. "Do you hear, Dmitri Dmitritch? I will come and see you in Moscow. I have never been happy; I am miserable now, and I never, never shall be happy, never!

Don't make me suffer still more! I swear I'll come to Moscow. But now let us part. My precious, good, dear one, we must part!"

She pressed his hand and began rapidly going downstairs, looking round at him, and from her eyes he could see that she really was unhappy. Gurov stood for a little while, listened, then, when all sound had died away, he found his coat and left the theatre.

IV

And Anna Sergeyevna began coming to see him in Moscow. Once in two or three months she left S——, telling her husband that she was going to consult a doctor about an internal complaint—and her husband believed her, and did not believe her. In Moscow she stayed at the Slaviansky Bazaar hotel, and at once sent a man in a red cap to Gurov. Gurov went to see her, and no one in Moscow knew of it.

Once he was going to see her in this way on a winter morning (the messenger had come the evening before when he was out). With him walked his daughter, whom he wanted to take to school: it was on the way. Snow was falling in big wet flakes.

"It's three degrees above freezing-point, and yet it is snowing," said Gurov to his daughter. "The thaw is only on the surface of the earth; there is quite a different temperature at a greater height in the atmosphere."

"And why are there no thunderstorms in the winter, father?"

He explained that, too. He talked, thinking all the while that he was going to see her, and no living soul knew of it, and probably never would know. He had two lives: one, open, seen and known by all who cared to know, full of relative truth and of relative falsehood, exactly like the lives of his friends and acquaintances; and another life running its course in secret. And through some strange, perhaps accidental, conjunction of circumstances, everything that was essential, of interest and of value to him, everything in which he was sincere and did not deceive himself, everything that made the kernel of his life, was hidden from other people; and all that was false in him, the sheath in which he hid himself to conceal the truth—such, for instance, as his work in the bank, his discussions at the club, his "lower race," his presence with his wife at anniversary festivities—all that was open. And he judged of others by himself, not believing in what he saw, and always believing that every man had his real, most interesting life under the cover of secrecy and under the cover of night. All personal life rested on secrecy, and possibly it was partly on that account that civilised man was so nervously anxious that personal privacy should be respected.

After leaving his daughter at school, Gurov went on to the Slaviansky Bazaar. He took off his fur coat below, went upstairs, and softly knocked at the door. Anna Sergeyevna, wearing his favourite grey dress, exhausted by the journey and the suspense, had been expecting him since the evening before. She was pale; she looked at him, and did not smile, and he had hardly come in when she fell on his breast. Their kiss was slow and prolonged, as though they had not met for two years.

"Well, how are you getting on there?" he asked. "What news?"

"Wait; I'll tell you directly . . . I can't talk."

She could not speak; she was crying. She turned away from him, and pressed her handkerchief to her eyes.

"Let her have her cry out. I'll sit down and wait," he thought, and he sat down in an armchair.

Then he rang and asked for tea to be brought him, and while he drank his tea she remained standing at the window with her back to him. She was crying from emotion, from the miserable consciousness that their life was so hard for them; they could only meet in secret, hiding themselves from people, like thieves! Was not their life shattered?

"Come, do stop!" he said.

It was evident to him that this love of theirs would not soon be over, that he could not see the end of it. Anna Sergeyevna grew more and more attached to him. She adored him, and it was unthinkable to say to her that it was bound to have an end some day; besides, she would not have believed it!

He went up to her and took her by the shoulders to say something affectionate and cheering, and at that moment he saw himself in the looking-glass.

His hair was already beginning to turn grey. And it seemed strange to him that he had grown so much older, so much plainer during the last few years. The shoulders on which his hands rested were warm and quivering. He felt compassion for this life, still so warm and lovely, but probably already not far from beginning to fade and wither like his own. Why did she love him so much? He always seemed to women different from what he was, and they loved in him not himself, but the man created by their imagination, whom they had been eagerly seeking all their lives; and afterwards, when they noticed their mistake, they loved him all the same. And not one of them had been happy with him. Time passed, he had made their acquaintance, got on with them, parted, but he had never once loved; it was anything you like, but not love.

And only now when his head was grey he had fallen properly, really in love—for the first time in his life.

Anna Sergeyevna and he loved each other like people very close and akin, like husband and wife, like tender friends; it seemed to them that fate itself had meant them for one another, and they could not understand why he had a wife and she a husband; and it was as though they were a pair of birds of passage, caught and forced to live in different cages. They forgave each other for what they were ashamed of in their past, they forgave everything in the present, and felt that this love of theirs had changed them both.

In moments of depression in the past he had comforted himself with any arguments that came into his mind, but now he no longer cared for arguments; he felt profound compassion, he wanted to be sincere and tender . . .

"Don't cry, my darling," he said. "You've had your cry; that's enough . . . Let us talk now, let us think of some plan."

Then they spent a long while taking counsel together, talked of how to avoid the necessity for secrecy, for deception, for living in different towns and not seeing each other for long at a time. How could they be free from this intolerable bondage?

"How? How?" he asked, clutching his head. "How?"

And it seemed as though in a little while the solution would be found, and then a new and splendid life would begin; and it was clear to both of them that they had still a long, long road before them, and that the most complicated and difficult part of it was only just beginning.

The Bet

Translated by S. Koteliansky and J. M. Murry

I

It was a dark autumn night. The old banker was pacing from corner to corner of his study, recalling to his mind the party he gave in the autumn fifteen years ago. There were many clever people at the party and much interesting conversation. They talked among other things of capital punishment. The guests, among them not a few scholars and journalists, for the most part disapproved of capital punishment. They found it obsolete as a means of punishment, unfitted to a Christian State and immoral. Some of them thought that capital punishment should be replaced universally by life-imprisonment.

"I don't agree with you," said the host. "I myself have experienced neither capital punishment nor life-imprisonment, but if one may judge *a priori,* then in my opinion capital punishment is more moral and more humane than imprisonment. Execution kills instantly, life-imprisonment kills by degrees. Who is the more humane executioner, one who kills you in a few seconds or one who draws the life out of you incessantly, for years?"

"They're both equally immoral," remarked one of the guests, "because their purpose is the same, to take away life. The State is not God. It has no right to take away that which it cannot give back, if it should so desire."

Among the company was a lawyer, a young man of about twenty-five. On being asked his opinion, he said:

"Capital punishment and life-imprisonment are equally immoral; but if I were offered the choice between them, I would certainly choose the second. It's better to live somehow than not to live at all."

There ensued a lively discussion. The banker who was then younger and more nervous suddenly lost his temper, banged his fist on the table, and turning to the young lawyer, cried out:

"It's a lie. I bet you two millions you wouldn't stick in a cell even for five years."

"If that's serious," replied the lawyer, "then I bet I'll stay not five but fifteen."

"Fifteen! Done!" cried the banker. "Gentlemen, I stake two millions."

"Agreed. You stake two millions, I my freedom," said the lawyer.

So this wild, ridiculous bet came to pass. The banker, who at that time had too many millions to count, spoiled and capricious, was beside himself with rapture. During supper he said to the lawyer jokingly:

"Come to your senses, young man, before it's too late. Two millions are nothing to me, but you stand to lose three or four of the best years of your life. I say three or four, because you'll never stick it out any longer. Don't forget either, you unhappy man, that voluntary is much heavier than enforced imprisonment. The idea that you have the right to free yourself at any moment will poison the whole of your life in the cell. I pity you."

And now the banker pacing from corner to corner, recalled all this and asked himself:

"Why did I make this bet? What's the good? The lawyer loses fifteen years of his life and I throw away two millions. Will it convince people that capital punishment is worse or better than imprisonment for life. No, No! all stuff and rubbish. On my part, it was the caprice of a well-fed man; on the lawyer's, pure greed of gold."

He recollected further what happened after the evening party. It was decided that the lawyer must undergo his imprisonment under the strictest observation, in a garden-wing of the banker's house. It was agreed that during the period he would be deprived of the right to cross the threshold, to see living people, to hear human voices, and to receive letters and newspapers. He was permitted to have a musical instrument, to read books, to write letters, to drink wine and smoke tobacco. By the agreement he could communicate, but only in silence, with the outside world through a little window specially constructed for this purpose.

Everything necessary, books, music, wine, he could receive in any quantity by sending a note through the window. The agreement provided for all the minutest details, which made the confinement strictly solitary, and it obliged the lawyer to remain exactly fifteen years from twelve o'clock of November 14th 1870 to twelve o'clock of November 14th 1885. The least attempt on his part to violate the conditions, to escape if only for two minutes before the time freed the banker from the obligation to pay him the two millions.

During the first year of imprisonment, the lawyer, as far as it was possible to judge from his short notes, suffered terribly from loneliness and boredom. From his wing day and night came the sound of the piano. He rejected wine and tobacco. "Wine," he wrote, "excites desires, and desires are the chief foes of a prisoner; besides, nothing is more boring than to drink good wine alone," and tobacco spoils the air in his room. During the first year the lawyer was sent books of a light character; novels with a complicated love interest, stories of crime and fantasy, comedies, and so on.

In the second year the piano was heard no longer and the lawyer asked only for classics. In the fifth year, music was heard again, and the prisoner asked for wine. Those who watched him said that during the whole of that year he was only eating, drinking, and lying on his bed. He yawned often and talked angrily to himself. Books he did not read. Sometimes at nights he would sit down to write. He would write for a long time and tear it all up in the morning. More than once he was heard to weep.

In the second half of the sixth year, the prisoner began zealously to study languages, philosophy, and history. He fell on these subjects so hungrily that the banker hardly had time to get books enough for him. In the space of four years about six hundred volumes were bought at his request. It was while that passion lasted that the banker received the following letter from the prisoner: "My dear gaoler, I am writing these lines in six languages. Show them to experts. Let them read them. If they do not find one single mistake, I beg you to give orders to have a gun fired off in the garden. By the noise I shall know that my efforts have not been in vain. The geniuses of all ages and countries speak in different languages; but in them all burns the same flame. Oh, if you knew my heavenly happiness now that I can understand them!" The prisoner's desire was fulfilled. Two shots were fired in the garden by the banker's order.

Later on, after the tenth year, the lawyer sat immovable before his table and read only the New Testament. The banker found it strange that a man who in four years had mastered six hundred erudite volumes, should have spent nearly a year in reading one book, easy to understand and by no means thick. The New Testament was then replaced by the history of religions and theology.

During the last two years of his confinement the prisoner read an extraordinary amount, quite haphazard. Now he would apply himself to the natural sciences, then would read Byron or Shakespeare. Notes used to come from him in which he asked to be sent at the same time a book on chemistry, a textbook of medicine, a novel, and some treatise on philosophy or theology. He read as though he were swimming in the sea among the broken pieces of wreckage, and in his desire to save his life was eagerly grasping one piece after another.

II

The banker recalled all this, and thought:

"Tomorrow at twelve o'clock he receives his freedom. Under the agreement, I shall have to pay him two millions. If I pay, it's all over with me. I am ruined for ever . . ."

Fifteen years before he had too many millions to count, but now he was afraid to ask himself which he had more of, money or debts. Gambling on the Stock-Exchange, risky speculation, and the recklessness of which he could not rid himself even in old age, had gradually brought his business to decay; and the fearless, self-confident, proud man of business had become an ordinary banker, trembling at every rise and fall in the market.

"That cursed bet," murmured the old man clutching his head in despair . . . "Why didn't the man die? He's only forty years old. He will take away my last farthing, marry, enjoy life, gamble on the Exchange, and I will look on like an envious beggar and hear the same words from him every day: 'I'm obliged to you for the happiness of my life. Let me help you.' No, it's too much! The only escape from bankruptcy and disgrace— is that the man should die."

The clock had just struck three. The banker was listening. In Ike house everyone was asleep, and one could hear only the frozen trees whining outside the windows. Trying to make no sound, he took out of his safe the key of the door which had not been opened for fifteen years, put on his overcoat, and went out of the house. The garden was dark and cold. It was raining. A keen damp wind hovered howling over all the garden and gave the trees no rest. Though he strained his eyes, the banker could see neither the ground, nor the white statues, nor the garden-wing, nor the trees. Approaching the place where the garden wing stood, he called the watchman twice. There was no answer. Evidently the watchman had taken shelter from the bad weather and was now asleep somewhere in the kitchen or the greenhouse.

"If I have the courage to fulfil my intention," thought the old man, "the suspicion will fall on the watchman first of all."

In the darkness he groped for the stairs and the door and entered the hall of the garden-wing, then poked his way into a narrow passage and struck a match. Not a soul was there. Someone's bed, with no bedclothes on it, stood there, and an iron stove was dark in the corner. The seals on the door that led into the prisoner's room were unbroken.

When the match went out, the old man, trembling from agitation, peeped into the little window.

In the prisoner's room a candle was burning dim. The prisoner himself sat by the table. Only his back, the hair on his head and his hands were visible. On the table, the two chairs, the carpet by the table open books were strewn.

Five minutes passed and the prisoner never once stirred. Fifteen years confinement had taught him to sit motionless. The banker tapped on the window with his finger, but the prisoner gave no movement in reply. Then the banker cautiously tore the seals from the door and put the key into the lock. The rusty lock gave a hoarse groan and the door creaked. The banker expected instantly to hear a cry of surprise and the sound of steps. Three minutes passed and it was as quiet behind the door as it had been before. He made up his mind to enter. Before the table sat a man, unlike an ordinary human being. It was a skeleton, with tight-drawn skin, with a woman's long curly hair, and a shaggy beard. The colour of his face was yellow, of an earthy shade; the cheeks were sunken, the back long and narrow, and the hand upon which he leaned his hairy head was so lean and skinny that it was painful to look upon. His hair was already silvering with grey, and no one who glanced at the senile emaciation of the face would have believed that he was only forty years old. On the table, before his bended head, lay a sheet of paper on which something was written in a tiny hand.

"Poor devil," thought the banker, "he's asleep and probably seeing millions in his dreams. I have only to take and throw this half-dead thing on the bed, smother him a moment with the pillow, and the most careful examination will find no trace of unnatural death. But, first, let us read what he has written here."

The banker took the sheet from the table and read:

"Tomorrow at twelve o'clock midnight, I shall obtain my freedom and the right to mix with people. But before I leave this room and see the sun I think it necessary to say a few words to you. On my own clear conscience and before God who sees me I declare to you that I despise freedom, life, health, and all that your books call the blessings of the world.

"For fifteen years I have diligently studied earthly life. True, I saw neither the earth nor the people, but in your books I drank fragrant wine, sang songs, hunted deer and wild boar in the forests, loved women . . . And beautiful women, like clouds ethereal, created by the magic of your poets' genius, visited me by night and whispered me wonderful tales, which made my head drunken. In your books I climbed the summits of Elbruz and Mont Blanc and saw from thence how the sun rose in the morning, and in the evening overflowed the sky, the ocean and the mountain ridges with a purple gold. I saw from thence how above me lightnings glimmered cleaving the clouds; I saw green forests, fields, rivers, lakes, cities; I heard syrens singing, and the playing of the pipes of Pan; I touched the wings of beautiful devils who came flying to me to speak of God . . . In your books I cast myself into bottomless abysses, worked miracles, burned cities to the ground, preached new religions, conquered whole countries . . .

"Your books gave me wisdom. All that unwearying human thought created in the centuries is compressed to a little lump in my skull. I know that I am more clever than you all.

"And I despise your books, despise all worldly blessings and wisdom. Everything is void, frail, visionary and delusive like a mirage. Though you be proud and wise and beautiful, yet will death wipe you from the face of the earth like the mice underground; and your posterity, your history, and the immortality of your men of genius will be as frozen slag, burnt down together with the terrestrial globe.

"You are mad, and gone the wrong way. You take lie for truth and ugliness for beauty. You would marvel if by certain conditions there should suddenly grow on apple and orange trees, instead of fruit, frogs and lizards, and if roses should begin to breathe the odour of a sweating horse. So do I marvel at you, who have bartered heaven for earth. I do not want to understand you.

"That I may show you in deed my contempt for that by which you live, I waive the two millions of which I once dreamed as of paradise, and which I now despise. That I may deprive myself of my right to them, I shall come out from here five minutes before the stipulated term, and thus shall violate the agreement."

When he had read, the banker put the sheet on the table, kissed the head of the strange man, and began to weep. He went out of the wing. Never at any other time, not even after his terrible losses on the Exchange, had he felt such contempt for himself as now. Coming home, he lay down on his bed, but agitation and tears kept him long from sleep . . .

The next morning the poor watchman came running to him and told him that they had seen the man who lived in the wing climbing through the window into the garden. He had gone to the gate and disappeared. Together with his servants the banker went instantly to the wing and established the escape of his prisoner. To avoid unnecessary rumours he took the paper with the renunciation from the table and, on his return, locked it in his safe.

The Kiss

Translated by Constance Garnett

At eight o'clock on the evening of the twentieth of May all the six batteries of the N——Reserve Artillery Brigade halted for the night in the village of Myestetchki on their way to camp. When the general commotion was at its height, while some officers were busily occupied around the guns, while others, gathered together in the square near the church enclosure, were listening to the quartermasters, a man in civilian dress, riding a strange horse, came into sight round the church. The little dun-coloured horse with a good neck and a short tail came, moving not straight forward, but as it were sideways, with a sort of dance step, as though it were being lashed about the legs. When he reached the officers the man on the horse took off his hat and said:

"His Excellency Lieutenant-General von Rabbek invites the gentlemen to drink tea with him this minute . . ."

The horse turned, danced, and retired sideways; the messenger raised his hat once more, and in an instant disappeared with his strange horse behind the church.

"What the devil does it mean?" grumbled some of the officers, dispersing to their quarters. "One is sleepy, and here this Von Rabbek with his tea! We know what tea means."

The officers of all the six batteries remembered vividly an incident of the previous year, when during manoeuvres they, together with the officers of a Cossack regiment, were in the same way invited to tea by a count who had an estate in the neighbourhood and was a retired army officer: the hospitable and genial count made much of them, fed them, and gave them drink, refused to let them go to their quarters in the village and made them stay the night. All that, of course, was very nice—nothing better could be desired, but the worst of it was, the old army officer was so carried away by the pleasure of the young men's company that till sunrise he was telling the officers anecdotes of his glorious past, taking them over the house, showing them expensive pictures, old engravings, rare guns, reading them autograph letters from great people, while the weary and exhausted officers looked and listened, longing for their beds and yawning in their sleeves; when at last their host let them go, it was too late for sleep.

Might not this Von Rabbek be just such another? Whether he were or not, there was no help for it. The officers changed their uniforms, brushed themselves, and went all together in search of the gentleman's house. In the square by the church they were told they could get to His Excellency's by the lower path—going down behind the church to the river, going along the bank to the garden, and there an avenue would taken them to the house; or by the upper way—straight from the church by the road which, half a mile from the village, led right up to His Excellency's granaries. The officers decided to go by the upper way.

"What Von Rabbek is it?" they wondered on the way. "Surely not the one who was in command of the N——cavalry division at Plevna?"

"No, that was not Von Rabbek, but simply Rabbe and no 'von.'"

"What lovely weather!"

At the first of the granaries the road divided in two: one branch went straight on and vanished in the evening darkness, the other led to the owner's house on the right. The officers turned to the right and began to speak more softly . . . On both sides of the road stretched stone granaries with red roofs, heavy and sullen-looking, very much like barracks of a district town. Ahead of them gleamed the windows of the manor-house.

"A good omen, gentlemen," said one of the officers. "Our setter is the foremost of all; no doubt he scents game ahead of us! . . ."

Lieutenant Lobytko, who was walking in front, a tall and stalwart fellow, though entirely without moustache (he was over five-and-twenty, yet for some reason there was no sign of hair on his round, well-fed face), renowned in the brigade for his peculiar faculty for divining the presence of women at a distance, turned round and said:

"Yes, there must be women here; I feel that by instinct."

On the threshold the officers were met by Von Rabbek himself, a comely-looking man of sixty in civilian dress. Shaking hands with his guests, he said that he was very glad and happy to see them, but begged them earnestly for God's sake to excuse him for not asking them to stay the night; two sisters with their children, some brothers, and some neighbours, had come on a visit to him, so that he had not one spare room left.

The General shook hands with everyone, made his apologies, and smiled, but it was evident by his face that he was by no means so delighted as their last year's count, and that he had invited the officers simply because, in his opinion, it was a social obligation to do so. And the officers themselves, as they walked up the softly carpeted stairs, as they listened to him, felt that they had been invited to this house simply because it would have been awkward not to invite them; and at the sight of the footmen, who hastened to light the lamps in the entrance below and in the anteroom above, they began to feel as though they had brought uneasiness and discomfort into the house with them. In a house in which two sisters and their children, brothers, and neighbours were gathered together, probably on account of some family festivity, or event, how could the presence of nineteen unknown officers possibly be welcome?

At the entrance to the drawing room the officers were met by a tall, graceful old lady with black eyebrows and a long face, very much like the Empress Eugénie. Smiling graciously and majestically, she said she was glad and happy to see her guests, and apologized that her husband and she were on this occasion unable to invite *messieurs les officiers* to stay the night. From her beautiful majestic smile, which instantly vanished from her face every time she turned away from her guests, it was evident that she had seen numbers of officers in her day, that she was in no humour for them now, and if she invited them to her house and apologized for not doing more, it was only because her breeding and position in society required it of her.

When the officers went into the big dining room, there were about a dozen people, men and ladies, young and old, sitting at tea at the end of a long table. A group of men was dimly visible behind their chairs, wrapped in a haze of cigar smoke; and in the midst of them stood a lanky young man with red whiskers, talking loudly, with a lisp, in English. Through a door beyond the group could be seen a light room with pale blue furniture.

"Gentlemen, there are so many of you that it is impossible to introduce you all!" said the General in a loud voice, trying to sound very cheerful. "Make each other's acquaintance, gentlemen, without any ceremony!"

The officers—some with very serious and even stern faces, others with forced smiles, and all feeling extremely awkward—somehow made their bows and sat down to tea.

The most ill at ease of them all was Ryabovitch—a little officer in spectacles, with sloping shoulders, and whiskers like a lynx's. While some of his comrades assumed a serious expression, while others wore forced smiles, his face, his lynx-like whiskers, and spectacles seemed to say: "I am the shyest, most modest, and most undistinguished officer in the whole brigade!" At first, on going into the room and sitting down to the table, he could not fix his attention on any one face or object. The faces, the dresses, the cut-glass decanters of brandy, the steam from the glasses, the moulded cornices—all blended in one general impression that inspired in Ryabovitch alarm and a desire to hide his head. Like a lecturer making his first appearance before the public, he saw everything that was before his eyes, but apparently only had a dim understanding of it (among physiologists this condition, when the subject sees but does not understand, is called psychical blindness). After a little while, growing accustomed to his surroundings, Ryabovitch saw clearly and began to observe. As a shy man, unused to society, what struck him first was that in which he had always been deficient—namely, the extraordinary boldness of his new acquaintances. Von Rabbek, his wife, two elderly ladies, a young lady in a lilac dress, and the young man with the red whiskers, who was, it appeared, a younger son of Von Rabbek, very cleverly, as though they had rehearsed it beforehand, took seats between the officers, and at once got up a heated discussion in which the visitors could not help taking part. The lilac young lady hotly asserted that the artillery had a much better time than the cavalry and the infantry, while Von Rabbek and the elderly ladies maintained the opposite. A brisk interchange of talk followed. Ryabovitch watched the lilac young lady who argued so hotly about what was unfamiliar and utterly uninteresting to her, and watched artificial smiles come and go on her face.

Von Rabbek and his family skilfully drew the officers into the discussion, and meanwhile kept a sharp lookout over their glasses and mouths, to see whether all of them were drinking, whether all had enough sugar, why someone was not eating cakes or not drinking brandy. And the longer Ryabovitch watched and listened, the more he was attracted by this insincere but splendidly disciplined family.

After tea the officers went into the drawing room. Lieutenant Lobytko's instinct had not deceived him. There were a great number of girls and young married ladies. The "setter" lieutenant was soon standing by a very young, fair girl in a black dress, and, bending down to her jauntily, as though leaning on an unseen sword, smiled and shrugged his shoulders coquettishly. He probably talked very interesting nonsense, for the fair girl looked at his well-fed face condescendingly and asked indifferently, "Really?" And from that uninterested "Really?" the setter, had he been intelligent, might have concluded that she would never call him to heel.

The piano struck up; the melancholy strains of a valse floated out of the wide open windows, and everyone, for some reason, remembered that it was spring, a May evening. Everyone was conscious of the fragrance of roses, of lilac, and of the young leaves of the poplar. Ryabovitch, in whom the brandy he had drunk made itself felt, under the influence of the music stole a glance towards the window, smiled, and began watching the movements of the women, and it seemed to him that the smell of roses, of poplars, and lilac came not from the garden, but from the ladies' faces and dresses.

Von Rabbek's son invited a scraggy-looking young lady to dance, and waltzed round the room twice with her. Lobytko, gliding over the parquet floor, flew up to the lilac young lady and whirled her away. Dancing began . . . Ryabovitch stood near the door among those who were not dancing and looked on. He had never once danced in his whole life, and he had never once in his life put his arm round the waist of a respectable woman. He was highly delighted that a man should in the sight of all take a girl he did not know round the waist and offer her his shoulder to put her hand on, but he could not imagine himself in the position of such a man. There were times when he envied the boldness and swagger of his companions and was inwardly wretched; the consciousness that he was timid, that he was round-shouldered and uninteresting, that he had a long waist and lynx-like whiskers, had deeply mortified him, but with years he had grown used to this feeling, and now, looking at his comrades dancing or loudly talking, he no longer envied them, but only felt touched and mournful.

When the quadrille began, young Von Rabbek came up to those who were not dancing and invited two officers to have a game at billiards. The officers accepted and went with him out of the drawing room. Ryabovitch, having nothing to do and wishing to take part in the general movement, slouched after them. From the big drawing room they went into the little drawing room, then into a narrow corridor with a glass roof, and thence into a room in which on their entrance three sleepy-looking footmen jumped up quickly from the sofa. At last, after passing through a long succession of rooms, young Von Rabbek and the officers came into a small room where there was a billiard-table. They began to play.

Ryabovitch, who had never played any game but cards, stood near the billiard-table and looked indifferently at the players, while they in unbuttoned coats, with cues in their hands, stepped about, made puns, and kept shouting out unintelligible words.

The players took no notice of him, and only now and then one of them, shoving him with his elbow or accidentally touching him with the end of his cue, would turn round and say "Pardon!" Before the first game was over he was weary of it, and began to feel he was not wanted and in the way . . . He felt disposed to return to the drawing room, and he went out.

On his way back he met with a little adventure. When he had gone halfway he noticed he had taken a wrong turning. He distinctly remembered that he ought to meet three sleepy footmen on his way, but he had passed five or six rooms, and those sleepy figures seemed to have vanished into the earth. Noticing his mistake, he walked back a little way and turned to the right; he found himself in a little dark room which he had not seen on his way to the billiard-room. After standing there a little while, he resolutely opened the first door that met his eyes and walked into an absolutely dark room. Straight in front could be seen the crack in the doorway through which there was a gleam of vivid light; from the other side of the door came the muffled sound of a melancholy mazurka. Here, too, as in the drawing room, the windows were wide open and there was a smell of poplars, lilac and roses . . .

Ryabovitch stood still in hesitation . . . At that moment, to his surprise, he heard hurried footsteps and the rustling of a dress, a breathless feminine voice whispered "At last!" And two soft, fragrant, unmistakably feminine arms were clasped about his neck; a warm cheek was pressed to his cheek, and simultaneously there was the sound of a kiss. But at once the bestower of the kiss uttered a faint shriek and skipped back from him, as it seemed to Ryabovitch, with aversion. He, too, almost shrieked and rushed towards the gleam of light at the door . . .

When he went back into the drawing room his heart was beating and his hands were trembling so noticeably that he made haste to hide them behind his back. At first he was tormented by shame and dread that the whole drawing room knew that he had just been kissed and embraced by a woman. He shrank into himself and looked uneasily about him, but as he became convinced that people were dancing and talking as calmly as ever, he gave himself up entirely to the new sensation which he had never experienced before in his life. Something strange was happening to him . . . His neck, round which soft, fragrant arms had so lately been clasped, seemed to him to be anointed with oil; on his left cheek near his moustache where the unknown had kissed him there was a faint chilly tingling sensation as from peppermint drops, and the more he rubbed the place the more distinct was the chilly sensation; all over, from head to foot, he was full of a strange new feeling which grew stronger and stronger . . . He wanted to dance, to talk, to run into the garden, to laugh aloud . . . He quite forgot that he was round-shouldered and uninteresting, that he had lynx-like whiskers and an "undistinguished appearance" (that was how his appearance had been described by some ladies whose conversation he had accidentally overheard). When Von Rabbek's wife happened to pass by him, he gave her such a broad and friendly smile that she stood still and looked at him inquiringly.

"I like your house immensely!" he said, setting his spectacles straight.

The General's wife smiled and said that the house had belonged to her father; then she asked whether his parents were living, whether he had long been in the army, why he was so thin, and so on . . . After receiving answers to her questions, she went on, and after his conversation with her his smiles were more friendly than ever, and he thought he was surrounded by splendid people . . .

At supper Ryabovitch ate mechanically everything offered him, drank, and without listening to anything, tried to understand what had just happened to him . . . The adventure was of a mysterious and romantic character, but it was not difficult to explain it. No doubt some girl or young married lady had arranged a tryst with someone in the dark room; had waited a long time, and being nervous and excited had taken Ryabovitch for her hero; this was the more probable as Ryabovitch had stood still hesitating in the dark room, so that he, too, had seemed like a person expecting something . . . This was how Ryabovitch explained to himself the kiss he had received.

"And who is she?" he wondered, looking round at the women's faces. "She must be young, for elderly ladies don't give rendezvous. That she was a lady, one could tell by the rustle of her dress, her perfume, her voice . . ."

His eyes rested on the lilac young lady, and he thought her very attractive; she had beautiful shoulders and arms, a clever face, and a delightful voice. Ryabovitch, looking at her, hoped that she and no one else was his unknown . . . But she laughed somehow artificially and wrinkled up her long nose, which seemed to him to make her look old. Then he turned his eyes upon the fair girl in a black dress. She was younger, simpler, and more genuine, had a charming brow, and drank very daintily out of her wineglass. Ryabovitch now hoped that it was she. But soon he began to think her face flat, and fixed his eyes upon the one next her.

"It's difficult to guess," he thought, musing. "If one takes the shoulders and arms of the lilac one only, adds the brow of the fair one and the eyes of the one on the left of Lobytko, then . . ."

He made a combination of these things in his mind and so formed the image of the girl who had kissed him, the image that he wanted her to have, but could not find at the table . . .

After supper, replete and exhilarated, the officers began to take leave and say thank you. Von Rabbek and his wife began again apologizing that they could not ask them to stay the night.

"Very, very glad to have met you, gentlemen," said Von Rabbek, and this time sincerely (probably because people are far more sincere and good-humoured at speeding their parting guests than on meeting them). "Delighted. I hope you will come on your way back! Don't stand on ceremony! Where are you going? Do you want to go by the upper way? No, go across the garden; it's nearer here by the lower way."

The officers went out into the garden. After the bright light and the noise the garden seemed very dark and quiet. They walked in silence all the way to the gate. They were a little drunk, pleased, and in good spirits, but the darkness and silence made them thoughtful for a minute. Probably the same idea occurred to each one of them as to Ryabovitch: would there ever come a time for them when, like Von Rabbek, they would have a large house, a family, a garden—when they, too, would be able to welcome people, even though insincerely, feed them, make them drunk and contented?

Going out of the garden gate, they all began talking at once and laughing loudly about nothing. They were walking now along the little path that led down to the river, and then ran along the water's edge, winding round the bushes on the bank, the pools, and the willows that overhung the water. The bank and the path were scarcely visible, and the other bank was entirely plunged in darkness. Stars were reflected here and there on the dark water; they quivered and were broken up on the surface—and from that alone it could be seen that the river was flowing rapidly. It was still. Drowsy curlews cried plaintively on the further bank, and in one of the bushes on the nearest side a nightingale was trilling loudly, taking no notice of the crowd of officers. The officers stood round the bush, touched it, but the nightingale went on singing.

"What a fellow!" they exclaimed approvingly. "We stand beside him and he takes not a bit of notice! What a rascal!"

At the end of the way the path went uphill, and, skirting the church enclosure, turned into the road. Here the officers, tired with walking uphill, sat down and lighted their cigarettes. On the other side of the river a murky red fire came into sight, and having nothing better to do, they spent a long time in discussing whether it was a camp fire or a light in a window, or something else . . . Ryabovitch, too, looked at the light, and he fancied that the light looked and winked at him, as though it knew about the kiss.

On reaching his quarters, Ryabovitch undressed as quickly as possible and got into bed. Lobytko and Lieutenant Merzlyakov—a peaceable, silent fellow, who was considered in his own circle a highly educated officer, and was always, whenever it was possible, reading the "Vyestnik Evropi," which he carried about with him everywhere—were quartered in the same hut with Ryabovitch. Lobytko undressed, walked up and down the room for a long while with the air of a man who has not been satisfied, and sent his orderly for beer. Merzlyakov got into bed, put a candle by his pillow and plunged into reading the "Vyestnik Evropi."

"Who was she?" Ryabovitch wondered, looking at the smoky ceiling.

His neck still felt as though he had been anointed with oil, and there was still the chilly sensation near his mouth as though from peppermint drops. The shoulders and arms of the young lady in lilac, the brow and the truthful eyes of the fair girl in black, waists, dresses, and brooches, floated through his imagination. He tried to fix his attention on these images, but they danced about, broke up and flickered. When these images vanished altogether from the broad dark background which every man sees when he closes his eyes, he began to hear hurried footsteps, the rustle of skirts, the sound of a kiss and—an intense groundless joy took possession of him . . . Abandoning himself to this joy, he heard the orderly return and announce that there was no beer. Lobytko was terribly indignant, and began pacing up and down again.

"Well, isn't he an idiot?" he kept saying, stopping first before Ryabovitch and then before Merzlyakov. "What a fool and a dummy a man must be not to get hold of any beer! Eh? Isn't he a scoundrel?"

"Of course you can't get beer here," said Merzlyakov, not removing his eyes from the "Vyestnik Evropi."

"Oh! Is that your opinion?" Lobytko persisted. "Lord have mercy upon us, if you dropped me on the moon I'd find you beer and women directly! I'll go and find some at once . . . You may call me an impostor if I don't!"

He spent a long time in dressing and pulling on his high boots, then finished smoking his cigarette in silence and went out.

"Rabbek, Grabbek, Labbek," he muttered, stopping in the outer room. "I don't care to go alone, damn it all! Ryabovitch, wouldn't you like to go for a walk? Eh?"

Receiving no answer, he returned, slowly undressed and got into bed. Merzlyakov sighed, put the "Vyestnik Evropi" away, and put out the light.

"H'm! . . ." muttered Lobytko, lighting a cigarette in the dark.

Ryabovitch pulled the bed-clothes over his head, curled himself up in bed, and tried to gather together the floating images in his mind and to combine them into one whole. But nothing came of it. He soon fell asleep, and his last thought was that someone had caressed him and made him happy—that something extraordinary, foolish, but joyful and delightful, had come into his life. The thought did not leave him even in his sleep.

When he woke up the sensations of oil on his neck and the chill of peppermint about his lips had gone, but joy flooded his heart just as the day before. He looked enthusiastically at the window-frames, gilded by the light of the rising sun, and listened to the movement of the passers-by in the street. People were talking loudly close to the window. Lebedetsky, the commander of Ryabovitch's battery, who had only just overtaken the brigade, was talking to his sergeant at the top of his voice, being always accustomed to shout.

"What else?" shouted the commander.

"When they were shoeing yesterday, your high nobility, they drove a nail into Pigeon's hoof. The vet. put on clay and vinegar; they are leading him apart now. And also, your honour, Artemyev got drunk yesterday, and the lieutenant ordered him to be put in the limber of a spare gun-carriage."

The sergeant reported that Karpov had forgotten the new cords for the trumpets and the rings for the tents, and that their honours, the officers, had spent the previous evening visiting General Von Rabbek. In the middle of this conversation the red-bearded face of Lebedetsky appeared in the window. He screwed up his short-sighted eyes, looking at the sleepy faces of the officers, and said good morning to them.

"Is everything all right?" he asked.

"One of the horses has a sore neck from the new collar," answered Lobytko, yawning.

The commander sighed, thought a moment, and said in a loud voice:

"I am thinking of going to see Alexandra Yevgrafovna. I must call on her. Well, goodbye. I shall catch you up in the evening."

A quarter of an hour later the brigade set off on its way. When it was moving along the road by the granaries, Ryabovitch looked at the house on the right. The blinds were down in all the windows. Evidently the household was still asleep. The one who had kissed Ryabovitch the day before was asleep, too. He tried to imagine her asleep. The wide-open windows of the bedroom, the green branches peeping in, the morning freshness, the scent of the poplars, lilac, and roses, the bed, a chair, and on it the skirts that had rustled the day before, the little slippers, the little watch on the table—all this he pictured to himself clearly and distinctly, but the features of the face, the sweet sleepy smile, just what was characteristic and important, slipped through his imagination like quicksilver through the fingers. When he had ridden on half a mile, he looked back: the yellow church, the house, and the river, were all bathed in light; the river with its bright green banks, with the blue sky reflected in it and glints of silver in the sunshine here and there, was very beautiful. Ryabovitch gazed for the last time at Myestetchki, and he felt as sad as though he were parting with something very near and dear to him.

And before him on the road lay nothing but long familiar, uninteresting pictures . . . To right and to left, fields of young rye and buckwheat with rooks hopping about in them. If one looked ahead, one saw dust and the backs of men's heads; if one looked back, one saw the same dust and faces . . . Foremost of all marched four men with sabres—this was the vanguard. Next, behind, the crowd of singers, and behind them the trumpeters on horseback. The vanguard and the chorus of singers, like torch-bearers in a funeral procession, often forgot to keep the regulation distance and pushed a long way ahead . . . Ryabovitch was with the first cannon of the fifth battery. He could see all the four batteries moving in front of him. For any one not a military man this long tedious procession of a moving brigade seems an intricate and unintelligible muddle; one cannot understand why there are so many people round one cannon, and why it is drawn by so many horses in such a strange network of harness, as though it really were so terrible and heavy. To Ryabovitch it was all perfectly comprehensible and therefore uninteresting. He had known for ever so long why at the head of each battery there rode a stalwart bombardier, and why he was called a bombardier; immediately behind this bombardier could be seen the horsemen of the first and then of the middle units. Ryabovitch knew that the horses on which they rode, those on the left, were called one name, while those on the right were called another—it was extremely uninteresting. Behind the horsemen came two shaft-horses. On one of them sat a rider with the dust of yesterday on his back and a clumsy and funny-looking piece of wood on his leg. Ryabovitch knew the object of this piece of wood, and did not think it funny. All the riders waved their whips mechanically and shouted from time to time. The cannon itself was ugly. On the fore part lay sacks of oats covered with canvas, and the cannon itself was hung all over with kettles, soldiers' knapsacks, bags, and looked like some small harmless animal surrounded for some unknown reason by men and horses. To the leeward of it marched six men, the gunners, swinging their arms. After the cannon there came again more bombardiers, riders, shaft-horses, and behind them another cannon, as ugly and unimpressive as the first. After the second followed a third, a fourth; near the fourth an officer, and so on. There were six batteries in all in the brigade, and four cannons in each battery. The procession covered half a mile; it ended in a string of wagons near which an extremely attractive creature—the ass, Magar, brought by a battery commander from Turkey—paced pensively with his long-eared head drooping.

Ryabovitch looked indifferently before and behind, at the backs of heads and at faces; at any other time he would have been half asleep, but now he was entirely absorbed in his new agreeable thoughts. At first when the brigade was setting off on the march he tried to persuade himself that the incident of the kiss could only be interesting as a mysterious little adventure, that it was in reality trivial, and to think of it seriously, to say the least of it, was stupid; but now he bade farewell to logic and gave himself up to dreams . . . At one moment he imagined himself in Von Rabbek's drawing room beside a girl who was like the young lady in lilac and the fair girl in black; then he would close his eyes and see himself with another, entirely unknown girl, whose features were very vague. In his imagination he talked, caressed her, leaned on her shoulder, pictured war, separation, then meeting again, supper with his wife, children . . .

"Brakes on!" the word of command rang out every time they went downhill.

He, too, shouted "Brakes on!" and was afraid this shout would disturb his reverie and bring him back to reality . . .

As they passed by some landowner's estate Ryabovitch looked over the fence into the garden. A long avenue, straight as a ruler, strewn with yellow sand and bordered with young birch-trees, met his eyes . . . With the eagerness of a man given up to dreaming, he pictured to himself little feminine feet tripping along yellow sand, and quite unexpectedly had a clear vision in his imagination of the girl who had kissed him and whom he had succeeded in picturing to himself the evening before at supper. This image remained in his brain and did not desert him again.

At midday there was a shout in the rear near the string of wagons:

"Easy! Eyes to the left! Officers!"

The general of the brigade drove by in a carriage with a pair of white horses. He stopped near the second battery, and shouted something which no one understood. Several officers, among them Ryabovitch, galloped up to them.

"Well?" asked the general, blinking his red eyes. "Are there any sick?"

Receiving an answer, the general, a little skinny man, chewed, thought for a moment and said, addressing one of the officers:

"One of your drivers of the third cannon has taken off his leg-guard and hung it on the fore part of the cannon, the rascal. Reprimand him."

He raised his eyes to Ryabovitch and went on:

"It seems to me your front strap is too long."

Making a few other tedious remarks, the general looked at Lobytko and grinned.

"You look very melancholy today, Lieutenant Lobytko," he said. "Are you pining for Madame Lopuhov? Eh? Gentlemen, he is pining for Madame Lopuhov."

The lady in question was a very stout and tall person who had long passed her fortieth year. The general, who had a predilection for solid ladies, whatever their ages, suspected a similar taste in his officers. The officers smiled respectfully. The general, delighted at having said something very amusing and biting, laughed loudly, touched his coachman's back, and saluted. The carriage rolled on . . .

"All I am dreaming about now which seems to me so impossible and unearthly is really quite an ordinary thing," thought Ryabovitch, looking at the clouds of dust racing after the general's carriage. "It's all very ordinary, and everyone goes through it . . . That general, for instance, has once been in love; now he is married and has children. Captain Vahter, too, is married and beloved, though the nape of his neck is very red and ugly and he has no waist . . . Salrnanov is coarse and very Tatar, but he has had a love affair that has ended in marriage . . . I am the same as everyone else, and I, too, shall have the same experience as everyone else, sooner or later . . ."

And the thought that he was an ordinary person, and that his life was ordinary, delighted him and gave him courage. He pictured her and his happiness as he pleased, and put no rein on his imagination.

When the brigade reached their halting-place in the evening, and the officers were resting in their tents, Ryabovitch, Merzlyakov, and Lobytko were sitting round a box having supper. Merzlyakov ate without haste, and, as he munched deliberately, read the "Vyestnik Evropi," which he held on his knees. Lobytko talked incessantly and kept filling up his glass with beer, and Ryabovitch, whose head was confused from dreaming all day long, drank and said nothing. After three glasses he got a little drunk, felt weak, and had an irresistible desire to impart his new sensations to his comrades.

"A strange thing happened to me at those Von Rabbeks'," he began, trying to put an indifferent and ironical tone into his voice. "You know I went into the billiard-room . . ."

He began describing very minutely the incident of the kiss, and a moment later relapsed into silence . . . In the course of that moment he had told everything, and it surprised him dreadfully to find how short a time it took him to tell it. He had imagined that he could have been telling the story of the kiss till next morning. Listening to him, Lobytko, who was a great liar and consequently believed no one, looked at him sceptically and laughed. Merzlyakov twitched his eyebrows and, without removing his eyes from the "Vyestnik Evropi," said:

"That's an odd thing! How strange! . . . throws herself on a man's neck, without addressing him by name . . . . She must be some sort of hysterical neurotic."

"Yes, she must," Ryabovitch agreed.

"A similar thing once happened to me," said Lobytko, assuming a scared expression. "I was going last year to Kovno . . . I took a second-class ticket. The train was crammed, and it was impossible to sleep. I gave the guard half a rouble; he took my luggage and led me to another compartment . . . I lay down and covered myself with a rug . . . It was dark, you understand. Suddenly I felt someone touch me on the shoulder and breathe in my face. I made a movement with my hand and felt somebody's elbow . . . I opened my eyes and only imagine—a woman. Black eyes, lips red as a prime salmon, nostrils breathing passionately—a bosom like a buffer . . ."

"Excuse me," Merzlyakov interrupted calmly, "I understand about the bosom, but how could you see the lips if it was dark?"

Lobytko began trying to put himself right and laughing at Merzlyakov's unimaginativeness. It made Ryabovitch wince. He walked away from the box, got into bed, and vowed never to confide again.

Camp life began . . . The days flowed by, one very much like another. All those days Ryabovitch felt, thought, and behaved as though he were in love. Every morning when his orderly handed him water to wash with, and he sluiced his head with cold water, he thought there was something warm and delightful in his life.

In the evenings when his comrades began talking of love and women, he would listen, and draw up closer; and he wore the expression of a soldier when he hears the description of a battle in which he has taken part. And on the evenings when the officers, out on the spree with the setter—Lobytko—at their head, made Don Juan excursions to the "suburb," and Ryabovitch took part in such excursions, he always was sad, felt profoundly guilty, and inwardly begged *her* forgiveness . . . In hours of leisure or on sleepless nights, when he felt moved to recall his childhood, his father and mother—everything near and dear, in fact, he invariably thought of Myestetchki, the strange horse, Von Rabbek, his wife who was like the Empress Eugénie, the dark room, the crack of light at the door . . .

On the thirty-first of August he went back from the camp, not with the whole brigade, but with only two batteries of it. He was dreaming and excited all the way, as though he were going back to his native place. He had an intense longing to see again the strange horse, the church, the insincere family of the Von Rabbeks, the dark room. The "inner voice," which so often deceives lovers, whispered to him for some reason that he would be sure to see her . . . and he was tortured by the questions, How he should meet her? What he would talk to her about? Whether she had forgotten the kiss? If the worst came to the worst, he thought, even if he did not meet her, it would be a pleasure to him merely to go through the dark room and recall the past . . .

Towards evening there appeared on the horizon the familiar church and white granaries. Ryabovitch's heart beat . . . He did not hear the officer who was riding beside him and saying something to him, he forgot everything, and looked eagerly at the river shining in the distance, at the roof of the house, at the dovecote round which the pigeons were circling in the light of the setting sun.

When they reached the church and were listening to the billeting orders, he expected every second that a man on horseback would come round the church enclosure and invite the officers to tea, but . . . the billeting orders were read, the officers were in haste to go on to the village, and the man on horseback did not appear.

"Von Rabbek will hear at once from the peasants that we have come and will send for us," thought Ryabovitch, as he went into the hut, unable to understand why a comrade was lighting a candle and why the orderlies were hurriedly setting samovars . . .

A painful uneasiness took possession of him. He lay down, then got up and looked out of the window to see whether the messenger were coming. But there was no sign of him.

He lay down again, but half an hour later he got up, and, unable to restrain his uneasiness, went into the street and strode towards the church. It was dark and deserted in the square near the church . . . Three soldiers were standing silent in a row where the road began to go downhill. Seeing Ryabovitch, they roused themselves and saluted. He returned the salute and began to go down the familiar path.

On the further side of the river the whole sky was flooded with crimson: the moon was rising; two peasant women, talking loudly, were picking cabbage in the kitchen garden; behind the kitchen garden there were some dark huts . . . And everything on the near side of the river was just as it had been in May: the path, the bushes, the willows overhanging the water . . . but there was no sound of the brave nightingale, and no scent of poplar and fresh grass.

Reaching the garden, Ryabovitch looked in at the gate. The garden was dark and still . . . He could see nothing but the white stems of the nearest birch-trees and a little bit of the avenue; all the rest melted together into a dark blur. Ryabovitch looked and listened eagerly, but after waiting for a quarter of an hour without hearing a sound or catching a glimpse of a light, he trudged back . . .

He went down to the river. The General's bath-house and the bath-sheets on the rail of the little bridge showed white before him . . . He went on to the bridge, stood a little, and, quite unnecessarily, touched the sheets. They felt rough and cold. He looked down at the water . . . The river ran rapidly and with a faintly audible gurgle round the piles of the bath-house. The red moon was reflected near the left bank; little ripples ran over the reflection, stretching it out, breaking it into bits, and seemed trying to carry it away.

"How stupid, how stupid!" thought Ryabovitch, looking at the running water. "How unintelligent it all is!"

Now that he expected nothing, the incident of the kiss, his impatience, his vague hopes and disappointment, presented themselves in a clear light. It no longer seemed to him strange that he had not seen the General's messenger, and that he would never see the girl who had accidentally kissed him instead of someone else; on the contrary, it would have been strange if he had seen her . . .

The water was running, he knew not where or why, just as it did in May. In May it had flowed into the great river, from the great river into the sea; then it had risen in vapour, turned into rain, and perhaps the very same water was running now before Ryabovitch's eyes again . . . What for? Why?

And the whole world, the whole of life, seemed to Ryabovitch an unintelligible, aimless jest . . . And turning his eyes from the water and looking at the sky, he remembered again how fate in the person of an unknown woman had by chance caressed him, he remembered his summer dreams and fancies, and his life struck him as extraordinarily meagre, poverty-stricken, and colourless . . .

When he went back to his hut he did not find one of his comrades. The orderly informed him that they had all gone to "General von Rabbek's, who had sent a messenger on horseback to invite them . . ."

For an instant there was a flash of joy in Ryabovitch's heart, but he quenched it at once, got into bed, and in his wrath with his fate, as though to spite it, did not go to the General's.

The Black Monk

Translated by Constance Garnett

I

ndrey Vassilitch Kovrin, who held a master's degree at the
University, had exhausted himself, and had upset his nerves. He
did not send for a doctor, but casually, over a bottle of wine, he
spoke to a friend who was a doctor, and the latter advised him to spend
the spring and summer in the country. Very opportunely a long letter
came from Tanya Pesotsky, who asked him to come and stay with them at
Borissovka. And he made up his mind that he really must go.

To begin with—that was in April—he went to his own home,
Kovrinka, and there spent three weeks in solitude; then, as soon as the
roads were in good condition, he set off, driving in a carriage, to visit
Pesotsky, his former guardian, who had brought him up, and was a
horticulturist well known all over Russia. The distance from Kovrinka
to Borissovka was reckoned only a little over fifty miles. To drive along a
soft road in May in a comfortable carriage with springs was a real pleasure.

Pesotsky had an immense house with columns and lions, off which the
stucco was peeling, and with a footman in swallow-tails at the entrance.
The old park, laid out in the English style, gloomy and severe, stretched
for almost three-quarters of a mile to the river, and there ended in a steep,
precipitous clay bank, where pines grew with bare roots that looked like
shaggy paws; the water shone below with an unfriendly gleam, and the
peewits flew up with a plaintive cry, and there one always felt that one

must sit down and write a ballad. But near the house itself, in the courtyard and orchard, which together with the nurseries covered ninety acres, it was all life and gaiety even in bad weather. Such marvellous roses, lilies, camellias; such tulips of all possible shades, from glistening white to sooty black—such a wealth of flowers, in fact, Kovrin had never seen anywhere as at Pesotsky's. It was only the beginning of spring, and the real glory of the flower-beds was still hidden away in the hot-houses. But even the flowers along the avenues, and here and there in the flower-beds, were enough to make one feel, as one walked about the garden, as though one were in a realm of tender colours, especially in the early morning when the dew was glistening on every petal.

What was the decorative part of the garden, and what Pesotsky contemptuously spoke of as rubbish, had at one time in his childhood given Kovrin an impression of fairyland.

Every sort of caprice, of elaborate monstrosity and mockery at Nature was here. There were espaliers of fruit-trees, a pear-tree in the shape of a pyramidal poplar, spherical oaks and lime-trees, an apple-tree in the shape of an umbrella, plum-trees trained into arches, crests, candelabra, and even into the number 1862—the year when Pesotsky first took up horticulture. One came across, too, lovely, graceful trees with strong, straight stems like palms, and it was only by looking intently that one could recognise these trees as gooseberries or currants. But what made the garden most cheerful and gave it a lively air, was the continual coming and going in it, from early morning till evening; people with wheelbarrows, shovels, and watering-cans swarmed round the trees and bushes, in the avenues and the flower-beds, like ants . . .

Kovrin arrived at Pesotsky's at ten o'clock in the evening. He found Tanya and her father, Yegor Semyonitch, in great anxiety. The clear starlight sky and the thermometer foretold a frost towards morning, and meanwhile Ivan Karlovitch, the gardener, had gone to the town, and they had no one to rely upon. At supper they talked of nothing but the morning frost, and it was settled that Tanya should not go to bed, and between twelve and one should walk through the garden, and see that everything was done properly, and Yegor Semyonitch should get up at three o'clock or even earlier.

Kovrin sat with Tanya all the evening, and after midnight went out with her into the garden. It was cold. There was a strong smell of burning already in the garden. In the big orchard, which was called the commercial garden, and which brought Yegor Semyonitch several thousand clear profit, a thick, black, acrid smoke was creeping over the ground and, curling around the trees, was saving those thousands from the frost. Here the trees were arranged as on a chessboard, in straight and regular rows like ranks of soldiers, and this severe pedantic regularity, and the fact that all the trees were of the same size, and had tops and trunks all exactly alike, made them look monotonous and even dreary. Kovrin and Tanya walked along the rows where fires of dung, straw, and all sorts of refuse were smouldering, and from time to time they were met by labourers who wandered in the smoke like shadows. The only trees in flower were the cherries, plums, and certain sorts of apples, but the whole garden was plunged in smoke, and it was only near the nurseries that Kovrin could breathe freely.

"Even as a child I used to sneeze from the smoke here," he said, shrugging his shoulders, "but to this day I don't understand how smoke can keep off frost."

"Smoke takes the place of clouds when there are none . . ." answered Tanya.

"And what do you want clouds for?"

"In overcast and cloudy weather there is no frost."

"You don't say so."

He laughed and took her arm. Her broad, very earnest face, chilled with the frost, with her delicate black eyebrows, the turned-up collar of her coat, which prevented her moving her head freely, and the whole of her thin, graceful figure, with her skirts tucked up on account of the dew, touched him.

"Good heavens! she is grown up," he said. "When I went away from here last, five years ago, you were still a child. You were such a thin, long-legged creature, with your hair hanging on your shoulders; you used to wear short frocks, and I used to tease you, calling you a heron . . . What time does!"

"Yes, five years!" sighed Tanya. "Much water has flowed since then. Tell me, Andryusha, honestly," she began eagerly, looking him in the face: "do you feel strange with us now? But why do I ask you? You are a man, you live your own interesting life, you are somebody . . . To grow apart is so natural! But however that may be, Andryusha, I want you to think of us as your people. We have a right to that."

"I do, Tanya."

"On your word of honour?"

"Yes, on my word of honour."

"You were surprised this evening that we have so many of your photographs. You know my father adores you. Sometimes it seems to me that he loves you more than he does me. He is proud of you. You are a clever, extraordinary man, you have made a brilliant career for yourself, and he is persuaded that you have turned out like this because he brought you up. I don't try to prevent him from thinking so. Let him."

Dawn was already beginning, and that was especially perceptible from the distinctness with which the coils of smoke and the tops of the trees began to stand out in the air.

"It's time we were asleep, though," said Tanya, "and it's cold, too." She took his arm. "Thank you for coming, Andryusha. We have only uninteresting acquaintances, and not many of them. We have only the garden, the garden, the garden, and nothing else. Standards, half-standards," she laughed. "Aports, Reinettes, Borovinkas, budded stocks, grafted stocks . . . All, all our life has gone into the garden. I never even dream of anything but apples and pears. Of course, it is very nice and useful, but sometimes one longs for something else for variety. I remember that when you used to come to us for the summer holidays, or simply a visit, it always seemed to be fresher and brighter in the house, as though the covers had been taken off the lustres and the furniture. I was only a little girl then, but yet I understood it."

She talked a long while and with great feeling. For some reason the idea came into his head that in the course of the summer he might grow fond of this little, weak, talkative creature, might be carried away and fall in love; in their position it was so possible and natural! This thought touched and amused him; he bent down to her sweet, preoccupied face and hummed softly:

"Onyegin, I won't conceal it;
I madly love Tatiana . . ."

By the time they reached the house, Yegor Semyonitch had got up. Kovrin did not feel sleepy; he talked to the old man and went to the garden with him. Yegor Semyonitch was a tall, broad-shouldered, corpulent man, and he suffered from asthma, yet he walked so fast that it was hard work to hurry after him. He had an extremely preoccupied air; he was always hurrying somewhere, with an expression that suggested that if he were one minute late all would be ruined!

"Here is a business, brother . . ." he began, standing still to take breath. "On the surface of the ground, as you see, is frost; but if you raise the thermometer on a stick fourteen feet above the ground, there it is warm . . . Why is that?"

"I really don't know," said Kovrin, and he laughed.

"H'm! . . . One can't know everything, of course . . . However large the intellect may be, you can't find room for everything in it. I suppose you still go in chiefly for philosophy?"

"Yes, I lecture in psychology; I am working at philosophy in general."

"And it does not bore you?"

"On the contrary, it's all I live for."

"Well, God bless you! . . ." said Yegor Semyonitch, meditatively stroking his grey whiskers. "God bless you! . . . I am delighted about you . . . delighted, my boy . . ."

But suddenly he listened, and, with a terrible face, ran off and quickly disappeared behind the trees in a cloud of smoke.

"Who tied this horse to an apple-tree?" Kovrin heard his despairing, heart-rending cry. "Who is the low scoundrel who has dared to tie this horse to an apple-tree? My God, my God! They have ruined everything; they have spoilt everything; they have done everything filthy, horrible, and abominable. The orchard's done for, the orchard's ruined. My God!"

When he came back to Kovrin, his face looked exhausted and mortified.

"What is one to do with these accursed people?" he said in a tearful voice, flinging up his hands. "Styopka was carting dung at night, and tied the horse to an apple-tree! He twisted the reins round it, the rascal, as tightly as he could, so that the bark is rubbed off in three places. What do you think of that! I spoke to him and he stands like a post and only blinks his eyes. Hanging is too good for him."

Growing calmer, he embraced Kovrin and kissed him on the cheek.

"Well, God bless you! . . . God bless you! . . ." he muttered. "I am very glad you have come. Unutterably glad . . . Thank you."

Then, with the same rapid step and preoccupied face, he made the round of the whole garden, and showed his former ward all his greenhouses and hot-houses, his covered-in garden, and two apiaries which he called the marvel of our century.

While they were walking the sun rose, flooding the garden with brilliant light. It grew warm. Foreseeing a long, bright, cheerful day, Kovrin recollected that it was only the beginning of May, and that he had before him a whole summer as bright, cheerful, and long; and suddenly there stirred in his bosom a joyous, youthful feeling, such as he used to experience in his childhood, running about in that garden. And he hugged the old man and kissed him affectionately. Both of them, feeling touched, went indoors and drank tea out of old-fashioned china cups, with cream and satisfying krendels made with milk and eggs; and these trifles reminded Kovrin again of his childhood and boyhood. The delightful present was blended with the impressions of the past that stirred within him; there was a tightness at his heart; yet he was happy.

He waited till Tanya was awake and had coffee with her, went for a walk, then went to his room and sat down to work. He read attentively, making notes, and from time to time raised his eyes to look out at the open windows or at the fresh, still dewy flowers in the vases on the table; and again he dropped his eyes to his book, and it seemed to him as though every vein in his body was quivering and fluttering with pleasure.

II

In the country he led just as nervous and restless a life as in town. He read and wrote a great deal, he studied Italian, and when he was out for a walk, thought with pleasure that he would soon sit down to work again. He slept so little that everyone wondered at him; if he accidentally dozed for half an hour in the daytime, he would lie awake all night, and, after a sleepless night, would feel cheerful and vigorous as though nothing had happened.

He talked a great deal, drank wine, and smoked expensive cigars. Very often, almost every day, young ladies of neighbouring families would come to the Pesotskys', and would sing and play the piano with Tanya; sometimes a young neighbour who was a good violinist would come, too. Kovrin listened with eagerness to the music and singing, and was exhausted by it, and this showed itself by his eyes closing and his head falling to one side.

One day he was sitting on the balcony after evening tea, reading. At the same time, in the drawing room, Tanya taking soprano, one of the young ladies a contralto, and the young man with his violin, were practising a well-known serenade of Braga's. Kovrin listened to the words—they were Russian—and could not understand their meaning. At last, leaving his book and listening attentively, he understood: a maiden, full of sick fancies, heard one night in her garden mysterious sounds, so strange and lovely that she was obliged to recognise them as a holy harmony which is unintelligible to us mortals, and so flies back to heaven. Kovrin's eyes began to close. He got up, and in exhaustion walked up and down the drawing room, and then the dining room. When the singing was over he took Tanya's arm, and with her went out on the balcony.

"I have been all day thinking of a legend," he said. "I don't remember whether I have read it somewhere or heard it, but it is a strange and almost grotesque legend. To begin with, it is somewhat obscure. A thousand years ago a monk, dressed in black, wandered about the desert, somewhere in Syria or Arabia . . . Some miles from where he was, some fisherman saw another black monk, who was moving slowly over the surface of a lake. This second monk was a mirage. Now forget all the laws of optics, which the legend does not recognise, and listen to the rest. From that mirage there was cast another mirage, then from that other a third, so that the image of the black monk began to be repeated endlessly from one layer of the atmosphere to another. So that he was seen at one time in Africa, at another in Spain, then Italy, then in the Far North . . . Then he passed out of the atmosphere of the earth, and now he is wandering all over the universe, still never coming into conditions in which he might disappear. Possibly he may be seen now in Mars or in some star of the Southern Cross. But, my dear, the real point on which the whole legend hangs lies in the fact that, exactly a thousand years from the day when the monk walked in the desert, the mirage will return to the atmosphere of the earth again and will appear to men. And it seems that the thousand years is almost up . . . According to the legend, we may look out for the black monk today or tomorrow."

"A queer mirage," said Tanya, who did not like the legend.

"But the most wonderful part of it all," laughed Kovrin, "is that I simply cannot recall where I got this legend from. Have I read it somewhere? Have I heard it? Or perhaps I dreamed of the black monk. I swear I don't remember. But the legend interests me. I have been thinking about it all day."

Letting Tanya go back to her visitors, he went out of the house, and, lost in meditation, walked by the flower-beds. The sun was already setting. The flowers, having just been watered, gave forth a damp, irritating fragrance. Indoors they began singing again, and in the distance the violin had the effect of a human voice. Kovrin, racking his brains to remember where he had read or heard the legend, turned slowly towards the park, and unconsciously went as far as the river. By a little path that ran along the steep bank, between the bare roots, he went down to the water, disturbed the peewits there and frightened two ducks. The last rays of the setting sun still threw light here and there on the gloomy pines, but it was quite dark on the surface of the river. Kovrin crossed to the other side by the narrow bridge. Before him lay a wide field covered with young rye not yet in blossom. There was no living habitation, no living soul in the distance, and it seemed as though the little path, if one went along it, would take one to the unknown, mysterious place where the sun had just gone down, and where the evening glow was flaming in immensity and splendour.

"How open, how free, how still it is here!" thought Kovrin, walking along the path. "And it feels as though all the world were watching me, hiding and waiting for me to understand it . . ."

But then waves began running across the rye, and a light evening breeze softly touched his uncovered head. A minute later there was another gust of wind, but stronger—the rye began rustling, and he heard behind him the hollow murmur of the pines. Kovrin stood still in amazement. From the horizon there rose up to the sky, like a whirlwind or a waterspout, a tall black column. Its outline was indistinct, but from the first instant it could be seen that it was not standing still, but moving with fearful rapidity, moving straight towards Kovrin, and the nearer it came the smaller and the more distinct it was. Kovrin moved aside into the rye to make way for it, and only just had time to do so.

A monk, dressed in black, with a grey head and black eyebrows, his arms crossed over his breast, floated by him . . . His bare feet did not touch the earth. After he had floated twenty feet beyond him, he looked round at Kovrin, and nodded to him with a friendly but sly smile. But what a pale, fearfully pale, thin face! Beginning to grow larger again, he flew across the river, collided noiselessly with the clay bank and pines, and passing through them, vanished like smoke.

"Why, you see," muttered Kovrin, "there must be truth in the legend."

Without trying to explain to himself the strange apparition, glad that he had succeeded in seeing so near and so distinctly, not only the monk's black garments, but even his face and eyes, agreeably excited, he went back to the house.

In the park and in the garden people were moving about quietly, in the house they were playing—so he alone had seen the monk. He had an intense desire to tell Tanya and Yegor Semyonitch, but he reflected that they would certainly think his words the ravings of delirium, and that would frighten them; he had better say nothing.

He laughed aloud, sang, and danced the mazurka; he was in high spirits, and all of them, the visitors and Tanya, thought he had a peculiar look, radiant and inspired, and that he was very interesting.

III

After supper, when the visitors had gone, he went to his room and lay down on the sofa: he wanted to think about the monk. But a minute later Tanya came in.

"Here, Andryusha; read father's articles," she said, giving him a bundle of pamphlets and proofs. "They are splendid articles. He writes capitally."

"Capitally, indeed!" said Yegor Semyonitch, following her and smiling constrainedly; he was ashamed. "Don't listen to her, please; don't read them! Though, if you want to go to sleep, read them by all means; they are a fine soporific."

"I think they are splendid articles," said Tanya, with deep conviction. "You read them, Andryusha, and persuade father to write oftener. He could write a complete manual of horticulture."

Yegor Semyonitch gave a forced laugh, blushed, and began uttering the phrases usually made use of by an embarrassed author. At last he began to give way.

"In that case, begin with Gaucher's article and these Russian articles," he muttered, turning over the pamphlets with a trembling hand, "or else you won't understand. Before you read my objections, you must know what I am objecting to. But it's all nonsense . . . tiresome stuff. Besides, I believe it's bedtime."

Tanya went away. Yegor Semyonitch sat down on the sofa by Kovrin and heaved a deep sigh.

"Yes, my boy . . ." he began after a pause. "That's how it is, my dear lecturer. Here I write articles, and take part in exhibitions, and receive medals . . . Pesotsky, they say, has apples the size of a head, and Pesotsky, they say, has made his fortune with his garden. In short, 'Kotcheby is rich and glorious.' But one asks oneself: what is it all for? The garden is certainly fine, a model. It's not really a garden, but a regular institution, which is of the greatest public importance because it marks, so to say, a new era in Russian agriculture and Russian industry. But, what's it for? What's the object of it?"

"The fact speaks for itself."

"I do not mean in that sense. I meant to ask: what will happen to the garden when I die? In the condition in which you see it now, it would not be maintained for one month without me. The whole secret of success lies not in its being a big garden or a great number of labourers being employed in it, but in the fact that I love the work. Do you understand? I love it perhaps more than myself. Look at me; I do everything myself. I work from morning to night: I do all the grafting myself, the pruning myself, the planting myself. I do it all myself: when any one helps me I am jealous and irritable till I am rude. The whole secret lies in loving it—that is, in the sharp eye of the master; yes, and in the master's hands, and in the feeling that makes one, when one goes anywhere for an hour's visit, sit, ill at ease, with one's heart far away, afraid that something may have happened in the garden. But when I die, who will look after it? Who will work? The gardener? The labourers? Yes? But I will tell you, my dear fellow, the worst enemy in the garden is not a hare, not a cockchafer, and not the frost, but any outside person."

"And Tanya?" asked Kovrin, laughing. "She can't be more harmful than a hare? She loves the work and understands it."

"Yes, she loves it and understands it. If after my death the garden goes to her and she is the mistress, of course nothing better could be wished. But if, which God forbid, she should marry," Yegor Semyonitch whispered, and looked with a frightened look at Kovrin, "that's just it. If she marries and children come, she will have no time to think about the garden. What I fear most is: she will marry some fine gentleman, and he will be greedy, and he will let the garden to people who will run it for profit, and everything will go to the devil the very first year! In our work females are the scourge of God!"

Yegor Semyonitch sighed and paused for a while.

"Perhaps it is egoism, but I tell you frankly: I don't want Tanya to get married. I am afraid of it! There is one young dandy comes to see us, bringing his violin and scraping on it; I know Tanya will not marry him, I know it quite well; but I can't bear to see him! Altogether, my boy, I am very queer. I know that."

Yegor Semyonitch got up and walked about the room in excitement, and it was evident that he wanted to say something very important, but could not bring himself to it.

"I am very fond of you, and so I am going to speak to you openly," he decided at last, thrusting his hands into his pockets. "I deal plainly with certain delicate questions, and say exactly what I think, and I cannot endure so-called hidden thoughts. I will speak plainly: you are the only man to whom I should not be afraid to marry my daughter. You are a clever man with a good heart, and would not let my beloved work go to ruin; and the chief reason is that I love you as a son, and I am proud of you. If Tanya and you could get up a romance somehow, then—well! I should be very glad and even happy. I tell you this plainly, without mincing matters, like an honest man."

Kovrin laughed. Yegor Semyonitch opened the door to go out, and stood in the doorway.

"If Tanya and you had a son, I would make a horticulturist of him," he said, after a moment's thought. "However, this is idle dreaming. Goodnight."

Left alone, Kovrin settled himself more comfortably on the sofa and took up the articles. The title of one was "On Intercropping"; of another, "A few Words on the Remarks of Monsieur Z. concerning the Trenching of the Soil for a New Garden"; a third, "Additional Matter concerning Grafting with a Dormant Bud"; and they were all of the same sort. But what a restless, jerky tone! What nervous, almost hysterical passion! Here was an article, one would have thought, with most peaceable and impersonal contents: the subject of it was the Russian Antonovsky Apple. But Yegor Semyonitch began it with "Audiatur altera pars," and finished it with "Sapienti sat"; and between these two quotations a perfect torrent of venomous phrases directed "at the learned ignorance of our recognised horticultural authorities, who observe Nature from the height of their university chairs," or at Monsieur Gaucher, "whose success has been the work of the vulgar and the dilettanti." And then followed an inappropriate, affected, and insincere regret that peasants who stole fruit and broke the branches could not nowadays be flogged.

"It is beautiful, charming, healthy work, but even in this there is strife and passion," thought Kovrin, "I suppose that everywhere and in all careers men of ideas are nervous, and marked by exaggerated sensitiveness. Most likely it must be so."

He thought of Tanya, who was so pleased with Yegor Semyonitch's articles. Small, pale, and so thin that her shoulder-blades stuck out, her eyes, wide and open, dark and intelligent, had an intent gaze, as though looking for something. She walked like her father with a little hurried step. She talked a great deal and was fond of arguing, accompanying every phrase, however insignificant, with expressive mimicry and gesticulation. No doubt she was nervous in the extreme.

Kovrin went on reading the articles, but he understood nothing of them, and flung them aside. The same pleasant excitement with which he had earlier in the evening danced the mazurka and listened to the music was now mastering him again and rousing a multitude of thoughts. He got up and began walking about the room, thinking about the black monk. It occurred to him that if this strange, supernatural monk had appeared to him only, that meant that he was ill and had reached the point of having hallucinations. This reflection frightened him, but not for long.

"But I am all right, and I am doing no harm to any one; so there is no harm in my hallucinations," he thought; and he felt happy again.

He sat down on the sofa and clasped his hands round his head. Restraining the unaccountable joy which filled his whole being, he then paced up and down again, and sat down to his work. But the thought that he read in the book did not satisfy him. He wanted something gigantic, unfathomable, stupendous. Towards morning he undressed and reluctantly went to bed: he ought to sleep.

When he heard the footsteps of Yegor Semyonitch going out into the garden, Kovrin rang the bell and asked the footman to bring him some wine. He drank several glasses of Lafitte, then wrapped himself up, head and all; his consciousness grew clouded and he fell asleep.

IV

Yegor Semyonitch and Tanya often quarrelled and said nasty things to each other.

They quarrelled about something that morning. Tanya burst out crying and went to her room. She would not come down to dinner nor to tea. At first Yegor Semyonitch went about looking sulky and dignified, as though to give everyone to understand that for him the claims of justice and good order were more important than anything else in the world; but he could not keep it up for long, and soon sank into depression. He walked about the park dejectedly, continually sighing: "Oh, my God! My God!" and at dinner did not eat a morsel. At last, guilty and conscience-stricken, he knocked at the locked door and called timidly:

"Tanya! Tanya!"

And from behind the door came a faint voice, weak with crying but still determined:

"Leave me alone, if you please."

The depression of the master and mistress was reflected in the whole household, even in the labourers working in the garden. Kovrin was absorbed in his interesting work, but at last he, too, felt dreary and uncomfortable. To dissipate the general ill-humour in some way, he made up his mind to intervene, and towards evening he knocked at Tanya's door. He was admitted.

"Fie, fie, for shame!" he began playfully, looking with surprise at Tanya's tear-stained, woebegone face, flushed in patches with crying. "Is it really so serious? Fie, fie!"

"But if you knew how he tortures me!" she said, and floods of scalding tears streamed from her big eyes. "He torments me to death," she went on, wringing her hands. "I said nothing to him . . . nothing . . . I only said that there was no need to keep . . . too many labourers . . . if we could hire them by the day when we wanted them. You know . . . you know the labourers have been doing nothing for a whole week . . . I . . . I . . . only said that, and he shouted and . . . said . . . a lot of horrible insulting things to me. What for?"

"There, there," said Kovrin, smoothing her hair. "You've quarrelled with each other, you've cried, and that's enough. You must not be angry for long—that's wrong . . . all the more as he loves you beyond everything."

Anton Chekhov

"He has . . . has spoiled my whole life," Tanya went on, sobbing. "I hear nothing but abuse and . . . insults. He thinks I am of no use in the house. Well! He is right. I shall go away tomorrow; I shall become a telegraph clerk . . . I don't care . . ."

"Come, come, come . . . You mustn't cry, Tanya. You mustn't, dear . . . You are both hot-tempered and irritable, and you are both to blame. Come along; I will reconcile you."

Kovrin talked affectionately and persuasively, while she went on crying, twitching her shoulders and wringing her hands, as though some terrible misfortune had really befallen her. He felt all the sorrier for her because her grief was not a serious one, yet she suffered extremely. What trivialities were enough to make this little creature miserable for a whole day, perhaps for her whole life! Comforting Tanya, Kovrin thought that, apart from this girl and her father, he might hunt the world over and would not find people who would love him as one of themselves, as one of their kindred. If it had not been for those two he might very likely, having lost his father and mother in early childhood, never to the day of his death have known what was meant by genuine affection and that naïve, uncritical love which is only lavished on very close blood relations; and he felt that the nerves of this weeping, shaking girl responded to his half-sick, overstrained nerves like iron to a magnet. He never could have loved a healthy, strong, rosy-cheeked woman, but pale, weak, unhappy Tanya attracted him.

And he liked stroking her hair and her shoulders, pressing her hand and wiping away her tears . . . At last she left off crying. She went on for a long time complaining of her father and her hard, insufferable life in that house, entreating Kovrin to put himself in her place; then she began, little by little, smiling, and sighing that God had given her such a bad temper. At last, laughing aloud, she called herself a fool, and ran out of the room.

When a little later Kovrin went into the garden, Yegor Semyonitch and Tanya were walking side by side along an avenue as though nothing had happened, and both were eating rye bread with salt on it, as both were hungry.

V

Glad that he had been so successful in the part of peacemaker, Kovrin went into the park. Sitting on a garden seat, thinking, he heard the rattle of a carriage and a feminine laugh—visitors were arriving. When the shades of evening began falling on the garden, the sounds of the violin and singing voices reached him indistinctly, and that reminded him of the black monk. Where, in what land or in what planet, was that optical absurdity moving now?

Hardly had he recalled the legend and pictured in his imagination the dark apparition he had seen in the rye-field, when, from behind a pine-tree exactly opposite, there came out noiselessly, without the slightest rustle, a man of medium height with uncovered grey head, all in black, and barefooted like a beggar, and his black eyebrows stood out conspicuously on his pale, death-like face. Nodding his head graciously, this beggar or pilgrim came noiselessly to the seat and sat down, and Kovrin recognised him as the black monk.

For a minute they looked at one another, Kovrin with amazement, and the monk with friendliness, and, just as before, a little slyness, as though he were thinking something to himself.

"But you are a mirage," said Kovrin. "Why are you here and sitting still? That does not fit in with the legend."

"That does not matter," the monk answered in a low voice, not immediately turning his face towards him. "The legend, the mirage, and I are all the products of your excited imagination. I am a phantom."

"Then you don't exist?" said Kovrin.

"You can think as you like," said the monk, with a faint smile. "I exist in your imagination, and your imagination is part of nature, so I exist in nature."

"You have a very old, wise, and extremely expressive face, as though you really had lived more than a thousand years," said Kovrin. "I did not know that my imagination was capable of creating such phenomena. But why do you look at me with such enthusiasm? Do you like me?"

"Yes, you are one of those few who are justly called the chosen of God. You do the service of eternal truth. Your thoughts, your designs, the marvellous studies you are engaged in, and all your life, bear the Divine, the heavenly stamp, seeing that they are consecrated to the rational and the beautiful—that is, to what is eternal."

"You said 'eternal truth.' . . . But is eternal truth of use to man and within his reach, if there is no eternal life?"

"There is eternal life," said the monk.

"Do you believe in the immortality of man?"

"Yes, of course. A grand, brilliant future is in store for you men. And the more there are like you on earth, the sooner will this future be realised. Without you who serve the higher principle and live in full understanding and freedom, mankind would be of little account; developing in a natural way, it would have to wait a long time for the end of its earthly history. You will lead it some thousands of years earlier into the kingdom of eternal truth—and therein lies your supreme service. You are the incarnation of the blessing of God, which rests upon men."

"And what is the object of eternal life?" asked Kovrin.

"As of all life—enjoyment. True enjoyment lies in knowledge, and eternal life provides innumerable and inexhaustible sources of knowledge, and in that sense it has been said: 'In My Father's house there are many mansions.'"

"If only you knew how pleasant it is to hear you!" said Kovrin, rubbing his hands with satisfaction.

"I am very glad."

"But I know that when you go away I shall be worried by the question of your reality. You are a phantom, an hallucination. So I am mentally deranged, not normal?"

"What if you are? Why trouble yourself? You are ill because you have overworked and exhausted yourself, and that means that you have sacrificed your health to the idea, and the time is near at hand when you will give up life itself to it. What could be better? That is the goal towards which all divinely endowed, noble natures strive."

"If I know I am mentally affected, can I trust myself?"

"And are you sure that the men of genius, whom all men trust, did not see phantoms, too? The learned say now that genius is allied to madness. My friend, healthy and normal people are only the common herd. Reflections upon the neurasthenia of the age, nervous exhaustion and degeneracy, et cetera, can only seriously agitate those who place the object of life in the present—that is, the common herd."

"The Romans used to say: *Mens sana in corpore sano.*"

"Not everything the Greeks and the Romans said is true. Exaltation, enthusiasm, ecstasy—all that distinguishes prophets, poets, martyrs for the idea, from the common folk—is repellent to the animal side of man— that is, his physical health. I repeat, if you want to be healthy and normal, go to the common herd."

"Strange that you repeat what often comes into my mind," said Kovrin. "It is as though you had seen and overheard my secret thoughts. But don't let us talk about me. What do you mean by 'eternal truth'?"

The monk did not answer. Kovrin looked at him and could not distinguish his face. His features grew blurred and misty. Then the monk's head and arms disappeared; his body seemed merged into the seat and the evening twilight, and he vanished altogether.

"The hallucination is over," said Kovrin; and he laughed. "It's a pity."

He went back to the house, light-hearted and happy. The little the monk had said to him had flattered, not his vanity, but his whole soul, his whole being. To be one of the chosen, to serve eternal truth, to stand in the ranks of those who could make mankind worthy of the kingdom of God some thousands of years sooner—that is, to free men from some thousands of years of unnecessary struggle, sin, and suffering; to sacrifice to the idea everything— youth, strength, health; to be ready to die for the common weal—what an exalted, what a happy lot! He recalled his past—pure, chaste, laborious; he remembered what he had learned himself and what he had taught to others, and decided that there was no exaggeration in the monk's words.

Tanya came to meet him in the park: she was by now wearing a different dress.

"Are you here?" she said. "And we have been looking and looking for you . . . But what is the matter with you?" she asked in wonder, glancing at his radiant, ecstatic face and eyes full of tears. "How strange you are, Andryusha!"

"I am pleased, Tanya," said Kovrin, laying his hand on her shoulders. "I am more than pleased: I am happy. Tanya, darling Tanya, you are an extraordinary, nice creature. Dear Tanya, I am so glad, I am so glad!"

He kissed both her hands ardently, and went on:

"I have just passed through an exalted, wonderful, unearthly moment. But I can't tell you all about it or you would call me mad and not believe me. Let us talk of you. Dear, delightful Tanya! I love you, and am used to loving you. To have you near me, to meet you a dozen times a day, has become a necessity of my existence; I don't know how I shall get on without you when I go back home."

"Oh," laughed Tanya, "you will forget about us in two days. We are humble people and you are a great man."

"No; let us talk in earnest!" he said. "I shall take you with me, Tanya. Yes? Will you come with me? Will you be mine?"

"Come," said Tanya, and tried to laugh again, but the laugh would not come, and patches of colour came into her face.

She began breathing quickly and walked very quickly, but not to the house, but further into the park.

"I was not thinking of it... I was not thinking of it," she said, wringing her hands in despair.

And Kovrin followed her and went on talking, with the same radiant, enthusiastic face:

"I want a love that will dominate me altogether; and that love only you, Tanya, can give me. I am happy! I am happy!"

She was overwhelmed, and huddling and shrinking together, seemed ten years older all at once, while he thought her beautiful and expressed his rapture aloud:

"How lovely she is!"

VI

Learning from Kovrin that not only a romance had been got up, but that there would even be a wedding, Yegor Semyonitch spent a long time in pacing from one corner of the room to the other, trying to conceal his agitation. His hands began trembling, his neck swelled and turned purple, he ordered his racing droshky and drove off somewhere. Tanya, seeing how he lashed the horse, and seeing how he pulled his cap over his ears, understood what he was feeling, shut herself up in her room, and cried the whole day.

In the hot-houses the peaches and plums were already ripe; the packing and sending off of these tender and fragile goods to Moscow took a great deal of care, work, and trouble. Owing to the fact that the summer was very hot and dry, it was necessary to water every tree, and a great deal of time and labour was spent on doing it. Numbers of caterpillars made their appearance, which, to Kovrin's disgust, the labourers and even Yegor Semyonitch and Tanya squashed with their fingers. In spite of all that, they had already to book autumn orders for fruit and trees, and to carry on a great deal of correspondence. And at the very busiest time, when no one seemed to have a free moment, the work of the fields carried off more than half their labourers from the garden. Yegor Semyonitch, sunburnt, exhausted, ill-humoured, galloped from the fields to the garden and back again; cried that he was being torn to pieces, and that he should put a bullet through his brains.

Then came the fuss and worry of the trousseau, to which the Pesotskys attached a good deal of importance. Everyone's head was in a whirl from the snipping of the scissors, the rattle of the sewing-machine, the smell of hot irons, and the caprices of the dressmaker, a huffy and nervous lady. And, as ill-luck would have it, visitors came every day, who had to be entertained, fed, and even put up for the night. But all this hard labour passed unnoticed as though in a fog. Tanya felt that love and happiness had taken her unawares, though she had, since she was fourteen, for some reason been convinced that Kovrin would marry her and no one else. She was bewildered, could not grasp it, could not believe herself . . . At one minute such joy would swoop down upon her that she longed to fly away to the clouds and there pray to God, at another moment she would remember that in August she would have to part from her home and leave her father; or, goodness knows why, the idea would occur to her that she was worthless—insignificant and unworthy of a great man like Kovrin—and she would go to her room, lock herself in, and cry bitterly for several hours. When there were visitors, she would suddenly fancy that Kovrin looked extraordinarily handsome, and that all the women were in love with him and envying her, and her soul was filled with pride and rapture, as though she had vanquished the whole world; but he had only to smile politely at any young lady for her to be trembling with jealousy, to retreat to her room—and tears again. These new sensations mastered her completely; she helped her father mechanically, without noticing peaches, caterpillars or labourers, or how rapidly the time was passing.

It was almost the same with Yegor Semyonitch. He worked from morning till night, was always in a hurry, was irritable, and flew into rages, but all of this was in a sort of spellbound dream. It seemed as though there were two men in him: one was the real Yegor Semyonitch, who was moved to indignation, and clutched his head in despair when he heard of some irregularity from Ivan Karlovitch the gardener; and another—not the real one—who seemed as though he were half drunk, would interrupt a business conversation at half a word, touch the gardener on the shoulder, and begin muttering:

"Say what you like, there is a great deal in blood. His mother was a wonderful woman, most high-minded and intelligent. It was a pleasure to look at her good, candid, pure face; it was like the face of an angel. She drew splendidly, wrote verses, spoke five foreign languages, sang . . . Poor thing! she died of consumption. The Kingdom of Heaven be hers."

The unreal Yegor Semyonitch sighed, and after a pause went on:

"When he was a boy and growing up in my house, he had the same angelic face, good and candid. The way he looks and talks and moves is as soft and elegant as his mother's. And his intellect! We were always struck with his intelligence. To be sure, it's not for nothing he's a Master of Arts! It's not for nothing! And wait a bit, Ivan Karlovitch, what will he be in ten years' time? He will be far above us!"

But at this point the real Yegor Semyonitch, suddenly coming to himself, would make a terrible face, would clutch his head and cry:

"The devils! They have spoilt everything! They have ruined everything! They have spoilt everything! The garden's done for, the garden's ruined!"

Kovrin, meanwhile, worked with the same ardour as before, and did not notice the general commotion. Love only added fuel to the flames. After every talk with Tanya he went to his room, happy and triumphant, took up his book or his manuscript with the same passion with which he had just kissed Tanya and told her of his love. What the black monk had told him of the chosen of God, of eternal truth, of the brilliant future of mankind and so on, gave peculiar and extraordinary significance to his work, and filled his soul with pride and the consciousness of his own exalted consequence. Once or twice a week, in the park or in the house, he met the black monk and had long conversations with him, but this did not alarm him, but, on the contrary, delighted him, as he was now firmly persuaded that such apparitions only visited the elect few who rise up above their fellows and devote themselves to the service of the idea.

One day the monk appeared at dinner-time and sat in the dining room window. Kovrin was delighted, and very adroitly began a conversation with Yegor Semyonitch and Tanya of what might be of interest to the monk; the black-robed visitor listened and nodded his head graciously, and Yegor Semyonitch and Tanya listened, too, and smiled gaily without suspecting that Kovrin was not talking to them but to his hallucination.

Imperceptibly the fast of the Assumption was approaching, and soon after came the wedding, which, at Yegor Semyonitch's urgent desire, was celebrated with "a flourish"—that is, with senseless festivities that lasted for two whole days and nights. Three thousand roubles' worth of food and drink was consumed, but the music of the wretched hired band, the noisy toasts, the scurrying to and fro of the footmen, the uproar and crowding, prevented them from appreciating the taste of the expensive wines and wonderful delicacies ordered from Moscow.

VII

One long winter night Kovrin was lying in bed, reading a French novel. Poor Tanya, who had headaches in the evenings from living in town, to which she was not accustomed, had been asleep a long while, and, from time to time, articulated some incoherent phrase in her restless dreams.

It struck three o'clock. Kovrin put out the light and lay down to sleep, lay for a long time with his eyes closed, but could not get to sleep because, as he fancied, the room was very hot and Tanya talked in her sleep. At half-past four he lighted the candle again, and this time he saw the black monk sitting in an armchair near the bed.

"Good morning," said the monk, and after a brief pause he asked: "What are you thinking of now?"

"Of fame," answered Kovrin. "In the French novel I have just been reading, there is a description of a young *savant*, who does silly things and pines away through worrying about fame. I can't understand such anxiety."

"Because you are wise. Your attitude towards fame is one of indifference, as towards a toy which no longer interests you."

"Yes, that is true."

"Renown does not allure you now. What is there flattering, amusing, or edifying in their carving your name on a tombstone, then time rubbing off the inscription together with the gilding? Moreover, happily there are too many of you for the weak memory of mankind to be able to retain your names."

"Of course," assented Kovrin. "Besides, why should they be remembered? But let us talk of something else. Of happiness, for instance. What is happiness?"

When the clock struck five, he was sitting on the bed, dangling his feet to the carpet, talking to the monk:

"In ancient times a happy man grew at last frightened of his happiness—it was so great!—and to propitiate the gods he brought as a sacrifice his favourite ring. Do you know, I, too, like Polykrates, begin to be uneasy of my happiness. It seems strange to me that from morning to night I feel nothing but joy; it fills my whole being and smothers all other feelings. I don't know what sadness, grief, or boredom is. Here I am not asleep; I suffer from sleeplessness, but I am not dull. I say it in earnest; I begin to feel perplexed."

"But why?" the monk asked in wonder. "Is joy a supernatural feeling? Ought it not to be the normal state of man? The more highly a man is developed on the intellectual and moral side, the more independent he is, the more pleasure life gives him. Socrates, Diogenes, and Marcus Aurelius, were joyful, not sorrowful. And the Apostle tells us: 'Rejoice continually'; 'Rejoice and be glad.'"

"But will the gods be suddenly wrathful?" Kovrin jested; and he laughed. "If they take from me comfort and make me go cold and hungry, it won't be very much to my taste."

Meanwhile Tanya woke up and looked with amazement and horror at her husband. He was talking, addressing the armchair, laughing and gesticulating; his eyes were gleaming, and there was something strange in his laugh.

"Andryusha, whom are you talking to?" she asked, clutching the hand he stretched out to the monk. "Andryusha! Whom?"

"Oh! Whom?" said Kovrin in confusion. "Why, to him . . . He is sitting here," he said, pointing to the black monk.

"There is no one here . . . no one! Andryusha, you are ill!"

Tanya put her arm round her husband and held him tight, as though protecting him from the apparition, and put her hand over his eyes.

"You are ill!" she sobbed, trembling all over. "Forgive me, my precious, my dear one, but I have noticed for a long time that your mind is clouded in some way . . . You are mentally ill, Andryusha . . ."

Her trembling infected him, too. He glanced once more at the armchair, which was now empty, felt a sudden weakness in his arms and legs, was frightened, and began dressing.

"It's nothing, Tanya; it's nothing," he muttered, shivering. "I really am not quite well . . . it's time to admit that."

"I have noticed it for a long time . . . and father has noticed it," she said, trying to suppress her sobs. "You talk to yourself, smile somehow strangely . . . and can't sleep. Oh, my God, my God, save us!" she said in terror. "But don't be frightened, Andryusha; for God's sake don't be frightened . . ."

She began dressing, too. Only now, looking at her, Kovrin realised the danger of his position—realised the meaning of the black monk and his conversations with him. It was clear to him now that he was mad.

Neither of them knew why they dressed and went into the dining room: she in front and he following her. There they found Yegor

Semyonitch standing in his dressing-gown and with a candle in his hand. He was staying with them, and had been awakened by Tanya's sobs.

"Don't be frightened, Andryusha," Tanya was saying, shivering as though in a fever; "don't be frightened . . . Father, it will all pass over . . . it will all pass over . . ."

Kovrin was too much agitated to speak. He wanted to say to his father-in-law in a playful tone: "Congratulate me; it appears I have gone out of my mind"; but he could only move his lips and smile bitterly.

At nine o'clock in the morning they put on his jacket and fur coat, wrapped him up in a shawl, and took him in a carriage to a doctor.

VIII

Summer had come again, and the doctor advised their going into the country. Kovrin had recovered; he had left off seeing the black monk, and he had only to get up his strength. Staying at his father-in-law's, he drank a great deal of milk, worked for only two hours out of the twenty-four, and neither smoked nor drank wine.

On the evening before Elijah's Day they had an evening service in the house. When the deacon was handing the priest the censer the immense old room smelt like a graveyard, and Kovrin felt bored. He went out into the garden. Without noticing the gorgeous flowers, he walked about the garden, sat down on a seat, then strolled about the park; reaching the river, he went down and then stood lost in thought, looking at the water. The sullen pines with their shaggy roots, which had seen him a year before so young, so joyful and confident, were not whispering now, but standing mute and motionless, as though they did not recognise him. And, indeed, his head was closely cropped, his beautiful long hair was gone, his step was lagging, his face was fuller and paler than last summer.

He crossed by the footbridge to the other side. Where the year before there had been rye the oats stood, reaped, and lay in rows. The sun had set and there was a broad stretch of glowing red on the horizon, a sign of windy weather next day. It was still. Looking in the direction from which the year before the black monk had first appeared, Kovrin stood for twenty minutes, till the evening glow had begun to fade . . .

When, listless and dissatisfied, he returned home the service was over. Yegor Semyonitch and Tanya were sitting on the steps of the verandah, drinking tea. They were talking of something, but, seeing Kovrin, ceased at once, and he concluded from their faces that their talk had been about him.

"I believe it is time for you to have your milk," Tanya said to her husband.

"No, it is not time yet . . ." he said, sitting down on the bottom step. "Drink it yourself; I don't want it."

Tanya exchanged a troubled glance with her father, and said in a guilty voice:

"You notice yourself that milk does you good."

"Yes, a great deal of good!" Kovrin laughed. "I congratulate you: I have gained a pound in weight since Friday." He pressed his head tightly in his hands and said miserably: "Why, why have you cured me? Preparations of bromide, idleness, hot baths, supervision, cowardly consternation at every mouthful, at every step—all this will reduce me at last to idiocy. I went out of my mind, I had megalomania; but then I was cheerful, confident, and even happy; I was interesting and original. Now I have become more sensible and stolid, but I am just like everyone else: I am—mediocrity; I am weary of life . . . Oh, how cruelly you have treated me! . . . I saw hallucinations, but what harm did that do to any one? I ask, what harm did that do any one?"

"Goodness knows what you are saying!" sighed Yegor Semyonitch. "It's positively wearisome to listen to it."

"Then don't listen."

The presence of other people, especially Yegor Semyonitch, irritated Kovrin now; he answered him drily, coldly, and even rudely, never looked at him but with irony and hatred, while Yegor Semyonitch was overcome with confusion and cleared his throat guiltily, though he was not conscious of any fault in himself. At a loss to understand why their charming and affectionate relations had changed so abruptly, Tanya huddled up to her father and looked anxiously in his face; she wanted to understand and could not understand, and all that was clear to her was that their relations were growing worse and worse every day, that of late her father had begun to look much older, and her husband had grown irritable, capricious, quarrelsome and uninteresting. She could not laugh or sing; at dinner she ate nothing; did not sleep for nights together, expecting something awful, and was so worn out that on one occasion she lay in a dead faint from dinner-time till evening. During the service she thought her father was crying, and now while the three of them were sitting together on the terrace she made an effort not to think of it.

"How fortunate Buddha, Mahomed, and Shakespeare were that their kind relations and doctors did not cure them of their ecstasy and their inspiration," said Kovrin. "If Mahomed had taken bromide for his nerves, had worked only two hours out of the twenty-four, and had drunk milk, that remarkable man would have left no more trace after him than his dog. Doctors and kind relations will succeed in stupefying mankind, in making mediocrity pass for genius and in bringing civilisation to ruin. If only you knew," Kovrin said with annoyance, "how grateful I am to you."

He felt intense irritation, and to avoid saying too much, he got up quickly and went into the house. It was still, and the fragrance of the tobacco plant and the marvel of Peru floated in at the open window. The moonlight lay in green patches on the floor and on the piano in the big dark dining room. Kovrin remembered the raptures of the previous summer when there had been the same scent of the marvel of Peru and the moon had shone in at the window. To bring back the mood of last year he went quickly to his study, lighted a strong cigar, and told the footman to bring him some wine. But the cigar left a bitter and disgusting taste in his mouth, and the wine had not the same flavour as it had the year before. And so great is the effect of giving up a habit, the cigar and the two gulps of wine made him giddy, and brought on palpitations of the heart, so that he was obliged to take bromide.

Before going to bed, Tanya said to him:

"Father adores you. You are cross with him about something, and it is killing him. Look at him; he is ageing, not from day to day, but from hour to hour. I entreat you, Andryusha, for God's sake, for the sake of your dead father, for the sake of my peace of mind, be affectionate to him."

"I can't, I don't want to."

"But why?" asked Tanya, beginning to tremble all over. "Explain why."

"Because he is antipathetic to me, that's all," said Kovrin carelessly; and he shrugged his shoulders. "But we won't talk about him: he is your father."

"I can't understand, I can't," said Tanya, pressing her hands to her temples and staring at a fixed point. "Something incomprehensible, awful, is going on in the house. You have changed, grown unlike yourself . . . You, clever, extraordinary man as you are, are irritated over trifles, meddle in paltry nonsense . . . Such trivial things excite you, that sometimes one is simply amazed and can't believe that it is you. Come, come, don't be angry, don't be angry," she went on, kissing his hands, frightened of her own words. "You are clever, kind, noble. You will be just to father. He is so good."

"He is not good; he is just good-natured. Burlesque old uncles like your father, with well-fed, good-natured faces, extraordinarily hospitable and queer, at one time used to touch me and amuse me in novels and in farces and in life; now I dislike them. They are egoists to the marrow of their bones. What disgusts me most of all is their being so well-fed, and that purely bovine, purely hoggish optimism of a full stomach."

Tanya sat down on the bed and laid her head on the pillow.

"This is torture," she said, and from her voice it was evident that she was utterly exhausted, and that it was hard for her to speak. "Not one moment of peace since the winter . . . Why, it's awful! My God! I am wretched."

"Oh, of course, I am Herod, and you and your father are the innocents. Of course."

His face seemed to Tanya ugly and unpleasant. Hatred and an ironical expression did not suit him. And, indeed, she had noticed before that there was something lacking in his face, as though ever since his hair had been cut his face had changed, too. She wanted to say something wounding to him, but immediately she caught herself in this antagonistic feeling, she was frightened and went out of the bedroom.

IX

Kovrin received a professorship at the University. The inaugural address was fixed for the second of December, and a notice to that effect was hung up in the corridor at the University. But on the day appointed he informed the students' inspector, by telegram, that he was prevented by illness from giving the lecture.

He had hæmorrhage from the throat. He was often spitting blood, but it happened two or three times a month that there was a considerable loss of blood, and then he grew extremely weak and sank into a drowsy condition. This illness did not particularly frighten him, as he knew that his mother had lived for ten years or longer suffering from the same disease, and the doctors assured him that there was no danger, and had only advised him to avoid excitement, to lead a regular life, and to speak as little as possible.

In January again his lecture did not take place owing to the same reason, and in February it was too late to begin the course. It had to be postponed to the following year.

By now he was living not with Tanya, but with another woman, who was two years older than he was, and who looked after him as though he were a baby. He was in a calm and tranquil state of mind; he readily gave in to her, and when Varvara Nikolaevna—that was the name of his friend—decided to take him to the Crimea, he agreed, though he had a presentiment that no good would come of the trip.

They reached Sevastopol in the evening and stopped at an hotel to rest and go on the next day to Yalta. They were both exhausted by the journey. Varvara Nikolaevna had some tea, went to bed and was soon asleep. But Kovrin did not go to bed. An hour before starting for the station, he had received a letter from Tanya, and had not brought himself to open it, and now it was lying in his coat pocket, and the thought of it excited him disagreeably. At the bottom of his heart he genuinely considered now that his marriage to Tanya had been a mistake. He was glad that their separation was final, and the thought of that woman who in the end had turned into a living relic, still walking about though everything seemed dead in her except her big, staring, intelligent eyes—the thought of her roused in him nothing but pity and disgust with himself. The handwriting on the envelope reminded him how cruel and unjust he had been two years before, how he had worked off his anger at his spiritual emptiness, his boredom, his loneliness, and his dissatisfaction with life by revenging himself on people in no way to blame. He remembered, also, how he had torn up his dissertation and all the articles he had written during his illness, and how he had thrown them out of window, and the bits of paper had fluttered in the wind and caught on the trees and flowers. In every line of them he saw strange, utterly groundless pretension, shallow defiance, arrogance, megalomania; and they made him feel as though he were reading a description of his vices. But when the last manuscript had been torn up and sent flying out of window, he felt, for some reason, suddenly bitter and angry; he went to his wife and said a great many unpleasant things to her. My God, how he had tormented her! One day, wanting to cause her pain, he told her that her father had played a very unattractive part in their romance, that he had asked him to marry her. Yegor Semyonitch accidentally overheard this, ran into the room, and, in his despair, could not utter a word, could only stamp and make a strange, bellowing sound as though he had lost the power of speech, and Tanya, looking at her father, had uttered a heart-rending shriek and had fallen into a swoon. It was hideous.

All this came back into his memory as he looked at the familiar writing. Kovrin went out on to the balcony; it was still warm weather and there was a smell of the sea. The wonderful bay reflected the moonshine and the lights, and was of a colour for which it was difficult to find a name. It was a soft and tender blending of dark blue and green; in places the water was like blue vitriol, and in places it seemed as though the moonlight were liquefied and filling the bay instead of water. And what harmony of colours, what an atmosphere of peace, calm, and sublimity!

In the lower storey under the balcony the windows were probably open, for women's voices and laughter could be heard distinctly. Apparently there was an evening party.

Kovrin made an effort, tore open the envelope, and, going back into his room, read:

"My father is just dead. I owe that to you, for you have killed him. Our garden is being ruined; strangers are managing it already—that is, the very thing is happening that poor father dreaded. That, too, I owe to you. I hate you with my whole soul, and I hope you may soon perish. Oh, how wretched I am! Insufferable anguish is burning my soul . . . My curses on you. I took you for an extraordinary man, a genius; I loved you, and you have turned out a madman . . ."

Kovrin could read no more, he tore up the letter and threw it away. He was overcome by an uneasiness that was akin to terror. Varvara Nikolaevna was asleep behind the screen, and he could hear her breathing. From the lower storey came the sounds of laughter and women's voices, but he felt as though in the whole hotel there were no living soul but him. Because Tanya, unhappy, broken by sorrow, had cursed him in her letter and hoped for his perdition, he felt eerie and kept glancing hurriedly at the door, as though he were afraid that the uncomprehended force which two years before had wrought such havoc in his life and in the life of those near him might come into the room and master him once more.

He knew by experience that when his nerves were out of hand the best thing for him to do was to work. He must sit down to the table and force himself, at all costs, to concentrate his mind on someone thought. He took from his red portfolio a manuscript containing a sketch of a small work of the nature of a compilation, which he had planned in case he should find it dull in the Crimea without work. He sat down to the table and began working at this plan, and it seemed to him that his calm, peaceful, indifferent mood was coming back. The manuscript with the sketch even led him to meditation on the vanity of the world. He thought how much life exacts for the worthless or very commonplace blessings it can give a man. For instance, to gain, before forty, a university chair, to be an ordinary professor, to expound ordinary and second-hand thoughts in dull, heavy, insipid language—in fact, to gain the position of a mediocre learned man, he, Kovrin, had had to study for fifteen years, to work day and night, to endure a terrible mental illness, to experience an unhappy marriage, and to do a great number of stupid and unjust things which it would have been pleasant not to remember. Kovrin recognised clearly, now, that he was a mediocrity, and readily resigned himself to it, as he considered that every man ought to be satisfied with what he is.

The plan of the volume would have soothed him completely, but the torn letter showed white on the floor and prevented him from concentrating his attention. He got up from the table, picked up the pieces of the letter and threw them out of window, but there was a light wind blowing from the sea, and the bits of paper were scattered on the windowsill. Again he was overcome by uneasiness akin to terror, and he felt as though in the whole hotel there were no living soul but himself . . . He went out on the balcony. The bay, like a living thing, looked at him with its multitude of light blue, dark blue, turquoise and fiery eyes, and seemed beckoning to him. And it really was hot and oppressive, and it would not have been amiss to have a bathe.

Suddenly in the lower storey under the balcony a violin began playing, and two soft feminine voices began singing. It was something familiar. The song was about a maiden, full of sick fancies, who heard one night in her garden mysterious sounds, so strange and lovely that she was obliged to recognise them as a holy harmony which is unintelligible to us mortals, and so flies back to heaven . . . Kovrin caught his breath and there was a pang of sadness at his heart, and a thrill of the sweet, exquisite delight he had so long forgotten began to stir in his breast.

A tall black column, like a whirlwind or a waterspout, appeared on the further side of the bay. It moved with fearful rapidity across the bay, towards the hotel, growing smaller and darker as it came, and Kovrin only just had time to get out of the way to let it pass . . . The monk with bare grey head, black eyebrows, barefoot, his arms crossed over his breast, floated by him, and stood still in the middle of the room.

"Why did you not believe me?" he asked reproachfully, looking affectionately at Kovrin. "If you had believed me then, that you were a genius, you would not have spent these two years so gloomily and so wretchedly."

Kovrin already believed that he was one of God's chosen and a genius; he vividly recalled his conversations with the monk in the past and tried to speak, but the blood flowed from his throat on to his breast, and not knowing what he was doing, he passed his hands over his breast, and his cuffs were soaked with blood. He tried to call Varvara Nikolaevna, who was asleep behind the screen; he made an effort and said:

"Tanya!"

He fell on the floor, and propping himself on his arms, called again:

"Tanya!"

He called Tanya, called to the great garden with the gorgeous flowers sprinkled with dew, called to the park, the pines with their shaggy roots, the rye-field, his marvellous learning, his youth, courage, joy—called to life, which was so lovely. He saw on the floor near his face a great pool of blood, and was too weak to utter a word, but an unspeakable, infinite happiness flooded his whole being. Below, under the balcony, they were playing the serenade, and the black monk whispered to him that he was a genius, and that he was dying only because his frail human body had lost its balance and could no longer serve as the mortal garb of genius.

When Varvara Nikolaevna woke up and came out from behind the screen, Kovrin was dead, and a blissful smile was set upon his face.